# THE
# BROTHERHOOD
# OF OLYMPUS
# AND THE
# DEADLIEST GAME

Written and Illustrated by

# GUY T. SIMPSON, JR.

For more information please go to the author's website:

## http://guysimpson.net

MYTHIC
PUBLISHING

ASGARD          GEHENNA          YELM

# DEDICATION

To the many members of the Brotherhood of Olympus
over the years, your tales will be told,

To my family for always believing in me,
even when I doubted,

To my father, my grandfather, and my uncle who are no
longer here, it's because of you that I wrote this book,

And to all of those that believed and trusted
—Dreams do come true.

*The Boys 1965*

# CONTENTS

# ACKNOWLEDGMENTS

I would like to gratefully acknowledge the many people who have been touched by the tale told within these pages and the members of my family whose echo can be seen in this story. I would also like to acknowledge my students, both current and past, for putting up with my stories throughout the years.

The team of Vicki Aden, Sarah Mulkey, Mike Munro, Dan Helms, Jerry Price, Linda Collins, Ryan Healy, and Cami Krise who humored me by reading the first draft of this work and helped me shape it to what it has become.

The team of dedicated English teachers who assembled the supplemental materials included in this edition, Rebecca Latham and Sarah Mulkey. My lovely editor, Becca Wolford. The fine folks at Mythic Publishing who gave my work an avenue to be read. My children, Taylor, Kathryn, and Guy, III, for listening to me ramble on and on about Brotherhood myths and legends and for being the most amazing children.

My best friend and wife, Rae for learning how to let me create this world while supporting my dream. And finally the author who inspired me all those years ago when I first read his work, the great J.R.R. Tolkien, without him the world would not be as rich and descriptive in my mind.


And of course the Fans of the Brotherhood of Olympus without whom none of this would be possible.

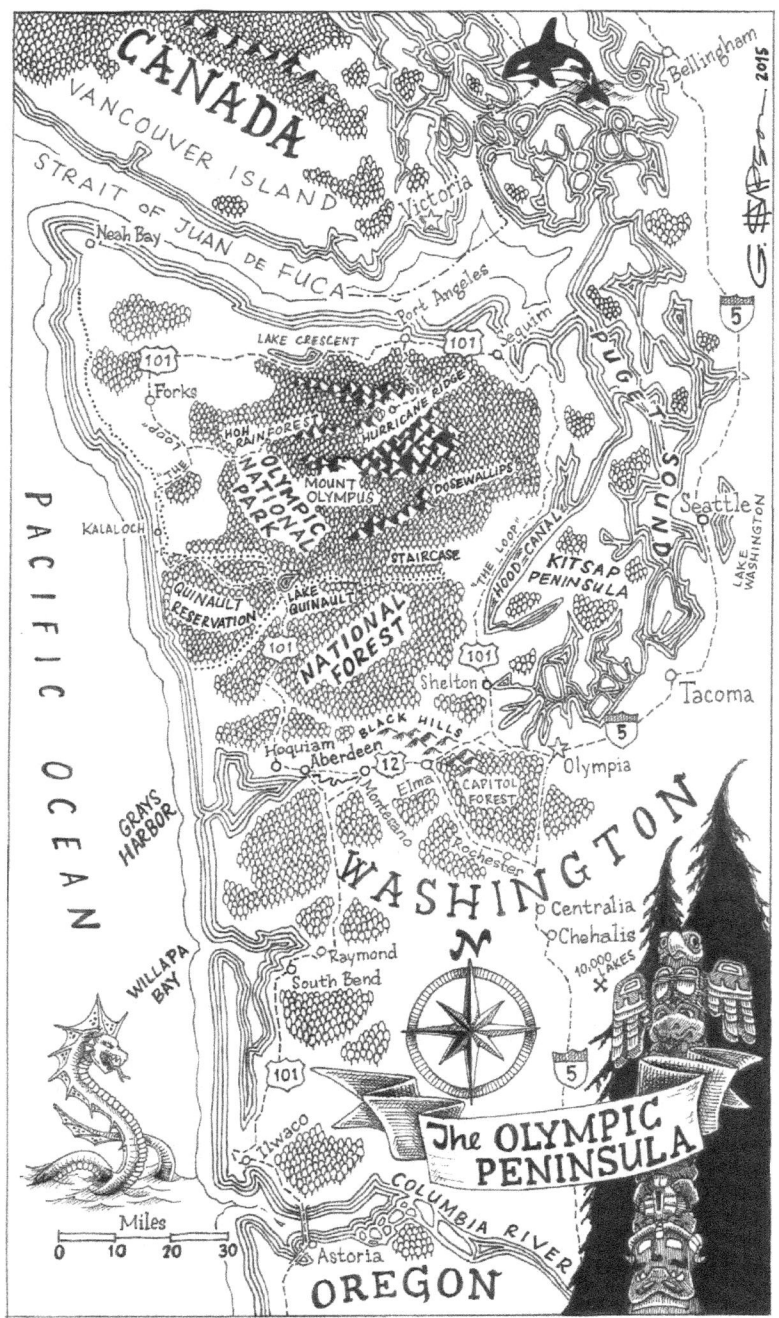

GRAYS HARBOR
WASHINGTON

1978
PACIFIC NORTHWEST
LEAGUE CHAMPIONS

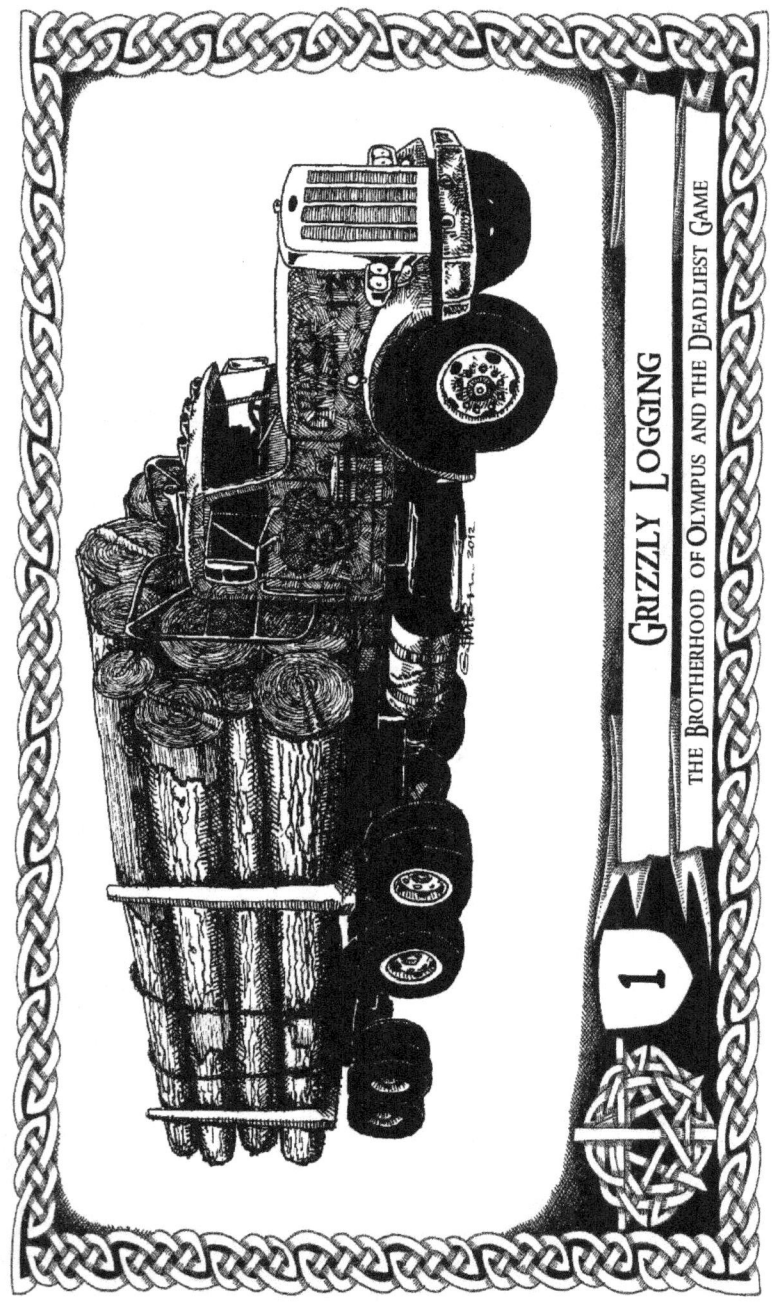

GRIZZLY LOGGING

THE BROTHERHOOD OF OLYMPUS AND THE DEADLIEST GAME

1

*This tale is based upon actual events...*

## The Unexpected News
## Chapter One
## January 13, 1978
## Cosmopolis, Washington

"Dad's wrong, I'm not a good-for-nothing lazy pot-head. And I will become something," declared Walter Reuss, as he down-shifted his yellow Chevrolet pickup with the loud audible whine of the transmission gears resisting his will. He quickly approached Highway 101, returning home from a trip into Montesano he should have made the day before to pick up his father's refilled oxygen and acetylene welding tanks. Those four long, cylindrical tanks jostled in the bed of the pickup as he forcefully decelerated. The berated scolding he took from his father for being lazy made him make the drive today and it had left him hurt and upset.

The canary yellow pickup glistened in a rare winter sun break through the moist gray clouds that hung in the sky like a shroud of indifference. Walter drove through the sweeping right curve of the Monte cut-off road bringing it to an end at a ninety degree angle to the highway. Traffic going both north and south was an unusual thing on this lonely stretch of two-lane roadway, but today that wasn't the case as he came to a stop with his left turn signal blinking.

The click-click-clicking of the turn signal kept time as he waited. The southbound traffic coming out of town ended, but the traffic going north into Aberdeen was still too heavy to risk pulling out in front of. He reached down and tuned his AM/FM radio finding one of the only stations that was strong enough to reach into the valley behind the forested hill.

I

"Great," he stated in irritation. "The Bee Gee's, anything but the Bee Gee's." Within moments he was singing along and tapping the top of his steering wheel.

Again he looked to the left. There were only two more cars headed towards Aberdeen. He felt an eerie feeling, somewhat like he was being watched, by more than one person, from more than one location. He cautiously glanced around the intersection but saw no one. Then, almost out of guilt, he adjusted the dial and found another radio station. The first car passed by with a whoosh.

The second car was familiar to him, a tan Dodge four-door sedan rapidly approaching. It was his mother heading into Aberdeen. They waved to each other as they exchanged smiles. As he watched his mother pass towards the forested hill beyond, a small Toyota sped past her in the opposite direction coming out of Aberdeen delaying his left turn home just a moment longer. He looked back to the left as he readied himself to go after the little foreign car. A fully loaded logging truck had rounded the corner by the weigh station. He knew he had enough time to pull out in front of the rapidly approaching truck, but he had those full tanks in the back of his pickup. He had always had an uncanny belief that he would someday die as a result of a welding or scuba tank accident, and would not risk pulling out quickly and banging those cylinders together. Today would not be that day, he thought as he continued to tap his hands to the song on the radio that he was now singing, patiently waiting for the logging truck to pass. He failed to notice that the log truck began to leave the lane on the road, heading towards the shoulder.

Walter finally turned his head to the left. He saw the log truck headed straight towards him, its massive front wheels throwing up the gravel on the side of the road as it barreled towards the middle of his yellow pickup.

"What the…!" Walter exclaimed in sudden horror. He rapidly shifted his truck into reverse and floored the accelerator, smoke from the burning tire rubber and dust from the dirt and gravel on the pavement billowed upward as the pickup surged backwards.

Adrenaline flooded his body, his pulse pounded in his head, and he became aware of the scent of gasoline and oil mixed with that of burning rubber. Over his shoulder he saw the oxygen and acetylene cylinders slide forward and bang into the cab of his pickup as he moved rapidly backwards. Those damn tanks.

With a sudden jarring impact the front of the Peterbilt log truck slammed into the front quarter panel of the pickup, mashing it down as its front right wheel careened upward over the hood of the smaller vehicle.

The force of the crash spun the pickup towards the trailer filled with logs. Walter felt the incredible pull exerted upon his body, the driver's side door flew open as the pickup twisted into the heavily laden load of logs. With all his might he held onto the steering wheel as he felt himself being ejected from the cab of the pickup. It happened so fast he had no time to think about his life, being upset with his father, whether or not he would amount to anything, or if he could have done anything different.

Humans are remarkable creatures capable of great things. Walter Reuss was such a human, but at that moment his strength failed and the violence of the accident took him. As he flew free from his pickup he struggled to see the welding tanks, hoping they would not blow up. He painfully thudded onto the highway, his glasses separating from his head, leaving him nearly unable to see. The world was dark and fuzzy. Thank heavens the tanks had not exploded. He began to exhale in relief. A millisecond later the massive tires of the truck trailer crushed the life from his young body.

It was nearly four o'clock on that Friday afternoon, and Drake Fraser was sitting on his unmade bed, getting ready to ride his bike to basketball practice at the junior high school. He wore gray sweatpants over his red shorts, red Converse high-tops, and a yellow t-shirt with the Latin words "Veni,

Vidi, Vici" printed underneath the profile of a Roman Centurion, in dark blue across the chest. His olive complexion suggested his partial Spanish heritage.

"Where's my sweatshirt?" Drake said to himself as he stood and looked around his small, dark paneled, almost closet of a room. He was thirteen and nearly six feet, four inches in height, with straight blackish-brown hair that was cut below his ears in what could be described as a rather bowl haircut.

"I'd never leave it at practice, it has to be here," he continued to rationalize to himself as he looked through the clothes hanging on the wooden bar that was his closet in one corner of the room. His dark brown eyes focused on the task at hand as he shuffled through the clothes scattered in loose piles on his floor.

"Somebody must've taken it," he concluded, and with that he exited his room closing the door behind him with a bit of a slam. Immediately outside his room stood the old metal shelving unit his father had gotten a few years ago that housed some of his favorite things—books. Not just any books, there were also two sets of World Book Encyclopedias on the bottom shelves. The older 1920 edition in its black and cool grey tweed covers, and the newer brown and white 1970 edition that he had read every page of, all twenty-one volumes. Drake stooped and ran a finger along the tops of the encyclopedias as he walked past them. Somehow this act had always reassured him.

"Mark!" he shouted, as he walked past the open stairwell towards the single bedroom at the end of the hall just beyond the little half bathroom on the second floor of the house. Drake was a painfully shy boy. He would rarely be heard talking to strangers and to him strangers included everyone who didn't live in the house with him. But with his brothers he could get loud. "Mark, did you take it?"

Drake swung open Mark's bedroom door, an action he would rarely do. Mark was his older brother, and not to be taken lightly. He was nearly sixteen and long regarded as the toughest of all the Fraser boys, having beaten all the other four in fights at some point in the recent past.

"What're you doing, dillhole?" Mark exclaimed to his brother, as Drake barged into his room. "Didn't you see my door was closed? What if I was naked?"

Mark was not naked, neither was he alone in his room. Sitting on his crisply made bed was their oldest brother Martin. Mark's bedroom was clean, organized, and sunlit from the large window at the far end. It might not be thought of as a teenage boy's room if not for the scantily clad women from a variety of magazines that hung on the walls.

"Did you take my sweatshirt, Mark?" Drake questioned again as Mark stood up from the single wooden chair in his room to face his younger brother.

"Why would I take your stinky sweatshirt, Drake?" Mark replied as he looked up at his younger brother. Even though he was older, he was only five feet, eleven inches in height. Everyone in the family was sure that he had stunted his growth when he started smoking cigarettes before the age of eleven with his uncle Wally. His features were very similar to his brother, though his straight blackish-brown hair was considerably longer than Drake's, parted in the middle and swept over his ears.

"You shouldn't talk," Drake retorted as he positioned himself closer to Mark, and pushed his right index finger against his brother's chest. "All your clothes stink of smoke."

Mark looked down at Drake's finger on his chest. Mark and Drake last fought just before Christmas four years ago, when they both wanted to sit in the front seat of the car on their annual trip through Aberdeen to look at the illuminated rainbow of lights homeowners had hung for the holidays. Mark won that fight, but they both lost and had to stay home while their other brothers went with their mother to see the lights. Mark knew that in the time since then, Drake had grown taller than him, had begun playing basketball, and had become physically stronger. His dominance over his brother was mostly perception, and not guaranteed should they fight again. Mark didn't want to lose that position.

"Drake," Mark stated calmly. "Move your finger. Besides, your sweatshirt's too big for me."

"Maybe you cut it up to make rags for when you work on cars," Drake insinuated as he refused to move. Mark had a history of taking his brother's things apart to see how they worked, or how he might be able to use the parts for something else he was working on. He was mechanically inclined, and driven to make money. He had begun working before last summer, first cleaning the Hoquiam Library and then later at a car dealership as a lot boy. Mark also felt unjustly persecuted because of some of his more questionable personal choices he made, spending many summer nights in his room as a result, and sometimes thought about achieving freedom from his family—he knew making money would help that happen.

"Little brothers," Martin interjected from his perch on the bed. "Come on guys, we're talking about a sweatshirt. It's not worth a fight."

"It's not just a sweatshirt," Drake snapped as he turned to face Martin removing his finger from Mark. "It's my school sweatshirt. It's my only sweatshirt, and I had to beg Mom and Dad to buy it for me. Unlike you two, I don't have a job so I can't just buy a new sweatshirt to replace it."

Martin was seventeen, the eldest of the five Fraser boys. He proudly stood six feet, four inches in height and was just barely taller than Drake. He possessed the same blackish-brown hair like his younger brothers, though his had a bit of a curl just below his ears. Unlike Mark and Drake, he had blue eyes like their father and a pasty white complexion that had benefited from years of avoiding chores outside. Most of his avoidance was so he could watch the science fiction television shows broadcast in the afternoons on the local independent stations. He was a television junkie who pouted and became vindictive if he didn't get to watch his shows. Both Mark and Drake had learned long ago it was easier to do Martin's chores than deal with him later.

"Do you have it Martin?" Drake queried.

"No," Martin replied quickly. "I'm in high school. I wouldn't wear a middle school sweatshirt, I mean seriously. I suggest you check with Dennis and Albert."

Drake thought of the logic in what they both had stated, and turned to leave the room.

"Close the door on your way out," Mark directed, reasserting his position above his brother. Drake did just that, but not too quietly, as he headed back past the stairwell toward the large room across the wide second floor landing from his small room. When they moved into Hoquiam from Central Park last year Mom and Dad had taken the larger bedroom downstairs, Martin took the other bedroom downstairs, and Mark got the medium sized room by the bathroom upstairs leaving Drake to either move in with his little brothers in the largest room, or take the very small room at the top of the stairs. Drake took the small room, and for the very first time he had a room without Mark.

"Which one of you took my sweatshirt?" Drake demanded as he entered the room.

The two boys in the room were on opposite sides, Dennis, the older one, was on the right laying on his bed, and Albert was on the floor to the left behind his bed.

"We didn't take anything of yours Drake," Dennis quickly stated in a very defensive manner. Dennis was not physically built like his three older brothers. He had turned ten in October, three years younger than Drake and four years behind him in school because Drake had skipped a grade. Dennis was also short for his age. His unkempt mane of dirty blonde hair and hazel eyes were a throwback to their Grandfather Reuss' Germanic heritage. Dennis had struggled with his health since his birth, had spent stretches of time in Children's Hospital in Seattle, and was babied by the rest of his family for fear he might hurt himself.

"One of you has to have my sweatshirt," Drake elaborated as he stood in the doorway of the large green-carpeted room. "I've already checked Martin and Mark, and they don't have it. That leaves you two."

"Maybe they lied," Dennis stated with a giggle as he looked across the room towards Albert. Dennis was a very bright kid, and rather calculating. He would always try and place himself on the winning side of a disagreement between his brothers.

"Albert?" Drake asked with a stern gaze. Albert had turned eight, just thirteen days ago, on New Year's Eve. He was already nearly as tall as Dennis, and shared the same hair, eye color, and skin complexion with his brother. However, his facial structure was much more similar to Martin and their father, Drake, Sr.

"What?" Albert responded with a question, a favorite tactic of his. As the baby of the family, Albert seemed to be an attention-deprived child. But that was truly not the case, since he was typically the first his parents thought of, and the most likely to do something to annoy his older brothers to get that attention he craved.

"What are you doing behind your bed?" Drake focused his question.

"Nothing," replied Albert as he raised his hands to illustrate that he was not hiding anything. With a sudden lurch a gray mass waddled out from behind his bed.

"Is that Monique?" Drake demanded to know. "In my sweatshirt?"

"She wanted to try it on," Albert said with a laugh. Dennis giggled along with his little brother.

The small dog in the extra-large sweatshirt turned towards the sound of Drake's voice and tried to run to him with a clumsy stumble. Drake quickly moved to her and picked her up, working her head out of the thick gray material. She licked his face as he began to remove her from the garment.

"If I had more time," Drake lectured as he got the white poodle free of his clothing and released her to run down the stairs, "I'd hurt you for hurting her."

Albert fell down like he had been shot by Drake into a pile of loose clothes on his floor and made a series of odd faces, much to the delight of the laughing Dennis.

"Oh great," Drake smelled his sweatshirt as he began to put it over his head while walking towards his room. "Now my sweatshirt smells like a stinky dog."

With the exception of the misused clothing, Friday was the same as Thursday, which was the same as any school day for quite some time. The Fraser boys loved each other, and demonstrated it to each other in peculiar the ways they had come to know.

What was different was happening downstairs, unbeknownst to the boys. The telephone had rung about forty minutes earlier waking their mother, Sophia from her slumber. She was a Licensed Practical Nurse who worked the graveyard shift at a nursing home. She slept during the day when her children were in school, though occasionally she slumbered into the evening. She was thirty-five, stood five feet, six inches, and had similar dark Spanish features that both Mark and Drake possessed, and had been married to her husband since she was sixteen. Life for her always seemed as though it was focused on her family, and sometimes she wondered about what she might have missed out on by marrying so young.

After the phone call woke her up, she called her husband at work, and pleaded with him to rush home. Dad did just that, arriving home and disappearing into the master bedroom at three forty-five. He worked as a commissioned insurance agent and had some flexibility in his schedule. He was nearly five years older than his wife, and four inches taller. He had the same blackish-brown hair that was most common in the Fraser family, though his was parted on the right and had a dab or two of Brylcreem in it to hold up the flip at the front. Most of the boys had mimicked that style for at least one of their school pictures in the past.

At four o'clock, both parents came out of their room and stood anxiously in the sparsely decorated living room. The Frasers were not a wealthy family, spending much of their time hovering around the federal poverty line for their family size. Working-class poor was how young Drake described them with his socio-economic vocabulary. Their household belongings reflected that distinction. A long, floral patterned sofa was across from a green re-upholstered arm chair and dingy yellow recliner. There were five different colored beanbag chairs piled in one corner, one for each of the boys, and a large nineteen inch color television set against the far wall with its rabbit ears antennae splayed wide.

"Boys!" Mom yelled. "Come down here!"

No one responded, which was not unusual, few were the times when any of the boys came on the first call from their parents.

"Martin, Mark, Drake, Dennis, and Albert!" she exclaimed. "Come down here!"

Dad walked to the stairway entry and shouted, "Get your butts down here right now! Stop ignoring your mother!"

They could tell that there was movement upstairs. The floorboards creaked revealing someone was at least walking towards the stairway.

"Boys, your father and I have something to tell you!"

Drake emerged from the corner of the landing at the middle of the stairway and was being followed by Mark and Martin. He turned and looked at them ominously upon hearing the last call from their mother. They had long feared what would happen to their family if their parents split-up and divorced. Many of the kids the Frasers knew in school were facing such problems as the financial woes of the deflating timber industry, which crippled the local economy and made the stress of marriage and maintaining a family all escalate to a breaking point. Divorce. They could not ever imagine a time where they would not be close to each other, and divorce was the ultimate fear for all the Fraser boys, except maybe Mark, who at times secretly thought it might be kind of cool to get two Christmases, and it would definitely remove him from some of the family responsibilities and consequences he dreaded without it being his fault if it all went wrong.

There was a palatable sense of dread as they walked down the stairs past the landing in the middle and flashes of their lives being disrupted cascaded through their minds. Slowly the boys crossed the hall and entered the living room. The older boys sat upon the sofa while Dennis and Albert came down the stairs into the living room and flung themselves into the pile of beanbag chairs with a raucous swoosh.

"Boys," Mom began, as she looked at her husband for reassurance and then continued, "we have some bad news to tell you."

That could not be good, they thought, and even Mark in all his coolness began to respond like his brothers. They were like deer caught in the headlights. All those dark thoughts of divorce came flooding over them even disrupting Mark's happy-go-lucky view of it all. They knew their parents fought and argued. It had gotten worse after their dad got hurt on the job seven years ago and lived his life in pain and on prescription painkillers. But through it all they had hoped that this day would never come. There had to be some way to keep the family together. This could not be the end to the only normal they had ever known. Their hearts stopped as they waited for their mother to continue. But she could not. She began to visibly sob.

"This afternoon," Dad took over as he comforted his wife with a hug, "your Uncle Wally was killed in an accident."

The shock of that statement kicked the floor out from underneath the Fraser boys. This was so much worse than divorce. Walter Reuss was only nineteen, and his twentieth birthday was almost a month away. He was so close in age to his older nephews that they had been raised as more like brothers. He was the one they all looked up to. He was their idol. He was always there for them. He was one of them. He was dead. He was gone.

Sadness flooded their hearts and minds. They had not experienced a death in their immediate family except when their maternal great-grandfather, Hector La Madrid, died on the same day that Albert was born in 1969. But that was so long ago, they were so young then, and Wally had been there to help them through it. Wally could not do that this time. He had left them. Tears flowed. Martin saw his mother begin to cry in earnest and realized it was not a joke and he began to sob uncontrollably. This set off both Dennis and Albert into some loud crying and wailing. Mark felt the dam of his coolness break. Of all the people in his life, he admired Wally the most. He wanted to be like him, and now Wally was gone. Mark cried for the first time in years.

Drake, always the introvert, pulled into himself as his emotions welled up inside. He was the one who was always teased for being quick to cry and he knew this would be no exception. There was a sudden pain in his right temple and somewhere in the back of his mind he flashed back to a time when he was five years old and playing tackle football with his brothers, cousins, and Wally in a grassy field behind his great-grandparent's house in the country. He had cried to get a chance to play. They all had ragtag football helmets and makeshift shoulder pads that had been repaired to their current state of usefulness by their grandfather. Even Drake had found some football gear to look the part, though his helmet was at least two sizes too big. Reluctantly the older boys let him play, even though he was a big crybaby. Drake had been determined to play and prove he wasn't a baby. Mark had been teasing him the whole time calling him a crybaby and a sissy. He was put on the team against Wally and Mark, and they played hard and fast. Drake did his best and tried to make tackles but somehow always seemed to miss. When his team got the ball they always ignored him and never included him in the offensive plays. Finally, when Wally got the ball near midfield heading for a touchdown all alone with only Drake to beat, Drake did it. He dove at Wally as he ran past him latching his arms around his uncle's right leg. Drake slid down Wally's calf as his uncle continued forward, his arms finally holding firm to Wally's foot and ankle. Wally was big enough to push onward, Drake's oversized helmet turned to expose his face, allowing Wally's right heel to bump into Drake's nose as he took each step on his path to the end zone. Drake held on for all he was worth, but he could not stop his uncle from scoring. As soon as Wally yelled touchdown, Drake released his grip and immediately noticed that his nose was bleeding a lot out of both nostrils. The dreaded double-barreled nosebleed, worst of all nosebleeds, and known to all of them to cause more deaths to five year olds then lightning strikes every year. Drake rolled over, holding his nose under the single bar of the facemask, blood covering his face and hands, and he began to cry. Wally sensed the danger of the situation and knew that if Drake continued to cry that loudly someone would come out of the house and see his nephew covered in blood and as the oldest, he would get in serious trouble. So he did what he thought was right and best for him in the situation. He bent down and said to Drake, "crying only makes it hurt worse." And Drake quieted and eventually even stopped crying.

Now, eight years later, Wally was gone, dead, and if ever Drake would not be called a crybaby, this was that time. In his head all he heard was Wally saying, "crying only makes it hurt worse." And Drake cried not a single tear over the death of his beloved uncle. In fact he cried no more until after the birth of his first child long into the future. Such is the power of words. Wally's words haunted him, but had Wally known the impact those six words would have on the day of his death, he would have taken the punishment and allowed his nephew the release of emotion all those years ago.

"We need to go out to your grandparent's house," added their father stoically. "Go get your coats and put the dog out so we can go."

The boys began to numbly stumble upstairs for their jackets, except Drake who already had put his jacket on over his sweatshirt to ride to basketball practice. He turned at the bottom of the stairs and went towards the back door calling the dog while making a clicking noise with his mouth, "Monique! Come on, let's go outside." The dog was still a bit traumatized by being forced into his sweatshirt and did not come to the door. Drake went and got her in the back of the hallway. Monique growled at a shadow in the hallway as Drake carried her through to the kitchen to take her outside.

Mom turned to Dad and clutched him in a deep hug and sobbed.

It was a long, quiet ride on US Highway 101 through South Aberdeen, Cosmopolis, and over the Cosmopolis Hill. It was never called the Cosmopolis Hill though since locals referred to Aberdeen's smaller neighbor as Cosi, just as they referred to Montesano as Monte. Each member of the family was lost in grief and introspection to varying degrees. It was only when the van began the long decline that slowly turned to the right before turning one final time to the left and the end of the descent from the hill on the southern outskirts of town that they began to stir uneasily from their silence. They all knew the way, having driven this way hundreds of times over the years to their grandparent's house out near Brooklyn. They all knew the end of the Cosi Hill, but had never felt this way upon reaching the final sloping curve of the roadway. Towering Douglas-firs lined the hill on both the uphill and downhill sides of the road. The imposing trees blocked the coming convergence of US 101 and the cut-off road to Montesano. The cut-off road came to an end in a tee intersection within one hundred yards of the bottom of the hill.

Dad used to tell the boys stories of how he used to go to the small clearing along the north side of the cut-off road to ride a timber company bus out into the forest every day with his father-in-law and brother-in-law. These park-and-ride timber stories always dealt with having to get up and be there by four o'clock in the morning, but his favorite revolved around the time he had tied their Uncle Richard's bootlaces together while Richard napped on the bus after being out late the night before. He loved that story, but now he doubted that his boys would ever recall that story when looking at that little clearing again.

As the van rounded the final curve and cleared the trees they saw the Grays Harbor County Sheriff and Washington State Patrol cars sitting on both sides of the road, their blue and red lights flashing. A State Trooper in his wide-brimmed hat was standing in the middle of the intersection directing traffic. Dad slowed the van to a crawl as they approached the scene before them. A large, diesel semi tow-truck had arrived, its flashing yellow lights pulsing slightly out of time with those of the police cars. There was also an ambulance and two volunteer fire department trucks there with their hoses still on the ground, and their red lights flashing to their own rhythm. It was an overwhelming orchestra of colored strobe lights.

And then they saw it. Lying on its side was the burned out shell of the cab of a blue diesel logging truck, a Peterbilt 359 with a spilt load of logs that crushed some of the cars parked in the park-and-ride clearing beneath it. Immediately behind the twisted trailer with one of its "U" shaped stakes still standing upright defiantly was the twisted remains of Uncle Wally's yellow 1967 Chevrolet stepside pickup. Its front end was crushed and twisted, as if the logging truck ran up over the hood on the driver side and spun it into the back end of the trailer and the twenty-to-thirty tons of logs it hauled at the time of the accident.

To the passengers of the Fraser van, it seemed the longest four hundred foot drive of their lives. It didn't help matters when the State Trooper stopped traffic on US 101 to let waiting cars on the cut-off road turn left towards Artic, Brooklyn, and Raymond. The tear stained eyes of the boys stared at the accident scene out the driver side windows. Their souls were crushed by the stark reality of the accident. The words their father had spoken earlier that afternoon were just words, but now there could be no mistaking it. Uncle Wally was dead.

Drake thought it was odd that the singular event of a moment in time could have such an impact on another individual, or in this case a family. He wondered how this all made sense in the grand scheme of things, and started to ponder the mysteries of life. Through all of his logical thoughts a vast sea of pain raged within him like a typhoon, but somehow he pushed it down, deeper and deeper. Drake finally turned away and looked into the forested hollow on the opposite side of the road. He thought he saw a little glint of sunlight reflecting off a piece of yellow metal beneath the trees in a small patch of what appeared to be clover. That was a curious thing, but in the long run it did little to take his mind off of the raging storm of pent-up emotions in his heart and soul.

The House of Reuss

The Brotherhood of Olympus and the Deadliest Game

2

**The La Madrid Gift**
**Chapter Two**
**January 13, 1978**
**Brooklyn, Washington**

There were already close to twenty cars in the driveway at the house of Henry and Isabella Reuss when the Fraser van pulled into the packed gravel of the great sweeping round-a-bout driveway. Mom had not grown up here. The house was built in 1970. However, she had spent a lot of time in the valley where her parents now lived, because the neighboring acreage was owned by her paternal grandparents. The two-story ranch style house was painted yellow, it had white trim work near the eaves and windows, and its brown wooden front door was centered on the bottom floor. A large unfinished and unpainted wooden shop with two massive garage doors stood back a bit behind and to the left of the house from the road. Beyond the shop the property stretched out into an apple orchard towards a creek that emptied into North River, which ran the length of the property down a steep embankment some one hundred and fifty feet behind the house. Cars were now parked in the yard and in the driveway filling most of the available space in front of the house. Dad had to pull the van into a grassy spot beside the shop next to the apple orchard. As they opened the side doors to the van and began to pile out, Martin wondered out loud where their grandparent's dog was at.

"Where's Buddy?" blurted Martin inquisitively. Buddy was no ordinary dog, he was a very large Saint Bernard who could look eye-to-eye with Martin when he stood up upon his hind feet and put his front paws on Martin's shoulders as if they were dancing. The extended family had been raising the large breed of dogs for the past few years and Buddy was the son of the Fraser's Brandy and their Aunt Carmen's Brunhilda. Wally had named him and went with the alcohol naming pattern the Fraser's had used in naming their Saint Bernards. He named him Budweiser but everyone simply called the big loveable dog Buddy. Now he was nowhere to be seen, which was highly unusual given his protective nature of the property and the sheer number of visitors.

"Must be off chasing cats or something," replied Dad as he came around the side of the van by everyone else. "You know how much he loves to wander off."

"But he doesn't usually go far," continued Martin. "And he never misses the chance to greet company."

Mark and Drake silently concurred with Martin as they all walked between the parked cars to the sidewalk in front of the house. The glass storm door opened out to the right and the wooden front door opened in to the left, a curious thing that the ever curious mind of Drake pondered every time he entered his grandparent's house. Inside the front door the hallway went forward past a long shuttered folding closet door on the right and turned to the right in front of an open bathroom door. Sitting guard in the hallway was a large, crocheted orange and black striped cat beanbag that was used as a doorstop. That large handcrafted feline looked like an odd prototype of a similar orange cat that would begin to grace newspaper comics the following year. Immediately to the right inside the front door was the start of a steep set of five stairs to a landing with a stylized pentagonal stained glass window cut into the interior wall and a small round window, similar in concept to a porthole to the right on the exterior wall, before the stairs continued to the left with the same perilous slope to the second story. A low hanging globe light was suspended at the end of a long swag chain above the middle of the landing. So steep were the steps that Dennis still refused to walk up or down them, he would sit on the steps and move up or down the stairs one step at a time on his butt.

They climbed the stairs, each in their own manner, and turned to the right into the living room that had large windows along the northwest and northeast walls. From here, the whole of the valley could be seen and any cars driving down the road could be spotted nearly a mile away. It had always seemed the safest place the Fraser boys had known. In fact, after their father was hurt on the job, during the spring of 1971 into the winter of 1972, all seven of the Frasers had lived on the ground floor in the space below the living room and behind the stained glass window. It was in many ways their home away from home.

Around the living room sat the Reuss' and many of their extended family. Grandpa and Grandma, Henry and Isabella sat in chairs that faced towards the windows but were separated by the pathway into the dining room on the far southern wall. On couches along the other walls and in the chaise below the windows that ran parallel to the road sat many family and friends. Folding metal chairs that Henry kept in the closet at the base of the stairs filled in the open areas around the room.

Mom came in and immediately hugged her parents and then her siblings, in turn. She was the eldest of the four Reuss children. She was four years older than her brother Richard, twelve years older than her sister Carmen, and sixteen years older than Walter. She had married Drake, Sr. the year after Wally was born and given birth to Martin the following year. Wally and her boys spent a lot of time together as they grew up, even though she often treated him as a son, she always loved Wally as her baby brother.

Her father, Henry, was of German stock—Prussian more precisely. He was big burly man, about six-foot-two with a receding gray hairline, a quick smile, and twinkle in his blue eyes. He met his wife of thirty-eight years in high school and they were married soon after.

Mom's mother, Isabella, was born in Madrid, Spain and

was still a fiery Spaniard underneath her demure grandmotherly image. She was a petite brunette, maybe five-foot-two, with brown eyes, and a dark olive complexion. Her parents, Hector and Lorenza La Madrid, immigrated from Spain in 1925. Their life in Europe was something they did not talk much about, but rumor had it that they were either of arcane gypsy blood or Spanish royalty. The La Madrid family had moved to Aberdeen for reasons even Mom didn't know. Her mother seldom talked about it, save for stories of Mom's grandmother telling them they had to stop speaking Spanish and speak English now that they were Americans. Her grandmother had died of tuberculosis a month after Wally was born, and she had spent much of Mom's teen years in and out of a sanitarium for the disease. Her grandfather moved in with the Frasers in his elder years, before his death on New Year's Eve 1969. Old Hector was quite fond of little Drake, and would often laugh at the little boy as he did precocious things, like falling asleep while eating dinner and continuing to lift spoonful's of mashed potatoes into his mouth without waking. He spent a lot of time with her middle child, and his last words were, "watch over little Drake, he's a special one." Because of the queerness of the La Madrid arrival and the secrets within the family, many locals regarded them with awe and skepticism. They were a dark family, and many had gifts of foresight and were generally much more aware of spiritual things than most people.

Mom had always believed that her mother could read her mind, and occasionally thought she heard her mother telling her things even though she was not talking to her. Mom didn't feel she was gifted like others in her family, and felt that she was rather normal, except for an acute sense of empathy that helped her in her chosen profession as a nurse. She was not sure if any of that passed on to her own children, though she expected something might develop in both Mark and Drake because of their obvious La Madrid genetic traits, but neither seemed to show any signs of such things. Her sister Carmen was much more in tune to the mystical. She had the La Madrid gift. A very young Carmen had predicted that Sophia would meet the man she would marry the night Sophia met Drake, Sr. at the Harborena Skating Rink in Hoquiam. She also had correctly informed her older sister that she would be the mother of five boys. But when it came to the La Madrid gift, her baby brother Wally was the real inheritor of the family secrets. And that was what much of the side discussions that afternoon in her parent's living room focused on, Wally and his special abilities.

Many of the stories overhead in the living room were completely new to the Fraser boys because their father did not like to hear any talk about supernatural or occult things in his house. Most of the people in attendance had known Wally since he was a little boy, and the stories they shared reflected this.

"Of course," one of Mom's uncles stated, "it was widely known that Wally was color blind and could really only see the color yellow. That's why they painted the house yellow, and why he painted his pickup yellow."

"He dropped out of school after eighth grade," added another relative on the other side of the room. "He said he was bored and didn't want to waste his life in school."

"He was born in the caul," an elderly woman near the boys said before turning towards them and continuing, "born with a veil he was indeed, and that's very rare and special."

"What does that mean?" asked Martin to the woman.

"Well, my boy," answered the woman, "it means he was born with a gift of psychic abilities."

"Are you serious?" Martin responded loudly. There was a long pause in the room.

"Yes, it's true." Isabella Reuss replied across the short side of the room. "Wally was born with a veil."

"He was an unusual child," she continued, as Henry got up and headed into the kitchen through the dining room. "He would always tell us stories about what he used to be when he was alive before he was born to us, where he used to live, and remarkably when he was quite young, four or five years old I believe, he told me one day when we drove by the Montesano cut-off road, he said 'Momma, I am going to die right here someday, with scuba tanks before I am twenty-one.' And I told him, that's nice dear, but I think you have a long time before then and you might change your mind. You might want to live to be old and wise. And we laughed about it the rest of the way into Aberdeen. But, he was right. He did die right there where he said he would. I drove by just before the accident and saw him sitting there waiting to turn, we waved to each other. And I saw the truck as it came around the corner by the weigh station, but I didn't know. I just didn't know. I don't understand, he was still so young, he had so much to live for."

The boys saw their grandmother breakdown into tears as she repeatedly said, "I just don't understand."

Dennis told his mom that he had to go to the bathroom, and she knew he didn't want to walk by the open staircase to get there alone.

"Drake," Mom began, "help Dennis get by the staircase to the bathroom."

"But Mom," responded Drake in mild protest. "He's ten years old, and he should be able to walk by the stairs by himself."

"Drake," Mom replied quickly, "just do it. Help your brother go potty."

"Awww," whined Drake. "This isn't fair, why can't Martin or Mark do it."

"Drake, I am not going to say it again," Mom rebutted.

"Come on Dennis," Drake finally stated as he started walking with his little brother to the hallway that contained the staircase to the lower level of the house.

Across the hall from the stairs was the main entrance into the kitchen. The hallway beyond was filled with hanging picture frames and larger picture collages on corked boards. Halfway down the hallway there were doors on both the right and left hand sides. The door on the right was the upstairs bathroom, and the door on the left opened into Carmen's old room. Further down the hallway, there were two final doors. On the right hand side at the end of the hall was their grandparent's room door and at the very end of the hall was their Uncle Wally's room.

Drake walked next to Dennis and went between him and the stairs to keep him from getting scared. Once he had gotten his brother past the stairway he knew he had to stay to help him back. Dennis walked into the bathroom and locked the door with a click. Drake stood and looked at the rows of photographs and picture collages on the wall. Nearly everyone in the family was represented at least twice. Strangely, he felt a pull to go open Wally's door, almost like Wally might be in there and all this fuss and bother was just a bad dream. But there was something else, a darker pull, like maybe Wally was there, but not in any corporeal form. Drake's heart began to race. He imagined the spectral Wally calling out to him, beckoning him to walk down the hall to his room. Drake took a step in that direction, then another.

There was a swirling fog thudding in his head keeping the beat of his bounding pulse. In the midst of the fog, he began to hear faint voices. Drake tilted his head as he listened. The voices were calling out, a chorus of voices slowly harmonizing into a single phrase, 'come to us,' and he began to walk down the long hallway towards his uncle's door. Suddenly one voice rose above the din, cutting through the fog in his mind.

"Where are you going?" Grandma said to him. Drake was confused, it was though his grandmother was next to him, but the voice was not coming from the living room, it seemed to be in his head pushing the beckoning chorus of voices aside. "Drake?"

Drake thought, "I thought I felt Wally calling me to his room."

"Yes, my dear, you did," Grandma's voice sounded in his mind. "But, he is in no condition for visitors tonight. Come get me and Grandpa some more coffee and then sit with me so we can talk some more about your gift, and what Wally has given you."

Drake turned and walked back outside the bathroom. He waited a moment longer and Dennis emerged from the bathroom.

"Did you wash?" Drake queried.

"Yes," replied Dennis with a sassy attitude. "I always wash."

Drake knew that wasn't true. He turned and paused for a moment because he saw a shimmering, translucent, terrified image of his oldest brother standing in the doorway of Aunt Carmen's old room across the hall. As suddenly as the ghostly image had appeared, it faded, and as it did any memory of it washed away from his mind.

He escorted Dennis past the stairs, and then headed over and got his grandparents' coffee cups and went into the kitchen to refill them. Upon his guarded return, he was careful not to spill any of the hot coffee he carried in mugs in both hands. He ever so carefully set the cups down on the coasters on the table. He got a thank you from both grandparents, and then sat down in a metal chair next to his grandmother. Quietly they sat there, as the discussions and stories ebbed and flowed through the large room filled with family and friends.

"Now then," Grandma's voice wafted like a melody in his mind, "let's talk about my grandson, shall we?" In the grief of the day, Drake finally managed a small smile, as his grandmother began to talk to him in his mind. All he could recall later was the feeling that his grandmother had talked with him, the details were lost, only the warmth of the sharing lingered.

Downstairs, some of Wally's friends had gathered and were sharing the grief of loss and their memories of their friend. Mark and Martin had found their way down to this group of older guys and stood listening to the conversation. Kevin, who lived on the Montesano Cut-Off Road, was one of the first people on the scene of the accident. He told the tale of what he saw when he arrived. He saw Wally's twisted pickup, its driver side door open, and the steering wheel bent nearly out the door. In the middle of the northbound lane of US 101 was the crushed body of Wally in a pool of blood. He saw the Peterbilt truck on its side and heard a man yelling from inside it. He ran to the truck and climbed up on its upturned side. He saw the face of the driver, a man sinking in the terror of the fire that was spreading inside the cab, and was able to open the door and grab the driver by the arms and began to pull him from the flames. He thought the driver began to slide up out of the cab and then said it felt like something pulled him back into the flames. Another man rushed over to help him and they both pulled on the driver, again he rose out of the flames only to be pulled back in by a greater force. Kevin showed his wrapped and bandaged hands. "I got second and third degree burns trying to pull him out, but I couldn't, something kept pulling him back in."

"Maybe it was his seatbelt," surmised Joe. "Or he had his foot stuck on the gear shift?"

"No," replied Kevin in a matter of fact tone. "I was still there when they got the fire out and pulled the old guy from the cab. He was dead, burned alive, and I will never forget the screaming as the fire took him. The firefighters said there was nothing inside that could've held him in. His truck didn't have any seatbelts and I know what I felt. Something pulled him back in."

"Maybe your burns just made it seem like something was pulling him," Joe theorized. "Pain can make a lot of things seem different then they really are."

"Maybe," Kevin responded half-heartedly and completely unconvinced.

Mark and Martin looked at each other, their eyes wide in amazement, their minds shocked by Kevin's story. Kevin was not one to embellish stories, and he was not prone to pain. A few months ago they had seen him pull out his pocket knife and cut a large wart off the back of his hand without any reaction when he was at their grandparent's house. According to Mark, that made him one of the coolest people he knew, right up there by Wally and himself, of course. Whatever it was that pulled the log truck driver back into the cab didn't matter, what was important to Martin was that something did. He knew he would have to tell Drake about it later and see what his brainy little brother thought about it.

"That's all messed up, man," added a curly brown haired teen from the corner below the stained glass window. He was a stout eighteen year old, standing no more than five feet, eight inches in height. Unlike his kin, he was thickly built and wore thick red suspenders over a blue flannel shirt, to hold up his worn blue jeans—a fashion look that was quite common in the grungy attire of the timber industry. "The bottom line is Wally is dead. Arguing or speculating about the other guy isn't going to change that fact."

Up until this point Ralph Reuss, Wally's younger cousin by a year, had not commented on any discussions. Ralph was the son of Henry Reuss' younger brother John. Ralph fit between Wally and Martin age-wise, and primarily hung out with just those two boys. Ralph's family lived on the other end of the valley a little over a mile away, behind the home of Jacob and Beatrix Reuss, the Fraser boy's great-grandparents.

"Wally was like a brother to most of us here," Ralph continued to share as he leaned back against the wall beneath the intricate window. "The truck driver killed him, in my opinion. And I say if something helped that bastard die in the crash, then that's karma. It's justice on a biblical scale, an eye for an eye, man."

Many of the friends of Wally gathered in the room, nodded in agreement with the words of the shaken Ralph. Martin and Mark looked at each other. Though they were as deeply hurt by the loss of Wally as anyone else there, something about Kevin's story told them it wasn't biblical justice that killed the truck driver. At that moment they both shared a chill that sent gooseflesh down the lengths of their arms and made the hair on the back of their necks bristle.

"Did you feel that?" Martin quietly asked his brother.

"Yeah," Mark responded with a shiver. "You too? That was weird."

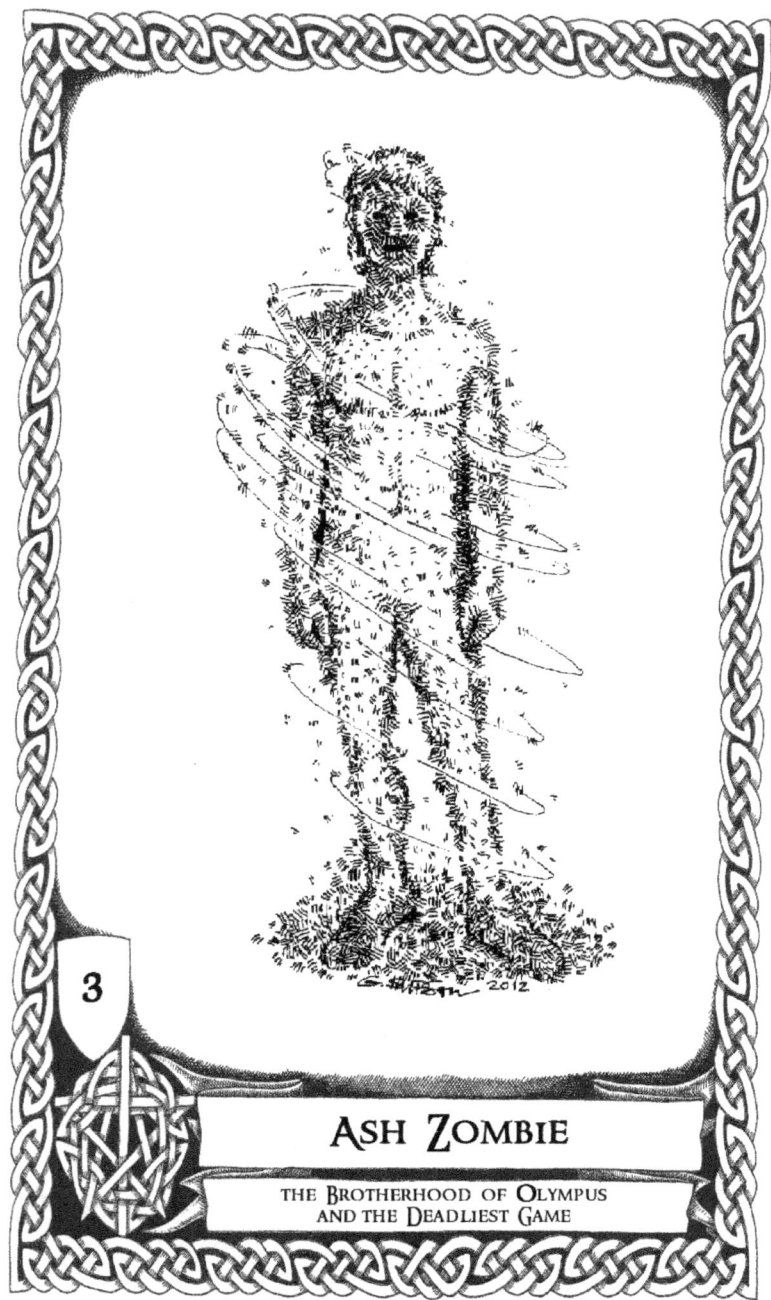

**3**

## ASH ZOMBIE

THE BROTHERHOOD OF OLYMPUS
AND THE DEADLIEST GAME

**Only the Good Die Young**
**Chapter Three**
**March 20, 1978**
**Hoquiam, Washington**

In the weeks that followed the tragic death of Walter Reuss, time passed and life continued, but the wounds lay bare in his friends and family and did not heal. The relationships between the Fraser boys had strained and began to tatter and unravel on the edges.

Mark had become more withdrawn from his brothers and began to slide academically. He had been a 'B' student or higher since he entered junior high back in Aberdeen, but now he no longer cared about school, and it was increasingly difficult to complete any assignment or turn in any homework. His focus had become his car. Two days earlier Mark celebrated his sixteenth birthday, and today he had skipped school and went to the Department of Motor Vehicles office to take his driving test with his mother. He was officially able to drive the car he had purchased in February from Kevin, Wally's cool friend, for two hundred dollars. Mark had spent nearly every waking moment of his free time out in the driveway or garage working on that old 1964 Chevrolet Impala. He hadn't even humored any attempts at offers for help from Martin or Drake.

Mark's car was his vehicle of escape from his family and their rules, his life, and the dark nightmare that pursued him since that day in January. He had begun to plan his departure. He didn't care about school, nor did he desire to go to college or anything like that anymore. All he wanted was to get away. He figured he would have to get his car running well, and then save up enough money to drive somewhere far away and get his own place. He would have to wait until after summer when he could get re-hired by the car dealer.

Perhaps he could outrun the darkness surrounding his soul. He found it increasingly difficult to trust his brothers, he was always annoyed by Dennis and Albert, even before all of this, and Martin had begun to act weird. It was his relationship with Drake that really suffered. Mark and Drake had shared a bedroom for most of their lives. They were remarkably so similar in looks as little children that many thought they were twins, especially once Drake grew as big as Mark. All through elementary school in Central Park they were nearly inseparable. He had to admit that he liked being with his crybaby, brainy, younger brother.

But that was all somehow different now. He didn't want to make that connection with Drake anymore, perhaps because he feared the hurt that he felt from the loss of Wally, and didn't want to repeat it when he left the family behind including Drake. Rather than think about emotions and junk like that, he kept himself busy.

Today was no exception. Mark was busy in the garage, removing the bolts in the motor mounts under the hood of his car. He had gotten Wally's small block Chevy 283 engine out of the wrecked pickup from his grandfather and was going to put it in his rebuilt Impala. The rhythmic clicks of his ratchet wrench echoed off the stripped engine block and reverberated in the chilly garage. The radio droned softly in the background so he didn't bother his family in the house, or someone might come out and yell at him. March was always a cold and wet month in Washington, gray refrigerated drizzle Drake had called it, and Mark certainly agreed. It was about eight-thirty, the sun had set over an hour earlier, and the temperature was in the low forties. His goal for the day was to get the old engine out and, if all went well, get the new one in.

He was lost in thought about the 'ongoing investigation' over the cause and fault of his uncle's accident. He had heard his father talking to his grandfather, in his dispassionate insurance agent voice, as to why they hadn't released any of the substantial life insurance money. Apparently the family of the log truck driver got a hold of Wally's driving record and had pushed that the cause of the accident was Wally's, and that this overgrown juvenile delinquent had killed their loved one. According to them it was practically murder. The official accident reports and forensic evidence had been sealed, and no one had access to any of the information.

Mark knew what this was. It was an attempt by society to make his uncle, his idol, out to be a bad guy. He was being framed. He knew Wally wasn't a bad guy, he was rough around the edges, and didn't like to conform to what others thought he should be or do, but that didn't make him a bad guy, and it most certainly didn't make him a killer.

His ratchet wrench fell out of his hand and through the engine well down to the cement floor of the garage with a metallic clang. He climbed off the front fender of the car and scooted underneath the front end of the Impala reaching out for the fallen wrench in the shadows beneath the car. The heavy scent of automobile oil and grease wafted over him as he lay upon the cold gray floor. Curiously, he heard an odd clicking sound that was like a distortion of his ratchet wrench faintly echoing in the garage.

Everything went dark.

For what seemed like minutes, Mark laid there, attempting to figure out why everything went black. Then finally it dawned on him that one of his brothers must have flipped the breaker switch for the power in the garage. He looked out under the car to see if the light of the street lamps was still softly lighting up the darkened evening sky. He saw nothing, no shade differentiation at all, nothing but black. He reached up to pull himself out from under the car, and his hand went through the air rapidly. He had anticipated some resistance when he touched the underside edge of the car, but it was not there. He took both hands and raised them up, there was nothing above him. His heart pounded heavily in his chest. This wasn't right.

"Martin!" shouted Mark. "Drake! Come on you guys, what the hell are you doing, this isn't funny! Turn the lights back on you dillholes!"

He was greeted by nothing but silence and the oppressive darkness. He decided to stand and find his way to the wall, and the light switch, or the breaker box. The wall should have been within ten, no more than twelve steps in any direction he went. But there was no wall ahead of him. He knew the garage wasn't that big, and he was sure he had taken at least twenty steps and in a pretty straight line too, so he knew he wasn't walking in circles. And where was his car?

"Drake!" he snapped. He knew this was out of Martin's capabilities, only his brainiac little brother could have pulled this off. Seconds passed into minutes and still he moved forward through the darkness with a hand extended hoping to find the missing wall.

He stopped and pondered for a moment. Perhaps he should head back to where he started before he got lost in the darkness. He took great care in turning exactly a hundred-eighty degrees by pivoting his feet one at a time into ninety degree angles, heel to heel. He began to slowly move back towards where his car should have been. Behind him he heard that same clicking sound of his ratchet wrench in the distance. No, it wasn't the same, it was irregular, not the fast metallic click that comes as the wrench pulls back, it was almost like someone was moving it a little at a time, and in uneven lengths. Maybe like Morse code, long and short bursts of clicking. He turned to face the noise and saw what appeared to be a dimly lit glow in the far darkness. Overcome by his weariness of the dark he threw caution to the wind and sprinted towards the light.

Mark was the strongest of all the Fraser boys, and they all knew that. Martin wouldn't challenge him physically, and he was still able to intimidate Drake, mostly due to the years of being on top at the end of any physical fight, both play and real. He knew, after watching Drake get stronger and more agile by playing basketball that the time would come when his now bigger little brother would one day be able to best him. Today wasn't that day.

"Drake!" he shouted as he ran towards the faint glow. "I'm going to kick your butt!"

He ran hard and fast. His side began to ache. He painfully realized that smoking cigarettes was not helping him stay fit. He pulled up and began to walk in the darkness. His deep ragged breathing masked any other noise he might have heard. The pain in his side was intense. He bent over at the waist and put his hands on his knees.

It was at this point that he began to sense that someone was watching him. He cautiously looked around himself without moving his head, not thinking that in the shroud of darkness no one else could have seen him moving. He was shocked to see that the faint glow was now behind him.

"Drake?" Mark queried, and then paused. "Alright, you win, you got me. Now turn the lights on."

The dim glow began to grow brighter, turning increasing lighter and lighter in shades of gray. Within the illumination, he heard that odd clicking sound.

"Drake?"

No response came from the glowing light.

"Okay, if it isn't Drake, then who is it?"

The clicking intensified to an almost painful level and then stopped suddenly. It was replaced by a disembodied voice that echoed upon the air itself.

"Mark. It's good to see you." said a vaguely familiar voice.

"Who are you?" Mark asked.

"You don't know?"

"No, who are you?" Mark demanded.

"I'm hurt. You were always my favorite nephew."

"Wally?" Mark said in disbelief.

"Yes Mark, it's me, your uncle Wally."

"Why can't I see you? Where are you?" Mark questioned.

In a sudden answer to his question, a cloud of gray, ash-like powder swirled in the air rising up from the ground below the glowing light. The cloud swirled and danced upon itself and rose up to above Mark's height. In the middle of the swirling mini-tornado of gray dust a form was taking shape. It was a rough invisible form, but damp enough that the ash stuck to it as it swirled around. The shape became more solid looking, from the ground to the top of its head, and to Mark's surprise it looked like Walter Reuss, his uncle.

Mark's eyes began to blink as moisture clouded his vision. Tears ran down his cheeks and he walked towards Wally.

"Why? Why?" he sobbed and began to cry in earnest.

"Why what Mark?" replied the ashen gray form of Wally.

"Why did you have to die?" Mark started. "Why am I here now? Why do you look that way?"

"Well, to start with. I look this way, because I am dead. Two months dead."

"You're all covered in gray soot. Shouldn't you be, I don't know, more like a zombie?" Mark stated.

The ashen form of Wally looked down at itself, then held up and turned its right arm in front of the hollow spaces where his eyes should be. It slowly turned its arm the other direction and then moved its fingers in a flexing motion.

"Hmmm, made of ash, I must've been cremated."

"Yeah, I guess so." Mark reasoned that was correct.

"Second question, you're here because I need to talk to you. I need you to understand, so you can do what needs to be done."

"What do you mean?" Mark said, he was more of a 'just the facts' kind of guy and he was already tiring of the riddle like dialogue.

"And your first question last, I died because I had to. It was my fate. I always knew I would die there. Besides, what happened to me was a catalyst for the things you all must now do. There are things you're meant to do, you and your brothers, which you wouldn't be able to do if I was still alive. My death will make you go and do great things. Besides, it's like that Billy Joel song, *Only the Good Die Young*, I never really liked it when I was alive. But. now I guess I was just too good, so here I am… What are you gonna do, right?"

"This makes no sense," Mark argued, fighting back tears. "You have no idea how messed up things are without you. Dad's all bent out of shape by the insurance company. They haven't paid your life insurance. And there's talk that Grandpa and Grandma are going to be sued for millions of dollars by the truck driver's family because, get this, you killed him. And now you show up and say you had to die for my brothers and me to do something? Wally, that's just crazy!"

"Mark. All of that will take care of itself. The truck driver was a nice guy. We hung out for a while after the crash. Trust me, I didn't kill him. Mark, I need you to listen to me. This is very important for you and your brothers. Remember when you, Marty, Drake, Ralph, and I used to hang out. Play football, go hiking in the woods, and stuff like that? We were special, the five of us, we all loved each other like brothers. I had to come back to help you. Now that I'm gone, you're the one they'll look up to."

"Wait," Wally said as his form turned and looked around. "Who are you? What do you want? "

With a look of fright upon his ash formed face, Wally turned back to Mark.

"Mark," Wally began urgently. "Run!"

The ash spun loosely for a couple of seconds and then reformed into the shape of Wally.

"Run?" Mark responded. "Run where?"

"Mark, never mind. You don't need to run," continued the ash zombie in a slightly higher tone, like Wally's voice had suddenly changed from a baritone to a tenor. "You must do something important."

"What Wally?" Mark asked. "Why is your voice different?"

"There is no time for questions now. You mustn't trust your brothers anymore. Martin and Drake are too upset over my death and may start to do odd things. You've always been the rational one. You know what you need to do. What you desire more than anything else. You have to get away from them. You mussst leave them."

From somewhere, just out of his frame of reference, the sudden thought of what it would mean to leave smacked Mark in the face with a very cold dose of reality. He would have to pay for everything, food, rent, clothes, gas, insurance, cigarettes, everything. He imagined himself poor, disheveled and homeless, living out of his broken down car in some backwater town in Nebraska. He had no idea why Nebraska popped into his mind. He hadn't ever even been there.

"I can't leave," Mark responded. "Wally, how would leaving my family make things better?"

The image of Wally began to lose focus, the ash that covered his hollow form began to move again and then it fell in one big pile on the ground before him with a whoosh.

"Wally!" Mark shouted painfully.

Mark stooped and put his hands in the ash and tried to somehow reform his uncle. Tears fell and the ash burned his wet eyes. He closed his eyes so tight they hurt. In that self-imposed darkness he heard his pulse racing in his head. From his squatting position he slowly fell backwards onto the dark ground, his hands on his eyes. He forced himself to take a deep breath to calm himself. There was a sudden tugging on his leg and he reacted with a startle.

As he sat up he smacked his head into the underside of his car and dropped his ratchet wrench on the cement floor with a familiar clang. He held his throbbing head with his oily hand. He looked out under the car towards his feet.

"Were you sleeping?" Dennis asked with wide eyes, amazed by the startle he caused his brother. Mark never jumped at any scary movie, or at any attempt by his little brothers to jump out at him from inside the closet, something both Dennis and Albert enjoyed doing. "Mom said you need to get your car back outta the garage before she goes to work."

"Did she get called in early?" Mark began to protest as he

scooted out from under the car, grabbing his twice fallen wrench on the way out. "It's only eight-thirty, dillhole."

"No it isn't," Dennis replied with attitude as he headed back to the door into the kitchen. "It's past ten, dillhole."

Dennis ran the rest of the way into the house to avoid being chased and caught. Still, he was ever so pleased with himself for making Mark jump like that under his car.

Mark sat there, rubbing his head. Dennis must have been right, he must have been asleep, that is the only way all of what just happened made sense. It was all a bad dream, a nightmare. He had convinced himself of that and then he realized what he was hearing softly in the background. KGHO, the only good FM radio station they had in Aberdeen, in his opinion, was playing a Billy Joel song. That song was *Only the Good Die Young*. Mark sobbed quietly in the garage.

4

## MORDGEISTS

THE BROTHERHOOD OF OLYMPUS
AND THE DEADLIEST GAME

**I'll Always Be Young**
**Chapter Four**
**April 14, 1978**
**Hoquiam, Washington**

Of all the Fraser children, Martin was perhaps the most affected by the death of his uncle. Wally had been the closest thing Martin had to an older brother. Due to the closeness of their age, and the amount of time Martin's mother spent with his grandmother when Martin and his brothers were quite young, the two boys, uncle and nephew regarded each other as much more than that. Martin knew he didn't have the same type of kindred spirit relationship with Wally that Mark did, but he believed that his bond with Wally had been stronger then that of his younger brother. In his mind, Martin was convinced that his relationship with Wally would survive beyond death.

The three months that followed the death of Wally Reuss had left a deep emotional crevasse in the psyche of Martin. He had withdrawn from his limited social network of friends and coworkers and had been wracked by dark menacing dreams making it difficult for him to get rest at night. Martin began to fear the coming of darkness because his nighttime was filled with horrors the like of which he had never before imagined. He had always been fascinated by science fiction, fantasy, and horror movies but now it seemed as though those fictional accounts had not prepared and for the reality that he faced every night in his dreams.

He did not remember dreaming on the night of Friday, January thirteenth. The following night while he slept, he watched as a silent observer to the events of the day before. It was though he was a ghostly apparition that fluttered from one location to another to bear witness to the tragedy that had befallen his family. He had no power to intervene. He had no voice to object. He had no choice but to watch it over and over again, as his screams of protest reverberated in his mind. Every night since then, it had been the same thing, with the worrisome exception that each night tended to get more vibrant, more real, so much so that Martin could smell the fragrances and aromas at each location. He found himself paying attention to the dialog that was occurring around him. It was always the same, yet he heard more of it each night, especially from the people on the periphery of his nightmarish vision.

Martin had also taken notice of a couple gray, shrouded, cloud-like figures that seemed to slowly emerge from the shadows more and more every night. They seemed to be present at the crash scene, in their house when their parents told them the news, and at their grandparent's house during the time after they arrived that day. These specters seemed to be observing what was happening and talking to each other, and over the weeks that passed, Martin began to hear their conversation. At first it was a gibberish clicking and long vowel sounds that made no sense at all, but parts of the nuances of their discussion began to make sense to him, and like a student immersed in a foreign language there comes a time when words and phrases are completely understood. It had taken three months, but this night in his dream state, Martin finally understood.

As he lay down to sleep that night, Martin had tried to rally his feelings of dread into those of an investigator, or explorer. If he didn't think of the scene that would unfold again before his eyes, but could focus on the spectral forms and their discussion he might be able to get a clue as to why he was stuck in this re-occurring nightmare. He tossed and turned fitfully for nearly two hours before he finally was overcome with the fatigue and drifted off to sleep. It seemed as though only moments had passed before he felt the chilled January wind as he materialized on the side of Highway 101 facing Wally's truck as it idled, waiting to turn left onto the road. He could see Wally's face. He was mouthing words to a song blaring on his radio. As Martin focused he could hear the words.

*I've faith in you,*
*You've always cared for me,*
*You've been a candle burnin' bright,*
*Guiding me in from the night,*

Martin could not believe it, Wally hated disco music, but he was singing along to the Dudes of Funk. He watched as his grandmother's car, moving at fifty-five miles per hour, seemed to pass from right to left before him, in slow motion.

"Haaaath click-ita, click, click, click." There they were again, talking to each other. The specters hovered on the other side of the road standing next to Wally's yellow pickup. Martin could see them gesture to his grandmother as she drove past. "Saaaach hisss mother."

A red Toyota whizzed by from right to left momentarily blocking his view. He did a double take, what did that thing just say?

Martin's eyes opened widely, he had never understood their language before, and suddenly parts of it made sense. He saw the logging truck rumbling past the weigh station. He knew what was coming next.

Wally watched his mother drive to the base of the Cosi Hill and disappear behind the massive stand of Douglas-fir that concealed the highway.

*You may not know,*
*how much I care,*

As Martin looked toward the log truck, he saw for the first time a gray mist push itself into the truck. One of the specters was inside the truck with the driver. The loaded log truck began to leave the lane on the road, heading towards the shoulder. Martin screamed to Wally to move, to look back down the road, to see his fate and somehow tonight, to avoid it. No one heard him.

Wally turned. He saw the log truck headed straight towards him, its massive front wheels throwing up the gravel on the side of the road as it barreled towards the middle of the yellow pickup. Wally's face showed his alarm and he stopped singing along to the radio. He rapidly shifted his pickup into reverse and floored the accelerator, smoke from the burning tire rubber and dust from the dirt and gravel on the pavement billowed upwards as the pickup moved backwards.

*But I need you to know I do,*
*And it's me that needs to share,*

The front of the Peterbilt log truck slammed into the front quarter panel of the pickup, mashing it down as the wheel careened upward over the hood of the smaller vehicle.

*How much I love you dear,*
*You need to know,*

The force of the impact spun the pickup into the trailer filled with logs, violently throwing Wally under the massive tires of the truck trailer. Martin closed his eyes. He couldn't watch anymore.

*'Cause your world is filled with fear...,*

The music stopped. The log truck was still moving into the park-and-ride area of the hollow beside the intersection, but was now nearly on its passenger side as it slid into the parked cars and trucks below it. The sound of the crash had been tremendous. It seemed to get louder every time Martin witnessed it. He saw the beat up blue and primer gray Chevy Impala of Wally's friend Kevin speed down the cut-off road towards the accident. Both specters stood together again and watched Kevin's car approach.

"Kathooorg clickety, heee shall bear witness," the specter uttered as it pointed a long skeletal hand towards Kevin as he jumped from his car while it screeched to a halt.

Martin watched Kevin run towards Wally's pickup and witnessed his abject horror as he saw Wally's crushed lifeless body on the highway.

"Help me!" a voice shot out from the overturned log truck. "Somebody please help me!" Kevin turned to see the face of the log truck driver rise up through the open driver's side window. Smoke poured out of the cab of the truck, covering the driver in a gray shroud.

Kevin sprinted towards the log truck. Another car came to a sudden stop. It had been less than a mile behind the log truck heading towards Cosmopolis. Two men jumped from the car, one ran towards Wally on the road, the other chased after Kevin to help him as he neared the underside of the truck. Kevin jumped up, grabbing the running board step of the cab and pulled himself up onto the side of the truck. The other man followed his lead, but was unable to pull himself up and hung on the side of the truck. Kevin quickly gave him a hand and pulled him up into the hot, choking tower of smoke that reached a hundred feet into the sky.

Kevin forced open the door and then he and the other man found the driver inside the opened side of the truck. They both grabbed an arm and began to hoist him out. Martin saw the specters shift again, one moved rapidly on the wind towards the overturned truck, the billowing fabric of its cloak trailing behind it. It passed through the metal cab into the smoking hulk of the log truck. The two men on the top side of the truck pulled the driver almost completely free. Martin could see his legs coming out of the opened door. Suddenly, it was as if part of the gray billowing smoke latched on to the driver's legs and pulled him back into the burning cab of the truck.

"No, no, noooooooooooooo!" shouted the driver as he disappeared back inside the inferno below. Kevin lunged into the cab of the truck and pulled on the driver again, and again, each time he felt he was losing his tug of war with the fire raging inside. Finally, he realized he could do no more, with one last sorrowful look into the eyes of the driver, he let go. Kevin pulled his charred and bloodied arms and hands from the truck and was helped down by the other man who had helped attempt the rescue of the truck driver.

The log truck driver cried out in anguish as his life tragically ended in the fire that consumed him. Kevin and the other man broke down and collapsed on the roadway after distancing themselves from the log truck in case it exploded. Kevin turned to look at the dead body of Wally and began to cry.

"Blaaasch, it issss all in place," the specter hissed. "Thaaaaa five are now undone."

Martin was stunned by what he saw and heard. What did it mean? He saw for the first time, the role these specters had in the events of Friday the thirteenth of January. They had made it all happen.

With that thought he faded into the living room of his house. He saw the raw emotion on his parent's faces. He watched as Drake led them down the stairs to the fateful announcement. They had dreaded the thought, they each had fully thought the news they would be getting that day was one of the break-up of their family, not the one they got.

"Chaaack, keeega, here they come." The specters were in the shadows of the hallway.

"Heeeeee isssss the one," hissed a specter as it pointed its boney finger at Drake. "Muuuust destroy himmmmm."

Mark followed Drake into the room.

"Breaaaaaak easy thissss one," the boney finger pointed at Mark. Martin emerged from the shadow of the hallway.

Monique was in the hall, she growled at the specters and they moved out of the shadows and into the living room.

Seeing himself always brought an odd sensation to the dream. There was some level of cognition in him, almost as though he could see himself watching the scene. But if this was truly a re-enactment why had he not felt himself that afternoon when this scene happened in real life?

"Heee warned usss thisss one has sight, may seeeee ussss, mossst dangerousss," the narrating specter added as it pointed at Martin. Martin wondered if that was why he was seeing all of this over and over again in his dreams.

Dennis and Albert bounded in and dove on the bean bag

chairs. Martin watched as his parents told their tale of the death of Uncle Wally. He studied the faces of his brothers and himself as they reacted to the news. For the past few weeks he knew what came next, one of the specters touched the right side of Drake's head as the three of them sat on the long floral couch. But tonight, as it pulled its hand back, there was a glowing tendril of light that came out of the side of his brother's head that wiggled and wrapped itself around the spectral finger as it was moved away from Drake.

"What the hell was that?" Martin thought out loud, but no one heard him.

The specters floated back into the shadows of the hallway. Martin watched the rest of the conversation unfold. He could recite the dialog from memory. While watching himself cry, Martin concluded that he should avoid crying in the future because he was not very attractive when he cried. All his family cried in that moment and yet Drake, the family crybaby somehow didn't. He hadn't noticed that Drake didn't cry in all the times he had watched this scene. They mechanically walked, devoid of emotion, to get their coats in their rooms. Except Drake who unsuccessfully tried to call Monique to the back door. Drake went and picked up Monique, carrying her on his right forearm, her front legs crossed in the palm of his hand. Martin was curious to see the reaction of the little poodle and the specters again, to see if she had somehow seen them or sensed them. Drake walked through the hallway by the specters. They recoiled and hissed at Monique as she was carried past. Monique turned her head as she neared the kitchen and growled at the specters. She had noticed them.

Martin began to feel the cold January breeze as he faded out once again. He re-materialized in the crowded living room of his grandparents' house. He watched as his relatives and their friends talked about the life of his uncle Wally. Something was different tonight, he felt like there was something he has never noticed before lingering in the living room. A breeze picked up coming straight from the living room windows, like someone had cast them open during a storm. It blew him towards the stairway and the hall beyond, down towards the bedrooms. In the three months he had experienced this dream everything had always been the same. Only the clarity had changed. Each night it was a little more vibrant, a little more real, but always the same. Martin felt himself drifting down the long hallway towards Wally's room. He was being pulled by some unseen force. The dream wasn't right anymore. This was totally different, tonight something's were out of sequence, and he had never gone down the hallway before. He would only hover at the far end and see the shadowy specters outside Wally's room.

The newness of this sensation scared him. Before him stood his uncle's bedroom door, and the unknown beyond it. Down the hallway he moved, and as he rapidly neared the solid wood barrier his hands went up to protect him. He passed through the oak, feeling the texture of the wood as he slipped through it. He thought that should have hurt but it didn't. On the other side of the door standing at the foot of the bed was Wally.

"I knew you'd come to me," the illuminated and ghostly form of Wally stated. "Of all my nephews, you're the one who'd seek me out."

"I don't understand," Martin gasped. "You can see me?"

"There are many things that we don't understand. Many mysteries in the world around us, many worlds that we don't even know exist even beyond the ones of myths and legends, and many beings with motives we fail to understand who won't just let us be," replied Wally.

"Marty," Wally continued. "We were chosen, you, me, Ralph, Mark, and Drake, to do something special. But there are greater powers at work here, for both good and evil and everything in between, and some of them didn't want us to achieve that purpose. But now I'm dead and all of that's broken, and we will never become what we were meant to be. So it's up to you and your brothers to do what we couldn't. You'll have allies, amazing allies actually, trust me I've seen 'em. And in time, you'll see 'em too."

"Why? Why? It doesn't make any sense. None of this makes any sense. We were chosen? Greater powers? What do you mean?" Martin continued and began to sob. "Why did you have to die? We need you, I need you. I'm lost without you."

"I've something else I have to do now, beyond here, another role to play, a challenge to overcome. I just hope I'm up to that challenge. Marty, you're not lost, you're right here, and I'm in a better place now. Someday after you've lived a long, full life you'll be there too. But when you get there you'll be an old fogey and as for me, I'll always be young."

Martin began to feel himself be pulled back through the door.

"No, wait, I need to know!" Martin shouted as he passed back through the door.

He drifted back down the hall stopping for a moment outside his aunt's old bedroom right across from the bathroom. He watched as Drake helped Dennis past the stairway towards the bathroom. Behind him he noticed the shadowy, gray form of the specters as they moved through Wally's bedroom door into his room just as he had moments before. He noticed that Drake turned his head towards Wally's room at the far end of the hall immediately after the specters passed through it. Silently Drake began to walk down the hallway towards his uncle's room. As Drake neared the door he came to a stop, as though he was listening to something on the other side of it. His hand reached for the brass doorknob, and then Drake turned and stood silently for a moment. Don't do it Drake, Martin pleaded to himself, the specters are in there. For some reason Drake walked back towards the bathroom. Perhaps his brother had heard his plea to avoid the bedroom.

Dennis opened the door and emerged from the bathroom. Drake asked him if he washed his hands, and the two of them began to walk down the hall towards the living room with Drake on the stairwell side. But, when Drake turned to go, he stared to his right and looked right into Martin eyes. He paused for just a split second, and Martin was sure that his brother had seen him.

"Braaackasg clickesty, Succorbenoth will be pleased by what weeeee have done for himmmmmmmmm," hissed one of the specters as they re-emerged from Wally's room. They floated down the hall a few feet and then came to stop, the cloudy shapeless form began to stop swirling and Martin noticed a skull-like face emerging from within one of them. Very long, sharp teeth were fixed in its boney jaw. Set within two incredibly dark cavities flickered red glowing eyes that peered down the hall at Martin.

"Carrouuush, you therrrre," it announced. "You can seeeeee us huuuman?"

The specters floated rapidly towards him, their skeletal hands outstretched and grabbing for him. Martin screamed a terrible scream.

With a sudden start and a thundering pulse, Martin awoke from his nightmare drenched in sweat, to find himself back in his dark bedroom. He looked at the red glowing numbers on his clock. It was 2:05 AM. He always woke up at 2:05 AM. Wally's watch was broken in the accident and it was forever stuck on 2:05, Martin understood the symbolism, he just wished it was later so he could get more sleep sometimes. Tonight's dream had been so different. He jotted down his recollections from the dream in his spiral notebook beside his bed. He had questions that needed answers. He had to know who or what the specters were working for. He wrote down the name he heard, but he really didn't need to because from that night onward the name 'Succorbenoth' was forever etched upon his soul. He did not sleep again that night.

HOQUIAM PUBLIC LIBRARY

THE BROTHERHOOD OF OLYMPUS AND THE DEADLIEST GAME

5

**Lilacs and Roses**
**Chapter Five**
**April 15, 1978**
**Hoquiam, Washington**

The stories that Martin had shared with him had energized his curiosity in ways that he didn't know it could be. It began the day after Wally's death, with the story of something pulling the truck driver back into the burning cab of the log truck. Martin also shared his recurring dream, how the details intensified every night, and then last night how he heard the ghostly images talking and what they said. Drake loved to know everything there was to know about everything, and this was a new frontier to him. A fresh horizon to study, and from his collection of books he knew that this was quite clearly within the definition of paranormal or the occult.

Armed with that knowledge, an art pad for making sketches, and a few notebooks to record his findings he trekked the seven blocks to the Hoquiam public library. It was a lot closer then the Aberdeen library and Drake liked its ambiance better. The library opened at 10:00 AM on Saturdays, and Drake was there when the doors were unlocked. He traipsed through the doorway, doing his best to avoid eye contact with the librarian, Miss Furfur. She worked the library alone on Saturdays, so he knew if he was going to check anything out he would have to talk to her, which was of course, nearly impossible. He made his way back to one of the larger heavy wooden tables beyond the rows and rows of books. Few people ever bothered him back in his corner of the library. He put his coat on the back of the chair, spread his notebooks out and set his art tablet off to the left side of his work space. He removed two pencils from a secret pocket inside his coat and looked to verify that they were still up to his sharpness requirement. They both passed inspection.

Drake spent the next hour perusing the books on the shelves. His interests seemed varied: art, history, medieval weaponry, music, and when he was sure no one was looking, the occult and paranormal. He pulled a number of books and carried them back to his corner and found that most of the information was virtually useless. Where was the encyclopedia of the occult? There wasn't a handy reference book like that he could turn to so he could look up 'Succorbenoth' and these other things Martin had told him about. However, he did get some useful information about astral projection, demonic possession, and some other cool things.

Just before noon, one of the neighborhood girls came in the library and happened to come back into Drake's corner. It was Rachel Finnegan. According to Drake, Rachel was a pesky girl, and like all girls she had cooties. Drake could rationalize this was probably not the case, but he held some words like powerful talismans melded to his body through eldritch magic.

When he was in elementary school in Cosmopolis, the year that his family lived with his grandparents, he rode the bus with Wally, his cousin Ralph, and both his older brothers. On a particular day, he remembered getting on the bus to go home and a nice, friendly girl from his class who had long blonde hair asked him to sit with her. He did so without thinking. His brothers, uncle, and cousin teased and taunted him the whole way home, even after the bus stopped to let the very embarrassed little girl off at her house. Wally had said, "Girls have cooties!" For some reason, Wally's words possessed such power in Drake's life. Wally's words bound him like links of dense iron to those notions, and he carried those heavy chains with him everywhere he went.

Rachel was a healthy, full of life, inquisitive, and slightly random thirteen year old girl. She was tall, though much shorter than the imposing Drake, and graceful, most of the time. There was radiance in her blue eyes that lit up a room if she was happy, and she was always happy to see Drake.

"Hi Drake," she bubbled. "Whatcha doin?"

"Looking stuff up," he replied without looking up.

Rachel noticed the art tablet and wanted to look at Drake's pictures, he always drew the best pictures of anyone she knew.

"Any new pictures?" she asked as she grabbed the tablet and flipped it open. Drake had moved his left hand in a slight motion like he intended to stop her, but he conceded and let her look at his drawings.

"Yes, a couple," he replied.

Rachel flipped through the drawings. She noticed how they seemed to get better as they went along, like Drake learned to draw better and better with each picture. However, the subject matter was not what she would have liked, it was full of monsters and hideous creatures that were combinations of other animals, and weapons, and fighting, and death. She looked at a picture of a very detailed horse carrying a heavily muscled man wearing intricate armor.

"Draw me a picture," Rachel cooed.

"Of what?" flatly replied Drake.

"A unicorn," she quickly responded, "or a unicorn with wings."

"I can't draw anything with hooves," Drake retorted, and then thinking ahead where the winged unicorn was going. "Or anything with feathers."

"Oh," replied the hurt girl. Her eyes looked down. "I get it, you don't like me."

"That's not it at all Rachel," Drake began to reply. "Girls have cooties."

"I get it Drake," Rachel cut him off. "I get the whole cootie thing, but it's kind of old. That's so second grade. It isn't real, and I don't understand how you can't just let that go. The older boys were just jealous of you, I mean."

"Drake," a very feminine voice cut through the tension in the back corner of the library. Miss Furfur emerged from the shelves of books, smiling an intoxicating smile. "How's the research going?"

"Okay, Miss Furfur," Drake stammered, struggling to make letters connect to form words and words to connect to form sentences in her presence.

"What are you researching?" the heavenly voice continued, as Miss Furfur looked at Drake's notes. "Succorbenoth and the occult? Drake, I am surprised, you've never looked up anything like this since I started working here in January. A new hobby, perhaps?"

"I think he's just looking up more gross monsters to draw," added Rachel.

Miss Furfur bent down towards Drake. That image was one of his best memories of being thirteen. She was dressed in a tight, above the knee, tweed skirt, a pink satin blouse, and matching pink precariously high heeled shoes that he wondered how she walked in, but was so glad she did. On top of that, her legs were encased in stockings with seams that ran up the back of her leg. She smelled of fresh roses. Her long black hair was stacked somehow on top of her head and she had things that looked like knitting needles stuck in her hair. She was as close as someone could come to being an angel, and in Drake's mind she was not a girl, she was like an evolutionary step above girls, and he knew without any doubts that she did not have cooties.

"Succorbenoth is a daemon, Drake," Miss Furfur stated, barely above a whisper. "Daemons are the lords and rulers over lesser demons and devils."

Drake looked into her eyes through her large eyeglasses. Her eyes were magical, like they were simultaneously reflecting a fireworks show and the most tranquil lake he had ever seen. They were framed by the smokiest of blues on her eyelids and thick black eyeliner. Her eyes were like a work of art. He felt light-headed.

"I do have some reference books in the basement that are from the occult section. And one in particular on daemons," Miss Furfur added. "Would you and your little friend like to go look at those, Drake?"

"Sure," interjected Rachel.

"She's not really my friend, more like an acquaintance," Drake responded.

"Follow me," the librarian stated as she rose and elegantly walked, one foot going completely in front of the other, making her hips sway from one side to the other. Drake hurriedly grabbed his notebooks and his drawing tablet and began to walk behind the angel in pink and tweed.

"You don't need to come," Drake quipped to Rachel.

"Of course I do," Rachel added as she kept pace with him. "I am a scientist, duh. Did you know when I grow up I wanna be just like Dr. Quincy on TV. Except a girl, obviously."

"Obviously," Drake thought, with cooties.

They went down the stairs to a darkened room. Miss Furfur turned on a light and went to an old, almost ancient looking door on the back wall of the library. She produced a large skeleton key and proceeded to unlock and open the door with a loud creak. She looked inside the musty old room and found a chain hanging from a single light fixture suspended in the middle of the room. The illuminated globe swayed back and forth after it clicked on, lighting the room in a very bright but uneven swash of electric light. The room looked like it should've been lit by thick candles. In the middle of the room stood a tall wooden table that had been assembled without the use of any nails or screws. It should've been in an antique store.

"How old is this?" Rachel asked.

"Very old," Miss Furfur answered. "Very few people ever see these special books."

"Well," Rachel added, "that's exciting, isn't it Drake?"

Drake nodded, his eyes studying the contents of the room, all those leather bound tomes of knowledge sitting there before him.

"Here we are," she said, pulling a couple books down from a shelf as she adjusted her glasses. "This is the one you'll want to start with, Drake. If you need anything else, call for me."

As Miss Furfur walked out of the room and back through the larger basement room beyond, Drake followed her with his eyes. There was that sashaying walk again. Rachel watched Drake and how he watched the librarian.

"Do you think I would look better with glasses?" Rachel asked him.

"Sure," he responded, not fully aware of what she asked.

"Hmmm, my dad said if you stare at the sun you can hurt your eyes," she continued. "Maybe I should do that so I can get glasses."

"Isn't your dad a leprechaun?" Drake said, without thinking about what he just said. "I mean you're Irish, right, Finnegan is an Irish name, but you never celebrate St. Patrick's Day, you never wear green. It's like you're boycotting your heritage. It's just odd."

"My dad isn't a leprechaun," Rachel answered, a spark in her eyes. That was perhaps the longest thing Drake had ever said to her, way more than a single sentence. "He says we are not Irish either. My parents have never bought anything green for me. If they did I'd wear it. And, my dad said St. Patrick's Day is a made up holiday and not even Irish to begin with, he says it's a Catholic holiday, not a leprechaun day at all."

Drake nodded his head, as he flipped through the demonology book Miss Furfur had handed him. It was old, and bound in reddish, thick leather. He was thinking, 'how will I find Succorbenoth in this?' Parts of it looked handwritten, and it didn't appear to have a table of contents. The pages fell open under his hand and he looked at where it stopped.

"Succorbenoth!" he gasped. "How did it do that?"

"Do what?" Rachel responded.

"Watch," Drake explained as he took the book, closed it and began to open it up. "I was thinking about finding Succorbenoth in this book and it just opened right to it, look."

The book opened to some detailed explanation of an exorcism, Drake turned a couple pages, and then a few more until he found the page on the daemon he sought.

"Weird," stated Rachel her tone dripping of sarcasm. "You don't usually see that behavior in an old book."

Rachel giggled as Drake began writing stuff down in his notebook. She watched him write and smiled. Drake looked up at her.

"Look," he said. "If you want to help see if you can find anything in any of these books about ghosts or specters that appear before someone dies, or are seen when someone dies."

"Okie Dokey Loki," she chirped and began cracking books open. "You know, you're a very weird boy."

"Thank you," he replied and went back to recording information about Succorbenoth.

They stood in that room, at the tall table for nearly two hours. Rachel showed Drake numerous references of ghosts and specters that are noted to appear before, or at the scene of accidents. She also came across a scary version of a specter from medieval Germany known as a mordgeist that worked as kind of like an evil mercenary for daemons and other nasty things. Drake drew a picture of this one and Rachel thought it was a very good picture, but also very scary.

Drake looked like he was finished with his research. He closed the last book he was looking through and folded shut both his notebook and art tablet. Rachel looked up at him and finished writing down the last bit of information she was gathering for him. She closed the book and handed him the notebook and pencil.

"So," Rachel started, "just outta curiosity, why're you so interested in all of this weird occult stuff? I mean it's cool, like vampires and monsters in the old black and white movies are cool, but it's also kind of weird to take it to this level. I mean, I like vampires, a lot, okay maybe even a little bit more than a lot, but I've never gone into secret rooms in the library to find out more about them."

"Maybe you should," Drake replied dryly.

"Maybe you should get your head outta books sometime and look at the world around you."

Drake looked at Rachel. He was hurt and didn't know how to respond. So, he collected his things and walked out of the room and towards the stairs that led up to the library above them.

"If you paid attention," she continued to herself, "you would have realized I know all about your cootie story, I've heard you tell it before. And do you realize how embarrassed I was, do you even remember that I was there? Duh, stupid head, I was the girl on the bus with you in second grade, Drake Fraser. Argh! Sometimes you make me soooo mad. And I don't know why you like that Miss Furfur so much. Maybe I need to get high heeled shoes."

As Rachel said that, she dropped the first book Drake was using, the demonology tome, and it opened to the heading of Furfur. She looked down at what was written.

"Furfur, a Daemon Countess of Hell, a greater succubus, she commands twenty-six legions, often appears as an angel with a flaming tail."

Oh no, she thought. 'Drake Fraser, you like a daemon, you're like the smartest boy I know, maybe even the smartest boy in the whole world. But geez, you need to get your head out of books and pay attention to what's going on around you.'

Rachel hurried after Drake, after she'd made sure to put that last book away exactly where the librarian had grabbed it. She didn't want Miss Furfur to see what she had just discovered. She found Drake in his corner of the library getting his coat. He had a couple books from upstairs to check out, and was starting to head to the main desk where Miss Furfur waited.

"So," she said, "I'm sorry if I made you mad, I didn't mean it. Sometimes you just make me all flustered. Drake, do any of those books you got have anything about protection from daemons?"

"I think so."

"You think I can borrow it at school on Monday?"

"Sure. Why? You've developed a sudden interest in weirdness?"

"No. Just making sure I know what I need to know to help what I have always been interested in."

"Sometimes you don't make any sense at all, Rachel."

"You either, Drake."

"Are you ready to check out, Drake?" the heavenly voice of Miss Furfur lifted him up, and he did his best to avoid looking at her as he blushed.

"Yes," he squeaked in a barely audible tone, as he handed her the stack of books.

"These are good choices," the librarian added as she stamped the check-out cards, placing each in the little card pocket inside the books. "Anything for your little friend?"

"No," Rachel responded.

"Drake," Miss Furfur added, "if you ever want to go back into that archive room in the basement, just let me know. You're such a good kid."

"Thank you Miss Furfur," Drake managed to say after standing silent for a brief moment. He turned and sort of ran out the door, down the stairs in front of the library, and off on his way home.

Rachel walked out the door, looked back inside at the librarian and saw her smile and wave to her. She turned and looked at Drake running down the road.

"You are such a weird boy, Drake Fraser," lamented Rachel with a heavy sigh.

TEN THOUSAND LAKES

THE BROTHERHOOD OF OLYMPUS AND THE DEADLIEST GAME

6

**Ten Thousand Lakes**
**Chapter Six**
**June 16, 1978**
**Hoquiam, Washington**

During the last few weeks of school, the Fraser boys, like students everywhere, lost focus on academics. Mark continued to be plagued by his inner demons and guilt. The cryptic message from the ash zombie about him having to leave his brothers because he could no longer trust them and that leaving was the only way for him to achieve his destiny began creeping its way further and further into his heart.

Martin had taken Drake's notes and drawings he gathered at the library and had used it to his defense. Martin had learned that the specters he had seen were known as mordgeists and historically worked for a greater entity. Drake's drawing was very close to what he had seen night after night in his sleep. He did not have the dream every night any more, and in fact he had not had it since mid-May and in some ways missed it because he wanted to know more about the doings of the mordgeists, and he desperately wanted another chance to talk to Wally. That one night, that one version of the dream in which he was seen by the mordgeists, was the only time he got to talk with Wally.

Drake had been in the locked archive room at least once a week since the middle of April. He was occasionally joined by Rachel, who had become almost obsessed with magical charms and demonic protection devices. Drake always teased her that as the daughter of a leprechaun she should be interested in lucky charms, not magical charms. She did not find that as funny as he did. Drake was enjoying his acquisition of knowledge of the paranormal. Not only was he learning new, interesting things, but he got to spend more time with the dreamy librarian. Miss Furfur had put her hand on the back of his arm on Saturday, May thirteenth. Drake was pretty sure this was not a casual brush of her hand on his arm. She touched him, and he was sure that her hand lingered on his arm for nearly half a minute. That moment joined his very short list of good things that he experienced as a thirteen year old.

Summer was the favorite season for both Dennis and Albert because it usually meant that all three of their older brothers would be free more and they would get more time with them. Dennis had a new favorite word, dillhole, which he loved to call everyone, though mostly under his breath so he wouldn't get in trouble. He had convinced Albert that he had to wait until he was as old as Dennis to use it, which unfortunately he never actually could be since they aged at the same rate. Furthermore, he rather seriously told Albert that if you used it before you were old enough then God would kill you. Then you would spend forever stuck below the bathroom floor at Sunday school, and little boys would pee on the floor because they didn't know how to aim. Both boys had seen this first hand, and the urine would soak through the creaky wood and drip on you. Albert was terrified of that prospect and made sure he didn't even think the word in his head.

Albert's new favorite pastime was dressing Monique, their white miniature poodle, in baby clothes that he had found in a box in the attic—much to the chagrin of Drake, who was growing more and more close to the spunky little dog. A year ago before they moved into town, they had gotten her as they gave away the last of their Saint Bernards, Ginger-ale and Freddy Fudpucker. Ginger was a good dog, much like her mother Whiskey, but Freddy, he was a monster who chewed everything and refused to be trained. They had all been confused how their mother had named him, since it seemed more like a trick to get them to say a bad word on accident, but she assured them all that he was named after an alcoholic drink, just like the other Saint Bernards they had owned.

Monique was such a huge transition from the large, slobbery, shedding, but mostly gentle animals they had loved. She was small, had curly white hair, and was a ball of energy who loved to play with the Fraser boys, though she was growing leery of Albert and she had a horrible under bite. It was this flaw that brought her into their family. In March, Dad moved his insurance office out of Aberdeen and into Montesano, the county seat, because of the market decline in Aberdeen and the cheaper rent in Montesano. A family in Montesano, who raised and showed purebred poodles, gave Monique to him for being a good guy and helping them with their insurance needs. She came with the name Monique. They were told she was a French poodle. It took them awhile to be able to say Monique, though they felt safer struggling over it, then attempting Fudpucker in front of their parents. Drake had begun calling her Mo, for short, and the others quickly followed suit.

Mom, who had turned thirty-six ten days earlier, called them all to the living room that afternoon to get ready for dinner. The boys were excited and hungry. She had made fried chicken, one of the few dinners her children always clamored for more of, and was typically only a Sunday night treat.

This dinner would be interesting, because both Mom and Dad had some news to tell the boys, but this news they thought would go over quite well, a lot better than the news six months ago. Drake and Mark came downstairs and set the table. It was Martin's turn but they knew he wouldn't come do it and they were hungry for fried chicken. The table was an old hardwood, darkened with age, and with two long leaves that extended it out to seat ten around it. Mom had found it in the former penthouse of Edward Finch, on the fifth floor of the old Finch Building years earlier when she was doing some re-upholstery work and got it for very little money. The boys quickly learned that not only was it big and heavy, it also had the most amazing ledge on the inside of the hand carved decorative bottom of the tabletop. This ledge was where they would pack the gristle and other inedible dinner pieces after they removed them from their plates or mouths. Mom had been raised to expect her family to clean their plates, not to leave any food on them at the end of the meal. For the boys, this got easier when they got two things, a dog that was small enough to walk under the table without being seen, and this dinner table with the awesome ledge. The only icky part was when the ledge got full.

All seven members of the Fraser family sat down to dinner. The fried chicken went quickly, and it often turned into a race to get seconds, or if you were lucky, thirds. Albert had learned a unique dinner strategy. He only took a few bites out of each piece of chicken and then would reach for more. This upset his older brothers, but none of them would take the half eaten food off their little brothers plate, so his strategy worked. However, the consequence of the strategy was that it sped up the older Fraser boys to keep up with Albert. Dinner went quickly, at least the chicken part of it. The boiled potatoes and gravy were a favorite of Drake's and he would concede chicken for more potatoes any day.

As they finished gnawing on chicken bones, while Drake continued to build a large potato pyramid that he drowned in the greasy gravy, Mom intentionally cleared her throat.

"Boys, your father and I have some things to talk to you about."

They all looked up at their parents in various stages of being covered in chicken juices.

"You know that after he moved his office in Montesano business didn't get much better," Mom began.

"Actually, this has little to do with business, and more to do with them dinking around on your grandparent's insurance claim," their dad took over, "you all know that I've been their insurance agent for a few years, ever since I started selling insurance, right?"

The boys nodded, Drake continued to eat his potatoes.

"Well, after Wally died, after the accident, the adjusters still have not authorized the payment of the insurance."

Mom shook her head and looked down at her plate.

"I continued to fight for what was right, what they owed Henry and Isabella, your grandparents. Then the adjusters said they weren't going to pay because they didn't want to be part of a wrongful death lawsuit, and they wanted to settle out of court with the truck driver's family and remove themselves from any liability. Your grandparents didn't want Wally's name ruined, he didn't kill that man. But, that would leave your grandparents completely responsible for any money the court might award. I couldn't support that, I couldn't work for a company like that, so I quit two weeks ago. I packed up my personal belongings out of my office and left the rest for whoever would take over."

The older boys knew this was not good news. Painfully, they remembered the early 1970s when they had no money. Specifically the Christmas of 1970 would always be remembered as the one that almost wasn't. Only the generosity of a local charity adopt-a-family program was all that kept the tradition going that year for the Fraser family. The next two years were very lean times for the family. The older boys could foresee those meager years repeating now that their father was unemployed.

"But there is good news too, boys," Mom interjected after looking up and seeing the somber reactions in her children's faces, especially Martin, Mark, and Drake, who had suddenly stopped eating his potatoes.

"Yes, there is," continued their father. "When I first moved my office out to Montesano I met a couple guys at the Beehive restaurant when I went there for lunch. They were selling campground memberships at a new camping resort in Lewis County, south of Chehalis. One of the guys, John, was the manager, and he asked me if I was interested in coming to work for them. Back then I said no, but if anything changed in the future maybe I would. Well, when I decided to quit the insurance job, I called up John, and I started working for them that same day. I have already sold ten memberships, making more money than what I made in a month selling insurance."

"Tell them the really good part, honey," Mom cut in.

"I purchased a membership too, so this summer we'll be going camping down to the 10,000 Lakes Camping Resort as many times as we can."

"Does that mean we are not going to Hurricane Ridge this summer?" Mark questioned. The family always liked the camping trip known as the 'Loop,' starting out along the Pacific Coast of the Olympic Peninsula and going all the way around it, the Hoh Rainforest, Kalaloch, Forks, past the Strait of Juan de Fuca, Hurricane Ridge, Mount Olympus, Sequim, Dosewallips, and alongside Hood Canal, the Staircase campground, and the rest of western Puget Sound before heading back home. It was kind of a rough shaped oval if you looked at a map, hence the name, the 'Loop.'

"No," Mom remarked excitedly, "we'll still do the 'Loop,' just maybe not until August. Boys, 10,000 Lakes has a heated pool with a diving board, putt-putt golf, pool tables, it's amazing. You all are going to like it so much."

"A diving board?" squeaked Albert from behind his messy face.

"A diving board is cool," Mark added.

The boys smiled, except Drake, who went back to eating his boiled potatoes and gravy.

The following week passed quickly. Mark had arranged to start his job at the car dealership after they returned. Martin had got the weekend off from the grocery store. They packed up the travel trailer with their supplies and on Friday morning, the twenty-third of June, they departed Hoquiam.

It was approximately seventy-three miles to the campground. They stayed on Highway 12, rather than driving up through Olympia, and turned south at Elma. The road was old and narrow as they headed toward Oakville. Once or twice a year they would drive this way to visit their Grandma Van Zanten, usually around the holidays.

Selma Van Zanten was the mother of Drake, Sr. Born Selma Warren, she had been a robust and hardy woman of Northern European stock. Her twin sister Velma was more reserved and dignified. Their family had moved from rural Wisconsin in 1930 to seek cancer treatment for their aunt at the Virginia Mason Medical Center. The family found land and settled outside Montesano, near Satsop. The aunt survived for a few more years, dying in 1936. By then the Warren family had put down roots and stayed put. One of those roots put down was the chance meeting of Velma Warren and a dark mysterious man named Martin Fraser. Martin was intrigued by the uppity Velma when he bumped into the car she was riding in, or rather when the car bumped into him on the road in the middle of the night. No one in the car had seen him on the road, and then the next moment he was standing right in front of the car. Luckily he was able to dodge and took most of the impact as a glancing blow to the side of the heavy steel automobile. Velma was so silent and dignified, even in that moment of horror of running a man over in her car, that he was love struck. Some might say it was the result of the impact with the car that made him see the glowing halo around her, rather than the radiance of her beauty. The Warrens helped him into their car and drove him to their house to care for him until he was fit and ready to continue on his way.

Velma was returning from Montesano with some supplies for her train ride back to Wisconsin to visit relatives at the time of the accident. When Martin awoke the next day, he saw the same lovely apparition, except now she was more bold and daring, and she willfully flirted with the dashing man. They were married within a month's time and Selma Fraser was pregnant with her first child, Karl, in April of 1933. Velma wound up staying in Wisconsin until April of

1943. Martin was confused when she returned. Their resemblance was uncanny, and neither Velma nor his wife Selma had ever told him they were twins. Twins in nearly every culture were special. Martin took a special liking to that fact.

Martin Fraser was a complete mystery. He had no identification, and at times in the 1930s he didn't always respond when someone called him by name. Years later, when Drake, Sr. told his sons this story and drove by the place where his father was almost run down by his aunt, Mark asked if they were related to the people who lived down the driveway marked by a very old, and rusted metal sign that said, "Homestead of Martin Fraser." Their dad explained to them that the sign had been there for many years, before he was born even, and was a marker for the historical location of an early homestead. "And, no, you are not related to him." Young Drake, in the back of the car, his encyclopedic mind at work, recorded all of this and one day it would help lead him to a discovery of his true heritage.

Martin Fraser had died on Christmas Eve 1953 as his family gathered around him. Martin had announced he was being 'called home.' It was sudden and quite traumatic for sixteen-year-old Drake, Sr. watching his father struggle to breathe and flail so much so that he physically held his father's arms down while life slipped away from him. He would often tell the tale of his father's death and how he had to climb back into the house through the window above the chair in which his dead father sat because the front door was locked. It always unnerved his sons and he got some pleasure out of seeing their squeamish reactions.

Selma Fraser had remarried in 1957 to the dashing John Van Zanten, a railroad engineer for Burlington Northern. The Fraser boys would never have known he was not their grandfather, but John Van Zanten insisted on not being called grandpa, instead the Fraser boys knew them as Grandma Van Zanten and John.

By this time they were through Oakville and into Rochester, past the road their grandmother lived on, and Dennis was complaining about needing to go the bathroom.

Dad pulled the van and travel trailer off the road just past downtown Rochester at the Little Red Barn restaurant. The boys piled out of the van except Drake, who sat holding Monique. They rarely, if ever, stopped at restaurants, except to use their facilities. Ten minutes later they were merging onto Interstate 5 heading south towards Centralia.

They passed the Green Hill juvenile detention facility on the left. Mom had always told the boys if they didn't behave they would be sent there. Mark and Drake had devised numerous escape plans during their summer nights when they were sent to bed early for breaking some rule or another.

"If you boys don't behave this weekend," Mom began, "You will be spending a lot of time, right there."

Mark and Drake looked at each other and smiled with their eyes. Still the roll of razor sharp barbed wire at the top of the twelve foot chain linked fence was always imposing for any boy.

They exited I-5 at Napavine and spent the next twenty minutes snaking through narrow country roads built up as causeways to avoid flooding, and across a bridge that had a single paved lane over it with stop signs at either end to control traffic. They had been noticing the wooden, brown and orange painted signs announcing 10,000 Lakes with a bold arrow pointing in the direction they were headed.

"We're here," Dad stated as he pointed off to the right hand side of the van. "That is the sales office I work out of. And this next road is the main entrance to the campground."

The boys stared at the nearly new double-wide mobile home that was sitting in a tree-cleared opening. A green wooden lattice at the bottom covered its still-attached wheels and the jacks holding it up.

"Nice," said Mark with a noticeable hint of sarcasm.

The van slowed as they turned to the right and up a steep paved road. Through the alder trees to the right stood the sales office and further up the hill what looked like a larger wooden building with a big cement lot below it. A stand of Douglas-fir jutted out on the left before opening up to a hillside of miniature golf holes. The road split around a group of trees in the middle, a small carved brown bear sat at the edge of the roadway. To the left was the exit, to the right the entrance, marked 'One Way' with an arrow, which they followed. Dad kept the van in first gear the whole way up the hill. The trees in the center of the two roads cleared out and a guard shack stood between the entrance and the exit, yellow and black striped gates barred the entrance and exit. Mark conjured up images of border crossing gates he had seen in movies with a single arm that raised and lowered to control passage to and from a country. As they came to a stop in a thankfully nearly flat portion of the road outside the guard shack, the van sputtered from the load.

"Look," Albert squealed in delight as he pointed to the large wooden building to the right. It was easier to see through the sparse alders at the top of the hill. This was the lodge. In the large cement lot below the decking on the back was an in ground "L" shaped wonder, with a diving board. "There's the pool!"

The boys all looked to that side of the van. The ranger on duty, in his brown shirt and hat with a large orange "TL" embroidered on the front, came out and took the membership card from Dad. A few minutes later the ranger re-appeared with a cardstock hanger to be placed on the rearview mirror of the van signifying that they were registered guests. The van lugged them up an even steeper hill beyond the guard shack after the gate arm swung upward. They turned left at the top of the hill into the "A" section of the campground. The pavement gave way to brown hard-packed gravel that popped under the weight of the van tires. They turned to the right as the roadway came to a tee intersection. Little brown wooden signs, with an orange painted letter and number on each were on short four-by-four poles sticking out of the ground at the front end of each campsite. They passed 'A-20,' 'A-22,' and 'A-24' on the right, 'A-21' and 'A-23' on the left, before Mom tapped Dad on the arm and pointed at 'A-23.'

They pulled ahead, and then backed in to the campsite. Mom got out of the van to help Dad, and stood in the campsite where her husband could not see her in his mirrors, motioning the van backward. Dad craned his head to see his wife, and cursed her for doing it all wrong while he backed the trailer in while trying to avoid hitting her. The boys smiled to themselves. Their parents did this same routine every time they backed up the travel trailer. The boys jumped out when their dad announced they were here. They each helped set up their campsite in their own way. Mark and Drake helped with the blocking and setting jacks on the trailer, Dennis and Albert sat up folding lawn chairs around the fire pit, and Martin sat in the trailer and wondered how he was going to make it through a whole weekend without television.

THE SPIRIT BOARD

THE BROTHERHOOD OF OLYMPUS AND THE DEADLIEST GAME

The *Spirit* Board
**Chapter Seven**
**June 24, 1978**
**Napavine, Washington**

10,000 Lakes Camping Resort was all it was cracked up to be for the rambunctious Fraser boys. They spent the evening of the twenty-third sitting around the campfire telling ghost stories that were mostly lame, but the family sat and laughed and enjoyed each other's company, even the normally sullen Martin. They roasted hotdogs, and later marshmallows on green sticks Dad had cut and sharpened soon after their arrival.

They went to bed at nearly midnight, with both Mark and Drake choosing to sleep on the short seats in the van rather than cram into one of the fold out bunks in the trailer, or on the floor for everyone else to step on. Mark slept on the far back seat and Drake slept on the middle seat near the side doors. Mark's bench seat was longer than the one Drake slept on, but birth order had its privileges. Monique slept in the van with the two boys, and would spend most of the night curled up on the sleeping bag of Drake, on top of his legs or his chest.

That Saturday morning they had slightly burnt pancakes, fried eggs, and bacon for breakfast. The boys went off adventuring as soon as breakfast was done, leaving their parents alone to do whatever parents do without their children around.

"Don't lose Dennis or Albert," Mom cautioned them. "Or it's straight to Green Hill for all of you."

They wandered through the woods, Drake carrying Monique through the brambles she could not walk through, always making sure both Albert and Dennis were kept in the middle of their band. Mark and Martin led, next came Dennis followed closely by Albert, before Drake and Monique brought up the rear. Four hours later they reappeared, scratched, dirty and overwhelmingly hungry for the stacked plate full of peanut butter and jelly sandwiches Mom had made for them.

After lunch, and their tales of high adventure on their wilderness walk, they all went down and played miniature golf. Drake discovered the golf handicap of having a poodle on a leash while putting. Mark and Dad were neck and neck on the score coming back up through the second nine holes of the course. They were both taunting each other with every missed shot or flubbed stroke. Dad won, like he almost always did with any form of competition within the family.

Next on their agenda was the swimming pool. They went back up to their campsite and changed into their swimsuits in rapid order. Drake was not happy to have to leave Monique tied outside the trailer, but knew they could not take her into the pool area. She stood and silently watched them leave the campsite, before finding a place in the shade beneath the trailer to nap.

They had to enter the pool area through the bathrooms on the lower floor of the lodge. A large sign declared the first rule of the pool, 'All swimmers MUST shower before entering pool.' Three shower stalls were to the left of the door out to the pool. Mark, Martin, and Dennis quickly moved into the showers, leaving Albert and Drake standing by the long bench along the hallway that led out to the pool. There was a glass door where there would have been a fourth shower stall and Drake casually looked inside it. It was a room filled with two long wooden benches, one shorter in front of the taller along the back wall, thick vapors of steam, and to his surprise—three men. Drake took notice of the one large man who sat on in the middle of the lower cedar bench, wrapped in thick white towels, his long flowing white beard covering much of his upper torso, and he sported a single black eye patch. The image of the man assembled in Drake's mind as a pirate Santa Claus. The man in the sauna took notice of Drake and waved to him. Drake quickly moved in to the shower stall vacated by Mark, just as Albert did in the shower Martin left. Drake was kind of creeped out by the old man waving at him, and didn't share any of it with his brothers.

The pool was a blast for the boys, each taking turns with the other swimmers to use the blue fiberglass diving board. None of the Fraser boys actually dove into the pool in the traditional sense, instead they enthusiastically bounded off the springy board feet first into the deep chlorinated pool. The pool was marked as being '12 Feet' deep in the area by the diving board. The older boys went down all the way and touched their feet on the bottom before pushing off to the surface after each jump off the diving board. Neither Albert nor Dennis had the mass to make it that deep when they jumped into the pool.

Mom glided gracefully down the length of the pool doing a modified version of the sidestroke, keeping her head out of the water, she had always told the boys she could not go underwater without her nose plugged or water would come right up her nose and she would drown. She also kept to the far side to avoid the people jumping off the diving board. Occasionally the boys would come over and hang on their mother, amazed that she could just float, but they found she could not do that when they hung on her and she would scold them for getting water up her nose.

Dad didn't go in the pool, nor did he put a swimsuit on. The boys could not remember a time when they might have seen their father's bare legs. He always had pants on. And he kept his legend alive and wore pants again. He sat in a white plastic deck chair and snapped photos of his family having fun in the water with his Pentax thirty-five millimeter camera, reloading film numerous times that afternoon. Photography had always been a hobby of Dad's. His complete set of darkroom equipment was now in Martin's walk-in closet. Martin had inherited the photography bug from his father and had taken photography classes at school.

As daytime slipped into evening, the boys began to complain of hunger, and the family decided to return to camp for the evening. They dried off with their towels to varying degrees of success, and wrapped the towels around themselves as they headed back into the lower doors of the lodge. On their way through the shower rooms and basement of billiard tables and dart boards, they came to the top floor of the lodge. Behind a desk on the far wall, they had all sorts of things available for campers, some for sale, and some to check out. The boys saw a stack of board games and asked if they could check some out. Their parents nodded.

Martin and Drake looked through the games, hoping to find multiplayer games, beyond *Chutes and Ladders*, or *Candy Land*, which were near the top of the pile boxes. They settled on *King Oil*, *Risk*, and *Spirit*, the last being a box Martin found behind the stack of the other games.

The ranger working the front desk wrote down their membership number and name and each of the games they were checking out in a three ring binder.

"I didn't know we had this one," she said as she wrote down the information for *Spirit*.

"What'd you get?" questioned Dennis as they walked out of the lodge. He had hoped they might get *Chutes and Ladders*. He looked at their bounty, taking notice of the artwork on each. He had played with Drake's *Risk* game in the past and 'accidently' lost all the yellow bigger star pieces that signified more armies, though he never told anyone. He had never even heard of *King Oil* before, and *Spirit* was a black and white box that had ghosts on it touching a board between a boy and a girl. That one looked scary. "These look stupid."

"No one said you have to play, Dennis," Martin snapped.

After a dinner of spaghetti noodles, fried hamburger

crumbles, tomato paste and ketchup, they sat around the fire and talked about how awesome the day had been. The four oldest boys sat at the picnic table and played a game of *King Oil*. Mark won it, with more than a fair share of gloating.

As the night turned dark they realized they didn't have the light or time to play *Risk*. It had always turned out to be an epic scaled game for the Fraser boys, especially if their dad played. There was the twenty-two hour marathon game the day after Christmas when Drake had first got the game and it still had all the yellow pieces. Instead they turned their attention to the two bags of marshmallows their mom brought out of the trailer. They hungrily roasted marshmallows again, seven green sticks hovering over the fire at different elevations. They enjoyed watching their dad burn his marshmallows to a flaming crisp, then he would blow it out and peel and eat the charcoaled skin off the marshmallow and then stick the remaining glob of white confection back over the fire to roast again. Drake was the only one with patience enough to sit there until his marshmallow was a soft golden brown, warm, and gushy all the way through.

When Martin had his fill of marshmallows, which was after the second bag was opened, he sat and read the directions of *Spirit* by the light of the campfire. He nudged his younger brothers and one by one they retreated to inside the trailer with Martin. He explained to them that two people needed to sit with the board game in their laps, facing each other, like the directions said. Martin and Mark went first. They placed their fingertips on the planchette, or pointer, and waited for Martin to explain what was supposed to happen.

"I have seen a *Spirit* board before," Martin stated. "It's supposed to let you talk to the spirits, who use the board to answer questions. You put your fingers on the planchette lightly, and then the spirits will move it around, spelling things out on the board."

"Cool," replied Dennis.

"Okay," Mark added. "Let's do it."

Mark and Martin sat there, and the planchette barely

moved. Then a few minutes later they started arguing after it did move each saying the other had pushed it.

Mark got up, disappointed by the whole experience.

Mom walked into the trailer and told them they need to get ready for bed, it was nearly midnight. Only Albert seemed happy to oblige. Martin and the others stepped outside.

"Come on guys," Martin encouraged them. "Let's get this thing working. I bet if we ask to speak to Wally it'll work."

Mark stopped in his tracks, not so sure that asking to talk to Wally was a good idea, but then concluded he had to go out with them and make sure Wally didn't tell his brothers something different than what he told him a few months ago in his odd dream, just in case that was more than a dream.

Martin and Drake sat in two lawn chairs by the fire, Dennis and Mark close by. The *Spirit* board was between them, sitting on their knees, as they softly rested their fingers on the planchette.

"Is anyone there?" Martin began. Slowly and to the surprise of everyone the planchette began to slide over the surface of the game board, over the individual letters of the alphabet to the word 'YES' printed in the upper left corner of the board.

With wide eyes they all looked at each other.

"Are you Wally?" Dennis blurted. The planchette began to slowly circle on the middle of the board before gracefully sliding over the 'YES' once again. The boys were shocked, astounded, and slightly scared by that answer. Mark stood up and watched the planchette on the board skeptically.

"How do we know you're Wally?" Drake queried, the scholarly skeptic in him taking over. The planchette stopped for a moment, then it began to move and stop with its point over a letter in the alphabet, or one of the numbers arranged zero-to-nine below the arched alphabet, and then move and stop, again and again. It responded, "I. D. I. E. D. J. A. N. 1. 3. 1. 9. 7. 8."

"I died Jan 13 1978," Mark stated first, before his

brothers. "Everyone here knows that. That isn't proof."

The planchette slowly moved again, circling, then began to point at letters in increasing speed. "O. N. L. Y. T. H. E. G. O. O. D. D. I. E. Y. O. U. N. G."

Mark sat down, his face pale.

"What does that mean?" Dennis asked.

"It's Wally," Mark answered. He told me 'only the good die young,' like the Billy Joel song. Only he and I knew that."

Drake and Martin looked at each other with wide eyes.

"What do you want to ask it?" Drake began. "What kind of questions can we ask?" The planchette swung into motion again, gliding up to each letter and stopping in turn. "A. N. Y. T. H. I. N. G." Then it began to move again, "A. L. L. K. I. N. D."

"Does Martin have a girlfriend?" blurted Dennis. The planchette slid off again circling over the 'YES.'

Dennis began to laugh.

"Let's ask serious questions," Drake interjected. "Will I go to college?"

The planchette moved quickly to the 'YES.'

"What college?" Martin asked.

"L. E. L. A. N. D. S. T. A. N. F. O. R. D. J. U. N. I. O. R. U. N. I. V. E. R. S. I. T. Y." spelled the board in rapid succession.

"What's that?" Dennis asked. "What did it spell, it made no sense."

"Stanford," remarked Drake. "It's officially known as Leland Stanford Junior University."

"And you just happen to know that?" Mark added mockingly, knowing Drake most likely did know the official name of every university in the United States, at least the ones that were in the World Book Encyclopedia.

"Will I go to college?" asked Martin.

The planchette quickly slid over to the 'NO' in the upper right corner of the board.

"Why not?" Martin wanted to know.

"A. I. R. F. O. R. C. E." responded the planchette on the

printed game board.

"You're joining the Air Force?" Mark stated, more a question for Martin then the board. The planchette moved again, hovering over the 'YES.'

"Does Mark have a girlfriend?" Dennis shouted. The planchette shot across the board, and stopped on 'NO.'

Dennis laughed again, not sure why.

"Will I get married?" Martin asked. The planchette spun as if pondering how to answer this question, then moved to the 'YES' before sliding to the number '5.'

"You're getting married five times," Dennis laughed again. "Is that even legal?"

The questions continued, and the topics varied widely. An hour past midnight, they began to ask deeper questions, though some of the earlier ones returned as topics.

"Is Drake getting married?" Dennis stated, thoroughly enjoying the girlfriend-type questions.

The planchette quickly spelled, "1. 0. Y. E. A. R. S. T. O. D. A. Y."

Drake pondered this result. It said he would get married ten years today, did that mean in ten years on this date, or that he was married ten years today, which was nonsense since he was only thirteen.

"How many children will I have?" asked Martin. The planchette spun in circles before moving to the 'NO.'

"You aren't having any kids," giggled Dennis.

"Will Dennis have any kids?" Drake said, hoping it might quiet their little brother. The planchette moved very quickly to the 'NO.'

"Will I have any kids," Drake asked. The planchette moved to the number "3." Drake thought to himself, I don't even like kids, why would I want three?

"Why did you tell me to do what you did?" Mark finally asked. The planchette slid, slowly at first across the board, then picking up speed, "D. E. S. T. I. N. Y."

Mark was hit hard by that answer.

"What's a mordgeist?" asked Drake. The planchette spun

in a tight circle on the middle of the board. It then spelled, "H. E. R. E."

Drake and Martin looked at each other shocked.

"The mordgeists are here?" Martin stated with a note of alarm in his voice. The planchette responded, 'NO.' Then it moved again, deliberately, spelling out, "O. N. T. H. I. S. S. I. D. E." Then after a brief pause it spelled, "T. H. E. Y. A. R. E. H. E. R. E."

Martin and Drake released their fingers from the planchette and it slowly stopped circling on the board.

Mark, Martin, and Drake all looked at the board cautiously. It was now nearly two o'clock in the morning. Drake and Martin put their fingers back on the planchette.

"Does Drake have a girlfriend?" shouted Dennis with a squeal, loud enough that lights inside the trailer came on.

"Good job, dillhole," Mark chided his brother. "Now we're gonna have to go to bed."

The planchette was spinning under the fingers of Drake and Martin while Mark reprimanded Dennis, neither saw it spell out, "R. A. C. H. E. L. F. I. N. N. E. G. A. N." Martin saw the last part and thought it has misspelled 'again' like it was asking for clarity on the question, like it did a couple times during the night when he had asked silly questions.

"I should get one of these so we can ask more when we get home," Martin remarked. The planchette slid over to the 'YES.'

The trailer door cracked open.

"Boys," Mom sternly announced. "Get to bed, or it's off to Green Hill. Now!"

Dennis quickly scooted off into the trailer. The planchette slid around in large graceful circles around the perimeter of the board. It then began to spell again, "G. O. O. D. N. I. G. H. T. B. O. Y. S. S. E. E. Y. O. U. S. O. O. N."

"See you soon?" Mark questioned. "Creepy."

Drake and Martin stood up and set the board in its box again, placing the planchette on top of it before closing them both inside the box with the black and white top. Martin looked at the image on the cover of the game. The hand of the spirit was on the planchette moving it, or manipulating it. It didn't matter how, all Martin knew was that it worked, and he knew he needed to get one when they got back home from camping.

8

THE ARCHIVE

THE BROTHERHOOD OF OLYMPUS
AND THE DEADLIEST GAME

### If a Picture Paints a Thousand Words
### Chapter Eight
### July 1, 1978
### Hoquiam, Washington

When the Fraser family returned from their camping trip to 10,000 Lakes they quickly settled back into their summer routines. Dad drove each day in the green Datsun station wagon to 10,000 Lakes to sell memberships at the campground. Due to the eight-plus hours he worked each day and the nearly two hour commute each way, no one at home saw much of him. Mom was back to work, nightshift at the nursing home, sleeping during the morning until mid to late afternoon. The boys saw less and less of their parents and depended on each other more.

Mark started working at the car dealership as a lot boy again, washing and detailing cars. His favorite part was when he got to move them around on the lot and park them in a different order so it appeared to the car-buying public that the inventory there was always selling.

Martin went back to work at the grocery store and had begun to be trained as a checker, moving out of the helper clerk/stocker position. It meant a few more hours and, more importantly, a higher hourly wage. He purchased a used 1972 olive green Dodge Coronet. It was a four door sedan that Mark called a boat because of it width and size. Martin made numerous trips to all the stores in town that sold games or toys, looking for a *Spirit* board game to buy with absolutely no luck. He concluded that he would have to drive up to Olympia to get the game. He proudly got the neighbor boy,

Tom Adams, who was a grade younger than him, his old job at the grocery store. He made sure to show off his superior skills and abilities at work to impress his neighborhood friend. The new job changed some of his work friends too. He now was hanging out with older people who had parties that included beer and marijuana. Not wanting to look like he didn't belong, Martin quickly succumbed to the peer pressure and began to enjoy these parties as well. He also brought young Tom Adams along with him to most of the parties.

Drake was back to doing research and drawing. He was mystified by what he witnessed with the *Spirit* board, and wanted to know more, so much more. He desired to know how it worked, what made it work, if he could he replicate the process, and most importantly what or who was answering the questions. He had drawn a picture of Martin and himself holding the *Spirit* board on their knees with the ominous forms of the mordgeists in the background. It was a really good picture, but the concept was also quite scary.

Dennis and Albert spent much of their time pestering their brothers or lying sprawled out on the beanbag chairs playing the *Atari* video game system their dad had purchased for the family. Dennis began to spend time with Martin when he came in late after work as well. No one spoke of what they said or did, but Drake did notice that the relationship between Martin and Dennis had changed.

Drake asked Mark to drop him off at the library on his way to work, to save him the walk there. Mark didn't mind at all and told Drake to be ready to go early so they wouldn't make him late to work. On the drive, Drake shared his curiosity of the *Spirit* board with his brother. Mark feigned interest.

"I bet there's something about them in the old archive room," Drake stated excitedly.

"What old archive room?" Mark replied. "At the library?"

"Yeah, Miss Furfur, the librarian, showed it to me a few

months ago."

"Where in the library is this archive room?" Mark questioned.

"In the basement by the back wall," Drake quickly answered.

Mark pulled up to the corner in front of the library. Mark was very curious about this 'old archive room.' He had spent two months cleaning the library after it closed as a service project for one of his teachers at school. It taught him the meaning of work, and earned him a dollar fifty-five an hour. But he had never seen any old archive room.

"Come on Drake," Mark said as he turned off the ignition of his car and climbed out.

"You'll be late," Drake replied as he climbed out of the car.

"I'm not going in the library," Mark added as he walked around the side of the old red brick building. "I just want you to show me where this 'old archive' room is."

They walked to the far side of the library where they could see the back wall, and it was made of heavy gray stone in the foundation where the basement existed, then red brick above that where the first floor of the library was. Like many buildings in Aberdeen or Hoquiam, the first floor of the library was up a short staircase. This was due to the nearly annual flooding that took place in the old tidal mud flats of Grays Harbor upon which both cities stood.

"Look," Mark said as he pointed. "If there was a room in the basement on the back wall, shouldn't it be sticking out of the wall right there?"

Drake was puzzled.

"I got to go, or I'll be late for work," Mark said as he turned and headed back to his car.

"See you later, little brother!" Mark yelled out his window as he pulled away from the curb in his car. Mark enjoyed letting everyone know that his larger sibling was still his little brother. Drake waved and walked up the steps to the front door of the library.

Once inside the front door, he saw her, the angel of the library, Miss Furfur. Today she was in a tight gray skirt and a flouncy red blouse, and a different color of shoes than before, but they seemed the same in all other regards. Drake was sure the temperature of the library was about twenty degrees warmer than outside. Miss Furfur saw him enter and walked towards him from the back shelving behind the front desk. That walk of hers was mystifying to Drake, it made him even forget his own name.

"Drake," Miss Furfur said as she approached. Drake stood there dumbfounded.

"Drake?" she repeated. "Drake, are you okay?"

"Oh, yeah, I'm fine, thank you Miss Furfur," he replied, as he began to regain his senses.

"Do you want to go into the old archive room again today?"

"Yes, please."

"I can do that for you, Drake," she said as she turned and began to walk to the stairwell down to the basement. "Oh, by the way, your little friend is here sitting over in the corner, I think she's waiting for you."

"What little friend?" Drake replied as he began to walk behind her.

"That cute little blonde girlfriend of yours," Miss Furfur said over her shoulder as she reached the stairs.

"She is more of an acquaintance actually," he responded, now knowing exactly who Miss Furfur was alluding to.

Before he began down the stairs he was immediately aware he was being followed.

"Hullo Drake," Rachel's sing-song voice echoed into the stairwell. "Where've you been? Did you miss me? I haven't seen you since the last day of school. Whatcha looking for today, some new monsters? Did you draw me a unicorn yet?"

"Hi," he replied in an attempt to be nice and also as a calculated move to get her to stop talking. "And I told you I don't draw anything with hooves." He muttered to himself just loud enough to be heard. 'Or draw anything for girls with cooties, either,' he thought.

"Looking for anything in particular?" Miss Furfur asked as she produced the old skeleton key and unlocked the solid wooden door of the old archive room.

"Anything about *Spirit* boards, or divination," Drake replied.

"Hmmmmm," Miss Furfur said as she stepped in the room and turned on that bright, swinging single light fixture. "I think we do, oh yes, here you go, this book is all about divination."

She handed the book to Drake as he flashed a smile to her, and his dimples popped on his face. Rachel felt her heart skip a beat.

"I am not sure they have anything on *Spirit* boards in here, they are pretty new, but the concept is quite old. There are a number of brands of boards sold around the world that do the same thing, so they say. *Witchboards, Ouija* Boards, and many others," the librarian stated, "Though I have never actually seen one work. Have you, Drake?"

Drake almost responded, "Yes, I have" but he caught himself, it had seemed like Miss Furfur was fishing for information. Why would she want to know that? What difference would it make to her if he had seen it work like it did that night at 10,000 Lakes with his brothers?

"No, just curious," he replied.

"Okay, Drake," the librarian added, as she turned and walked away with that magical walk of hers. Drake noticed once again that thin line running up the back of her legs as she headed for the stairwell. "Let me know if you need anything."

"What's divination?" Rachel asked, as soon as she was sure Miss Furfur was out of hearing range headed up the stairs, her high heels clicking as she walked on the wooden stairs.

"Seeing the future," Drake replied. "Being able to predict the future, or see what will come to pass. Usually using something like *Tarot* cards, tea leaves, and junk like that."

"Is it true?" Rachel asked in genuine curiosity.

"Some people think so," Drake added, as he began to flip through the book the librarian had given him.

"If you could know anything about your future what would you want to know?" Rachel asked as she found a book on witchcraft and began to flip through it. She did like witches, and vampires. She knew of the Salem witch trials, of course, but most of her knowledge of witches came from television and the daily reruns of *Bewitched*. She never fully understood the premise of the television show when she watched it, and she watched it a lot because it was one of her favorite shows. If she was a witch like Samantha Stevens, then her stupid husband Darrin would just have to deal with it, or she would get a new husband with the twitch of her nose. Plain and simple, she would embrace being a witch and would not change for anyone. "Oh, there're spells in here. You think they really work?"

"I dunno," Drake answered.

Drake began to take notes in one of his notebooks, and Rachel actually was quiet for quite some time, scribbling things down in spiral notebook of her own. Drake happened to see the colorful unicorn on the cover and sighed under his breath, 'girls are so weird.'

Time slipped by as they quietly continued their research. Over an hour later, Drake was surprised by the long period of silence from Rachel. He had noticed from time to time that her head was bopping to some music that only she heard inside her head, making the loose ponytail in her long blonde hair sway this way, then that.

"You never answered," Rachel stated, as she became aware of Drake watching her.

"I said, I don't know if the spells work," Drake said as he remembered her last question.

"No, not that question Drake," Rachel giggled. "The one before. If you could know anything about your future what would you want to know?"

Drake stood and pondered. What would he like to know about his future, he did ask if he was going to college with the *Spirit* board, the pursuit of knowledge was very important to him.

"I guess if I am going to college and what one," he finally answered.

"Boring," Rachel remarked. "I'd want to know who I am marrying, and when we're getting married, and how many adorable babies will we have. That's what I'd wanna know."

"More boring," Drake retorted to her flight of fantasy.

"My wedding will be in June, of course," she continued. "I've always wanted to be a June bride. My bridesmaids will each wear a color of the rainbow, so when they all stand by me you will see the rainbow. And I will sing *When*, by Sourdough, to my husband. Do you know that song Drake?"

Drake shook his head. He thought she was mad with her detailed thoughts of a wedding, and what would she think if she found out she was just going to be some crazy cat lady and never get married, what would she think about divination then? Then she began to sing. One thing that Drake did know about Rachel was that she was an accomplished singer. She was a soprano, and she had qualified for many choir competitions at the state level through the high school, even though she was still in junior high. He admired this in her.

*When love is worth more than gold,*
*Then why am I not rich,*

Her voice lifted Drake above the hustle and bustle of daily life, like the true voice of an angel, so clear and melodic.

*The world doesn't seem to know the value of my love.*
*When it's darkest before the dawn,*
*Then where shall I go?*
*My home is empty until you fill it with your love.*
*And when my faith in life is fading fast,*
*You give me your love,*
*And that's a treasure bound to last.*

"Never heard that song," he responded truthfully. "You should become a singer, you're very good." The word he thought of was 'amazing,' but 'good' somehow slipped into its place as a much safer alternative.

Rachel blushed at the compliment.

"I think a singer also makes more money than Dr. Quincy, too. But I still don't know why you'd want to know about getting married and weird junk like that," Drake added.

Rachel looked at Drake as he returned to his note taking. She was pleasantly surprised he remembered her comment about being a medical examiner. It proved that he did listen to her. Deep inside her she thought, 'Someday, Drake Fraser, I really hope you do understand all the weird junk like that.' Drake smiled for a moment as he wrote. His dimples popped out, and Rachel swooned.

Drake and Rachel left the library late in the afternoon. Drake knew he had gotten a lot of valuable information about divination and the operation of medium devices like the *Spirit* board to share with his brothers. Rachel had written down a number of spells about protection from evil, making charms, and how to make someone fall in love with someone else. She was not sure if any of them would work, but she was more than willing to try.

Miss Furfur seemed cautious of them when they left, and Drake thought she went out of her way to avoid contact with Rachel, and he noted in his mind that was kind of weird.

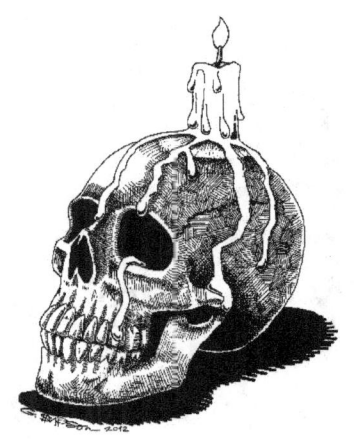

## Must be Your Lucky Day
## Chapter Nine
## July 6, 1978
## Aberdeen, Washington

Martin took Drake for a ride in his green boat of a car, on his day off from work, in another attempt at finding the elusive board game. This was the day they would drive up to Olympia and look for it at all the toy stores and department stores in the capital city. They knew there were two malls up there, South Sound Mall, and the newer Capital Mall. They would find it there, Martin knew. If not, he would drive further up the freeway to the much larger Tacoma and he would surely find the game there. One way or another today was the day Martin got the board game.

They began to drive down Simpson Avenue heading out of Aberdeen.

"Remember," Drake announced. "Dad wanted us to stop at Payless and get more film for his camera."

Martin rolled his eyes. The closest Payless Drug Store was back behind them on Myrtle Street that ran north and south and served as the official border between Aberdeen and Hoquiam. Aberdeen was on the east side of the street, Hoquiam was on the west.

"We can stop on our way back from Olympia," Martin stated.

"Depending on how long we are up there, Payless may be closed by the time we get back," Drake rationalized.

Martin thought of Drake's logic, he was right, they could be in Olympia, or beyond for quite some time, then the drive home would put them back after dark perhaps. Martin knew in his heart that Drake was almost always right. He flicked on his left directional and slowed to turn. Aberdeen had two main thoroughfares that headed east and west in a rough backwards 'S' shape. Entering town on Olympic Highway from the east, the road divided becoming first Wishkah Street then after the first of the 'S' turns the road changed into Alder Street, before finally becoming Sumner Avenue after the final part of the 'S.' Sumner was the longest of the three. Both one way street corridors were separated by a single city block and much of the downtown existed within this one block corridor running the length of the city. Heading west running parallel to each of the other three roads was Simpson Avenue which started in Hoquiam and was one of the longest roads in the cities before it turned into Park Street and then finally becoming Heron Street, and then rejoining Olympic Highway.

"We could probably get film in Olympia," Martin remarked as he turned left onto Sumner Avenue and headed west through Aberdeen.

"From like a camera store for a lot of money," Drake added. "You know he likes the Payless brand film, it works like *Fuji* film but is a lot cheaper. Do you know where Payless is in Olympia?"

"We're already heading back to Payless," Martin explained. "I'm just saying we could've found it up in Olympia too."

Drake nodded as he watched the homes and businesses pass by. The parking lot at Payless was nearly empty when Martin and Drake arrived. Drake noticed that the Payless sign on the front of the building was still on. The red letters glowed very faintly in the summer daylight. As Martin and Drake passed into the store the sign lights flashed brightly and then went off.

Near the back wall of the store was a sign that guided them to the 'photography' section. The boys moved quickly through the store, through different aisles, in a silent race to get to the film first. Martin easily won. In fact, he won too easily, so he turned to see where Drake was as he stood in front of a wall of film boxes all neatly arranged in little diamond shaped shelves.

Drake was behind him, in another aisle completely stopped, staring at something on the shelf. Martin grabbed the little boxes of film their dad had requested and walked over to see what his brother was doing.

"Drake," Martin stated as he turned the corner into the aisle, "the film's over here, and I already grabbed it."

Drake looked up from where he was looking on the bottom shelf and with wide eyes pointed to the games on the shelves. Drake always went down the toy and game aisle in any store if he had a choice, and today was no different, with the exception of the outcome.

"A *Spirit* board!" Martin exclaimed. "You found one, nobody in town had them at all, not even Payless when I was here last week, and today you just walk in and find it, Drake."

Martin quickly grabbed the familiar black and white game box as if he was fearful someone else might come in and contest him for the game.

"You are a good luck charm, Drake," Martin continued as he walked to the cashier at the front of the store, film boxes in one hand and the board game box tucked safely under his right arm. "This'll save me lots of gas money, since we don't have to drive to Olympia. And what's even better is we can go home and start using it."

Drake quietly took in what his brother was saying about him being a lucky charm, but Drake never told Martin what he saw as he turned and began down the long aisle that would become the toys and games after the main center aisle cut across them all. He was sure he saw the heavenly form of Ms. Furfur standing at the far end of the aisle, just about where he found the game. Normally, he would have turned and walked down another aisle if it were a girl he knew standing there, like Rachel Finnegan. Drake went out of his way to avoid talking to girls. But he wanted to see Ms. Furfur, not to talk to her or anything like that, but to pass by her, perhaps smell her perfume, and if she dared to talk to him, he imagined himself with a confident debonair smile smoothly saying, "How are you this fine day, Miss Furfur. Doing a little shopping at Payless today, are we?"

Unfortunately for Drake nothing like that came to pass. By the time he started down the second part of the aisle with the toys and games, Miss Furfur turned and went down the rest of the aisle rounding the corner towards the photography section. Drake increased his speed as he walked, which he imagined Martin doing as well as they raced to the back of the store. But as he neared where he saw Miss Furfur lingering, he caught her fragrance of fresh roses in the air and stopped. Then he saw the box on the bottom shelf and stood there, silently, trying to make sense of what just happened. He was not the lucky charm, Miss Furfur was.

The cashier, a kindly older man who could have been friends with their grandparents, was busy ringing them up on the cash register, looking at the price tags on each of the boxes of film, before entering the same number into the register. When he got to the game, he turned it over looking for the Payless price tag. It didn't have one. He smiled at the boys. He picked up the telephone handset, and dialed a number.

"Hi," the cashier said on the phone, as he turned and smiled at the boys again, holding up his index finger to them signifying he would be with them in just a second. "Do we have a price for a *Spirit* board game? Uh huh, uh huh, okay. So what is the price? Fourteen ninety-five, thank you."

The cashier hung up the phone and turned back to the boys, as he entered the price into the cash register, and totaled up the cost of their purchase.

"Thirty five sixty-seven," stated the cashier as he placed the more than a handful of film boxes into a bag. "You boys must be lucky. According to my manager we haven't had one of these games in stock since last Christmas, not sure how it got on the shelf. It didn't even have a price tag on it. It must be your lucky day."

He chuckled as he took the two twenty dollar bills Martin handed him and rang open the register, and began to count out their change. Martin and Drake exchanged curious glances at each other. Drake began walking for the door, as Martin held out his hand for the change.

"Four dollars and thirty-three cents," the old man counted out as he placed the money into Martin's hand. "Have a good day boys."

Martin quickly joined Drake outside by his car. Martin unlocked the door, climbed in, and then reached over and unlocked his brother's door.

The ride home was in silence, and it seemed to both boys that it was somehow longer than it should have been.

Drake went and rescued Monique from the hands of Albert, freeing her from the humiliation of being some oddly dressed baby-dog hybrid. He took her outside so she could potty. Then he picked her up and carried her back inside talking to her along the way, setting her down as he stopped in the kitchen where he filled a glass with ice from the freezer and then added water out of the tap. The ice clinked in the glass as he reached back down and picked up the poodle. Together they went down the hall and turned right before the stairwell and into Martin's bedroom.

None of the boys had a lavish bedroom. They all lived in a very spartan environment, and didn't have much more than the bare necessities. Martin was more of an exception, because he had begun to purchase things for himself after he started working for the grocery store soon after he turned sixteen. He had *Star Wars*, *Close Encounters of the Third Kind*, and *King Kong* posters on his wall. Drake was always drawn to the King Kong poster due to its artistic use of perspective, the massive ape stood with one foot on each of the twin towers of the World Trade Center in New York City, in his left hand he held a blonde woman, in his right a crushed shell of a jet airplane as two green army helicopters and another jet harassed him from above. It wasn't this that fascinated

Drake. What fascinated him was the city of New York that filled in the poster to the right of the great ape. The Empire State Building stood dwarfed in the background. He knew he needed to master perspective like this to be able to draw better.

Martin had a small white and silver marbled Formica dinette table and two old, red vinyl cushioned, silver metal chairs that oddly matched the table sitting against the wall opposite of his unmade twin bed.

"Martin," Drake announced, "are you here?"

Martin swung open the closet door, he stood within the closet, and the red light of the dark room inside it was still on.

"Did you just open up the door and ruin film?" Drake asked, as he turned and stepped towards the dark room.

"No," Martin replied hastily. "I was just in here looking at the *Spirit* board in the red light to see if I could make out anything odd on it. Kind of investigating it, before we use it."

Drake nodded.

"That was kind of weird," Martin continued. "In the store, I mean, that they haven't had one of these in there since Christmas and today it was there. What do you think, brainiac?"

Drake pondered what Martin said.

"It was kind of like it, the board I mean," Martin added, "like it wanted us to find it. This particular *Spirit* board was destined to be mine. So I wanted to see if there was something written or printed on it in like invisible ink, so I brought it in here."

Drake and Monique looked at him silently.

"But I didn't find anything," Martin finished. "Case closed. It's just a normal board game, just like the one we used at 10,000 Lakes. Are you ready to start? I figured I would write down anything we got from it, kind of like an experiment journal."

Martin walked past Drake and Monique, and set the board down on the table. He had an opened spiral notebook and a blue *Bic* ink pen lying next to it. At the top of the first page of the spiral notebook he wrote, '*Spirit* Board Experiment Journal.' He then quickly wrote the date and who was there on the first lines of the paper.

They turned the board so the short sides of the game faced them on opposite sides of the small table. Drake sat down, still holding Monique.

"You need both hands on the planchette," Martin instructed as he saw the poodle cradled in his brother's right arm.

"I'll use both," Drake replied. "Mo will just lay on my lap."

Monique did just that, she turned once and sat down on his lap in a slight curled up position and laid her head down.

Both brothers rested their finger tips on the planchette.

"Is anyone there?" Martin began. "Wally, are you there?"

The planchette sat motionless. Time crept slowly by.

"Wally," Martin said as he began to get frustrated. "Wally, are you there? We want to talk to you again."

With a loud bang the door between the kitchen and garage slammed shut and Monique bolted off Drake's lap, barking as her little legs sped her around the corner and out into the hall.

"Shut up Mo!" Mark yelled at the poodle as he walked past the bedroom doorway and turned to clomp up the stairs to his room.

"Mark's home," Drake stated.

The planchette began to slowly move under their fingertips, in large graceful circular motions it spelled out, "T. H. A. N. K. Y. O. U. C. A. P. T. I. A. N. O. B. V. I. O. U. S."

"Are you Captain Obvious?" Martin asked, ignoring the misspelling.

The planchette slid over to the 'NO' and then moved the pointer over to the far end of the board so it pointed at Drake.

"Wally," Drake began. "Is it you?"

'YES' was the rapid response from the board.

"Where are you?" Drake asked.

"E. T. H. E. R. E. A. L. P. L. A. N. E." the board responded.

"What is that?" Martin questioned as he quickly took his hands off the planchette to write it down.

"I have read about it," Drake responded. "In the archive room at the library, it is like a vapor or gaseous substance that connects some of the various planes of reality together. There were some references as to how humans might travel through the ethereal plane in those books, too."

"So," Martin said, as he thought really hard about what his brother just explained, "it connects things, binds us, and penetrates us. Kind of like the Force?"

"No," Drake replied shaking his head. "It gives no power, it's a place, like another reality, but it isn't like Earth. It's like a dark land of clouds and vapor that connect other planes of existence together. In theory, you could travel through the ethereal plane to the afterlife, Heaven, Valhalla, Mount Olympus, or whatever you believed existed."

"Cool, Wally told me about other worlds, beyond myth and legend existing in my dream," Martin added as he placed his fingers back on the planchette. "What's it like there, Wally?"

"D. A. R. K." the board spelled out quickly. "V. A. P. O. R. S."

"Creepy," Martin stated as he wrote down the response.

"E. X. C. E. P. T. L. I. G. H. T. F. R. O. M. Y. O. U." the board spelled without being asked.

"Except light from you?" Drake asked. "What do you mean, light from us? There's light from us in the ethereal plane?"

'YES' replied the board gracefully.

"The light from us," Drake continued, almost like he was thinking out loud. "It shines in the ethereal plane, and you can see it. What can you see?"

The planchette spun, and then spelled, "B. E. A. C. O. N."

"The light is like a beacon?" Martin added. He barely took

any time to write down the results in a frantic scribble on the spiral notebook paper.

"So," Drake inquisitively continued, "the beacon of light, comes from us. You see us?"

'NO' quickly responded the planchette on the board.

"What do you see then?" Drake asked again.

"L. I. G. H. T" the planchette spelled, before spinning in a tight circle. Then it began to spell again, "S. P. I. R. I. T. B. O. A. R. D."

"You see light," Drake began to respond as he tried to logically assemble the answer. "You see a beacon of light from us, through the board. You see this light in the dark vapor, and you see the board within the light, so you can guide the pointer to spell things out."

The planchette spun in tight circles then in a series of stabbing motions it responded over and over again, 'YES,' 'YES,' 'YES,' 'YES.' Then it returned to its tight little circle of movement.

"Where are the mordgeists?" Martin asked, remembering the discussion with the *Spirit* board at the campground.

"H. E. R. E." responded the planchette.

Both boys took their fingers off the planchette with deep sighs. The fear of the specters was real within them. But they had to know more, and returned their fingers to the white plastic of the planchette.

"They are here?" Drake questioned. "In Martin's room where we are?"

'NO' was the response.

"Then how are they here?" Drake queried.

"H. E. R. E. I. N. V. A. P. O. R." the planchette spelled out for them.

"They are there, with you," Drake answered. "Can they see the light too?"

'YES' was the quick response from the board.

"A. L. L. H. E. R. E. C. A. N. S. E. E. L. I. G. H. T." the planchette spelled out for them in explanation. That response troubled Drake. If 'all here can see light' that meant anything could come to the light of the board. And he recalled reading about some ethereal monsters that stalked the plane.

"Y. O. U. R. L. I. F. E. F. O. R. C. E. I. S. S. T. R. O. N. G." the planchette spelled quickly, pausing a moment before continuing. "B. E. A. C. O. N. V. E. R. Y. B. R. I. G. H. T."

Martin took his fingers off the planchette and wrote down the responses.

"So," Drake continued, trying to make sense of it all. He didn't wait for Martin to put his fingers back on the planchette before he began his next question. Martin hurriedly got his fingers back on the planchette as it began to move without him. "Our life force is strong, and it makes a very bright light that shines like a beacon from the board there in the dark vapors?"

'YES' was the quick response.

"Y. O. U. A. R. E. S. P. E. C. I. A. L." the planchette continued on its own again. "G. R. E. A. T. Y. O. U. W. I. L. L. D. O" it circled the board in large slow circles. "M. A. N. Y. H. E. R. E. F. E. A. R. Y. O. U."

Both boys were shocked by what they were reading. It was telling them that they were special, that they will achieve great things, and that there were things on the other side, in the dark shadows that feared them. It was a revelation to both of them. Martin felt it validated his opinion of who he was. Drake was uncertain he wanted anything to do with greatness or causing fear in anything, it all sounded like too much trouble.

"O. R. T. H. E. Y. W. I. L. L. T. R. Y. T. O. U. S. E. Y. O. U. R. P. O. W. E. R." the planchette continued to slide from one letter to the next.

"They will try to use your power?" Drake asked. "What do you mean? How will they try to use our power?"

The planchette stopped. It slowly moved to the ghost face on the lower right corner of the board, then moved upward in a big arch before it slid ever so slowly over the 'GOOD BYE' near the bottom of the board.

The planchette stopped moving and Drake removed his fingers. Martin began to write down what had been revealed.

"Why'd it say good bye to us?" Martin asked as he continued to write.

"Maybe," Drake explained, using his best logic based upon what he had read before, and just learned, "it was stopping and saying good bye because the longer we used it the more chance that something bigger or badder would see the light and come over and use the board. Maybe something was almost there, so it stopped. You saw how it pointed to the ghost face, maybe the mordgeists were coming?"

"Maybe," Martin responded. "But, either way, I need to know more, I was beginning to feel like I could sense this dark land of vapors. Like I could almost see who was pushing the pointer around on the board from the other side, but I'm not sure, because I don't think it was Wally."

Drake sat there and thought about the ramifications of what Martin had just explained. He knew, based upon his research, that all humans possessed some measure of psychic ability, some more so than others. Maybe Martin had some latent psychic power, like he had overheard about their relatives on the La Madrid side of the family, or had experienced firsthand with their Grandmother, back in January. Maybe that was what the board meant about them having power. Then he noticed that Monique had not come back. She was asleep, lying curled up on the tile floor just outside Martin's room. He wondered why she stopped there and didn't come back and lay in his lap again? She certainly was a silly dog, sometimes.

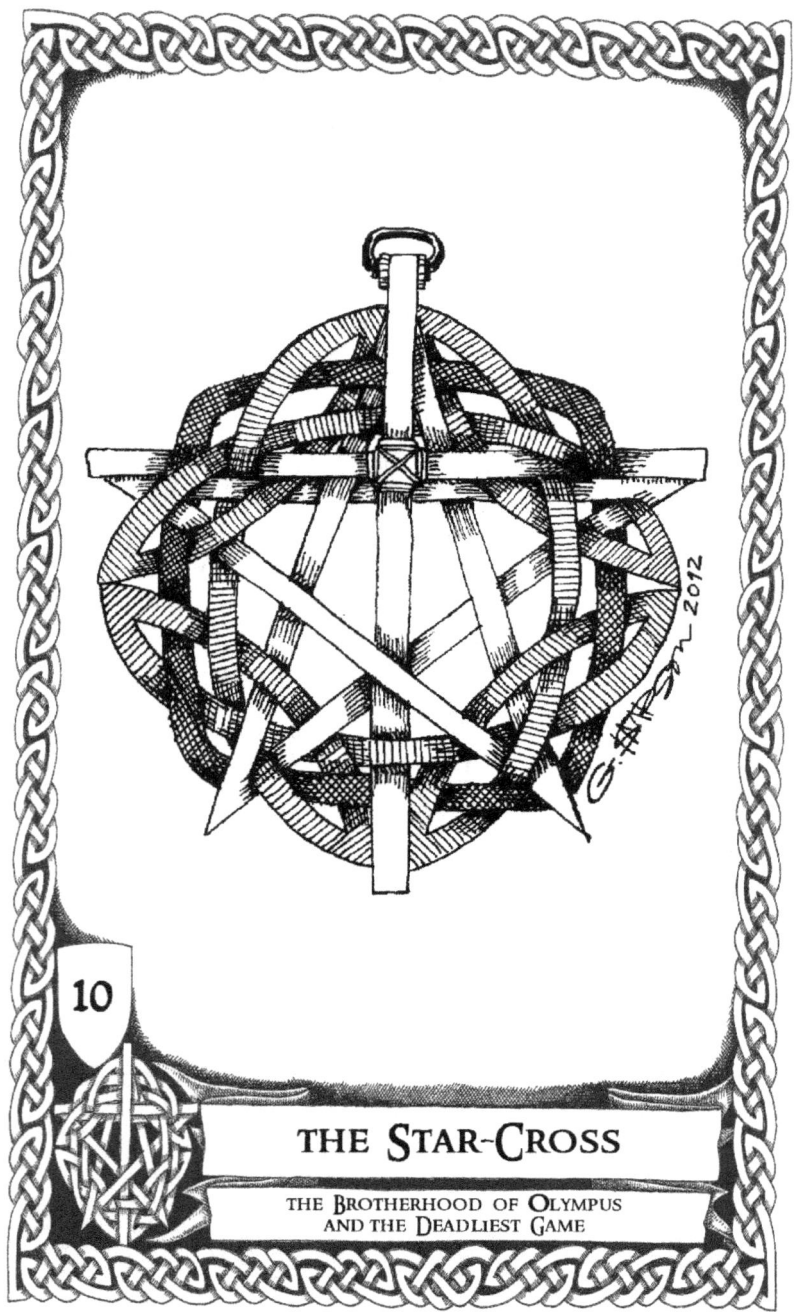

10

## THE STAR-CROSS

### THE BROTHERHOOD OF OLYMPUS
### AND THE DEADLIEST GAME

**Torn Asunder**
**Chapter Ten**
**July 14, 1978**
**Hoquiam, Washington**

As often as they could, after that first afternoon, Martin and Drake sat in Martin's room and experimented with the *Spirit* board. But, limiting their investigation into the unknown was the growing social life of Martin. He was spending more and more time with Tom Adams and his grocery store friends, so Drake made do with the free time by reading, researching, and drawing. He had even started going to the library at different times, and made the startling discovery that Mark was correct about the old archive room.

Yesterday, the thirteenth of July, Drake had visited the library in the evening before it closed. Miss Furfur was not there, it was the ancient Mrs. Madison with her short blue-gray hair, thick horn-rimmed glasses with the golden chain attached to keep them from getting lost, and the clear and utterly unmistakable fragrance of mothballs that followed her. She wasn't Miss Furfur, and she wasn't amused when Drake came up and asked permission to get the key and go into the old archive room in the basement.

"There is no archive room in the basement," the elder librarian told him. "That's just nonsense. Who told you there was an archive room, dear? Your older brother? One of the older neighborhood kids?"

Drake was stunned. Mark had tried to explain this to him earlier, but he had been in there, he knew it was real.

"Where're they now," the librarian finished, as she raised

her voice in hopes she might shame whoever it was that set Drake up for this silly prank. "Are they around here somewhere laughing at you for coming up and asking for the key to the archive room. They should be ashamed of themselves. Ashamed!"

Drake left the library feeling bewildered, Mrs. Madison shaking her head scornfully at the unseen perpetrator of the practical joke played upon the young boy.

He pondered it all as he fell asleep that night. It hurt his logical head, and he dreamt of a shiny black stone tower that stretched hundreds of feet into the sky before being lost in the angry, dark storm clouds. He was with four others, three of them he didn't recognize. There was an older man who might have been an Indian with thick framed glasses, a wild-haired, brown muscle-bound guy, and a red-haired woman were with him and Martin. Inside the tower they found a long, long hallway filled with doors that opened into places fantastical and wondrous, as well as places terrifying and foreboding. The destinations behind the doors perplexed him, but he was puzzled most by the long endless hallway inside this tall slender tower.

He awoke feeling like he hadn't slept much at all. The morning whisked by, as he absent-mindedly hung out with Dennis and Albert, and played a few *Atari* video games. After he fixed his little brothers lunch, he prepared to go to the library again. He knew Miss Furfur worked the library front desk on Friday afternoons. When he arrived, she was there, in all her angelic splendor, the sweet aroma of roses wafting into Drake's mind. She asked him if he would like to go into the old archive room again, he simply said yes, and walked with her to the heavy wooden door in the basement, and was left inside to do his research with that same, "If you need anything, please let me know." He appreciated the access to all of this knowledge, but the where's, why's, and how's of it all boggled his mind.

He finished quickly because he knew Martin was off work early today and they could do more investigation into the

*Spirit* board. He left and made sure he said thank you to Miss Furfur, and she thanked him for always brightening her day. He walked down the front stairs and began to walk home, with all of the oddities piling up in his mind. He had to sort them out, to make sense of them all, or he would have his sense of reality, his clear concept of logic and order turned on its side.

The sorting in his mind began with Miss Furfur. She came to work at the library in January, sometime after Wally had died. She was a vision of beauty and grace and she somehow was able to give him access to a hidden room of secret knowledge that the other librarians or even his brother Mark had no idea existed. But there was more. He was certain she was in Payless the day he found the *Spirit* board game on the shelf, though Martin said he had not seen any lady come around the aisle before he found Drake in front of the game. Who was she? What did she know? Why was she helping him learn about these dark otherworldly things?

Then there was the *Spirit* board itself. Why was it there that day in Payless, but not in their inventory? It spoke of dimensions, or planes of existence that he could only verify in myths and legends, or within the books in the secret archive room. Who or what spoke through the board to them? Were the mordgeists real? Were they just some image or amalgamation of things that manifested in Martin's repetitive dream, that dream that started this whole research into the paranormal, which he had discounted most of, until Martin told him of the moment in his dream that he was standing in Aunt Carmen's old bedroom and Drake had turned and stopped for a split second? It was like Drake had seen him. Drake recalled that moment on Friday, January thirteenth, and he did recall seeing a faint image of his brother standing there. He just never shared that confirmation to Martin. He held that bit of information secretly to himself as part of what motivated him to find out more, to figure out why, or how this was all happening. He knew if he verified it to Martin his brother would take it to another level and devote his whole life to trying to make sense of it, and in doing so drag Drake into the lifelong quest as well.

Drake had walked well past the roads he normally walked down to make his way home, but he hadn't noticed. He was nearly half a mile past his house and still walking in the wrong direction.

"Hey," a familiar voice rang out from the porch of the house he was striding past. The house, like most in Aberdeen or Hoquiam, was built up to withstand the floods. Its architecture was what Drake liked to call World War Two American, kind of a non-descript style built with frugality of resources. It was a quite popular style in the Grays Harbor region, though Drake would later realize that the style was more specific to the Northwest instead of being representative of the time period they were built in. They had cedar shake siding, many of which were painted in soft pastels, or stained in earth-toned hues. They also had stylized, yet cost effective woodworked trim pieces adorning the pitched eaves or porches, which in many cases were done entirely by hand by skilled millworkers who built many of these older houses.

This house had one exception to that style—it was painted a very bright, vibrant, almost royal shade of blue, and its trim was a pastel pink. Drake had always wondered who lived there, whenever his path took him by this garish house.

"Drake," the voice rang out again, as figures moved in the deep shadows of the screened porch. Drake stopped and turned.

"Did ya come to see me for my birthday?" she announced as she bounded off the porch and headed straight towards him, her long blond hair was free of the ponytail he always saw her wear, it cascaded in waves of curly brilliance. Of course, it all made sense, the oddly painted house was home to Rachel Finnegan.

"Thanks for coming to my birthday party," she squealed as she ran up and hugged him fully, quite to his shock. The smile on her face was brighter than the sun in the sky.

"Li...," he stammered, as she released her hug. "Library."

"I can't go to the library right now, silly," she replied. "It's my birthday! See there's my brothers Junior, and Patrick, and my baby sister Maddy, and my mom and dad." She pointed into the shadow of the porch, Junior and her mom both waved to him.

"No," he clarified. "I just came from the library, walking, and walking, I must've missed my turn."

"Oh," she stated as she thought for a brief moment. "That's okay, what's important is that you were here for my fourteenth birthday."

Drake managed a proto-smile, bringing his dimples out, and Rachel flushed.

"Wait right here," she added as she raced off to the porch and then into the house beyond.

While he stood there on the bright sunny sidewalk waiting for Rachel, he wondered why she was always so happy, and how long it was going to take him to get back home if she took much longer in her house.

With the same eruption of energy she burst out of the house, knocking little Patrick over as she darted past her siblings and down the porch steps. She held something fast in her left hand. A string flowed out of her grip.

"I made something for you," she said as she came to a stop right in front of him. "You have to promise, as my birthday present, that you'll wear it. Do you promise?"

Drake was not sure what to say, it could be anything, it could be ugly, or it could be girly, or worse, though he could not imagine anything much worse than that. But she stood there, that radiant smile, her eyes wide and happy. He nodded.

"Yay!" she shouted. Junior and Patrick came to look through or over the porch railing at their older sister. She opened her left hand and quickly tied the loose white string around Drake's neck.

Hanging from the string, as he looked down at his button up plaid shirt, was what appeared to be a woven wooden charm, made of a couple of different types of wood. It was a star, with a cross on top of it, with an intricate woven circle around it. The whole thing was a bit larger than a silver dollar and most of it was painted a bright blue.

"It's made out of lilac and rose wood," Rachel explained. "Did ya know that lilac has been used to protect people from haunted houses and a bunch of other stuff? And roses…"

"Rachel!" interrupted a gruff voice from the porch, as the form of Clancy Finnegan, Rachel's father, came out into the sun on the steps. His skin was weather-worn and freckled. He was a squat man, not short or stocky, just well-built and a bit shorter than his oldest daughter. He had close cut, curly red hair, full side burns, a wide nose, thin lips, and bright sparkly eyes hidden in the shadows of his thick red brows. "Come on big girl, it's your birthday, and the cake's waiting for you."

Rachel looked at Drake, smiled one last time, and then turned to run up the stairs. "Coming Daddy!"

Drake watched them slip into the shadows and then disappear inside the house. Only her father lingered, casting a curious glare at him as he turned and started back the way he came, into the shadows of the porch.

The odd, but kind of cool charm Rachel had given him swung across his chest as he walked. And as he walked he thought two divergent things. First, there is no way Rachel's dad wasn't a leprechaun. All he was missing was the green hat, jacket, and buckles on his shoes of course. And second, why would she give him something she made, and apparently made well, on her birthday? Girls were just so confusing, and weird. Then he smiled to himself as he realized he kind of liked weird.

Later that evening, as Martin and Drake used the *Spirit* board in Martin's room, the investigation took a turn that would forever alter part of their relationship as brothers.

Drake was thinking he would begin to ask some of the questions that he had been pondering, about the board, about

Miss Furfur, about all of this occult stuff. He thought if he could get some answers, he might be able to put the bigger pieces together and begin to make sense of it all.

Martin had taken a different approach. He had been asking the board for more information, more things it could do, and whether it could give them power.

'YES' was its response.

Martin turned and picked up a Coke bottle cap and placed it on the board.

"Can you move it?" he questioned.

The planchette spun slowly, and then slid quickly to 'YES.'

They sat in silent wonder as the bottle cap began to slowly twitch, and then began to slide across the board.

"Whoa!" Drake exclaimed. "Did you see that?"

Martin nodded.

"Can you lift it up?" Martin asked.

'YES' was the answer the planchette quickly gave. The bottle cap stopped and then rocked back and forth before starting to rise before it suddenly bent over in half with a pop. It dropped back on the board. The boys sat there with wide opened eyes, shocked.

"Can you teach us how to do that?" Martin asked.

The planchette spun in slow circles before lunging out to point at 'YES' in response.

"Cool," said Martin. He looked at Drake excitedly.

"Where is the old archive room at the library?" Drake asked deliberately.

"What archive room?" Martin responded. The planchette circled smoothly around the board in a giant oval, and then responded, "N. O. T. T. H. E. R. E."

"I know it's not there," Drake continued. "But I've been in it, I've seen the books, where is it if it's not here?"

The planchette stopped. Then it began to move again. Slowly and deliberately it spelled, "G. E. H. E. N. N. A."

"Gehenna? I have read about Gehenna, it is a place similar to Hell, or the Abyss, but it's a separate place. Kind of like the Moon is a separate place from Earth." Drake thought out loud. "But that isn't possible!"

The planchette spun upon itself, then began to spell again, "N. O. T. P. O. S. S. I. B. E. L. I. S. H. U. M. A. N. I. N. V. E. N. T. I. O. N."

Martin scribbled down the response, taking note of the misspelling of 'possible.'

"A human invention," Drake went forward. "Does that mean anything is possible? And since you used the word human, does that mean you're not human?"

The planchette quickly slid to 'YES' and then came to a complete stop, it began to move again towards the 'NO' and then suddenly slid to 'YES' before going on to spell, "N. O. T. H. U. M. A. N."

Martin was shocked. Drake's mind began to click, he now had some answers but he figured he had some more clarification to glean from the board. The second button of his plaid shirt popped open, the blue woven circle charm on the string was now visible against his skin.

"Who is Miss Furfur?" Drake asked.

"L. I. B. R. A. R. I. A. N." the planchette spelled out in spurts.

"She is more than just a librarian," Drake pressed. "Who is she, what does she want?"

"Y. O. U. R. P. A. T. R. O. N." slowly wobbled the planchette across the board, losing energy as it slid. Then it rapidly spelled, "Y. O. U."

"My patron?" Drake stated confusingly.

"Dude," Martin interrupted. "Whoever she is, the board just said she wants you."

"T. H. E. Y. C. O. M. E." The planchette spelled on its own, the boys had gotten used to it doing this. It had even begun to ask them questions over the last few times they used it.

"Who is coming?" Martin asked.

The planchette spun in a tight irregular oval, and then it moved with increasing intensity. "E. V. I. L." "E. V. I. L." "E. V. I. L." "E. V. I. L." After the last 'L' the planchette launched itself off the board and towards Drake, hitting the exposed charm hanging around his neck.

"Mom!" shouted Drake as he ran from Martin's room, down the hall to his parent's room. He opened the door, flicking on the light switch and awakening his sleeping mother. "Mom!"

"Drake?" Mom responded as she rose to an elbow. "What is it? Did I oversleep?"

She looked at the alarm clock on the dresser. She still had three hours before she had to be at work.

"The *Spirit* board, its evil, it just spelled evil, like twelve times then it attacked me."

"Martin!" Mom called. Martin was quick to respond, the quickest Drake had ever remembered him responded to the call from one of their parents with the exception of holidays, or when there was a television show on he wanted to watch.

"What Mom?" Martin said as he stepped into the room.

"Did the game just attack your brother?"

"Kinda."

"Go get the board," Mom commanded.

Martin brought the board and planchette into the bedroom.

"It's just a game," Mom stated. "Set it here, let's try it out."

Martin set it on the edge of her bed, Mom put her fingers on the planchette, and Martin joined her as he sat on the bed.

"Is the board evil?" she asked.

The planchette was painfully slow in beginning to move. Then it slowly slid to 'NO.'

"See Drake," Mom explained. "It's just a game, come here, take your brother's place."

Martin got up and Drake sat down on the edge of the bed, his feet on the floor. He leaned over to put his fingers on the planchette with his mother. The charm swung out from his shirt.

The planchette began to move easily beneath their fingertips. Then to Mom's amazement it spelled, "B. E. W.

A. R. E." Before rapidly spelling over and over, one four letter word. "E. V. I. L."

Drake and Mom both released the planchette in its third spelling of evil.

"I'm done," Drake announced. "It's evil, and I'm not using it any more. Martin, you need to get rid of it."

Martin stood there, looking at his younger brother and his mother, and he thought about the possibilities the *Spirit* board had offered, to teach him how to move things with his mind and more.

"Drake," Mom stated in an attempt to mediate the growing dispute, "it's just a game."

"No, Mom," Drake said as he pointed at the board on the bed next to her. "You need to get rid of it."

"No," Martin responded. "It's mine, I bought it, and I'm going to keep it."

"Fine," Drake yelled back at him. "But you can't use it by yourself, and I won't help you!"

"I can too," Martin snapped. "And I'll just get Dennis or Albert to help me."

Martin walked forward, grabbed the board, and stormed off to his room, slamming the door behind him.

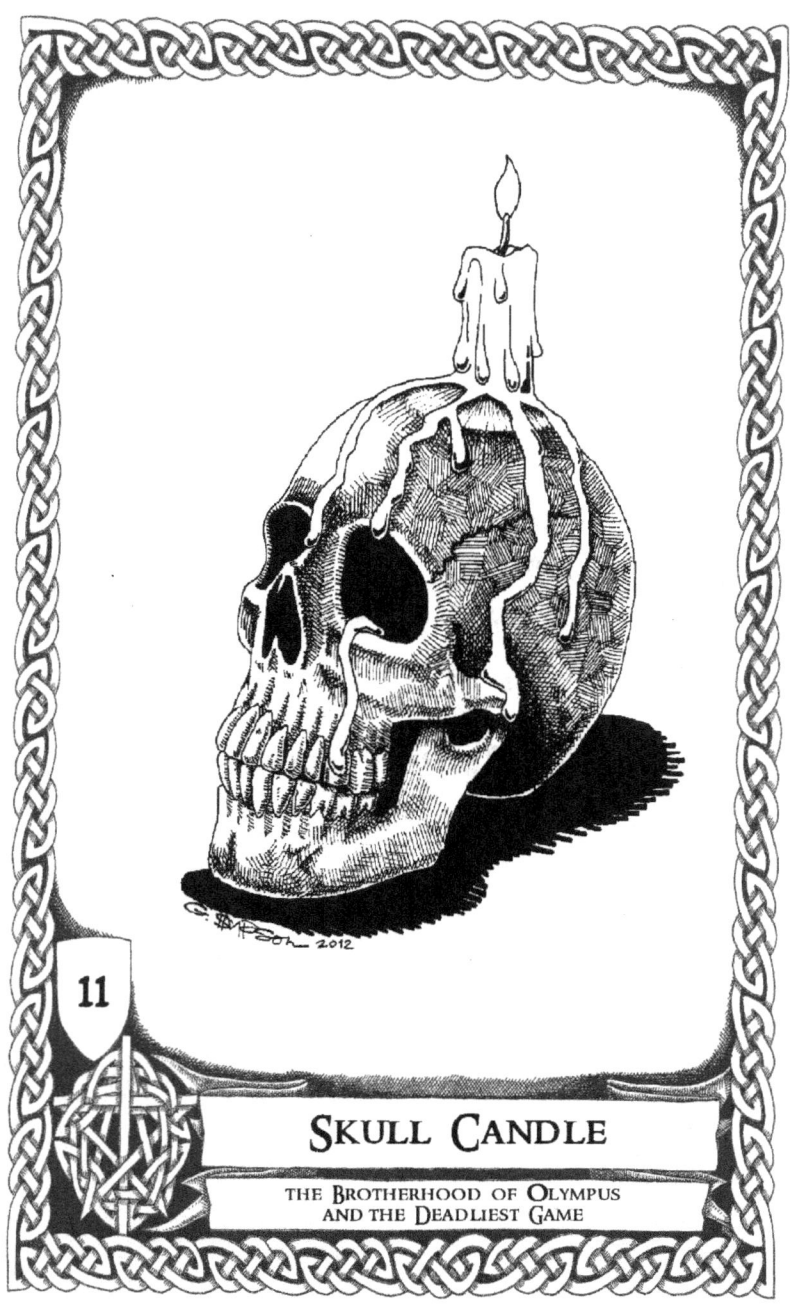

11

SKULL CANDLE

THE BROTHERHOOD OF OLYMPUS
AND THE DEADLIEST GAME

**Madame Chavali**
**Chapter Eleven**
**July 15, 1978**
**Aberdeen, Washington**

Drake and Martin had not spoken since the night before. Drake knew that Martin was making a mistake continuing to use the *Spirit* board, especially without him. He could imagine the sorts of things Martin might do in search of this mystic or psychic power he craved.

Drake played a few games of *Surround* and *Combat* with Albert on the *Atari* to keep him happy. Dennis was noticeably absent.

Drake made lunch for Albert and himself, and then decided he would go to the library. Miss Furfur worked on Saturdays, and he wanted to know information from her, though as he thought about it he doubted he could actually ask her the questions he wanted to.

He packed his notebooks and art tablet into his duffle bag and headed out, telling Albert to let anyone who asked know he went to the library. Albert nodded and sank back into the bean bag chair in front of the television.

The walk to the library was uneventful. Mid July in Grays Harbor typically meant blue skies and temperatures soaring into the seventies. The summer was mild, dry, and full of freshness and an abundance of life.

As he reached the stairs of the library, he heard his name.

"Drake," called the voice. "Pssst! Drake! Over here."

He knew this voice. It was Rachel Finnegan, again. Drake turned and walked over to where Rachel stood beside one of the large rhododendrons in front of the library. She was back far enough that she could not be seen from the door of the library or any of the front windows.

"Why are you hiding in the bushes?" Drake asked curiously.

"I'm not," she responded. "I was just waiting for you, and I thought this rhododendron was rather lovely so I came over to look at it."

He looked at her, shook his head, and began to turn back towards the library.

"Wait," she asked as she touched her hand to his arm, causing him to flinch. "I found another place to get some information for you."

"What do you mean?" he queried. "Where?"

"Did you know that there's a psychic bookstore in Aberdeen?"

"No," he said coolly.

"And they have tons of books about witches, and monsters, and devils, and junk like that," she added. "And psychic stuff too."

Drake was intrigued. He turned to face her again. She took that as acceptance.

"Let's go," she stated, and as she began to walk away from the library, Drake followed her. "I'll show you."

The walk was pleasant. When they crossed the long Simpson Avenue Bridge he gazed upward to avoid looking at the river far below him. High in the sky a series a cirrocumulus clouds drifted eastward, and Drake thought they were shaped like ducks. They were a group of ducks following a larger cloud that could very well be a turtle. He chuckled to himself. Rachel walked slightly ahead of Drake, with a visible bounce in her step. She talked the whole time about odd information, almost random topics Drake thought. Occasionally, she stopped to look into the large windows of the storefronts they passed. Drake noticed that most of these were girl related, which was different for him, since in his family only his mother was a girl, and nobody really thought of her as a girl, since she was just their mom.

They walked all the way down Simpson Avenue nearly to Aberdeen.

Finally as they neared Ontario Street, they turned south.

"I thought you said it was in Aberdeen?" Drake asked as they walked farther.

"Aberdeen, Hoquiam," Rachel said in response. "Hoquiam, Aberdeen, is there really a difference? Did we just pass through a gate, or wall, or fence? No, we didn't. That border is arbitrary. Anyway, we're almost there."

Drake shrugged and continued his walk with the odd girl.

Just behind the gas station on the corner of Simpson and Ontario, stood a building with two businesses in it, on the right was an auto body, or car detailing shop, Drake could not tell from their signs, but definitely car-related. On the left, the first part of the building they approached was a bookstore. The hand painted sign on the window read, "Vision Quest, Bookstore & Palm Readings." He had no idea this place even existed.

"Come on," Rachel said as she opened the door. Drake was standing looking at the front of the building like a lost child.

"Drake," Rachel continued. "Come on, we're here."

Drake snapped out of it and followed her into the bookstore.

The bookstore was dimly lit. In fact, it took a few moments for their eyes to adjust to the environment having just stepped in from the bright summer sunshine outside. Immediately Drake noticed the smoky fragrance wafting through the building. Incense he thought. Aunt Carmen has burnt some of that at his grandparent's house before.

Rachel began looking at trinkets and baubles that lined one counter of the store. Drake continued to look in awe at the assembled books, hardback and paperback, with subject matter ranging from astral projection to something called Zen philosophy. His mind raced through what he already knew, classifying the books in front of him, which ones he would have to read, and which ones could wait.

Rachel approached him. She nodded her head towards the back of the store. There were *Tarot* cards and other divination devices, including a *Spirit* board in a plastic wrapped box. They walked towards this section of the store, when suddenly they were startled by the appearance of a man in a multi-colored spiral tie-dyed tee shirt.

"May I help you find something?" he asked.

"No," Rachel responded. "I think we're just looking, right Drake?"

Off to the side of them, a candle ignited, followed by a gust of wind that forced the lingering aroma of incense past them leaving them with the smell of a match and a distinct floral aroma that Drake could not place.

"Mmmm," Rachel said as she turned to the candle. "I love lilacs."

"Did you say your name was Drake?" asked the voice of a woman in the darkness behind the candle. Drake thought she was obviously the one who lit the candle, but he didn't answer her question.

"Yes," Rachel answered as she pointed at him. "His name is Drake."

"Come closer," the woman stated. They both took steps forward. "Yes, yes, I see now. Your children will grow to be great and mighty, perhaps more mighty than you, Drake."

"Our children?" Rachel questioned, as Drake shook his head. "We're just friends, really."

"More like acquaintances," Drake added.

"Bah, it doesn't matter, what will be may be, and what may be will be," stated the woman still hidden in the shadows. "Who can say, unless you choose to do neither, then nothing will remain."

Drake did his best to follow her logic in his head, but he got lost. Rachel was still focused on the 'your children' statement, and looked at Drake. He had an intense look on his face so she knew he was contemplating all of what the lady had said to them. A few moments later she realized she was still staring at him, and then she blushed.

"Come here my children," the woman said. "I've been expecting you. Haven't we been expecting them Ray?" The tie-dyed tee shirt man nodded and turned to go back to the front counter of the store.

"Let me know if you need anything, Madame," Ray said as he departed.

Drake and Rachel approached a round table behind a curtain of beads, which they had not noticed until they were right in front of it. Drake pulled back the beaded curtain with a series of clicks as the beads hit each other. Rachel entered the room first, followed by Drake.

"Please have a seat," the woman asked them pleasantly.

"How do you know Drake?" Rachel asked as she sat in the chair to the left. Drake lingered for a moment as he got his bearings inside the beaded curtain. He noticed a variety of old leather-bound books with no names on them, journals perhaps. He also noticed a number of charts on the walls— birthdays, astrological signs, and Chinese birth year symbols. Drake was a dragon, and when he first found this out years ago, he concluded that must be why he was named Drake, since it is a shortened version of Dragon. But, he realized soon afterwards, that his father was named Drake too, and that was where his name came from. He also saw objects of intense fascination for him, most notably an ornately crafted silver-handled dagger lying on a table behind the dark lady, and next to the dagger, a full size human skull with a red candle half melted and securely attached to the top of it. It was like a Halloween decoration. The red melted wax ran down the skull like strings of red licorice, and Drake realized he was hungry.

"Please, sit down Drake," the woman offered again. Drake complied and sat to the right of Rachel.

The candle in the middle of the table flared and it became brighter in the beaded room. The candle was thick and sat in an ornate holder made of metal and glass. Beyond the candle sat a woman with jet black hair that hung loosely beside her exotic face. Her skin was olive, and her lips were full and vibrantly red. When she spoke there was a twinkle in her dark brown eyes. She was dressed in a white peasant blouse and had layers of multi-colored scarves attached to her. Drake was intrigued, but very cautious. Rachel was curious and intent.

"How do you know Drake?" Rachel asked again.

"Allow me to introduce myself," the exotic woman stated. "My name is Chavali, and I am a mystic. You came here seeking my counsel, did you not?"

"We came here cause she said this was better than the library," Drake finally spoke as he pointed at Rachel.

"How do you know Drake?" repeated Rachel with a smile.

"Bah," Chavali spoke. "My counsel you seek, for I have knowledge, knowledge of many things. Knowledge of the past, the present, and what may come. And this is what you seek, is it not?"

"Knowledge is good." Drake rationalized.

"But, how do you know Drake?" Rachel pestered.

"Did I not just say?" Chavali snapped. "I have knowledge of many things, gifted to me from the gods and others throughout time and space. Such is my power."

"Oh, so you knew we were going to show up here today?" Rachel said. "I mean, Drake and I."

"I knew you would show up," Chavali responded. "I thought sooner, or perhaps later, but did not expect today, otherwise I would have been more prepared for your arrival."

"Why is that?" Rachel asked. Drake listened intently.

"Drake, I have seen many things that may come to pass," Chavali spoke again. "Many will come to fear you, many to trust you, many to love you, many to hate you, but in all the strings of time I have seen, one thing is certain. Drake, you will be like a king, a king by your own hand. And for one such as me, who dabbles in the mystic arts, being on the good side of a great and powerful king is most wise."

"Interesting," Rachel continued. Drake's mind was contemplating what the mystic was saying. "So, like he will have a crown, and a throne and stuff? A castle?"

"Drake will walk the halls of many a castle, and he will break the doors of others, but his kingdom will be of his own making, a tower I foresee in all strings of time." The mystic responded.

"A tower is good," Rachel added with a smile.

"But, that is long from now," Chavali stated. "The knowledge you seek is about here and now, is it not?"

"Yes," Drake said as he slid forward in the wooden chair.

"There are many forces at work," the mystic began. "I cannot see them all. They are well hidden, pulling strings, but I do see ominous things, specters in black."

"Mordgeists," Drake interjected.

"A greater daemon I see too, Succorbenoth be his name. But there are more, more still, a black council, and even now they have your brother in their grasp," Chavali continued. Drake's mouth dropped open in amazement. "A battle shall be fought, and like the Teutonic knights of old your brothers must rise to this challenge or die."

"Teutonic Knights," Drake asked. "Who were they?"

"What do I look like," Chavali answered. "A library? Look it up. I only tell you what I see, I see what is open to me, not all things come into this light before me, so much I cannot see."

"Why do you talk in circles and stuff?" Rachel asked. "Is that a requirement for being a mystic?"

"Why are you so annoying," Chavali snapped back. "Irish?"

"I am not Irish," Rachel proclaimed, as she stood up and faced the mystic. "Thank you for being so polite, Miss Mystic, now we really need to be going."

Chavali bowed her head to Rachel. The young girl turned and walked through the beaded curtain back into the main part of the bookstore.

"Please," Chavali pleaded. "I sought no harm. You are in grave danger, and this test will change so much for so many, and whether you succeed or fail, much lies in the balance."

Drake hesitated, and continued to listen to the exotic woman.

"You are the key, Drake," Chavali shared. "Listen to your heart, keep your mind open, and hold the charm dear to you. Should you fail there will be great suffering. Do not let your brothers divide, only together can you pass this first test."

"Okay," he replied flatly.

"You must decide," Chavali continued as she reached out and put her hands around Drake's right hand on the table, the burning candle between her arms. Her hands were warm, relaxing to the touch, and Drake turned again to face her. "I know this all seems so complex and big, bigger than you, and right now it is, but it will not always be. The decision that awaits you, it is whether you believe all of this is real, which changes who you are as a logical person. But you must make that decision before moving forward. Trust yourself Drake."

Drake nodded. He rose up, cautious of his hand in Chavali's grasp. He didn't want her sleeves to catch fire on the candle.

"And," Chavali added, "please remember, I was nice to you, and should you have need of me, I shall make myself available as best I can."

She released his hand with her left hand, and then pulled her right hand up, still holding his. She bowed her head down and kissed the back of his hand.

"Pacea fie cu tine regele meu," Chavali said.

Drake removed his hand, bowed his head, and departed through the beads. He saw Rachel standing up front by the counter talking to Ray, the man in the tie-dyed shirt. She heard the beads, and turned to see him walking towards her. She walked up to him.

"Weird," she stated in a muted tone, meant only for his ears.

"Weird is a compliment, my dear!" shouted Chavali from the back. Rachel's eyes opened very wide. "One more thing Drake, dear. I keep seeing the name Bhutan before you, does that mean anything to you?"

Drake shook his head, and Rachel hit him on the arm with the back of hers.

"She can apparently hear a lot, but she can't hear you shaking your head," she said as she rolled her eyes.

Rachel and Drake left the bookstore, and began the long walk home. Drake had so much to think about. He wasn't sure he got answers from his visit with the mystic. He somehow felt he had more questions now than before. Twice now, the *Spirit* board and Chavali, had both said stuff about great power, and people being afraid of him. But this king by your own hands stuff was new, and who were the Teutonic knights? He would have to look that up. He didn't recall there being a mention of Teutonic knights in the encyclopedia. Maybe he'd become a knight, in all the stories he had read or heard you had to become a knight before you could become a king. That was a cool thought for a thirteen year old boy like Drake. He smiled to himself as he walked.

Rachel talked endlessly about the weirdness of that mystic lady in particular, and the whole trip to the psychic bookstore in general. She also proudly displayed her purchases, a box of *Tarot* cards and a green book that was titled 'Herbology.' She had used her birthday money to get these items, and that was part of the reason she suggested going there.

But deep inside her, she was troubled for Drake, his safety, and what all of this creepy stuff meant. She made up her mind, on that walk back along Simpson Avenue, the day after she turned fourteen, that she'd do whatever it took to keep Drake Fraser safe, even if that meant becoming a witch. Of course she would have to learn how to wiggle her nose.

And as she thought about what Chavali had said, she could see the future she described, the one where they had children. And Drake was a king living in a tower, which meant she would be a princess, or even a queen.

In her head the rest of the way home she sang.

*When love is worth more than gold,*
*Then why am I not rich...*

And she smiled.

**Brothers Divided**
**Chapter Twelve**
**July 28, 1978**
**Hoquiam, Washington**

Martin had continued his 'investigation' of the *Spirit* board in the weeks since he and Drake argued over the safety of the board game. Without his scaredy-cat little brother helping him or holding him back, he was poised to make great strides in his discovery of the spiritual phenomenon. To replace Drake, he easily enlisted Dennis to his cause. Dennis took this as a sign he was moving up in the family pecking order, passing Drake, which pleased him greatly. Dennis had taken this newfound position to mean that he didn't have to hang out endlessly with Albert anymore. He had matured above Albert even more than he already was, and Albert sadly acknowledged this change by playing more and more video games solo.

The good thing for Albert was he learned to play video games well that summer, which came with a caveat—he could easily beat anyone in the family on any of the games, but as his reputation of arcade domination grew, few were the times anyone challenged him. So in the end, his life grew emptier.

Drake had withdrawn into deep contemplation. He went to the library once, looking for information on the Teutonic knights and Bhutan. The later was easy enough. Bhutan was a country in the northern region of the Indian sub-continent, situated near India, Nepal, Bangladesh, and China. What Bhutan had to do with him was beyond him, way beyond him. In fact it made no logical sense at all. It did have an awesome flag of red and gold split diagonally with a white serpentine dragon in the middle. Drake knew dragons were cool, but not really relevant to his current situation at all. He did find a reference for Teutonic knights within the encyclopedia. He was shocked that he didn't recall it at the time. According to the encyclopedia, the Teutonic knights were founded during the 1100s in central Europe, modeled like the knights Templar and the knights Hospitallers. They went off on crusades of the Holy lands. A hundred years later they shifted their focus back to central Europe where they fought on the Baltic frontier and the Russian steppes, they were diminished in the 1300s, and lost all their holdings in 1618. Not much information, but a start.

Mark continued to separate himself from his brothers, spending as much time as he could at the car dealership, or working by himself on his car. He could not shake the insistence Drake had about this archive room at the library. He knew it didn't exist, but Drake was not prone to lying, and he had seen the odd research Drake returned home with. He was getting all that information somewhere, so he knew he was going to have to look into the matter further with his brother. Mark and Martin had stopped hanging out together after they got back from 10,000 Lakes. They had completely disconnected. He didn't even see his older brother that much anymore, with their competing work schedules, and Dennis and Martin doing whatever in his room until late at night.

In less than a week they would be heading north on their annual camping trip around the 'Loop.' Martin had already announced that he could not get the week and a half off needed for the trip, so he would be staying home by himself.

Dennis and Martin sat at the small Formica table, the *Spirit* board on the tabletop between them. The fingers of their left hands rested lightly upon the planchette. This new arrangement had allowed Martin to write more freely without breaking contact with the pointer. Dennis was doing quite well with the board. His energy was nearly as strong as

Drake's, but it wasn't consistent and the planchette would sit idle for stretches of time, frustrating Martin. Despite all the challenges, Martin was making all sorts of headway into the world of psychic powers.

"Wally, can we try doing that with the bottle cap now?" Dennis asked excitedly.

The planchette smoothly moved over to 'YES' and then slowly circled in the center of the board.

Martin picked up one of the bottle caps and set it on the *Spirit* board.

"What do we do?" Martin asked.

The planchette began to spell again, "T. H. I. N. K. M. O. V. E. I. T."

"We have to think about moving it?" Martin asked.

'YES' came the response. With their left hands still on the planchette, they both focused on the bottle cap and thought, move. After a minute or so, they gave up.

"Which way are you thinking of moving it Dennis?" Martin questioned his brother.

"That way," Dennis replied, pointing away from himself, towards Martin. "Which way are you thinking?"

"Just the opposite," Martin responded. "I think we are cancelling each other out. Think about moving it off the table to the other wall over there." He pointed to the wall with his King Kong poster by the window.

"Okay," Dennis replied. He closed his eyes and really thought hard about moving the bottle cap. With a sudden metallic pop the bottle cap smacked against the far wall just missing the window.

"Cool!" Dennis exclaimed.

"We did it," Martin added. "We did it by ourselves, way to go Dennis!"

'YES' the planchette moved to answer them. "B. Y. E. S. E. L. F. S."

"Dennis," Martin began excitedly as he placed another bottle cap on the *Spirit* board, "let's just think about lifting it up, not pushing it."

'YES' answered the planchette. "L. I. F. T. I. T."

Both Dennis and Martin focused their attention on the bottle cap. It wiggled slowly on the game board. With the grace of a newborn deer rising to its feet right after birth, the bottle cap jerked and lunged as it slowly rose upward. Climbing ever higher, it was soon level with Dennis' eyes, and then Martin's. Upward it went, and still they watched it in silent amazement. Dennis had not even taken a breath for fear of losing his concentration. Finally it bumped up against the ceiling, but it kept pushing upward, crushing the metal cap into a flat token and putting an equally deep depression into the ceiling plaster.

The bedroom door swung open with a thud, the bottle cap fell back to the table top, and both boys were shocked by what they had just accomplished and upset for being disturbed.

"Mom said dinner is almost ready," Drake announced as he stood outside the room.

"Don't interrupt us!" snapped Martin. "We're learning things beyond your ability and knowledge, and I don't want you in here."

"Yah, dillhole," Dennis added.

"It's beyond my ability and knowledge?" Drake responded feeling deeply hurt by the verbal attack. "Neither of you have the foggiest idea what my abilities or knowledge really are. You both know I'm way smarter than either of you."

"Whatever," Martin added. "If you're so smart how come you're not able to do telekinesis like me and Dennis? We can make things move with our minds."

"How do you know it was you that moved things and not the board?" Drake asked a question they hadn't considered.

"Get out of here," Martin snapped. "And close the door on your way out!"

"Close the door, dillhole," Dennis giggled to himself, finding courage to stand up to Drake in the company of Martin.

"I may not be able to do telekinesis, but at least I know

how to spell it," Drake said as he grabbed the doorknob, pulling the door closed. He opened it one final time in defiance. "Besides, I am going to be a king by my own hands."

The door slammed shut, and the planchette moved to 'YES' and then spelled out, "H. E. W. I. L. L. B. E. K. I. N. G."

Both boys watched the planchette, and read what it spelled. Dennis was crushed. Perhaps he had chosen the wrong brother to make a power play against. Martin was confused, he had thought all those praises and statements of being powerful and causing fear in things was solely directed at him. This changed everything. If Drake was to be king, what was he going to be? In a kingdom, there can only be one king. If Drake was going to be it, then what was left for him? Moisture welled up in Martin's eyes.

He would have to be powerful enough to prevent that. Drake was smart, athletic, and probably even physically stronger than him now, so he would have to have a greater power. Psychic power could be the solution he sought. That was a power that Drake could not master, without a gifted teacher at least, and the *Spirit* board would be Martin's instructor, or so he hoped.

"Can you teach me," Martin asked, "to be a powerful psychic?"

The planchette circled for what seemed like minutes before moving in multiple stabbing motions to the point on the board that said 'YES.'

"W. E. C. A. N. T. E. A. C. H." the planchette spelled in smooth circular motions. "C. A. N. Y. O. U. L. E. A. R. N."

"Yes," Martin responded. "I can learn. I can learn anything you are willing to teach me, I want to learn it all."

The planchette moved with a new passion, "I. T. W. I. L. L. B. E. D. A. R. K."

"I don't care how dark it is, I want to know it all," replied Martin.

"I. T. M. A. Y. B. E. D. E. A. D. L. Y." the planchette

spelled with a sinister undertone, almost like it was smiling, if the board was capable of such emotions.

"I don't care," Martin replied. "If I died, I'd be able to see Wally again. But I won't, I know I won't. I want to learn it all."

'YES' responded the planchette. It began to spell, "F. O. R. G. E. T. W. H. A. T. Y. O. U. K. N. O. W."

"Forget what you know?" Dennis asked. "What does that mean?"

"R. E. A. D. Y. T. O. B. E. G. I. N." the planchette spelled out its question.

"Yes," Martin replied. "I'm ready."

The lights in the room flickered and dimmed. The two coats of paint that had long ago sealed the window shut in his room snapped, popped, and creaked as the window frame lunged upward leaving the window open. An unseasonably cold gust of wind darted into the room raising the still forms of the drapes into green fabric arms that reached out into the room and rustled the pages of his spiral notebook, the posters on the walls, the hair on the boys' heads, and left both Dennis and Martin experiencing goose bumps on areas of their skin they had no idea got goose bumps.

About twenty-five minutes had passed since Drake asked Martin and Dennis to get ready for dinner. Drake sat in a bean bag chair by Albert playing a game of *Breakout* with him. The ricocheting pixilated square bounded off the paddle Albert was nimbly controlling, knocking out the rainbow-colored blocks across the top of the television screen. There was no denying it, Albert was now much better than Drake at the game. Lost in the mindless pinging of the game, Drake felt the hurt build that Martin had levied upon him. Maybe he was not so special after all. Madame Chavali was probably just a crazy woman who escaped from the big state mental hospital up by Tacoma. Soured by this whole line of thought, Drake glanced at his little brother in the bean bag chair beside him. His cherubic face stared at the geometric advancement of the game. Albert was so happy that Drake sat and played the video game with him that he smiled the whole time. Drake's eyes lingered as he thought, if only life could remain that simple.

Mom emerged from the kitchen and asked Drake to get his brothers for dinner, it was ready and already on the table. Drake rose from the bean bag chair and headed towards Martin's room. Only the five of them would be eating dinner together that night. Mark was working at the car dealership and wouldn't be home for dinner. It was not unusual for someone to be missing from the dinner table, with their father working in Napavine, their mother sleeping before work, or both older brothers off at work, yet somehow Drake wished Mark were there to help him deal with Martin.

Drake stood in front of the door. Monique had followed him, as she often did. Below the door, Drake could see lights flashing, almost like a strobe light. Monique growled at the door. Drake rubbed his hand over the charm Rachel had given him that hung around his neck.

Drake reached for the doorknob with his right hand. It was cold to the touch, very unusual for late July. He slowly turned the knob. Monique continued her rumbling, throaty growl. Drake swung the door open.

Inside the room he saw the lights flickering. His brothers were still sitting at the little table facing the *Spirit* board on the table top between them. The room was like a refrigerator. It was so much colder than the rest of the house.

Dennis sat with his eyes closed, his small fingertips on the planchette. Martin had sweat dripping from his forehead, which amazed Drake because of the cold temperature of the room.

Monique began to bark. She barked a furious, angry bark, in an unending pattern of growls and yaps.

"What're you doing?" Drake asked. "What's going on in here?"

Monique barked louder and more rapidly, standing just outside the threshold to the room.

"Dennis!" Drake shouted. "Martin! What are you doing?"

"Stop scaring the dog!" Mom yelled from inside the kitchen.

"I thought I told you not to come in here again!" angrily responded Martin. "Shut up you damn dog!"

Monique continued her barking, looking at shadowy places where no one stood in the room.

"Mom said dinner is ready," Drake replied. "This isn't right Martin, what're you doing?"

"You want to know what I am doing?" Martin responded. The lights returned to normal. Monique stopped barking but went back to the throaty growl.

"Look," Martin said pointing to his blue metal foot locker at the end of his bed.

Martin stared at it intently.

With a startling movement, Drake gasped. The foot locker began to rise off the floor. Monique barked once again, breaking the concentration of Martin and sending the foot locker crashing back onto the floor. Drake bent and quickly scooped up Monique in his arms.

"Hey!" Mom shouted as she came to Martin's room after hearing the loud crash, thinking her boys were fighting. "Knock it off in here!"

Mom came up and stood next to her tall son, who was now holding the poodle on his right arm, her two front feet crossed in his hand.

"There's no fighting in my house," Mom angrily commanded. "Do you guys understand?"

The boys all nodded.

"It's dinner time, come on and wash up, let's go." Mom added as she walked away.

Martin stared at Drake.

Dennis got up, placed a number of bottle caps in his pocket, and scooted past his older brother, patting Monique on the head as he left. She growled in response.

"Who has power now, little brother?" Martin asked with a

smile. "You saw some of my new ability, what do you think?"

Drake shook his head.

"Martin you shouldn't be doing this," Drake explained. "There's evil in that board, and it's using you, making you think it's helping you, when it's really just taking control of you, bit by bit."

Martin laughed.

"You don't understand," Drake tried to select his words carefully. "We can have great power, but only if we are united. We're brothers, and we're supposed to help each other be better, get stronger. Only then will we have real power. You have to believe me, this board is using you and dividing us."

Martin chuckled again.

"You're just jealous, Drake," Martin sneered. "One of us does have power now, and it isn't you. It's me, and it looks like I will be king, not you."

Drake took one final look at Martin and the *Spirit* board. It was the last he would ever see of Martin using the board. He turned with Monique still on his arm and walked away. Dread filled his heart, Chavali's words echoed in his mind, "Should you fail there will be great suffering. Do not let your brothers divide, only together can you pass this first test."

What could he do to get Martin to see the error in trusting the *Spirit* board? He needed Martin, he needed Mark, he needed Dennis, and he even needed Albert if they were going to overcome this growing sense of doom that hovered over them. If only they could all see it like he could, then they would understand. He also knew that the board game had to leave the house. As long as it was in the house he knew bad things might happen.

Probabilities and possibilities raced through his young mind. Finally he mused to himself that maybe it didn't matter, maybe it was all just a bad dream, and he would soon wake up and none of it had really ever happened. He shook his head wishfully. That wasn't very likely at all. Drake set

Monique down, washed his hands for dinner and went to the table.

It was a very quiet dinner. No one talked, and the boys didn't even look up at each other. Albert sadly thought he had done something wrong since no one would talk to him, or look at him.

"What did I do?" Albert asked.

"Be quiet and eat your dinner, Albert," Mom responded. "A little quiet never hurt anybody."

Later during the first week of August, Mark took Drake to watch the Grays Harbor Loggers play a baseball game at Olympic Stadium. The stadium was a prized relic of the region dating back to the 1930s. It had definitely seen better days, but still hosted the annual Loggers Playday every September, home football games for Hoquiam High School that meant every other year the annual Aberdeen versus Hoquiam football game that was the oldest continuous high school rivalry west of the Mississippi River, and of course minor league baseball.

Mark had gotten the two tickets from his boss at the car dealership and thought his little brother would like to go watch a professional sports game for the first time in person.

They sat together in the old wooden stadium watching the baseball game. Neither of the boys ever really played baseball, so some of the game was lost on them. They were very curious why there were cameras there filming things, no one in Grays Harbor ever did anything to get on the news, and the cameras didn't really look like news cameras anyway. Drake assumed it was because the Loggers were solidly in first place in the Pacific Northwest League and they might be drawing some attention of some sports broadcasters somewhere in the region.

It felt good for the two brothers to sit and just be together. It was kind of like old times for them. Drake knew the two of them would always be friends. During the fifth inning, Drake got up to go use the bathroom. He walked

messed up his hair.

The two of them got the beer keg righted on the hand truck and Drake shouldered the load as he started toward the stairs. Billy carried the bags of cups.

"Are you here with your Dad?" Billy asked.

"No," Drake answered. "My Dad's at work."

"My Dad's not here either," Billy replied. "He had to mow the lawn."

Drake laughed. He pulled the hand truck up the stairs, with a loud thump as it crested each step. Billy put one hand on the keg to stabilize it as it slowly made its way to the top of the stairs. Once he made it to the top he set the keg down.

"Hey," Billy said with a hug. "Thanks kid, for being a patriot and helping out your fellow Americans."

"I hope you achieve your dream," Drake said sincerely.

"Me too," Billy replied. Then he turned and looked at Drake. "You need to follow your dreams too Drake. Go after 'em. Don't let your life rush by until one day when you stop and look back and say, man I wish I would've, or I should've, or I could've. Seize the day kid. Be the best you that you can be, and don't ever let anyone tell you that you can't be what you want to be. Even if that's a pro ball player, or a comedian."

Billy raised his hand and Drake shook it one more time. Then Billy hugged him. Drake waved and started back down the stairs to the bathroom.

"Who wants a beer! Nice warm beer here!" Billy began to shout in the bleachers.

13

MOUNT OLYMPUS

THE BROTHERHOOD OF OLYMPUS
AND THE DEADLIEST GAME

**The Loop**
**Chapter Thirteen**
**August 10, 1978**
**Port Angeles, Washington**

They began their journey around the Olympic Peninsula, with a stop at the deep crystal blue waters of Lake Quinault for a picnic lunch. They didn't stay long, because their first overnight destination was at Kalaloch along the central coast and they wanted to get there before nightfall to set up the travel trailer. The drive around most of, and through the longer east to west of the Quinault Reservation always puzzled Drake. He thought it would be more scenic if the road from Ocean Shores connected to Kalaloch. Quietly though, Drake was more concerned about what they were all once told by John Van Zanten, their step-grandfather. John was a railroad engineer, and explained to the boys that there are still places, "dangerous locations where we engineers have to be very careful. Indian reservations. Do you know that some trains, the Indians call them 'Iron Horses,' still get attacked? Why, if you're not careful they will sneak right up on you. Hiding behind the trees, and then, BAM! You are shot clean through the belly with an arrow. Let me show you boys some of the arrows I pulled out of my locomotive." Drake listened to the story, saw the arrows, and filed it away. But on their drive though the Quinault Reservation, in the deep, roadway canyon carved out of the towering trees where the only sunlight streamed down through the ribbon of blue directly above the road, he saw a lot of trees. More than enough trees to hide an army of archers, and reason enough for him to be a bit anxious on this part of the drive.

"Are we there yet?" Dennis questioned. "I have to pee."

"Almost," Mom answered. "Wait just a little while longer, you don't want your dad to pull off to the side of the road here."

No we don't, Drake concurred, and it was obvious to him at that point that the Indian story was either true or at least their mother had heard of it, and was equally unsure of its truth.

They stayed at Kalaloch for three days. During that time, the four boys spent nearly every moment of daylight in the cold surf, running from the rolling waves, digging in the gray sand, or exploring the driftwood-laden dunes. The fresh sea air cleared their troubles away, and they felt like a complete family again, even though Martin was not with them. Occasionally, one of the boys, usually Mark or Drake, would turn and look for Martin to show him what they found or did, and then would realize he was not with them. It was at those times they missed their oldest brother. At night, when Mark and Drake crawled into their sleeping bags inside the van, they both found themselves wondering if life would ever be the same for them, like it had been every year of their lives, until this one.

"Do you suppose someone could live out on Destruction Island?" Mark asked Drake. The island was clearly visible out in the ocean, but little could be seen on it except the single man-made structure.

"Well it does have an old lighthouse on it." Drake replied sleepily. "So I guess at some point people lived there."

"I was just wondering," Mark added. "You know, like completely independent, grow your own food and everything."

"I think when the winter storms come it would be hard to keep anything on there that wasn't attached," Drake elaborated. "Livestock, supplies, people. Or even you."

The following morning was their last at the beach. Drake

made sure to take Monique out on the beach one final time. The little poodle loved the beach. She would run so fast that her feet were just a white blur and a rooster tail of sand shot out behind her. In great circles she would turn on the beach before coming to a sudden stop in front of one of the boys with her front feet laying spread on the sand, her butt in the air ready to run. She would taunt them, as she wagged her short tail, and faked like she was starting to go, until she would shoot off like a spring that had been wound too tight and start it all over again. It was difficult not to smile when he watched her on the beach. Drake kept that memory with him always.

They packed up and continued up the coast to the Hoh River Valley and the ecological majesty of the Hoh Rainforest, stopping along the way only to see the massive Duncan Cedar, the largest western red cedar in the world. It was four miles off Highway 101 and nearly everyone was put off by the gravel logging roads they traversed to get there. Drake was pleased they took the opportunity to visit the stately giant. He thanked it before they left, for allowing them a moment of its time, and hoped somewhere, somehow, that the tree might remember him in some distant future when he no longer existed.

The Hoh Rainforest was about eighteen miles off the highway, through National Forest lands and private property. The occasional 'watch for livestock on the roadway' signs broke up the bumpy monotony of the ride.

"Where would you go for ice cream if you lived here?" Albert asked.

"You'd make it yourself," Dennis quickly replied. "Dillhole."

"Hey," their mother interjected "knock that off back there Dennis, be nice to your brother. Besides, Forks in not that far from here. Maybe if you're good we will stop there and get ice cream when we drive through."

Their stay in the rainforest was almost always the same.

The boys would get up, adventure through the campground and surrounding wilderness, and come back to the campsite for lunch. After lunch, the family would do something together, usually a photograph-taking opportunity on one of the nature trails, or a walk along the swift moving river. One of their most memorable hikes was along the 'Hall of Mosses,' a less than a mile trail loop that took them through some of the most amazing forest in the world. The hanging green moss covered every tree, deciduous and evergreen, like the long beards of wizards. The ground and some of the moss covered trees sprouted multiple varieties of ferns. It was a green wonderland, and in some of the galleries of trees the trail opened up inside the vaulted ceiling of the forest like a primeval cathedral. This was as the world looked before mankind walked in it.

At night they would gather around their campfire, talk about the day's events, and bond as a family. The Frasers had always felt a kindred spirit to the land during their camping trips around this majestic wilderness. It filled them with awe. It recharged their souls with an Earth-centered focus. And it always brought them closer together as a family.

On their last day at the rainforest, Mark and Drake wandered in the campground and came upon the new amphitheater that was recently built to show video to campground visitors. The stage was built up of cement, but the backdrop was cedar, with a sturdy roof and sides that enclosed speakers. In the back, there were two large cedar doors that covered a large white projection screen. Painted on the doors was Raven, the mythical trickster spirit. He was depicted in stylized coastal art in three colors—black, blue, and red. The style was used by the new Seattle Seahawks when they made their helmet logo. In front of the stage were thirteen rows of benches in a curved, semi-circular fashion. To the right was a fire pit. Mark was first to bound up on the stage and with a smile he turned and did a mock bow.

"Thank you," Mark stated as he bowed again with a broad sweeping gesture with his arms. "Thank you."

Drake followed him up on the stage. He examined the artwork more closely, noticing the brush strokes on the surface of the wood. Mark dropped off the front of the stage and jumped up on the first bench. He looked back at his brother, and then jumped from one bench to the other all the way back to the projection booth built into the middle back four rows of benches. He looked to see if the little booth was locked. Mark turned to his brother still up on the stage.

"So all this will get wiped out when Mount Olympus erupts, huh?" Mark queried his brother. Drake turned away from the painting and walked to the center of the stage.

"Well," Drake began. "Unlike the larger Cascade Mountains to the east, featuring the five peaks of Adams, Saint Helens, Rainier, Glacier Peak, and Baker, the Olympics aren't volcanic."

"If they aren't volcanoes, then how did they get here?" Mark asked.

"The Olympic Peninsula," Drake started again as he stepped further out on stage, "geologically is one of the youngest regions of the contiguous United States. It was actually formed from the North American tectonic plate sliding over the top of the Pacific plate, scraping large seamounts, sedimentary rock, and vast amounts of sea floor basalt as it went until all of this rocky debris formed what we call the Olympic Peninsula. Kind of like a butter knife scraping the top of the butter dish and building up a series of butter ridges along it as it went."

"Oh," Mark replied. "That makes sense. Good thing Americans bought it from the Indians."

"Did you even pay attention at all in your Washington State History class?" Drake questioned as he shook his head. "This land, this peninsula, home to this rare temperate rainforest boasts some incredible flora and fauna. But it existed long before Americans arrived, and they didn't buy it from the Indians, they kind of took it, like every other invader has done to the people who lived in the land they invaded. Except the Americans didn't just kill them all, diseases did a lot of that for them."

"What's flora and fauna?" Mark questioned.

"Seriously?" Drake asked. "Plants and animals. Are you sure you're in high school?"

"Not everyone reads encyclopedias," Mark retorted. "Nor do they need to when they have a brother who did. Please continue, professor."

"The Indians," Drake started as he felt his confidence growing, "the indigenous people of the peninsula, the Chalat', Chehalis, Chimakum, Duwamish, Klallam, Makah, Queets, Quileute, Quinault, S'Klallam, Skokomish, Squaxin, Suquamish, and Twana had enjoyed the abundance of life present in the fertile land and waters of the region. Many of the tribes were of the Coastal Salish family and had similar customs, shared fishing villages, and inter-married. Among their oral traditions there was a great spirit, he was a 'Changer' or 'Transformer,' known as K'wati to the Chalat' and Doquebatl to the Klallam, who wandered the lands making noble people into great monuments, among other things. The Dosewallips River, for example, was named after a great Klallam chief changed into a mountain that rose at the headwaters of the river. He also changed the Quileute tribe into people from wolves. There was also a shared myth of a violent tribe, or monsters that lived in the mountains, such as the sésquac of Salish legend. All this helped keep people from exploring the interior of the peninsula. So much of the mountainous region is still barely more than mapped."

"So there've been people here for a long time, before Americans came?" Mark clarified. "Wolf people, that's kinda like werewolves isn't it? And this sésquac, is bigfoot right?"

"Yes," Drake replied. "To all of your questions, actually. These mountains have not always been the Olympics, though I cannot imagine another name being as fitting for them. According to the Duwamish people, the mountains were known as Sun'A-Do. Then in 1774, the Spanish explorer, Juan José Pérez Hernández was credited with the 'discovery' of Mount Olympus. Though, Pérez named it Cerro Nevado de la Santa Rosalía, which meant the Snowy Peak of St. Rosalia."

"Say what?" Mark interrupted. "That's not a name that will role off your tongue."

"That name didn't last long," Drake added. "In 1788, I believe, the English Captain John Meares gave it a new name when he 'discovered' it, that name was Mount Olympus. To Captain Meares Mount Olympus seemed to be a 'veritable home of the gods,' and that name has stuck, even though some people in the federal government tried to change the name in the 1800s to Mount Van Buren."

"That would have totally sucked," Mark announced.

"There is magic here, Mark," Drake continued. "These mountains, forests, river valleys, and ocean beaches, all possess a special magic. A magic few people could deny existed if they actually set foot in this most northwestern point of the lower forty-eight States. It's almost tangible enough to touch, like an undercurrent of electricity that moves through everything that is here."

"Drake," Mark stated after a silent pause. "Sometimes I worry about you, little brother. You know so much junk, someday your head is going to be full and someone is gonna ask you if you are hungry and want dinner. And all you will be able to do is tell them about flora and fauna and werewolves."

Mark laughed as he jumped down off the bench.

"Speaking of food," Mark began as he turned and began to leave the amphitheater. "Let's go get lunch."

As they finished their lunch a few deer wandered through their campsite, which wasn't uncommon. The Frasers had stayed there for four days. They were noticeably saddened to leave the Hoh River Valley.

Mom had perked them up by talking about stopping in Forks for ice cream. The boys all thought that was a great idea. That day's drive was not one of the longest of their trip around the 'Loop' but it always seemed to take longer. They stopped at a drive-in restaurant and got milkshakes.

For many miles after they left Forks, they drove down Highway 101 through the Sol Duc River Valley, skirting along the riverside. They crossed a few bridges and had the river that curled like a snake back and forth through the thick trees of the valley, appear on the opposite side of the van each time they crossed one. Eventually they drove along the long southern shoreline of Lake Crescent. The peaceful clear waters of the lake stretched for miles out the driver's side of the van.

"You know," Dad began with a dark chuckle, "in the 1920s there was a family from somewhere near Forks, on their way home from Port Angeles. In August too, I think. The Warren family was returning from vacation, driving by this very lake, and they disappeared from the face of the Earth. Now, rumors and folklore says that they might have driven off to Mexico, or someplace else. But, we all know that the lake took them on a more permanent vacation, one that they are still on today."

Albert did not find that story very funny as he peered out the window at the rippling lake to the north of them. He would not like this vacation to end that way and paid very close attention to his dad as he drove the rest of the way around the lake shore.

Their dad picked up an eight track tape and slid it into the player mounted below the dash. The Chattanooga Boys Greatest Hits played in an endless loop as they drove. The boys found themselves singing along out of boredom and a form of localized brainwashing. The four of them did a mock version of the four part harmonies recorded on the tape, in a crude sing-a-long style, to the same eleven songs, over and over.

Some of the songs made Drake sit and wonder as they sang along.

*Back when we were young we had amazing dreams,*
*Our words and ideas were gonna change the world.*
*Or perhaps the world might change to accept our dreams,*

To Drake, this brought to the front of his mind his visit to the psychic bookstore and the fight he had with Martin. Perhaps all of it was just that, it really didn't matter because they were just kids living in Hoquiam, not even rich kids, or special kids. The Fraser boys were just working-class poor kids, not the sort of people who go around changing the world.

Drake pushed these thoughts from his mind. Most of the songs on that eight track tape were somber, almost depressing, but there was one that was sure to make them smile. Soon enough *Shadows from the Sun* would start up again, and they would do their best to sing along, but they really were not that good.

*Seeing shadows from the sun move across my floor,*
*Playin' chess by myself with nothin' but pawns,*

They all understood what it meant to be bored enough to just sit and watch the shadows move across the floor, or to count the tiles on the floor. They knew the futility of playing a game that you could never win because you were missing all the pieces but one kind, or just the yellow pieces of a *Risk* army. Though Albert always seemed to start to giggle at that line, he would explain it as, "How could you play chess with just pawns, what kind of card is a pawn, is that like an ace?" Albert it seemed believed that there chess was a card game, like *Go Fish.*

*Watchin' Mister Rogers, and drinkin' beer,*
*My life ain't perfect, but I got nothin' to fear.*

When the bass voice rumbled 'Rogers' Albert would giggle completely through the next line of the song, and it would bring a smile to everyone in the van to hear his cherubic laughter. As soon as he finished his laugh, after the second chorus, he would bring seriousness to the forefront.

"Why're they watching *Mister Rogers?* I'd rather watch *Captain Kangaroo*, or *Scooby Doo*, or just regular cartoons like *Bugs Bunny.*"

Then his brothers would laugh at his feigned seriousness.

They arrived in Port Angeles late in the day, then turned

south on Heart of the Hills Road and headed back into the National Park. They always visited Hurricane Ridge, sometimes camping here, before heading back down the eastern side of the peninsula.

They stayed at the campground below Hurricane Ridge inside the National Park. On the drive up to the ridge, the road was wide and well maintained, and its grade was not overly steep, so the van climbed upwards with ease. Behind them to the north, as they climbed the roadway, they could see across the Strait of Juan de Fuca and see the southern end of Vancouver Island, the city of Victoria, and the nation of Canada. At the top of the ridge, standing there, they looked out at Mount Olympus and its four glacier-covered peaks rising up from behind the tops of closer mountains. There was a solemn majesty to the mountain. It stood like a monument, or a holy cathedral of nature. There was an almost tangible air of divinity present, just under the surface of reality like inspirational harmonious energy pulsating within the rhythms of nature. Some have described a similar thing when visiting Neolithic monuments, such as Stonehenge, throughout Europe, or the pyramids of Egypt or Mesoamerica.

"Do you feel that?" Mark said as he turned to Drake. "There is energy here."

"Yeah," Drake responded as he wondered if this was why John Meares had named the peak Mount Olympus.

For most of the rest of the day they spent much of their time on the trails around the high ridge itself. The warm summer sun on the mountain meadows covered in seasonal wildflowers fueled the colorful palette of blooms.

"I can't help but think that this is what it would have been like to film *The Sound of Music*," Mom told her boys. "Being up here on Hurricane Ridge in the summertime, it truly is a special place."

On the second day at the campsite below Hurricane Ridge, Mom drove the van into Port Angeles to replenish their food supplies. She returned with a surprise. She had decided she would cook pork chops for them that evening. Her boys loved eating meat that allowed them to use their hands—fried chicken, hamburgers, hotdogs, and that list included pork chops.

The dinner that evening was great. The boys ate eagerly, saving the bones for Monique. They had given her one, but didn't want to give her anymore for fear she would bury them and then they would have all sorts of wildlife in the campsite that night digging for her elusive bones. Drake stated that he would give them to her later in the van.

After roasting marshmallows over the campfire, Mom urged them all to go to bed. They would be packing up early in the morning and continuing on their way around the peninsula. Drake and Mark climbed into the van. Drake had given Monique her pile of pork chop bones on the vinyl floor mat of the van. She sat down and began to chew on them. Her favorite bones were from Albert, because he left the most meat behind.

Mark and Drake wedged their pillows behind their shoulders. They could not see each other over the seat of the van, but they had done this same thing every night. They would talk of what they did that day, where they were going the next day and occasionally just life in general. Maybe it was the majestic mysteries of Mount Olympus that brought out the conversation, but neither Mark nor Drake could remember why they started talking about the library and the elusive archive room.

"So," Mark began to frame a question in his mind, "this archive room in the basement, what's in it?"

"Books," Drake answered.

"Duh," Mark responded. "It's a library. I meant what kind of books? Why aren't they out in the rest of the library?"

"These books seem old," Drake replied. "They are all hardbound, mostly leather, kind of like what you'd see in the movies in an old library in a castle or something."

"What's in these books?" Mark asked. "Any about cars? I could use a book about Chevy's."

"No," Drake chuckled. "The books are about paranormal things, magic, dimensions, other planes of existence, ghosts, and monsters, that kind of junk."

"Hmmmm," Mark thought. "And you can only get in the room when the new librarian's there? Mrs. Madison said she'd never seen it?"

"Yeah," Drake responded. "She said you or Martin wanted to make me look stupid in front of her, asking for a key to something that didn't exist."

Mark thought about the importance of books and knowledge to his brother. Kind of like the value of cars to him.

"So you know," Mark began. "I think, once the new librarian figures out that you know that the room isn't really there, you probably will never get into it again."

"That'd suck," Drake answered. "There's so much information in those books, and I've barely had any time to read them, all I've done is jot down a few notes from a couple of them."

"How many books are in there?" Mark wondered.

"Lots," Drake replied sleepily. It had been a long day, and he was quickly succumbing to his fatigue.

"Could I get most of them in a couple bags, like maybe Dad's Coast Guard duffle bag?" Mark continued.

"Sure," Drake nodded with his eyes closed. "Maybe two duffle bags. But that'd be stealing."

"Think of it this way, Drake," Mark explained to his drowsy brother. "The room isn't really there, is it?"

"No," Drake agreed.

"Then you aren't really taking anything from the library, are you?" Mark added.

"Guess not," yawned Drake. Below him he could hear the grinding of Monique's teeth on the pork chop bones. "Mo, be quiet."

The poodle looked up at him, turned her head softly to

the side, and then began to chew on her bones again.

Mark pulled out his red transistor radio, extended the antenna and turned the dial on, only to be met by static. He was afraid he might be limited to AM stations that would bounce off the atmosphere, like how they could listen to KYA out of San Francisco from time to time in their bedroom in the old house in Central Park.

He kept it on FM, because FM stations played better music, and many of them played music all night instead of signing off. He slowly rolled the dial. Drake thought it sounded like a war movie where the radio guy kept turning the dial, hoping to find the right frequency and get reinforcements. Suddenly, right around 100 FM, Mark struck gold.

"Here's *Bhutan*, by Mjolnir, the Hammer of the Thor, on 99.9 KISW, Seattle's Best Rock," the radio disc jockey stated. The song started to play and Drake dozed further to sleep, vaguely hearing the music, but he did pick up one word before he fell asleep. Bhutan. Where had he heard that before?

In his dreams that night, Drake felt himself flying. He looked out over the horizon and saw the tops of the mighty Douglas-firs that he skimmed above. He was heading south, he could tell from where the first quarter moon stood in the sky. Before him rose the mountain. He climbed higher and higher, but never leaving the closeness to the tops of the forest below him. He saw the four peaks of Mount Olympus approaching, and the meadows of Hurricane Ridge were now behind and below him. Clouds had gathered above the mountain, but they didn't look like normal clouds, these looked almost electrified. He picked up speed and shot forward towards those odd clouds above the peak.

He felt the moisture of the vapor as he entered the clouds with a whoosh. Then everything turned bright, like right after a flash bulb went off, and he could not see. He was aware that he was sitting now, no longer flying. Where he sat, he didn't know, it was still nearly painfully bright, except it didn't hurt. Then he was aware that he was no longer alone. He was not afraid of whoever was watching him, they meant him no harm. But he did have the feeling of standing in front of a judge, a teacher, or some other authority figure that he knew he was not on an equal standing with. He began to notice movement above him in the near distance, and the brightness began to fade.

He sat cross legged on a platform, and below him he could see the stars through the gaps in the clouds. Across from him rose a half circle platform which stood ten feet above where he sat. It was about fifteen feet away from him. He imagined from above it would be like a giant letter 'C' with the platform he sat on being a dot in the middle of the 'C.' Above the top of this raised platform he saw movement. There were people sitting on the top of the platform looking down on him. He could not tell how many people sat there, but he was sure it was a lot. It felt like there was more than could possibly sit on the surface of the platform itself. He sat quietly, peering into the bright mist, hoping to get a better look at the people sitting above him.

He smelled the mixing of fragrances reminiscent of incense, and the unmistakable scent of fresh roses combined with the crispness of the mountain air.

"Welcome," a warm voice spoke. "Drake, son of Drake, son of Martin the Nameless."

"We have waited long to meet you," a female voice that sounded like a fresh spring breeze continued from his right.

Normally, Drake wouldn't have spoken. He was not that type of person, he was shy and book smart, not very social, and he knew that. But, this was a dream, so he was not bound by those waking limitations.

"Where am I?" Drake asked, as he looked around the raised platform hoping for a clear glimpse of who sat there. "Who are you?"

"Is it not clear, my boy?" stated a booming masculine voice from nearly right in front of him. "Look around yourself. You sit high upon Mount Olympus, home of the gods."

"So," Drake quickly began, taking advantage of his dream confidence, "you all are gods? That means you must be Zeus, and the lady over here, is she Aphrodite or Athena perhaps?"

Drake knew a lot about ancient mythology and the pantheons of gods and goddesses that once existed in the world.

"No," burst the booming voice in answer. "I am not Zeus, he could not make it, but he sends his regards, I am known by many names, but we have no time to hear of me this night. Tonight we gather to give you heed, and through our counsel, help you find your way."

Drake stared at the looming shape of the man speaking. He seemed to be wearing a broad chest plate of golden armor and possessed immensely thick shoulders that were covered in a dark cape. The most noticeable things about him were the long golden spear he held in his right hand, the braided white beard that covered part of his golden armor, and an eye patch that covered one of his eyes. As he spoke his features became clearer. When he stopped speaking he returned into the white mists and was no more than a vague silhouette. Something about this man was familiar to Drake, he almost felt like he had seen him before, but could not place where.

"This isn't the right Mount Olympus though, we aren't in Greece," Drake rationalized.

"This is a sacred land, grandson of Martin the Nameless," a voice to the left began. "For many generations the people who lived here never came into the mountains, for fear of what resided here, and out of respect of the land, respect of their elders, and respect of the spirits. This mountain is just as good as the other one that bears its name. In my opinion, it's even better. Here we do not limit the counsel to only one race. All are welcome here if they be willing to honor the sanctity of the mountain. Here we gather all who would come to give you counsel, god, demigod, daemon, or native spirit such as I, Doquebotl."

Drake saw that this figure was dressed in what looked like clothes made out of cedar bark, and lined with white fur. He had a wide, dark face, seasoned from the sun and the feathers of a great eagle in his long hair. Next to Doquebotl, Drake saw the black hair and angelic face of Miss Furfur, which further cemented the knowledge that this was a dream. Why would the librarian be above him on Mount Olympus? What was she, according to Doquebotl, a 'god, demigod, daemon, or native spirit?'

"Let me explain," the booming voice stated, "since this matter is very close to my heart. You have a choice to make, my boy. You see long ago, there were always those who would hear the noble call and defend the masses. Heroes of old they were. In my realms, both here on this world and beyond, a group of knights formed a special Brotherhood. They were a secret order of the Teutonic knights, Livonian to be precise. Great warriors they became and they championed the world against mighty foes, driving them back into the darkness, defeated, shamed, and licking their many wounds. Unfortunately, like many things mankind makes, he also unmakes, and the knighthood fell to corruption and avarice. The guiding principle of this Brotherhood was love. Love of the Earth, of humanity, of goodness, of brotherhood. It was also bound to five people, five brothers, five knights. There must always be at least five, a pentacle, or the Brotherhood could fall. They each must possess strengths that balance the others' weaknesses. The last Brotherhood faded into antiquity quite some time ago, in 1469. Long have those of us here worried for the fate of your world. But, most of us have agreed long ago to let mankind, uhm…"

"Grow," a female voice from near the bearded one-eyed god spoke. "Mature, and become the masters of their own destiny."

"Yes," the bearded god continued. "Master their destiny. That is what they shall do. For over five hundred years, there has been no Brotherhood on Earth, but that all was set to change, for there are dark times approaching. Those who were defeated by the last Brotherhood have finally arisen again, and they have gained allies. There are, in fact, forces that might rival our own, who are finding their way into your world once again. Walter, brother of your mother, was to be the leader of this new Brotherhood, but as you may know, not everyone thinks this Brotherhood was a good idea. There are many of great power who will go to great lengths to stop the rebirth of the Brotherhood. Walter died because of this. But you, my boy, must now lead. You must form this new Brotherhood of Teutonic knights and stand ready to defend the world."

"Why?" Drake asked the most obvious question in his mind. "Why me, why should I?"

The bearded god pointed his spear to his left, and a very dark skinned figure rose. She appeared to have more arms than she needed, and had massive white wings that stretched out from her obsidian shoulders. Drake struggled to recall his knowledge of Mesopotamian and Indian myth. He thought he knew of her, but her identity escaped him.

"Let me show you why, son of Drake," the multi-armed entity spoke, as she came forward and touched Drake's right hand with one of her own ebony hands. With a start, Drake saw that he was no longer sitting in the counsel of the gods. He stood in the sky above the mountain, held there with the black goddess. He recognized the four unique peaks—this was Mount Olympus, but it had no snow on its peaks. The glaciers were gone. So were the trees of the forest, and the wildflowers of the mountain meadows. In their absence the ground had turned brown. The winds swept through the valleys of the mountain, picking up dust and sands from the burned and wasted lands. Beyond, to the east, the Cascade Mountains rumbled and red molten rock showered into the sky, lighting up the gray and black volcanic clouds that stretched as far as the eyes could see into the atmosphere. There was no green. There was no life. The land was a desolate wasteland. Drake turned and looked at the expressionless face of the goddess.

"All the Earth suffers the same," she stated, sensing his questions from the look upon his face. "The seas have boiled leaving little water. Water sustains life."

"And the people?" Drake pleaded.

"Most died," the ebony goddess answered. "Those who survived are now claimed by the dark gods who reside in netherworlds, they have remade the Earth into a netherworld."

Hell on Earth, he thought. Drake felt tears begin to well in his eyes.

"This can't be," he snapped. "Why didn't you and the gods above Olympus stop this?"

In answer to his question, the winged goddess turned and released his hand. Drake was once again sitting on the pedestal before the gods of Olympus.

"The old days have passed. We cannot be involved in the happenings of the land," Doquebotl spoke sadly. "We abide by the Covenant of Reason that set man upon his path of enlightenment, to do otherwise would jeopardize our own realms."

"At least," the bearded god interrupted, "we cannot be directly involved. Who's to say that we cannot help guide, or provide resources to, let's say a champion, or a Brotherhood of champions, those who will take up the call and defend Earth from those dark powers that seek to destroy it."

"So that future I just saw isn't guaranteed?" Drake asked.

"Do you really want to know?" another voice asked, opposite the ebony goddess. "What would you give to stop it from coming to pass? You have much to trade."

"Brother Raven," Doquebotl interrupted, "the grandson of Martin the Nameless does not need to be trifled with. Do you not seek the continuation of the world as we all do here, so assembled?"

"Yes," squawked Raven. "I also desire to be free of the restrictions of the Covenant of Reason. Forgive me, grand son of Martin the Nameless, I sought no injury upon you."

"You have already begun your journey," the big bearded

god continued. "You are gathering ancient knowledge and learning what must be learned. You can prevent that bleak future from coming to pass, should you desire to."

"I do," Drake heard himself say.

"Good," the bearded god said with what appeared to be a smile. "Then I give to you this first token of assistance from those who sit above Olympus."

Drake suddenly felt a solid piece of wood materialize in his hands.

"You possess the Staff of Orkan. Guard it well," the bearded god explained. "It has dominion over the storm, and will also guide you to where you need to go. It has many special abilities, which you may come to know."

Drake looked at the thick quarterstaff in his hands. Both ends were capped in silver metal, and along the length of the staff were carved Nordic runes.

"One last thing, son of Drake," the black multi-armed goddess spoke. "Our message to you is quite clear, and in time, you will come to remember, should you seek out the truth. And perhaps, as I have foreseen, you may one day be welcome here among us. But for now, all of this will be but a fleeting memory. I wish you well upon your journey."

She bowed low to Drake, as did a number of the other non-distinguishable gods, demi-gods, daemons, and spirits present.

"All hail!" bellowed the one-eyed god. "The return of the Brotherhood upon the Earth. All hail the return of the Brotherhood of Olympus!"

Drake stretched his arms over his head. Over the back of seat he was laying on, he heard Mark adjusting his radio. The static going in and out, until he found a station.

"Here's *Bhutan,* by Mjolnir, the Hammer of the Thor, on 99.9 KISW, Seattle's Best Rock," the radio disc jockey stated. And the music started.

*Starlight shines down upon my head,*
*The moon points my way,*

*I seek the gods long thought dead,*
*To hear of their plight,*
*I sit before those who've always led,*
*But now they cannot fight,*
*They tell me tales of woe and dread,*
*A future full of fear,*
*I must lead an army for which I was bred,*
*If I choose not to lead,*
*The souls of man to dark gods be fed,*
*The world will surely bleed,*
*What I learned I couldn't share,*
*Belief and faith has deserted man,*
*We've lost our way in Bhutan...*

Drake listened to the words, now the lyrics had a different meaning then when he'd heard the song before, and fell into a restful slumber.

The next morning, the sun shown in the van windows and woke both boys up as they slowly stretched the sleepiness away.

"Damn it," Mark said. "I left my radio on last night. I think the battery is dead. Maybe Mom has a nine volt battery in the trailer?"

Drake sat up.

"I had an awesome dream last night," he explained to his upset brother.

"Good for you," Mark replied. "But your awesome dream doesn't help my radio."

"I flew," Drake continued. "Yeah, I flew, and hmmm."

Mark looked at Drake. It looked like his mind had slipped out of gear.

"Guess it wasn't such an awesome dream after all," Mark stated, "if you can't remember any of it."

Drake sat silently, struggling to remember his dream. The more he thought the more the images slipped out of his mind. He finally looked down, dejected. His folded blue jeans on the floor bore an unusual pattern upon them.

"Ewwwwwww!" Drake exclaimed.

Upon his nicely folded blue jeans were arranged every single one of the small pieces of the pork chop bones. Monique had somehow placed them in a pattern in such a way that no two of them touched. Each was at least a half an inch from the other. This was no easy feat, since the bones varied in shapes and sizes, and it was dark last night, and she had no hands.

"Mo," Drake announced. "How did you do that?"

"More important question, is why?" Mark said as he leaned over the back of the seat and stared at Drake's pants. "At least she didn't do that to my pants."

Mark laughed. Drake picked up one of his pillows and threw it at Mark. Mark returned fire. Mark quickly found his camera and snapped a couple pictures of the assorted bones on Drake's pants. The boys laughed more, and then they dressed for the day ahead of them. Mark climbed out of the van, and took Monique out with him, so she could potty. Drake began to pile his stuff in the back of the van with Mark's. He started to roll up his sleeping bag when he found a long piece of wood in the long crack of the seat. It was a staff, with metal caps on each end. Along the wooden staff were carved Nordic runes. Drake was shocked. This seemed familiar somehow. He knew he needed to keep it, and keep it safe. And he looked forward to going home so he could translate the runes upon the staff. Drake hid the staff in a blanket on the back floor of the van underneath all his stuff.

He picked the bones off his pants, and slowly slid them on, noticing the nice pattern of stains upon the leg. He exited the van.

"Hey Mom," he heard Mark shout when he saw Drake exit the van. "Guess what Mo did with all the pork chop bones last night?"

"What did she do?" Mom asked.

Drake heard the family laugh inside the trailer.

He turned and looked at Monique.

"Thanks a lot, dog," he said to her.

**14**

TO PROTECT AND SERVE

THE BROTHERHOOD OF OLYMPUS
AND THE DEADLIEST GAME

**The Deal**
**Chapter Fourteen**
**August 18, 1978**
**Hoquiam, Washington**

Martin had spent much of the first week his family was gone on their big, around the 'Loop' camping trip working at the grocery store. He had taken a little bit of time to train his new found psychic abilities. He had even learned to use the *Spirit* board by himself, without the support of one of his little brothers. It was not as smooth as it was with the energy of another living being, but it still worked.

He tried not to think about how upset he was with Drake, or even the disappointment he felt toward Mark. They had not even talked since they came back from 10,000 Lakes, and he knew it was all Mark's fault. Why had his brothers turned out to be such losers?

He found himself enjoying his time with Tom at work, and then at the parties they went to after work. They went to the apartment of Annie, one of the cute women that worked at the store. Both Martin and Tom thought that she was very nice to them, and perhaps there was more to this niceness than just being a good hostess.

After the consumption of a lot of beer, and the smoking of a couple grams of hash, Tom upped the ante. The talk had been centered on having a huge party on Saturday the fifth, but they didn't have a place to host it.

"Martin can host it," Tom announced with a drunken smile. "His family's out of town for a couple weeks. Right

Martin?"

Martin looked stunned. Even in his current state of impairment he knew that was not a good idea. Annie came over and rubbed her hands up Martin's back.

"Can you have a party Martin?" she asked. "That'd be so awesome, and I know I would be there."

Martin's head flushed of all its sensibilities.

"What do you say, buddy?" Tom asked. Martin thought about his family. He was sure they were enjoying themselves without him. In fact they probably didn't even miss him. It wasn't fair of them to go off and leave him. A wicked smile crossed his face.

"Sure," Martin began. "Let's party at my house on Saturday!"

"Woo who!" Annie exclaimed as she came really close to Martin's face. He could smell her perfume, and feel her body pressing into his. He felt so alive. Every nerve in his body was on fire. Then as she began to separate from him she gave him a quick brush of her lips over his.

Later that night as Tom and Martin drove back home, Tom began to talk about the party plans. Martin had his head lost in the clouds.

"We need money for beer," Tom said. "And some weed. How much do you have Martin?"

"Not much," he responded. "We don't get paid until next Friday. What about you?"

"I'm tapped out, dude," Tom replied.

"My party's going to suck," Martin realized.

"Dude, that's harsh," Tom began to chuckle, "cause Annie really digs you, and you're going to completely blow it with her by having a lame party."

"If only I knew someone with some extra money," Martin said as he drove down Wishkah Street. "I could borrow some from them."

"Face it dude, you're going to blow it with Annie," Tom laughed. Then he sat up, and became very serious. "I know someone with a lot of money you could borrow from."

"Who?" Martin inquired.

"You," Tom said as a matter of fact.

"How, is that?" Martin asked as they turned onto Alder Street. "I told you I am broke."

"Not when you're working at the store," Tom said rubbing his index finger to the side of his head. "You have lots of money in your register when you work. What if you like just took a few dollars every time someone bought something. Then however much you took, you could give back next week when you got paid, by sticking it in your register. You'd be a little short one day, a little over another, it balances out. I'll even split paying it back with you, fifty-fifty."

Martin thought as he drove. That didn't sound too bad. They would just be borrowing the money from the store, not stealing it, and Tom would pay back half of it. And the best part would be they would have an awesome party, and he might get to know Annie a whole lot better.

"What do you think?" Tom asked. "Sound like a plan?"

"Yeah," Martin said as Alder Street turned into Sumner Avenue. "That sounds like a plan."

Friday at work went as planned. Martin found it quite easy to put extra money in an envelope he kept in the register drawer. At the end of his shift he closed everything out and took his envelope home. Tom had waited in the parking lot for Martin to get a ride home and to see how much money he had made. Martin sat in his car and counted the cash. He had two hundred thirty-five dollars, and it looked like they were going to have an amazing party.

Saturday, both Tom and Martin prepared for the party. They went shopping, then paid someone over twenty-one to buy them alcohol, lots of alcohol. Tom took Martin to a friend of his who took them to another friend where they purchased a large quantity of marijuana.

"This party is going to beyond awesome," Tom announced.

Martin agreed.

On Saturday, August fifth, the party at the Fraser house was awesome for all those who attended. A few drunken guests vomited on the carpet in the living room. A couple people broke a few of Mom's family heirlooms. Tom got so completely inebriated that he passed out in the yard on his way to his house across the street. And Annie spent the night in Dad and Mom's bedroom. Martin, according to the very hung-over Tom, claimed he spent the night in his parent's room too.

On Monday, August seventh, Martin and Tom were arrested by the Hoquiam Police Department when they came in to work that afternoon. Tom's parents came and got their son who, like Martin, was still a minor, from Jail. Martin knew that his parents were on vacation and wouldn't be back for over a week. He called and talked to his grandmother, Isabella, who somehow knew that he was in trouble and together with his grandfather they came in and got Martin out of jail.

Martin and Tom both lost their jobs at the grocery store, though Martin stood up and told the police detective that it was all his idea, and that Tom had nothing to do with it.

Tom supported that statement, so all the charges against Tom Adams were dropped by Friday, August eleventh. Tom's parents told him he was never to see the delinquent criminal Martin Fraser again. Mrs. Adams was furious over the whole fiasco. She had been a grade school friend of Sophia Fraser, and had been pleased when the Frasers moved in across the street from them a last year. She no longer felt that way.

Martin spent that week at his grandparent's house, living in exile. He was not sure how his life had spiraled out of control. He wished more than anything now that he had taken the time off and gone on the camping trip with his family. But, he could not change the past.

The police detective in charge of this case, Sean Franklin, was a graduate of Montesano High School, class of 1957, with Drake Fraser. They spent much of their high school careers being right next to each other on classroom roll sheets and locker assignments. He knew the Frasers, and he was friends with Martin's uncle Karl. They still went hunting together, and in fact he had dated Martin's aunt Rebecca right after high school. He knew he had to wait until Drake and Sophia returned from their vacation before proceeding with the case. He told Martin he had to stay at his grandparent's house, and not to even think about leaving the county. Martin was very compliant to that directive.

Detective Franklin spent a day assuring the owners of the grocery store, a kindly older couple who were always philanthropic for the greater Grays Harbor area, that he would take care of this whole matter for them. They were deeply hurt by the actions of Martin Fraser. They thought he had been such a nice boy whenever they had seen him at work in the store. How could he have stolen from them? They had wanted Martin to be in jail with the other crooks and thieves, not staying with his grandparents. The thing that bothered the detective the most was thinking about how it was going to go when he had to tell Drake and Sophia about their oldest son.

In the afternoon of Thursday, August seventeenth, the Fraser family backed their travel trailer into the driveway, happy to be home from a very long, but refreshing vacation. Mark and Drake made note of the fact that Martin's car was on the street beside the house. One of the advantages of living on the street corner was more parking.

The boys began unloading stuff from the trailer and the van. Drake was careful to take all his stuff, including the hidden staff, upstairs to his room. Mom had called for all the dirty clothes so she could start laundry, but first she had asked all her stinky sons to take showers. She said the house smelled terrible, and they needed to freshen up. While she was unpacking things in the kitchen, she came across a note, written by her mother. It told her that Martin had gotten in trouble and was staying with them, and when she got home to call. Scared and frantic she called her parents' house.

Mark and Drake noticed their mother on the phone as they made trips into the house and back out to the trailer. They also noticed that a few minutes into phone conversation she broke down into sobbing tears. Mark and Drake were curious and concerned for their mother, unaware of what was going on.

"Mark," Mom asked through her tears after she hung up the telephone, "get your father. I need to talk to him."

Mark hurried out through the garage and out to the trailer, where Dad was putting things away in the storage compartments on the back side of the trailer.

"Dad," Mark said as he came around the back of the trailer, "Mom said she needs you in the house. She was on the phone, crying."

Dad looked up at his son, and felt the honest compassion Mark was sharing. He quickly stood up, and rushed inside to his wife.

The next half hour was filled with tension for Mark and Drake. They had no idea what was going on. Dennis and Albert were taking turns flooding the bathroom as they played in the shower.

"I think they are going to use all the hot water," Drake stated to Mark, trying to break the tension.

Soon after, their parents emerged from their bedroom. Mom grabbed her purse and got in the van and left. Dad came out, his eyes red, and got in his Datsun station wagon and left. Before he left he told his sons in the garage, "Finish putting the camping stuff away, and make sure your brothers get some dinner. I'll be home later." He then did something he never did. He kissed both Mark and Drake on the forehead.

"What was that about?" Mark asked his little brother. "Dad never kisses us."

"Do you think something happened to Martin?" Drake pondered. "His car is out on the street behind the house. Is he at work?"

"I don't know," Mark said sadly. "Just makes me think of that day in January, and Wally."

Drake could not imagine that. He could not deal with the loss of his brother, eight months after the loss of his uncle who was like a brother to them all. That was unthinkable. He hoped to God that was not the case.

"Come on," Mark said as he walked into the house. "We have a lot to get put away, and I'll make dinner for the fish boys in there."

Drake noticed that water had begun to seep outside the bathroom door.

"Hey!" Drake yelled at the door. "You guys are flooding the house, knock it off!"

Drake saw a towel fall on the growing puddle of water under the door. Dennis and Albert were not taking showers at all he thought, it seemed they were just playing in the tub. Drake shook his head and walked upstairs to his room. He unwrapped the staff from inside the blanket once he closed his door. He gazed at the intricate carved runes on the surface of the wood. He was awed by the craftsmanship of the staff. He had no idea how he got this staff, but it was eerily familiar to him, and he thought after he translated the runes he might remember more.

Mark made fish sticks and tater tots for dinner. The four of them sat at the table and joked with each other into the evening. Drake cleaned up the kitchen after dinner, and they all sat and watched television, falling asleep where they sat.

Mom brought Martin to the police station, where Dad had been talking to Detective Franklin. The Detective had filled him in on all of the details of the crime, with the possible involvement of the neighbor boy Tom Adams. Martin's subsequent confession to the criminal charge of theft, and his claim that he did so all by himself, freeing Tom from further charges. And ultimately, where the grocery store owners were in their view of the charges, what they wanted done, and the prosecution of the thief.

The detective called the store owners on the phone, and explained to them the special circumstances in the case, and hoped that they would be willing to make a deal with the police department that would save face for everyone involved. Dad and Detective Franklin finally got the grocery store owners to agree to a deal, one that was difficult for Martin and the family, but would keep him out of jail, and would see that all the charges were dropped.

Mom and Martin were escorted back to Detective Franklin's office. Outside the door, Martin looked into his mother's eyes, he began to cry.

"Stop it now," Mom stated. "We're going in to see what we can do to help you."

Martin hugged his mother. Then she opened the door and walked into the small office with a large wooden desk in the middle. There were two wooden chairs in front of the desk, Dad got up from one and walked over to the side of the desk motioning for Martin and Mom to sit down.

"Sophia," Detective Franklin began. "I am so sorry we have to meet this way. Martin, you have put your parent's in a very difficult spot. You know that right? This is a small community, people know each other, doing what you did is going to impact your family for the rest of the time they live on the Harbor. You're looking at a number of months in jail, after spending time at the Green Hill facility for juvenile offenders until you turn eighteen in October."

Martin's world continued to collapse around him. He missed the irony of the Green Hills reference, and the taunt his mother had always made to her boys. Mom didn't, and thought that this was God's way of getting back at her for saying that to her boys so many times in the past. You have to watch what you wish for, because you might not like it once you get it.

"Mr. and Mrs. Greenfield," the detective continued. "The store owners have said they want to see you prosecuted to the full extent of the law. That would put you in incarceration until sometime in late 1979, depending on the leniency of the judge."

"I'm sorry," Martin erupted as tears flooded his eyes. "I didn't think about the consequences, I was going to pay the store back, I was only borrowing the money."

"No, son," the detective interrupted. "What you did wasn't borrowing, you stole. And now you have to face the music for your actions."

Mom wiped the tears from her eyes, and squeezed Martin's right hand with her left.

"Here's the thing, Martin," the detective continued. "I've known your father since, grade school I suppose. I still go hunting with your Uncle Karl. Hell, I even dated your Aunt Rebecca for a while, son, we could've wound up being related. I don't want to see you sit in jail over this. You wouldn't finish high school. You'll never find a job. Face it, your life would never, ever be the same. Now, because I know your Dad, I have talked to the Greenfield's and they've agreed to drop the charges against you, on two conditions."

Mom's eyes perked up, she didn't want her son to endure the life of an ex-convict. If there was a deal to avoid it, she wanted him to take it.

"The first condition is you have to pay back the money you stole," Franklin explained.

"Yes sir," Martin answered.

"The second condition is tomorrow, your parents are going to take you down to the recruiter's office and you will be joining the United States military."

"I don't want to join the military," Martin said. "Mom?"

"Son," Franklin went on. "You only have two choices, the deal on the table or jail. I suggest you think about it. I'll step outside for a few minutes while you discuss it with your folks."

Detective Franklin got up from his chair touched his hand on the shoulders of both, Mom and Dad as he left the office.

"Mom," Martin sobbed. "I can't go in the military, I'll die."

"Drake," Mom pleaded. "There has to be another option?"

"Honey," Dad responded as he shook his head. "Believe me I spent the last few hours talking options, trying to save him from jail. Sean and I both spent time in the service, and this may be the best thing for Martin. It'll certainly force him to grow up."

"It's your choice," Mom told Martin.

"Actually, it's not," Dad interrupted. "He's still a minor, and we're held liable for his stupid decisions. We'll have to pay restitution, it's our responsibility. My mind is made up. Tomorrow morning we go and sign you up, your only choice in the matter is whether you want to join the Army or the Navy."

Martin flinched because he thought his dad was going to hit him as he explained things to him wildly waving his arms.

Mom cried. Martin sobbed in deep rasping breaths but produced no tears. Dad stood with fire in his eyes, hurt and angry that his son could publicly humiliate him this way.

Detective Franklin re-entered the office.

"Have we decided?" the detective questioned.

"Yes," Dad answered. "We'll take the deal. Martin will be joining the military tomorrow."

LUCKY CHARMS

THE BROTHERHOOD OF OLYMPUS AND THE DEADLIEST GAME

15

**Changes Bearing Gifts**
**Chapter Fifteen**
**October 31, 1978**
**Hoquiam, Washington**

August was a month of turmoil for the Frasers, and a month of new beginnings. Martin had gone to the military recruiter's office. He had decided to join the United States Air Force, and then came back to pack up his belongings. He moved the cardboard boxes of his possessions to the attic of his grandparents' workshop. He left Washington State and his childhood behind on August twenty-second. He boarded an airplane for the first time in his life at Seattle-Tacoma International Airport and was off to Lackland Air Force Base (AFB) in Texas to begin basic training. His brothers and mother stood and watched the plane leave, disappearing into the clear azure sky.

No one spoke on the long van ride home. Mom was forced to deal with her long opposed fear of her son's growing up and moving away. She knew the time was coming, because her boys were getting so big. But Martin still had another year of high school. She had anticipated his graduation in June and then Martin heading off to college perhaps the following autumn. Here it was, a year early, and it ripped at her heart to have her eldest son move away.

None of the younger boys ever heard the whole story why Martin decided to drop out of school and join the Air Force, all they knew was that he did.

When they got home they started moving their belongings from one room to another. With Martin gone, Dennis and

Albert were finally going to get their own bedrooms, much like Mark and Drake did when they first moved into this house. Mark was not moving out of his bedroom by the bathroom upstairs. And that suited him fine.

Mom had decided that they would move out of the first floor bedroom that was below Mark's to the larger space that had been Dennis and Albert's, giving the parents the biggest bedroom in the house. Dennis would be moving into the space that used to be Martin's, and Albert would move into Drake's old closet of a bedroom. Drake would move into the newly painted lavender room his parents had occupied giving him more room for his drawing desk and his stacks of books.

The transition took some of the edge off the loss of Martin. Drake was not sure whether he and Martin were back on speaking terms before he left, but before he boarded the plane Martin had asked him to watch the upcoming premiere of *Battlestar Galactica* and let him know how it was. He coldly thought Martin would be missing the television more than his brothers.

August waned and September began in a flurry of activity as the family prepared to get the boys ready for school. Drake started high school and had to put up with Rachel Finnegan being in both his Washington State History and Freshman English classes.

Before they knew it, September twenty-second was upon them, and Drake celebrated his fourteenth birthday with his grandparents, aunts, and uncles. Life was returning to normal for the Frasers, or at least the new normal, the one without Martin being there. Martin wrote letters to Drake frequently asking for recaps on his favorite television shows, and playing a game of tic-tac-toe on the letters they sent back and forth to each other. Martin shared his news of basic training, and when the six and a half weeks were up, he graduated Basic Military Training as a member 3702 Squadron, Flight 359. He informed them that he was staying at Lackland AFB to begin technical school, to be trained to be an SP, or Security Police. He would then be assigned an Air Base somewhere and would guard the installation. He seemed happy, at least in the tone of his letters.

The *Spirit* board sat idle inside a box in the attic of Henry and Isabella Reuss' workshop out in Brooklyn. It was not happy being idle, of course, having done so much with Martin and Dennis. It missed them.

Martin began having nightmares about the board, and was actually sent to a medical clinic on Lackland AFB to be treated for this problem.

Dennis began sleeping irregularly, and took ill. His history of respiratory illness had haunted him since birth. And this became a terrifying ordeal for the Frasers. Dennis was hospitalized in mid-October due to an undiagnosed upper respiratory illness. They had thought that he might be allergic to something that had been left in Martin's room, the film developer, or one of the other darkroom chemicals perhaps.

Mom and Dad argued more, partially due to the cost of having Dennis in the hospital, but there seemed to be more. She accused him of always being gone, he rebutted that he had to be gone to make the money needed to keep the family going.

Mark was just Mark. He locked himself outside the problems of the rest of the family, and got by with his car, his few friends at school, and his thoughts of where his future would take him someday.

Albert, now alone in his own room, became more alone in everyday life. Martin was gone, Dennis was in the hospital, and he didn't like school that much. Only Drake seemed to take any time for him. He knew though that the start of basketball season loomed in early November and he'd lose time with Drake, too. Albert was sad.

Drake had enjoyed going back to school. Learning was fun for him. He enjoyed most of his teachers. A couple teachers kind of bothered him though, because to them teaching just seemed to be a job, and not a true passion. He had begun going back to the library, and on occasion went into the old archive room if Miss Furfur was there. He thought there was something else about her that he couldn't put his finger on since the summer time. But like most thoughts in a teenage boy's mind, it was quickly replaced by something else.

He did find a book in the library on all types of Nordic runes that allowed him to translate the inscription carvings on the staff, which were written in an Elder Futhark. He learned its name, the Staff of Orkan, which was Norwegian for Hurricane. That made a lot of sense, since he got it at Hurricane Ridge. He found that he had to study parts of the Norwegian language to understand some of what was written on the staff, but much of the inscriptions were in languages he didn't have a key to unlock. Regardless of his limited grasp of all that was written upon it, the staff became his prized possession.

During the fourth week of October, Dennis took a turn for the worse. Drake told his teachers that he was going to have to miss some school because they were going to be moving Dennis up to Children's Hospital in Seattle. A certain blonde-haired girl happened to overhear Drake and his English teacher talking.

Rachel Finnegan decided she needed to act.

Drake returned to school Tuesday morning, October thirty-first. Rachel was very happy to see him. She boldly decided to sit with him at lunch. Drake usually sat by himself or with some of the other brainy kids. She thought that might change during basketball season, when he would hang out with the jocks. Rachel sat with the band, choir, and drama kids. She knew lunch would be the only time she could talk to him, semi-privately.

When lunch came, Rachel got her sack lunch out of her locker, and another larger brown paper bag. She walked in the cafeteria and saw Drake sitting alone at a table. He usually was quick through the lunch line, and always had hot lunch because he got it free like many of the students at the school who were in the government sponsored free and reduced lunch program due to poverty.

As she approached him, her mind raced with what she was going to say. They had become sort of friends through their time at the library, and their trip to the psychic bookstore. But they didn't socialize at all in school. Drake never even looked at her, or said hi, or anything. And she waited for him to make the first move, to acknowledge her. But it never happened. Today had to be different.

She sat down across from Drake. Tuesdays were chili and cinnamon roll day in the cafeteria, and Drake was busy dipping his cinnamon roll into his bowl of chili.

"Hey," Rachel stated as she opened her lunch bag, setting the larger brown bag on the seat next to her. Drake looked at her perplexedly.

"So," she continued, "you like cinnamon rolls."

Drake looked at her, stopped chewing, and looked side to side around him, thinking someone must have sent her to talk to him. He looked back down but didn't start to eat again.

Rachel opened up her sandwich bag and began to eat. Drake glanced at her. She continued looking at him, her legs moving to some unheard music. She still watched him, even while she ate. Drake put his food down, figuring his lunch was over.

"Are you done?" Rachel asked, shocked because he had just started.

"Guess so," Drake muttered. Rachel stopped eating and looked at him mournfully.

"Is it because of your brother?" she asked. "I know he's very sick, and in Seattle." Drake sat silently.

"Well," she went on, "you remember when I got that book for my birthday? You know when we walked to the bookstore together?"

Drake nodded.

"That herbology book helped me make these," she said as she pulled the larger brown bag up and sat it on the table in front of Drake. "I know what's wrong with your family, I've seen…"

She turned looking to see if anyone was within earshot of what she was about to say.

"I've seen," she began again, "who's out to get you, that's why I gave you the charm. I think she, or it, is now trying to get to your family to hurt you. I mean, look how sad you are, it isn't fair."

"What's in the bag?" he asked.

"I made two charms to go above your doors, you only have two doors into your house don't you?" she replied. He nodded. "Good, there's also some red pepper in a silk bag in there. You need to sprinkle it around the outside of your house."

"Okay," he mumbled.

"Make sure you do it today, after school," she added. "There's something about Halloween that makes me feel like you need to do this fast."

"Okay," he mumbled again.

"Promise?" she asked.

"Okay," he said.

"Great," she responded and started to eat again. Her feet moving to that unheard music, and still she looked at him. "What's wrong, aren't you going to finish your lunch?"

"I can't eat," Drake said under his breath. "If someone watches me, it creeps me out."

"Oh," she said, as she looked down at her food. "I won't watch you then."

Drake saw her look down and began to eat again.

"You certainly are a weird boy, with very odd rules," she said as she sat happily in that moment across the table from the boy she cared for.

Drake went home after school with the bag Rachel had given him, and started by sprinkling the ground red pepper around the house. He then went into the house and hung the small woven charms above the front and back doors using thumb tacks. He shook his head and went to his room to read.

He went to bed early that night after dinner. Mark took Albert trick-or-treating. With his room right behind the front porch, he expected to hear all the trick-or-treaters throughout the night. To his surprise, he didn't hear a single one. That meant the candy his mom bought would be theirs to split. He did think it was odd that no one stopped that night. He knew the porch light was on, and they had some Halloween decorations on the porch. He slept easily that night for the first time in weeks.

At 11:40 PM, in a hospital room in Seattle, Dennis Fraser woke up out of his fever induced coma. He said he was hungry, and when he found out it was Halloween, wanted to know if he could go trick-or-treating.

## Carmen of the La Madrid Family
### Chapter Sixteen
### January 13, 1979
### Brooklyn, Washington

Martin had finished his Technical School on Friday, December twenty-ninth. He received word of his post assignment that afternoon. He had requested McChord AFB outside Tacoma, Washington. McChord was the closest AFB in proximity to his officially listed hometown of Aberdeen, or where he currently lived with his grandparents in Brooklyn since his dad kind of kicked him out. His second choice was Fairchild AFB outside Spokane. He received his second choice. He got eighteen days of leave before he had to report to his new base assignment. He would spend his leave at home.

Martin was excited to return home to Hoquiam and a little nervous as well. He knew that his relationship with his father had been damaged and didn't know what to do to fix it, except be the best Airman he could to prove to his father that he was dedicated to this. He also knew that the relationship with his brothers was strained. He missed them terribly. He thought back to the summer before, when he was so mad at Drake and so disappointed in Mark. Only Dennis stuck with him, and poor Dennis had been so sick while he was gone. He hoped that the weekly letters he exchanged with Drake had helped rebuild the bridge with his little brother.

Martin arrived on a commercial airline flight at Seattle-Tacoma International Airport on New Year's Eve 1978. He was picked up at the airport by his mother and two youngest brothers. It was basketball season and Drake was tied up with practices and holiday tournaments throughout the Christmas Break from school. Drake had slept in that Sunday morning because his basketball team had played three games the day before and he was very tired. As the tallest player on the team, his coaches played him as much as they could to get him the experience he needed to become a better player.

Martin was disappointed that Drake wasn't at the airport to pick him up, but quickly blew it off because he was home. He hugged his mother for minutes, and minutes, then in turn gave each of his little brothers a hug, picking them up off the floor. They carried his big green military duffel bag, both Dennis and Albert, one at each end instead of slung over the shoulder the way Martin had been carrying it.

When they arrived at the house, Mom insisted that Martin could sleep on the couch, at least for a night, before taking his stuff out to Brooklyn and getting his car. It was Albert's ninth birthday as well and it was good to have them all together for the celebration.

They had fried chicken that Sunday night, like old times. Albert still didn't finish the meat on each piece of chicken before grabbing more. They talked as a family. They laughed, they teased, they taunted each other, and for that moment in time they were a family again.

After dinner, the birthday cake, and unwrapping presents, Dad went to bed, since he had to drive to Napavine to work in the morning and wasn't planning to stay up to see the ball drop on television anyway. With a new sense that her eldest son was an adult, Mom and Martin drank some cocktails while the rest of the boys laid around waiting for the clock to strike midnight.

As they watched Dick Clark count down to the start of the New Year, they all silently hoped it would be a better year than 1978 had been to the Frasers. Drake pointed out that they were watching the past become the future since the television broadcast was recorded from the Eastern Time zone. Everyone else decided that the New Year had not made Drake less weird. Then Mark went outside and lit a string of one hundred firecrackers he bought at Taholah on the Quinault Reservation in early July and had saved for this night.

Soon afterwards, they started drifting towards their bedrooms, and Martin snuggled into a blanket on the couch. He was home, and yet he would never be at home there again.

The first week of January, Martin took his old boat of a car into the car dealership where Mark worked during the summer and bought a 1977 Datsun B-210 hatchback. It would get him much better gas mileage on his drives across the Cascades to his duty station and back home. It was also a two seat car, so he didn't have to drive any of his little brothers anywhere for his mom while he was home. He did give each of them a ride in the metallic blue car. It was the newest car they had ever ridden in. It did take Martin a bit of time to learn to handle the shifting of a manual transmission on the floor, instead of on the column like the family van was.

He visited his old high school, in uniform, to show off for his brothers. He also wanted to see some of his classmates who he had not seen since the previous June. He even ran into his old neighbor, Tom Adams.

"Hey Tom," Martin said as he saw him walk past in front of the parking lot. Tom turned, saw Martin and looked like he was seeing a ghost.

"Martin?" Tom responded. "How are you? You look official, and a bit scary. I didn't recognize you at first and thought I did something to get in trouble."

"I'm doing well," Martin replied. "I got stationed at Fairchild, over by Spokane. I got a new car, a Datsun B-210." He pointed out in the visitor spots.

"Cool," Tom responded. "So did you hear about me and Annie?"

"No," Martin stated, not sure he liked where this was headed. "What about you and Annie?"

"Oh, we've been going out together since October. She quit her job at the grocery store after they fired us. She said that was all wrong."

"Tom," Martin clarified. "You know she graduated from high school two years ago. She was old for me, why is she dating you?"

"Guess she felt sorry for me after you left for the Air Force. You know, I've never told anyone about the trouble we got in," Tom added. "I do wanna thank you for taking the blame for it all though. My mom wanted to kill me at first. Now she just wants to kill you."

Martin stood there dumbfounded.

"Hey," Tom said as he started to leave. "Maybe I'll catch you later, there's a party at Annie's this Friday, maybe you can show up, it'll be like old times."

"Maybe," Martin said, he made a feeble attempt at a wave. What god of fate did that to him? How was it that the guy who comes up with the idea to steal the money in the first place not only gets away with the planning of it, and the spending of it, but then gets the girl they both liked? That made no sense at all.


The second week of January was much like the first for Martin, except that he stayed out in Brooklyn more. He was not sure why. He had unpacked many of his things into the house. Grandpa and Grandma Reuss had let him move into Wally's old room at the end of the hall upstairs.

As Martin pondered the dark, foreboding feelings he was experiencing he was reminded of the time of the year. It was nearing the one year anniversary of Wally's death. And here he was now, living in Wally's old room, at least while he visited on leave. He pulled out the *Spirit* board and felt a wave of confidence and power as he held it. He had forgotten the feeling that slim piece of pressboard with the lacquered paper on the front gave him.

He sat in Wally's old room and held the board. He had made it to one of Annie's parties last week and felt a bit out of place. Kind of like he had grown or matured, and the rest of the people he used to hang out with, or admire, hadn't. He didn't want to go to any parties this weekend, so he figured he would just stay at his grandparents' house until Sunday the fourteenth.

On Saturday evening, Aunt Carmen visited her parents and sat and chatted with Martin until late in the evening. Carmen clearly carried the Spanish heritage of her mother. She had flowing dark hair, engaging brown eyes, and a disarming loveliness about her that made her approachable. She was six years older than Martin, and had spent much of the early 1970s as what Dad called a 'hippie.' Carmen preferred the term flower child. Carmen had always possessed the La Madrid gift, and she sensed the dilemma in Martin and the struggles he was facing. They talked and talked, and it was good for Martin to have someone listen to him on that level.

Martin finally shared his stories about what he had learned in his experiments with the *Spirit* board. Never one to shy away from the paranormal, Carmen asked Martin if he still had the board.

"Yeah," Martin responded. "I got it down in the bedroom."

"Well, get it out," Carmen said, shooing him down the hallway with her hand. "Let's see what this thing can do."

Martin quickly returned with the board, the planchette and his spiral notebook. They moved a chair so they could face knees to knees with the board on their laps.

"Oh, god," Carmen stated with a laugh. "I haven't used one of these in years. I hope I remember how."

"Hello there," Martin said as they both put their finger tips on the planchette. "Is there anyone there?"

The planchette did not move.

"We want to speak to Walter Reuss," Carmen asked. "Wally, can you hear me? It's your sister. If you are out there, answer me."

The planchette slowly started to move. It glided over the surface of the board in a tight circle.

"Wally, are you there?" Martin asked.

The planchette spun to some letters and began to spell, "N. O. T. W. A. L. L. Y."

"You're not Wally?" Carmen asked. "Where's Wally?"

The planchette replied, "O. U. T. S. I. D. E."

Carmen thought about that answer, yes, Wally was in some sense outside. His cremains were buried in the backyard along the riverbank below the big leaf maple tree he had loved to sit under. There was a simple granite memorial marker on the spot he was buried.

"Just outside, or buried outside?" Carmen questioned.

The planchette was straight to the point, "B. U. R. I. E. D."

"So to talk to him, we need to go outside to his grave? That is creepy." Martin responded.

The planchette wasted no time, sliding over to its response, 'YES.'

Carmen looked into her nephews eyes. Saw his hurt.

"Can you handle that, Martin?" Carmen asked.

"Going out to Wally's grave?" he replied.

"Yeah," she answered.

"I guess so," Martin stated. "Yeah, I think so, if we get to talk to Wally."

'YES' responded the planchette, then it spelled, "T. A. L. K. T. O. W. A. L. L. Y. A. T. G. R. A. V. E."

"Well then," Carmen said bringing her hands up off the planchette. "That settles it. I'll get a lantern. Make sure you put your coat on, it's cold out there."

Carmen went downstairs into the garage and came back with a lantern. She had also put her coat on, and a stocking cap. Martin had grabbed his coat out of the bedroom, and they walked down the stairs and out the back sliding glass door. Carmen started the lantern when she got to the large moss covered maple tree.

Carmen had a blanket under her arm that she spread out over the top of the grave marker.

"There," she said. "That should help keep our butts from getting wet."

They sat down on the blanket with their legs crisscrossed in front of them, the lantern beside them, and the *Spirit* board on their knees. Martin had his spiral notebook to his right on the edge of the blanket. It was a chilly January night. Their breath came out in waves of fog.

"Ready?" Carmen asked her nephew.

"Yeah," Martin replied. "I'm ready."

They placed their fingertips upon the planchette, and it began to move immediately.

"Wally," Carmen asked. "Are you there?"

'YES' came the reply from the planchette.

"What did I give you for your third birthday?" Carmen questioned, knowing that this was a trick question.

'NO' came the response of the planchette. Then it spelled, "G. I. F. T."

"That is true. I didn't give you a gift." Carmen stated.

"I. D. I. D. G. E. T. S. L. I. N. K. Y. D. O. G." the planchette spelled.

Carmen looked up at Martin. She had tears forming in her eyes.

"He did get a slinky dog," Carmen said sadly. "I'd forgotten."

"Wally," Martin began, "have you been using this board with me before?"

The planchette slid quickly in response to Martin's question. "H. I. M. A. R. T. Y."

Only Wally used to call Martin 'Marty' when they were little kids. Martin had forgotten how much he missed his uncle. Tears began to flow unabated down his cold cheeks.

'NO' the planchette answered the second part of his question. "O. T. H. E. R. S. U. S. E. W. I. T. H. Y. O. U."

"Others used it with me?" Martin clarified.

'YES' then it spelled out, "B. U. T. I. W. A. R. N. E. D. Y.

O. U."

"How did you warn him, Wally?" Carmen asked.

"M. A. D. E. I. T. S. P. E. L. L. E. V. I. L." the planchette answered. Martin felt crushed. He had been so hard on Drake for refusing to use the board after that. Drake had been right.

"W. I. L. L. T. E. L. L. Y. O. U. S. E. C. R. E. T. S" the planchette spelled for them.

"What kind of secrets will you tell us, Wally?" Carmen stated.

"Y. O. U. W. I. L. L. H. A. V. E. 2. K. I. D. S." the board offered.

"I'll have two kids?" Carmen said. "I don't think I'll ever want kids."

"P. R. E. G. N. A. N. T. N. O. W." the planchette informed her. Carmen laughed.

"I don't think so," she answered. "Good try. What else do you have?"

"Martin, you should write these things down, so we can see how accurate these predictions are," Carmen directed her nephew.

"D. R. A. K. E. S. R. W. I. L. L. D. I. E. 2. 0. 0. 4." The board offered.

"My dad will die in 2004?" Martin asked.

'YES' came the response.

"What about me," Carmen asked.

"2. 0. 4. 8." was the response.

"Wow," Carmen replied. "That is a long time from now, I guess I am okay with that."

"And me?" Martin asked.

The planchette spun in a great circle, over and over again, before spelling out, "M. A. N. Y. T. I. M. E. S."

"What?" Martin exclaimed. "What the hell does that mean?

"J. A. N. 1. 3. 1. 9. 8. 4." The planchette spelled as it kept moving. "O. C. T. 3. 1. 1. 9. 8. 4"

"Wait," Martin asked, he was freaked out by this response.

"I am going to die twice, so soon? Why not 2048 like Carmen?"

"D. R. A. K. E. T. O. O." the planchette freely moved under their fingertips. Martin didn't like to see that his little brother was going to suffer the same fate as him.

"Will we die in a car accident?" Martin asked, "since we die together?"

'NO' the board replied. "N. O. T. T. O. G. E. T. H. E. R."

"Oh," responded Martin. "Then how?"

"S. A. M. E. D. A. T. E." was the response of the planchette. "W. A. R."

Martin immediately assumed that meant Drake would join the Marine Corps, like he always talked about after seeing war movies. Drake liked their uniforms and their official song. The other part of that answer meant that in 1984, the United States must be at war with someone, for them both to die in the military.

"Who will be president in 1984?" Carmen asked, hoping to get some clarity as to why they would be at war.

"R. E. A. G. A. N." the planchette responded.

"Ronald Reagan?" Carmen replied. "Well, that would explain why we would be at war, probably with the Soviets."

'NO' the board responded. "O. L. D. G. O. D. S."

"Old gods?" Martin stated. "That makes no sense, how could we be at war with old gods?"

"D. E. F. E. N. D. O. L. Y. M. P. U. S." the planchette spelled out.

"Okay," Martin said as he laughed. "That is just crazy. We are going to die in Greece fighting old gods over Mount Olympus?"

'NO' the board answered quickly.

"Who'll be president after Reagan?" Carmen questioned the board.

"B. U. S. H." was the quick reply.

"Who's that?" Martin asked Carmen.

"Former C.I.A. Director," Carmen answered. As a flower

child she had always been politically active and new the opposition well. "He's probably worse than Reagan."

"M. A. R. 2. 8. 1. 9. 7. 9." The planchette spelled out, followed by, "3. M. I. L. E. I. S. L. A. N. D." The planchette spun in its tight circle before finishing its prediction, "N. U. C. L. E. A. R. M. E. L. T. D. O. W. N."

"A nuclear meltdown?" Carmen questioned. "On March twenty-eighth this year?"

'YES' was the response.

"Oh my god," Carmen gasped. As an activist she'd protested the growing nuclear power industry in the United States. "That's horrible."

For the next hour and a half, Martin and Carmen asked questions about things and dates, items humans usually never get to know, nor have the opportunity to know until they have come to pass. Martin recorded this forbidden knowledge on five pages of his spiral notebook. It was a very comprehensive list that covered events over the next fifty years. Some of the events, like the crazy war against old gods, made little sense at all. Other information was painfully clear.

Finally the planchette told them, "I. T. I. R. E. D."

"And we are very cold," Carmen responded.

"I. S. T. O. P." the planchette spelled out for them more clearly. "E. V. I. L. C. O. M. E. S."

"Who is coming?" Martin asked. "Who is this evil?"

"S. U. C. C. O. R. B. E. N. O. T. H." the board replied. "H. E. H. A. T. E. S. Y. O. U."

Martin removed his fingers from the planchette and it slid to a stop. The temperature around them dropped dramatically just then, so much so that they could feel the moisture on their skin begin to freeze.

"I think I'm done now," Carmen announced as she hurriedly stood and stretched out her cold cramped legs.

They quickly picked up their things and headed back into the warmth of the house through the sliding glass door. Once inside, Carmen thought about the information they possessed.

"Let me have the list," she stated. "I will put it in an envelope, and we will see if any of it starts to happen. I mean what are the odds that there will be a nuclear meltdown or hostages taken in Iran, or Ronald Reagan elected president."

"Not likely," Martin agreed, kind of. "I guess."

Martin tore out the five pages and gave them to Carmen. He looked at the dates of his 'deaths,' still confused and troubled by that piece of information before he let it go into her hands.

"Well, nephew," Carmen stated, "it's late, and I have to get home to my husband. He probably locked me out when he went to bed."

Martin smiled at her. He took the board and headed up the stairs to bed. Carmen went out into the driveway and climbed in her car.

She started up the motor and adjusted the heater, turning it all the way up to take the chill out of the air inside her car. She buckled her seat belt and looked up in the rearview mirror. Looking back at her in the mirror was the completely white, dead face of her younger brother, Wally.

She screamed and turned to look behind her. No one was there. She turned the dome light on and checked the backseat for an intruder. Nothing. A feeling of panic rushed through her. She immediately reached over and locked the passenger's side door and her door. Her heart pounded.

She did her best to calm herself. It had to just be her hyper aware senses, set on edge from all the *Spirit* board activities during the night.

She then put the car in reverse and backed out of the driveway, pulling out on the main road, and heading off towards her house. She turned the radio on, adjusting the dial as she drove, looking for some music to ease her nerves.

She found a static-filled station out of Olympia that was playing some music. She didn't recognize the song, but that didn't matter, she was lost in thought about why Wally would make himself visible to her in that way. Why scare her? What purpose would that serve? They had always been close, and it made no sense that he would deliberately scare her. Her car thumped as she drove over the abrupt edges on both sides of the short bridge that spanned the creek that fed into North River.

As she drove she noticed wispy images in the trees, taking shape out of the low lying fog. Like random spirits rising from the gray mists, they wandered toward the river ahead of her. Having the La Madrid 'gift' had always made her aware of spectral things, and occasionally she had seen ghosts, or other entities, but never in this magnitude. Soon she had traveled many miles and was well on her way home. But the spectral migration toward the river had intensified. The ghosts all headed toward the bridge in the dark distance ahead of her.

She kept looking forward trying to avoid looking out at the apparitions. She focused her attention on the road. She didn't want to know if they saw her as easily as she saw them. Once she got to the bridge the road narrowed considerably.

She began to cross the second bridge of three she had to cross to get back onto Highway 101, before she could finally get home. This was an old, rickety bridge that the county always said it was going to replace, but never did. She saw something moving ahead of her in the dark umbra of the headlights of the car. The apparitions had stopped at the bridge, unable to cross the water. She slowed down, unsure what could be on the narrow bridge ahead of her. There appeared to be three or four animals, large animals, oddly shaped deer, or maybe hunched over people on the right hand side of the bridge. She slowly neared the middle of the bridge. Whatever was out there was in the road so much that she had to drive near the far side to give them room. As she began to pass them, they suddenly rose up and lunged at the side of the car. Their twisted faces pressed against the windows. Their charred and pock-marked skin pulled taut over their skulls giving the impression of plastic surgery gone wrong. The tight skin revealed smiling mouths filled with hundreds of sharp teeth, their eyes were completely red, and had an unnatural glow, and their long boney fingers ended in talon-like claws. They tried to open the doors as they pressed on the car. In her mind she heard their terrible rasping voices calling to her, "Let us in, give us the child."

"There isn't a child in here!" Carmen shouted.

She reacted instinctively as she floored the accelerator and the car shot away from her attackers. She drove so fast that she almost lost control and crashed on the corner following the bridge. Her heart pounding fast from the fright of the attack and near crash she realized that she needed to slow down enough to drive home safely, but she was still way over the speed limit. She didn't drive straight home after that. She drove all the way into Montesano, and then looped back around to her house, for fear she might be followed.

It took an hour before she got home, in what usually took only twenty minutes. As she settled herself from all the visions that had plagued her that night, she realized that her brother had saved her by appearing in her mirror and making her lock her doors, which she never did when she drove those back country roads. She had no idea what those things were, but felt they were probably related to that *Spirit* board and the monsters it had made mention of. She knew she could not tell her husband because he didn't believe in the supernatural like she did. He'd just tell her to stop drinking so much wine, like he always had when she attempted to talk to him about paranormal stuff in the past. She'd certainly warn Martin, though. And she'd keep that list of predictions safe and hidden.

As she neared her driveway, she felt nauseated. It was a strange feeling, something she'd never felt before. She came to an abrupt halt and she swung open the door and threw up on the gravel road. She never got sick. Something was wrong. No, something was different. Then it hit her perceptive mind.

"Oh my god," she exclaimed. "I'm pregnant!"

The unnatural voices she'd heard wanted the child. At the time, she didn't know what they meant, but now she realized those things on the road were not after her, they were after her unborn child. Like a mother bear, her emotions flared. She'd never allow anything to harm her child and she'd take every precaution possible to make sure that never happened. From that day forward there had always been a gray area in the aura of the land where Carmen resided. No bright spots giving away powerful life forces to the keen-sighted, no dark spots revealing lingering evil, just gray, an area free of perception, like a cloak that rests over the gentle forested area. No evil walked there. It was a safe island in the sea of psychic energies and the spirit of the land.

Carmen took out the five folded pages of predictions. The *Spirit* board was right about the first thing on the list, she was with child. She hoped to God it was wrong about Ronald Reagan, and the war that would take the lives of Martin and Drake. Yes, especially, that one.

**17**

# INNOCENCE LOST

### THE BROTHERHOOD OF OLYMPUS
### AND THE DEADLIEST GAME

The Coming Storm
Chapter Seventeen
May 5, 1979
Brooklyn, Washington

It was a gray, drizzly day. Not too chilly, but not warm either. Spring in Western Washington was a weatherman's nightmare. It would be sunny for a few minutes, down pour rain, or hail the next. It would switch in an instant to mist or just drizzle a bit, and then be back to sunshine depending on the apparent emotional stability of the myriad of clouds that continually pushed in over the state from the Pacific Ocean. Henry Reuss had always told people 'you know you're in Washington in the spring, if you looked out the windows on all four sides of your house and the weather was different out each of them.' This was one of those days.

Today was a celebration. It marked the fifty-fifth birthday of Isabella Reuss. People began arriving at Henry and Isabella's house late in the afternoon. Isabella's sister, Eileen, who was fourteen years younger, actually arrived the night before.

Dad had left work early that day so that they could arrive on time for dinner at five o'clock. The Fraser's van pulled into the gravel driveway of the Reuss house ten full minutes early. It was one of the first times any of them could recall that they had arrived early to an event.

"Wouldn't have happened if Martin was here," Mark stated as they came to a stop, much to the chagrin of Mom in the front passenger's seat, forcing her to turn and scowl at her son. "What? I'm just saying that if Martin was here we'd have had to wait for some TV show to end or something, and we would've been late."

"He has a point," Dad said in defense of Mark as he touched Mom's arm. She let it go.

They piled out of the van. Mom inspected the boys to make sure they had not become un-presentable during the ride. She had inspected them before they left their house as well. Albert had to change his shoes that time because he reported for that first inspection in his rubber boots. Mom had explained to them that this was their grandmother's birthday, and there would be pictures taken and they had to look nice. They passed her quick onceover, and headed towards the front door. Dennis pressed the doorbell. Drake stared at the storm door, its hinges on the right, and the front door behind it with the hinges on the left. He shook his head, some things he imagined were meant to be secrets.

Once inside they climbed the stairs, with Dennis coming up last, scooting backwards one step at a time. Drake walked up slowly, keeping pace with his younger brother in case he needed help.

At the top of the stairs, a flurry of hugs awaited them.

"You're early!" exclaimed Isabella as she hugged her grandchildren and gave them a quick peck on the cheek. Mom flashed Mark a stern look. He got the message and didn't comment about being early like he had in the van.

They put their jackets in on the bed in Carmen's old room and returned to the large window-filled living room. Drake noticed that the gathered family were smiling and talking, and enjoying each other's company, with the exception of his grandfather. Henry sat in his chair stoically, looking at his relatives, and glancing outside watching the road to their house in the distance.

Richard Reuss and his new wife of three months, Jan, and her daughter Jennifer, who was Dennis' age, came up the stairs to join the throng. Richard was followed by his younger sister Carmen, and her husband Steve. Nearly everyone fawned over the pregnant bulge Carmen showed off proudly.

Drake stood in the long hallway, filled with photographs. He thought to himself, as he saw Jan, and Jennifer, and his pregnant Aunt Carmen, that the family had turned the corner in a philosophical way. The long months of sadness and sorrow after the loss of Wally had passed, and the family, like a flower, was beginning to bloom again... to grow, to move forward, and he did just that as he went in and joined his large extended family for dinner.

After dinner, they brought out a large chocolate cake with too many candles burning on it.

"Take some of those candles off of it," Isabella demanded. "I'm not, that old!"

The family laughed, and Isabella blew out the candles with two breaths and a round of clapping.

"What did you wish for, ma?" Richard asked.

"I'm not telling," Isabella said with a smile. "If I did, it wouldn't come true."

The cake was cut, and cold vanilla ice cream was scooped out and put on plates with each piece of cake. Mark stood in line to get his plate, and when he got there Isabella touched his hand.

"Take this one in and give it to Grandpa," she stated, "and ask him if he wants any coffee. Thank you Mark."

Mark collected two plates, one for him, and one for his grandfather then he headed out into the living room.

"Here's some cake Grandpa," Mark said, as he held out one of the plates.

"Oh," Henry said as he turned away from the window. "Thank you, Mark."

Henry took the plate. Mark sat down in the chair next to him.

"Grandma wanted me to ask you if you wanted any coffee," Mark remembered.

"No, I'm okay," Henry answered. He continued to glance out the window, as if he was watching for someone to drive down the road towards their house.

They sat in silence together eating the birthday cake. Finally Henry turned to Mark.

"You know," he stated somberly. "This is your Grandma's second birthday without her son. I should've never scolded him that day and made him drive into Monte."

It hit Mark like a ton of bricks. Henry sat quietly, disengaged from the rest of the family, looking off in the distance hoping to see someone driving down the road late for the party. He hoped to see Wally come home. The pain in his heart made tears form in his eyes. All the troubles that each of them endured at the loss of Wally paled to the man who lost his son, and believed that all of this was his fault. Mark put down his plate and hugged his grandfather deeply. Henry, somehow sensing the reason for the hug, returned it. Together they cried.

The moment was broken by the ringing of the phone. Mom assumed it was finally Martin calling to wish his grandmother a happy birthday. Carmen answered the telephone. She talked to whoever it was for a moment, then with her hand over the mouthpiece, called her father over to the phone.

Everyone was quiet, unsure who would be calling to talk to Henry. Carmen answered their looks of confusion by silently mouthing one word, "Lawyer."

The family sat as silently as possible while Henry talked on the phone. Most of the conversation was one sided, with Henry nodding, or saying brief things like, yes, or no.

Minutes later, Henry hung up the telephone.

"Who was that Henry, and why didn't they wish me a happy birthday?" Isabella teased with a giggle.

"That," Henry answered grimly. "Was our attorney calling to let us know that the truck driver's family is filing their wrongful death suit against us in court tomorrow, for two million dollars."

A hush fell over the birthday party. Henry, Isabella, Sophia, Richard, and Carmen all came together in a family hug. The mood turned somber. Henry explained that the insurance company, the one Dad used to work for, had settled with the family and in doing so made it look like they admitted the fault of the accident was Wally's. Their family then decided to file the wrongful death suit against them, Henry and Isabella. The lawyer had told him that the process was going to take some time. After the suit was filed it would be a while before it got assigned a judge and was placed on the docket. It could be a few months or more, before it actually went to trial.

"We'll lose everything," Isabella sobbed.

"Our house, or property, our cars," she looked down the hallway at all the photographs. Drake had drifted back down the hallway and stood there by himself. "And we'll lose all our special memories. That's not fair, and it's not right. We lost a family member in that accident too."

Tears flowed down Isabella's cheeks.

The phone rang again, this time it was Martin calling to wish his grandmother a happy birthday.

Drake stood in the hall, looking at a single photograph on the wall. It was one on a cork bulletin board, held there by three red pushpins. The tacks were not through the photo, but rather pushed in tightly on the edges to keep it in place. Along the left hand white margin of the photo was a date imprinted on the film, 'SEPT 1965.' The photo was black and white, and it was of the boys—Martin, who was holding his baby brother Drake, Mark, Wally's dog Tippy, Wally, and their cousin Ralph. The five of them, and the dog, sat in the field of what appeared to be DeWitt Park in Cosmopolis. As he stared at this one old, black and white image, the singularity of the moment began to open memories that he was unsure from where they originated. Memories of knighthood, and gods, and of brotherhood flooded his mind. There before him sat the Brotherhood as it was intended, in that single photograph, now so horribly unable to happen.

He knew in an instant what he had to do. He walked down to the kitchen where Mom was now talking on the phone to Martin. She had taken over the telephone conversation with Martin after he finished talking to Grandma.

"I need to talk to Martin," Drake said to Mom. "Mom, I need to talk to Martin."

Mom looked up at her son, and sensing his determination, she said her good-byes to Martin and handed Drake the phone.

"Martin," Drake said into the phone. "It's Drake, we have to talk."

"What's wrong?" Martin's voice crackled over the phone line.

"I know now why all of this has been happening," Drake answered. "But first we have to stop this lawsuit. If only there was some proof that Wally didn't cause the accident."

In a phone booth on Fairchild AFB, Martin felt a tug upon his soul.

"I know how we can find out," Martin replied. "Or at least we will have an idea how to get the evidence we need."

"How's that?" Drake questioned.

"When I come home next month on leave, I'll use the *Spirit* board on Wally's grave again, and I'll ask him to tell me what happened, or how we can prove it wasn't his fault."

"I'm not sure that's a good idea," Drake responded. Then the thoughts of the Brotherhood pushed forward. "But if that's what we need to do, then so be it."

"So why is all of this happening?" Martin asked.

"I think you may know," Drake answered. "But I can't go into it until later. Okay?"

"Okay," Martin replied.

"You want to talk to anyone else?" Drake asked.

"Yeah, let me talk to Aunt Carmen," Martin said.

Drake set the phone down, sought out Carmen and pointed to the phone. She acknowledged his silent directions and walked to the telephone.

Drake returned to the photograph down the hallway. He stood, looking at the old image and letting the memories and knowledge flow over him like a warm shower of goodness. This was his destiny, and now he must rise up to face it.

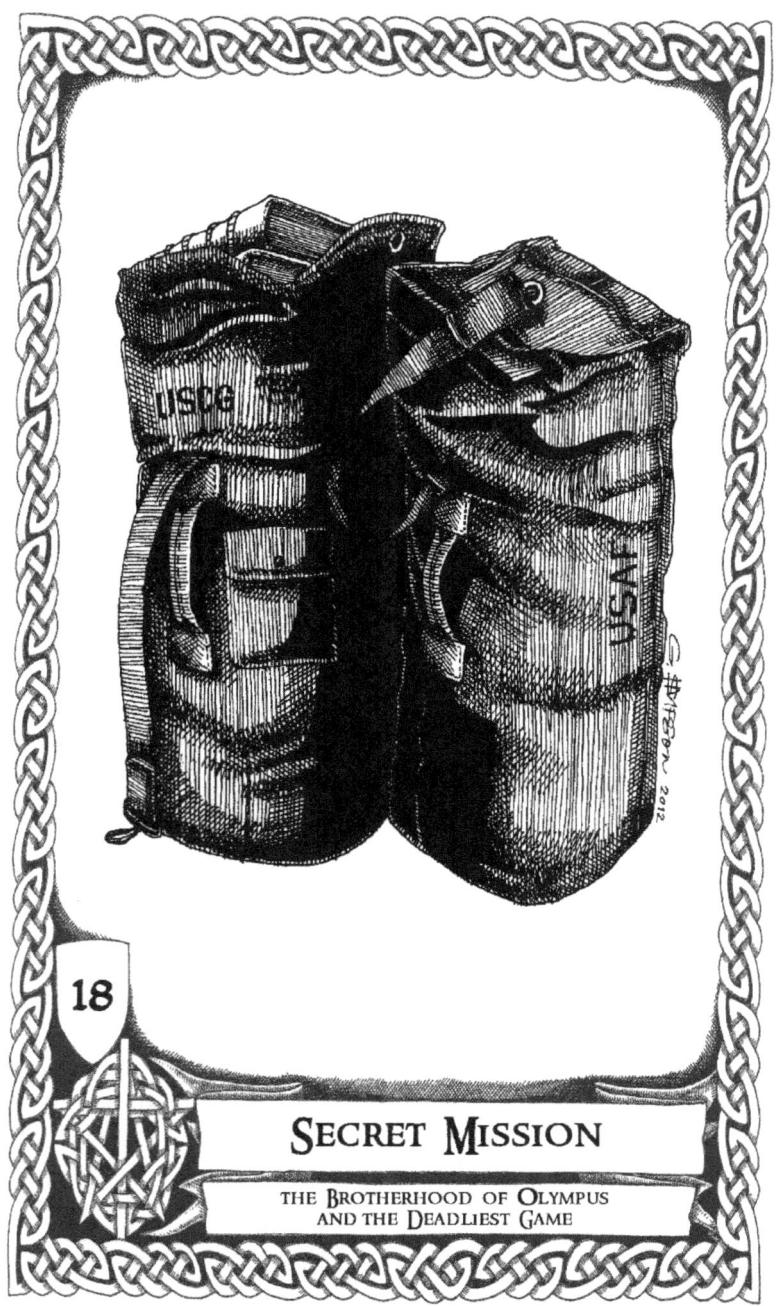

18

## SECRET MISSION

THE BROTHERHOOD OF OLYMPUS
AND THE DEADLIEST GAME

## Of Presidents and Librarians
## Chapter Eighteen
## June 7, 1979
## Hoquiam, Washington

Since his moment of epiphany in May, Drake had attempted to get as much information as possible from the library to assist him in assembling the vague memories and thoughts that he now possessed. Unfortunately, Miss Furfur was seldom at the library anymore. He had only gotten access to the archive room once during the whole month. Things got worse when old Mrs. Madison told him that Miss Furfur would be leaving the library, and her last day was going to be Saturday, June ninth.

Frantic at the looming loss of his special resource room, Drake recalled what Mark had talked to him about in the van that night on Hurricane Ridge. The necessity for 'borrowing' those books in the archive room took on new meaning if he would never have access again after the ninth of June.

Drake approached Mark, to see if he even remembered the conversation. Mark did, and said he would help his brother out, except he couldn't do it on the ninth, but he had to do it two days earlier on the seventh, because he was working swing shift from three to eleven o'clock on both the eighth and ninth at his new job at Danny's, the twenty-four hour restaurant on Wishkah Street in downtown Aberdeen.

During lunch at school on Wednesday, Drake sat at the same table he always sat at. Rachel had been joining him on a fairly regular basis since Halloween. She sat across from him on this day. This day was odd for Drake in a lot of ways.

211

The first being that as he sat there, other students, not the upper classmen, but his freshman classmates were walking up and congratulating him. He'd do his best head nod, in recognition and then try to keep eating. He really didn't like people looking at him eat, or talking to him while he ate.

Of course he knew the reason why they were bothering him. Earlier in the day, the high school had end of the year assemblies for each of the classes. At the junior, sophomore, and freshman assemblies they planned for the coming year by nominating and electing class officers. At the freshman assembly only one boy was nominated for president, which was how it would have stayed had it not been for that exceptionally weird girl across the table from him. Out of nowhere Rachel stood up and nominated Drake for sophomore class president. The ballots were made by running Xerox copies, and by the end of the assembly that featured cheerleaders, a band performance, and lots of talking from teachers, the ballots were handed out and people cast their votes as they left the assembly by slipping the folded ballots into the box on the chair by the door.

Just before lunch, the Principal had announced the voting results for each set of class officers. Drake knew he would not win, he didn't want to win, he'd even voted for Sam Bates who was nominated against him for president. When the principal started naming the winners over the intercom, Drake sat silently in his art class. The principal started with the sophomore class before moving up to the next grade level.

"And next years' sophomore class president is Drake Fraser," the principal's voice announced. Drake was sure he hadn't heard that correctly.

"Hey man," Bill who sat at the same table next to him said with a smile. "Way to go Mister President. Just so you know, I voted for you."

"Me too," Mike said from across the table.

"That's absolutely fantastic," Mr. Dore said in his Australian accent, as he came up and patted Drake on the back. "You're going to be an awesome president Drake."

Drake almost died at the thought. Being class president would mean speeches and other icky stuff like that, or standing up in front of hundreds of people looking stupid, and that wasn't going to happen. He would have to figure a way out of the whole thing. It was a fiasco waiting to happen.

Lunch, therefore, wasn't fun for Drake. He sat and was planning his last trip to the archive room, and he had no time for his classmate's congratulations. He circled the seventh of June on his calendar in his binder.

"Thanks Rachel," Drake said with dry sarcasm.

"You're welcome," she chirped back. She noticed the circled date. "What's on the seventh?"

"Nothing," he responded, like he did most of his 'conversations' with Rachel in single words.

"Oh," she responded. She knew him better than that.

"Hey, Fraser, congratulations," a freshman boy said who walked by. Drake thought he might have been on the football team. Drake did his head nod.

Sometimes he wished he'd never met that blonde Irish girl. He smiled to himself when he thought that because he knew she'd get upset. She looked at his smile and somehow knew it was meant for her, but for entirely different reasons. She smiled with him.

The next day at school was more of the same, and might have actually been worse if Drake had taken the time to listen to the buzz that was being said around him. But he was a man on a mission. He was so focused on the Library that he was completely ignoring the boring things he had to do on the second to the last day of school. He went through the motions and made sure his locker was cleaned out. He had gone to the school library with his English class to make sure that all their textbooks and library books were turned in. He did his best to avoid Rachel, but Ms. Stamper had them line up alphabetically. Finnegan, then Fraser. That doomed him.

He ignored her. Perhaps when he was forty he would forgive her for nominating him for president. She talked to him in line. Maybe when he was fifty he would forgive her.

The day took forever to end. Drake rode home in Mark's car. They planned their library visit like a military exercise. They had a map and precise times drawn up for each step of the maneuvers. Drake would enter the library and gain permission to the archive room after Miss Furfur returned upstairs, then he'd go and open the side door by the alley. Mark would enter with the two military duffle bags that they'd load the books in. Mark would leave back through the door, and Drake would close the archive room and leave up through the main entrance at nearly closing time, leaving Miss Furfur no time to check the room. And if no one came in on her last two nights and got access to this room that shouldn't be there in the first place, then no one would ever know they illegally checked those books out. Drake had waffled on the whole taking of the books for months, but when he realized that if he didn't act soon he would lose access to them, he re-evaluated it. To him, it became a moral question. Would you take something that isn't yours if you knew it could help you save people? Was saving lives worth that? Finally Mark had helped him settle this internal debate.

"You aren't taking them, I am," Mark explained. "And if you don't like it I will punch you right in the eye."

Mark's determination had helped wash his hands of the guilt he was feeling. Besides, if the *Spirit* board was right, the books actually belonged to a library in Gehenna, which was a neighboring realm of Hell. Would the gods frown on stealing something from Hell if it could save people? Thank heaven for Mark, making it all so clear for him.

"Right in the eye," he said making a fist.

"Which eye?" Drake replied.

"Does it matter?" Mark stated. Drake thought a moment. No it wouldn't matter at all. Either eye would hurt.

The library closed at eight o'clock. The boys drove to the library and parked a block away. Mark had explained that the get-away car had to be parked far enough away that it couldn't be seen. It was nearly seven o'clock. Mark got the two olive green canvas duffle bags, one was their Dad's and the other was one Martin had left at the house when he came home from leave the first time. They walked around the corner and then split up, both knowing the plan.

Mark headed around towards the alley and the backside of the library, not wanting to look suspicious and invite any police to come and visit him. He got to the back door, and peered into the darkened library basement. There was no door on the back wall, so the archive room wasn't really there. This wasn't going to work at all. He sat down and waited for the lights to come on.

Drake walked up the sidewalk, and started up the stairs. He glanced around to make sure he was not being followed and felt something like what he imagined James Bond felt like when he went on secret missions. He opened the door and found Miss Furfur at the front desk. She lit up upon seeing him.

"Drake," Miss Furfur said. "I'm so happy to see you, I wasn't sure I was going to get to see you before I left. You know this Saturday is my last day here, right?"

"Where are you going?" Drake asked wistfully, his mind floating on the pleasant fragrance of roses.

"Why, back home of course," she replied.

"Oh," he answered. "Where is home? I thought you were from Aberdeen?"

"No," she said looking into his eyes and smiling. He had no defense for her. "My home is far from here, very far in fact. I think I'll miss Aberdeen and Hoquiam. I've enjoyed my time here. But my work's nearly done, and I must return home, my family has missed me."

"May I go into the archive room, Miss Furfur?" Drake inquired as he broke free from her charms, for a moment.

"Absolutely," she replied as she turned and walked, Drake would miss that walk, those high heeled shoes, and those seams that ran up the back of her legs and much more as he followed her towards the stairwell. "Oh, by the way, your pesky acquaintance is here waiting for you."

Drake turned to look, but it was too late. Rachel Finnegan joined him from the back shelves of books.

"Hullo Drake," she said as she walked in step with him. Drake felt ambushed. He didn't like Rachel at all since the election at school, and now she might ruin the plan.

"You don't need to be here," he said to Rachel as they started down the stairs.

Miss Furfur turned on the lights. The plan was in action. They approached the old heavy wooden door of the archive room. Miss Furfur pulled out the large skeleton key and unlocked the room, gracefully stepping in and turning on the light with a clink of the metal chain. Miss Furfur turned and exited the room, passing so close to Drake that his heart felt like it stopped beating. He inhaled her fragrance. Time stopped. Then he heard her heels clicking on the floor as she began to walk away.

"Let me know if I can assist you in any way, Drake," she said as she walked.

Mark saw the light come on. He quickly got to his feet and peered into the window by the door. He could see the librarian walk across the room. She was a very attractive woman, not like old Mrs. Madison who was there when Mark had to clean the library. No wonder Drake liked coming to the library so much. Then he saw the back wall again, the same gray stone wall that he'd peered at in the dark just moments ago before the light came on. But now there was a thick, wooden door in the middle of it. Mark was shocked and he stood there, mouth open, and forgot to hide. The librarian turned and saw him. Their eyes locked on each other. Mark had failed. He turned away and stood in the shadow of the building cursing to himself.

Drake waited to hear Miss Furfur walk up the stairs. There was a very long pause, and then he heard the sound of her shoes going up the old stairs. He had no time to explain to Rachel, the plan was in action and he had to act. He stepped out of the archive room, leaving Rachel inside it for a moment. To his surprise he was not alone in the basement.

Mark stood there dumbfounded.

"How'd you get in?" Drake whispered excitedly. This wasn't part of the plan.

"The...," Mark stammered, "the librarian, she stopped and unlocked the door. The door was locked, Drake, I couldn't have gotten in. But she unlocked it with a key. And then she opened the door and told me to come in."

"What?" Drake screeched in a loud whisper. "The plan is ruined, she knows you're here."

"Drake," Mark said, suddenly realizing what he needed to do, "she let me in, she saw the duffle bags, she told me to make sure I got as much as we can before I left. Of course she knows the plan. I think she's in on our plan somehow. Don't ask me how, it just seems like it, like she knew we were going to do this, and she's letting us."

"That's just great," Drake snapped in his whisper voice. "All I know is I'm not going to jail for this, no Green Hill for me, you got it?"

"Got it," Mark said as he walked up to the open wooden door. He stopped and felt the stone wall, then the heavy wood of the door. "This is amazing. This door wasn't here before she came down here."

"Drake," the voice inside the room sounded. "What're you doing out there? Who're you talking to?"

Mark's eyes went wide, he pointed into the archive room, and silently mouthed to his brother, 'Who's that?'

"I am talking to my brother," Drake said to Rachel in the room as he walked back inside. "I told you Rachel, you shouldn't be here."

"Hi, Drake's brother," Rachel said, extending her hand to Mark. Mark reached out and did a soft handshake, dropping one of the large duffle bags in the process. "My name's Rachel. Rachel Finnegan. Drake and I have English together."

Mark looked at Drake and mouthed, 'She's cute.' Drake mistakenly nodded in agreement, he thought she had cooties too.

"So," Rachel began, "Drake's brother."

"Mark," interrupted Mark.

"Mark," Rachel continued, "what're you doing here tonight? I've never seen you at the library with your brother before. Why do you have those army bags?"

"Well," Mark said, hoping he could explain it all, "I'm here with these bags tonight to take all of these books. Yep, that pretty much explains it. Guess it wasn't that hard to explain it all after all."

"What?" she responded in shock at the whole plan. "You can't do that. That's stealing."

"Technically," Drake replied, "he is taking something that isn't really here. This room doesn't exist, Rachel. When Miss Furfur isn't here, this room isn't here. And I got news for you, Miss Witchy-poo, Miss Furfur is leaving here on Saturday. That means no more archive room, and no more research books, unless Mark takes them tonight."

"Stealing," Rachel said in her defense, "is still stealing regardless of who you steal from, or why."

"Think of it as more of an extended check out," Mark added. "We'll return them when we're through with them, right Drake?"

"Yes," Drake said. "On my word of honor."

Mark began to load books into the first bag.

"Be careful how you stack them so you don't damage them," Drake directed. "And it should help get more in if you stack them neatly."

"Oh," Mark added. "The librarian also told me to take all that I can."

"Figures she would," Rachel chided. "She's a daemon, and daemons are pure evil."

"What?" Drake and Mark said together.

"She's not a daemon," Drake continued. "An angel

maybe, but not a daemon."

"She's a daemon," Rachel replied. "Her name is one of the books in that bag."

Mark looked up at Drake, raised his eyebrows. "No time to check now."

"Listen, Rachel," Drake said. "If you're going to turn us in, go do it, if not please get out of the way so we can get these books loaded before the library closes."

"Fine," Rachel finally stated after she looked at both brothers, noticing their similarities and their differences. "But I want to get this book from you when you leave."

Rachel pointed to a book. It was a spell book for witches and warlocks.

"I'll borrow it from you," she said. "For a little while."

Drake looked at her. Then shook his head and began to help load books into the second duffle bag. A few minutes later they were putting the last couple books into the bags. Mark folded over the canvas, inserting the metal hook through the four grommets. Then he clipped the shoulder strap to the hook. The bags were really heavy. Mark dragged one over to the door before returning for the second.

Drake was busy writing a note. When he finished, he folded it and left it on the table inside the empty archive room. He turned off the light and closed the door as Rachel stepped out with him. Mark was over by the door, both extremely full duffle bags leaning against the wall.

Mark opened the door and dragged the first bag out without leaving the basement, and then he turned and did the same to the second bag.

"When you get out," Mark instructed his brother, "come out to the back to help me carry these bags, they're really heavy."

"Okay," said Drake at the same time Rachel responded with her, "Okie Dokey Loki."

Drake and Mark both raised their eyebrows and looked at each other. Mark closed the door and stood outside.

"Let's go," Drake said as both he and Rachel climbed the

stairs one last time together.

They walked to the front desk. Rachel was surprised that Drake stopped to talk to Miss Furfur. It was nearly eight o'clock.

"Drake," Miss Furfur's voice lilted on the air. "I'm so pleased that you stopped to say good-bye before you left."

"I wish you didn't have to go," Drake said.

Rachel stood facing the front door. She rolled her eyes.

"Eighteen months is a long time to be away from your family, Drake," the librarian stated.

"I know," Drake said, looking down.

"Don't worry," she said, as she reached out and put her hand on Drake's shoulder, touching his hair as her hand passed. "I'm positive I'll see you again."

"Really?" Drake said, looking back up into those magical eyes.

"I'm very sure," Miss Furfur stated. Rachel made a gagging motion with her finger. "Good-bye Drake."

"Good-bye," Drake replied as he turned and walked to the front door where Rachel waited, "Miss Furfur."

Drake opened the door.

"Oh, Miss Finnegan, a moment of your time please," the librarian stated, as Rachel turned to face her. "Come here, please."

Rachel walked towards the desk. Fear rushed through her mind, she was certain the library daemon lady had seen her mocking gestures. The door closed behind Drake.

"Miss Finnegan," the taller librarian said as she leaned over to look Rachel eye-to-eye. "I know, we both know, who we both are, and neither one of us is fooling the other. So I'm going to make this perfectly clear. When Drake Fraser grows up, he's going to be all mine."

"Ewwww," Rachel replied. "You're like old and stuff."

"Older than you might think, my dear," the librarian responded. "But mark my words, if you stand in my way, it will be the last thing you do. Got it, Miss Finnegan?

"Oh," Rachel said as she stared into the eyes of the

librarian, and a feeling she had never known filed her. It wasn't fear, it was hatred. She hated this thing pretending to be a librarian. "I got it, Miss Daemon."

Rachel turned and walked out of the library. She knew she was just threatened and challenged over the affections of a boy who apparently didn't even like her. It didn't matter, she wasn't going to let Miss Furfur, the daemon lady, bully or threaten her. Not if it was the last thing she did.

She found the brothers lugging the heavy duffle bags back towards the street where she assumed they had a car parked. She followed along until they stopped next to a blue car. Mark pulled out his keys, unlocked the car and then opened the back door.

"This wouldn't have been so hard," Mark said through his heavy breathing, "if we didn't park so far away, Drake."

Drake looked at Mark in disbelief. It was Mark's get-away car part of the plan that put the car so far away.

"Let's put them in the back," Mark told Drake.

"Mark," Rachel started. She knew now that she would need that spell book more than she originally thought. No one threatened her. And no one was going to take Drake from her. Even if he didn't realize he needed her just yet. She was willing to be patient, which was completely against her nature. Or just maybe she could make him realize he did like her. "Make sure you take that book out for me."

Mark looked over at Drake. Drake nodded.

"Okay," Mark said, as he unclipped the strap and opened the duffle bag. He knew that witchcraft book was near the top. He grabbed it and pulled it out. "There you go."

"Thank you Mark," Rachel cooed, hoping Drake was paying attention. "You know for a thief, you're not that bad looking."

Mark was flabbergasted. Drake was shocked, but did his best not to show it.

"Drake," Rachel said. "Make sure you use some more of the pepper, the charm might be wearing off. You have to keep it fresh."

Drake nodded.

"You got a fungus problem?" Mark asked Drake.

Drake shook his head, sometimes Mark could be such a dolt.

"Do you need a ride?" Mark asked Rachel as he and Drake climbed into the car.

"No," Rachel responded, clutching her book to her chest. "I'm good. I'll see you at school tomorrow, Drake. Good night, Mark."

Mark started his car and pulled away from the curb.

Behind them, Rachel continued to stand there holding the book. Further behind her, on the edge of the library lawn, a dark shape spread enormous webbed wings and took to the air.

"If he thinks I am a witchy-poo now," Rachel said to herself, "just wait Drake Fraser, just wait."

Mark looked in his rearview mirror, thinking he saw a large shadow move over the road far behind them.

"Dude," Mark said to Drake, "I think your girlfriend likes me."

"She's not my girlfriend," Drake replied. "She's more of an acquaintance."

Deep inside though, Drake wasn't sure that was all she was to him anymore.

**19**

## SEE THE TRUTH IN CLOVER

THE BROTHERHOOD OF OLYMPUS
AND THE DEADLIEST GAME

The Eyeglasses
Chapter Nineteen
June 27, 1979
Grays Harbor County, Washington

The month of June had been busy. School had ended and summer vacation had started, much to the enjoyment of the youth of Grays Harbor, the Fraser boys included. A trial date for the wrongful death suit had been set for August twenty-third. Miss Furfur never showed up for work on Saturday, June ninth, her last scheduled day at the library, and no one knew why. Mark began working five days a week at Danny's from three o'clock to eleven o'clock, every day except Wednesdays and Thursdays. Martin came home on two weeks leave on June twenty-fourth. Drake spent his days reading the books he had acquired from the archive room at the library. He had not seen Rachel Finnegan since the last day of school, and her absence from his life made his anger towards her fall away. A curious change was transforming him. In fact, he was now actually looking forward to being sophomore class president in the fall. His knowledge on the paranormal had soared to new heights, as had his understanding of the ancient Teutonic knights and their secret Brotherhood with a mission to protect the Earth from threats from beyond. Dennis was happy to see Martin come home, and had gone out and spent the night at their grandparents' house to hang out with Martin on Monday, June twenty-fifth. Albert, now significantly taller than Dennis, was still just Albert. Nothing shook Albert of his 'don't worry, we'll be fine' attitude. Although despite his apparent lackadaisical attitude, he had become increasingly independent and self-sufficient over the last few months.

On Monday evening, Martin and Dennis had gotten out the *Spirit* board and taken it out to the big leaf maple tree that stood above Wally's grave. Martin's efforts that night were focused on figuring out what they could do to prove that Wally was not at fault in the fatal accident over a year and a half before. Much of the other contact with the other side was about how much the *Spirit* board had missed both boys, and how much it looked forward to teaching them more. Martin knew that they weren't communicating with Wally, because of how the board was responding. It was so different then the last time he used it on the grave in January with Aunt Carmen. He wanted specific information, and the board was being evasive.

"Stop," Martin yelled at the board. "I need to talk to Wally Reuss, not you, you damned mordgeists! Stop taunting us with knowledge we can't have, and let Wally talk!"

Martin took what he had learned of telekinesis and forced it back through the planchette into the ethereal plane imagining the mordgeists being pushed away from the board. Dennis and Martin both heard an audible scream upon the wind.

The planchette sat silent for long minutes.

"They're gone," Martin said as he thought about the other dimension. His ability to use his psychic resources had grown.

"Wally," Dennis began, jumping at the opportunity, "Wally, are you there?"

The planchette slowly moved, circled, and then slid over to 'YES' in response. Dennis smiled at Martin.

"How can we prove you weren't at fault in the accident?" Dennis asked.

The planchette spun in a medium sized circle around the center of the board. "F. I. N. D. M. Y. G. L. A. S. S. E. S." it spelled in response. "G. L. A. S. S. E. S. S. E. E. T. R. U. T. H."

226

"Whoa," Dennis said. "If we find his glasses, we'll see what happened. Where are they, in the house?"

"They never found his glasses," Martin explained. "He had them on when the truck hit his pickup, but they weren't on his body when they put him in the ambulance. They're gone. No one ever found them."

"A. T. S. I. T. E." the planchette spelled out.

"Where at the site?" Martin questioned.

"D. O. N. T. K. N. O. W." the planchette responded before continuing, "C. A. N. T. S. E. E. T. H. E. R. E."

"Will we find them," Dennis asked, "if we look?"

"YES," came the answer.

"M. U. S. T. G. O." the planchette informed them.

"Wait, Wally," Martin pleaded. "How can we stop the lawsuit?"

The planchette slid quickly over the board, spelling out, "M. U. S. T. B. R. E. A. K. A.N.D.B.U.R.N.E. V. I. L."

"We must break and burn evil?" Martin questioned. "I don't understand."

The planchette slowly slid over the words, 'GOOD-BYE' and then sat unmoving.

On Wednesday, June twenty-seventh, Martin drove in to Hoquiam to get Mark and Drake to go out to the accident site and look for Wally's missing glasses. Mark wasn't happy about having to drive out there and use his gas, but they couldn't all fit in Martin's Datsun. Drake, on the other hand, was resistant for another reason.

"All five of us have to go," Drake said.

"It won't take all five of us to look along the side of the road for a pair of glasses," Mark answered. "The three of us can fit in my car."

"Actually," Martin said, "I need to take my car too so I can drive up to Olympia afterwards, I have a date with this girl I met named Beth."

"See," Drake explained. "If we're already taking two cars then we need to take all five of us."

"Why?" Martin questioned.

"I don't know," Drake responded. "I'm not sure. I just know that something inside me is saying we all need to go. Whatever happens today is meant for all five of us."

"What do you think?" Mark said to Martin.

"Drake's probably right," Martin replied. "Again."

Mark shook his head, and then started walking towards the kitchen and the garage beyond.

"Whatever," Mark said. "I'm leaving, so the runts better get out here if they're riding with me."

"Dennis! Albert!" shouted Drake. "Let's go! Mark's leaving and we have to go with him!"

Albert and Dennis hurried out the door. Drake went in, checked the house making sure the television and the lights were turned off, and made a quick detour to his room then made sure he locked the house, with Monique inside. He left with his brothers, carrying a long object wrapped in a blanket that he tucked behind the front seat of Mark's car. He just wished he had a better understanding why all five of them had to be there. He hoped that it wasn't so they could all die together.

Dennis rode with Martin, having beat Albert out the door and to the little blue Datsun. Albert and Drake rode with Mark.

The ride out over the Cosi Hill was uneventful, and there was absolutely no sense of dread or foreboding in any of the Fraser boys. When they came down the Cosi Hill and saw the accident site, they realized how much it had changed in eighteen months. The State had recommended the intersection be reconfigured to prevent future accidents. They planned on adding turn lanes and had already cut down some of the tall Douglas-firs that used to line the roadway, opening up lines of sight to reduce the chances of an accident like the one that claimed Wally's life from happening again.

Too little, too late, thought Mark as he pulled into the gravel park-and-ride lot in the elbow of the intersection. Martin was right behind him. The five boys got out of the two cars and stood together for a moment.

"The *Spirit* board said the glasses are here," Martin explained. "No one ever found them. But the board said if we find them, and it said we would find them, we can see what really happened at the accident. Then we would break the evil and the lawsuit is toast."

Drake kind of felt like he was playing basketball and Martin was acting in the role of the coach, telling his players what they needed to do to win the game. Except he wasn't overly inspired by Martin's coach talk, he hoped it wouldn't affect the outcome of the 'game.'

They immediately began to scour the area, looking in the ditches, the gravel shoulders, the bushes along the east side of Highway 101. Minutes turned to hours, and they had walked the whole side of the highway. They had found no sign of any eyeglasses. Albert and Dennis were complaining of hunger. Martin was losing hope. He knew the glasses had to be there.

The wind turned and blew to the west. Drake walked out into the intersection and stood where his uncle had sat in his pickup. He mentally watched the crash unfold around him, and from what he knew of where the pickup ended up, and where Wally ended up on the highway, he thought of the physics of the problem. If Wally was thrown from his truck with such force that he bent the steering wheel and he landed out in the highway, then his glasses would have had to follow that same trajectory. He made an imaginary line across the highway with his arm, and looked down at his fingertips like they were a site on a gun. There, across the road, stood a thick stand of Douglas-firs. The afternoon sun was shining down upon them, small beams of light breaking through the branches lighting up the boughs as they gently swayed in the wind. A few of these sunbeams made it all the way down to the ground. And to Drake's amazement one of them did, right were his fingers were pointing. The sight gave him sudden chill. There was a little hollow under the branches, and clover filled the hollow in a short carpet of green. There in the midst of the clover, the sunbeam dancing upon it, was a piece of yellow metal. Wally's glasses were golden. He had just gotten new ones the month before his death.

Drake knew in an instant that he had found the lost glasses. He smiled to himself, looked both ways, and then crossed the road. He didn't take his eyes of that glowing piece of metal as he crossed the highway, or when he went down the gravel shoulder and into the weed-filled ditch beyond. The wind shifted again, blowing back to the east, bringing the scent of the trees and the clover to his senses. Steadily he made his way through the bramble of underbrush and blackberry briars that stood between the road and the trees.

Drake thought to himself that he had seen this sight somewhere before, a moment of déjà-vu filled his senses, perhaps it was a dream he had before. He heard his brothers arguing behind him about being hungry and tired. He cleared the briars and stepped into the clover.

Suddenly a feeling of dread, of terrifying panic, flooded him. He heard a voice, a ghostly voice that echoed around him.

"They are not for you. Get out! Flee these woods!"

A cold gust blew at him from the clover and nearly toppled him. He regained his posture, looked at the piece of yellow metal about fifteen feet ahead of him, turned one more time, and stepped back into the clover.

"Be gone boy!" shouted the voice as the wind came again, although this time he could see the wind and it took the form of a human skull and it rushed at him with an evil cackle. Drake broke, turned, and as fast as he could manage he ran through the briars and brambles and up out of the ditch and into the road. He stood there, his heart pounding loudly in his chest. He turned and looked back at the clover-filled hollow. It was again a serene scene of natural beauty, except that one sunbeam was still shining directly on that piece of yellow gold metal.

"I found them!" Drake shouted, as he walked to the west

side of the road again closest the glasses. "They're over here!"

His brothers all stopped bickering and kicking rocks and ran over to the other side of the road with him, after a couple cars drove past.

"Where?" Dennis asked.

"Right there," Drake said pointing to the glint of yellow metal in the sunbeam.

"Why didn't you get them?" Martin asked.

"I can't," Drake said. "There's something in there that won't let me get them."

"Dennis," Martin snapped, "come on, you and I'll go, we used the *Spirit* board and it told us we'd find them."

Martin and Dennis bounded down the gravel shoulder and into the deep ditch beyond. They started to cross through the brambles and briars where Drake had just been.

"What's in there, Drake?" Albert asked, somewhat nervously.

"Well," Drake explained, hoping to not scare his baby brother more than he already was, "it was like a wind, but I heard it tell me to 'get out.' And then I saw it, and it was kind of scary."

"Even for you?" Albert asked. Drake nodded. "Oh, that must be really scary then."

Mark and Albert watched in anticipation, not knowing what to expect as Martin and Dennis made it through the blackberries and up to the edge of the clover. Drake hoped whatever was there, would leave his brothers alone.

The winds swirled into the gravel of the ditch throwing up dust and tiny rocks into the air. Martin and Dennis stepped into the clover at the same time.

"Be careful!" shouted Albert.

Both Martin and Dennis came to a sudden stop.

"Get out!" a disembodied voice yelled at the two of them.

"Did you hear that?" Martin asked Dennis. Dennis nodded with wide open eyes.

"Mark, Drake, did you hear that?" Martin shouted back to

the road.

"Hear what?" Mark yelled back.

"One more step," Martin said to Dennis.

Martin lifted his foot and pivoted further into the clover. Dennis was locked in fright and didn't budge.

"I said, get out!" the voice shouted as the shape in the wind formed on the far side of the clover and sped towards the two boys. Martin turned before it and began to run. Dennis fell over backwards, his eyes rolled up in his head. Martin ducked down to grab his brother as the cackling skull blew past him, leaving his blood chilled. Martin partially dragged and carried the slack form of Dennis through the blackberries and the brambles with great urgency.

On the roadside, Mark and Albert saw the skull apparition for the first time as it rushed at Martin and Dennis. Albert began a scream that lasted for minutes. Both Mark and Albert turned and ran towards Mark's car. Luckily there was no traffic at the time, because neither boy stopped to look both ways before crossing. Drake went down into the ditch to help Martin carry Dennis up to the shoulder of the road.

Drake quickly checked for Dennis' pulse and he found it throbbing in his neck.

"He's not dead," Drake yelped.

"Help me get him to my car!" Martin yelled. "We have to go, we have to go now!"

Drake grabbed Dennis under his shoulders, Martin grabbed his feet, and it was a much nicer way to carry him then how Martin had virtually dragged him through the blackberry briars.

As they reached Martin's Datsun, they noticed Albert shouting at them as his scream finally ended.

"Hurry!" Albert screamed, he pointed out the window of Mark's car up the Cosi hill. Near the top a black tangle of churning wind filled with all manner of debris was moving down the hill towards them. "They're coming!"

20

FLIGHT TO THE BRIDGE

THE BROTHERHOOD OF OLYMPUS
AND THE DEADLIEST GAME

**Flight to the Bridge**
**Chapter Twenty**
**June 27, 1979**
**North River, Washington**

Drake loaded Dennis in Martin's car. He looked at Martin, but his brother had no solutions to offer. Suddenly it came to him as he looked back up the Cosi hill at the swirling mass of debris. "Aunt Carmen! We need to get to Carmen's!"

Martin nodded, jumped in his car, and quickly started it up.

Drake ran over and jumped headlong into the open passenger side window that Albert had just vacated. Mark gunned the engine and gravel sprayed as they spun out of the park-and-ride and onto the highway heading southbound on 101. Martin and Dennis in the blue Datsun were right behind him, emerging from the cloud of dust and gravel.

"Where're we going?" Mark shouted to Drake, as his brother finished sitting up after his dive into the car.

"Aunt Carmen's," Drake excitedly responded. "She's the only one I know that can help us."

Mark nodded. Albert sat looking out the back glass. The black twirling mass of wind and debris had made it to the bottom of the hill. Albert looked at it. He thought it was like a tornado the way it seemed to spin upon itself.

The black tornado began to close the distance between them as they turned the corner to the right beside the old weigh station. As they drove onward, Albert made a startling discovery. It was cutting through the forest, tearing out trees and logs and adding them into its death spiral. It was taking a short cut, closing faster on them.

"How far to Aunt Carmen's?" Albert asked.

"Not that far, a few miles," Mark snapped as he gripped the wheel, the speedometer reaching ninety.

Albert looked behind them. Martin was keeping right up with them, and the death tornado was still closing as it cut through the trees.

Fortunately for the boys Highway 101 was relatively straight once they passed the weigh station. Mark pressed the accelerator hard and the speedometer edged over one hundred. He knew he could outrun Martin's Datsun, but he didn't want to leave his brothers behind.

On the straightaway, the cars began to move ahead of the churning mass of black death. They zipped by Clark's Restaurant, and were rapidly approaching the Artic Tavern heading towards the North River Bridge.

"You cannot escape!" a hollow voice echoed through both cars. Martin began to visibly sweat. Mark began to think of options.

"We can't lead this to Carmen's house!" Drake exclaimed. "It will destroy her house, maybe even her, and her baby."

Mark nodded. The options clicked in his head.

"Logging roads," Mark said. "We'll lead it up one of the old logging roads."

Mark turned to the left, and shot down Artic Road just past the Tavern. Behind him, Martin was confused, he didn't know why they would head away from Carmen's, but he followed his brother's car. Maybe Drake had figured out a solution.

"What is it?" Mark demanded.

"I don't know!" shouted Drake.

"It's like a tornado, but its evil, it's a death tornado, and it's hunting us," Albert explained. "Look, it's picking up pieces of stuff as it comes after us."

They crossed a bridge over a creek that fed into North River and sped up the hill beyond it. The death tornado behind them slowed as it crossed the water, almost like it was afraid to cross, then it was on their side and speeding after them again.

Drake took notice of the behavior.

They sped down the road, over an old slide area, and down into a valley. They skidded to the left and up a logging road. The death tornado seemed to go through the houses in the valley without disturbing them, but it crossed the valley straight into the woods that shrouded the logging road they were on.

Mark expertly drove them around the narrow dirt and gravel road as the climbed up, and up a hill. The seething mass of evil closed on them over land, ripping stumps out of the ground as it passed over them.

"The river!" Drake shouted.

"What?" Mark said as the sounds of his tires squealed on the gravel that shot out from underneath them.

"It was slow to cross the creek," Drake began. "I think it won't be able to cross the river, it's too wide."

Mark saw Drake's line of logic. It could work, and it was possible. None of them had ever tried to outrun a 'death tornado' as Albert called it, before.

"Only one problem, little brother," Mark answered. "The river is back the other way."

Drake looked ahead up the winding gravel road. He saw a landing, one that the logging company had used to pull logs up before loading them onto trucks to be hauled down these very same roads back into town and the lumber mills there.

"That landing," Drake said as he pointed ahead of them. "If we turn there and drive right back at it, it may not realize what we did. By the time it passed us we would be heading back to the bridge. I just hope it takes time for it to turn."

Mark nodded and sped towards the landing. As he approached the landing he started tapping his brakes to let Martin know that he was beginning to stop so he would not drive right into the back of his car. Mark's Impala slid sideways in the gravel as he came to a stop facing back down the hill. Martin slammed on his brakes and skidded to a stop.

Seeing Mark's direction, Martin quickly threw the Datsun in reverse and backed up, then spun back around to idle next to Mark.

"The river!" shouted Drake out his window to Martin. "I don't think it can cross the river!"

"Drake!" Martin shouted back. "That means we have to drive through it!" Drake nodded grimly.

"Stay close!" Mark yelled as he punched the accelerator spraying a huge tail of gravel and dust behind them. Martin sped off right with him. They had cleared the landing and started down the road.

The seething mass of blackness and debris rounded the corner. It had overshot them, and was partially behind them when it hit. As the blackness swirled before them violently, their cars began to rock at the force of the wind. Inside the death tornado, they saw swirling apparitions, ghosts, and skeletons mixed with the logs, trees, rocks, and other debris. Skeletal hands whipped at the side of the doors, spectral faces moaned as they spun by the cars. Albert covered his ears, and put his head down, no longer looking out the back glass of the car.

"No, no, no," Albert whimpered to himself over, and over.

Mark's car was suddenly hit by a charred log sideways, nearly tipping it on its side. Mark skillfully kept the car on two wheels until he was able to land it back down on all four in the coming corner with a very loud crash that jostled them like they had never been before. Martin saw this and thought his brothers were going to die. He was relieved when he saw Mark regain control of his car, although somewhere inside him he realized Mark was going to be pissed off about the damage his car just took.

Their strategy worked, for the most part. The debris buffeted them. It cracked Martin's windshield in two places and it left them shaken. Seeing the things inside the blackness was worse than the physical damage their cars took as they cut through the back side of it.

The three oldest boys knew they were very lucky, had they not gotten behind it, and gone straight into it, they wouldn't have made it.

Drake turned and looked back into the backseat. Albert lay in a fetal position, his hands over his ears, his eyes squeezed painfully shut. He continued his whimpering as well.

"No, no, no," he whimpered.

"Albert!" Drake yelled at him as he shook him with his left hand. "Albert, come on, we made it. Get up. We need you to keep a look out for it!"

"Okay," Albert finally said as he peeked out of one of his eyes.

Downward the cars sped along the dusty gravel road. Albert rose up and peered out the back of the car again. Although this time he kept his head lower, shielding himself with the backseat.

"It's back!" Albert squealed as he ducked lower behind the headrest of the back seat.

"Let us know if it's getting closer," Drake asked him. "Got it?"

"Yep, got it," he shot back.

They launched out of the gravel road in a cloud of dust, nearly hitting a car heading the opposite direction on Artic Road. Martin was not as fortunate and did clip the back end of the car with the driver's side tail light of the B-210, cracking the light in a shower of red plastic on the road. The driver of the other car stopped and turned to look at the crazed hit and run driver as they sped away. He then began to roll up his window as he saw the massive black cloud moving towards him. He covered his head as a tree inside the storm slammed into his car, tipping it completely over on its roof in the ditch.

At dangerously high speeds the Frasers sped back down Artic Road towards the North River Bridge. The death tornado kept pace with them, moving down the middle of the road.

"Go, go, go!" Albert shouted. "It's gonna get Martin!"

Luckily, Mark's Impala squealed over the short bridge over the creek at the start of the road. Martin was right behind them. The blackness slowed and spun in on itself as it began to cross the bridge. They slid to a sudden stop in the gravel before making the quick left turn south out onto Highway 101. The bridge was right there in front of them. The tornado cut across the median and up the hillside. It was nearly upon them. Albert saw the spectral faces again and dropped back on to the seat. He reached down and grabbed the blanket Drake had brought and pulled it over his head. Albert's action freed the wooden shaft of the rune carved Staff of Orkan. Drake saw it, and he remembered.

"Mark," Drake said quickly. "Stop on the other side of the bridge. Make sure you're clear from the edge of the bridge though."

Mark nodded, not knowing what his brother was thinking, but so far he had been right and they were still alive. The car bounced and shook as it sped over the old bridge. As soon as Mark was over the bridge he turned towards the shoulder and slammed on his breaks, coming to a sideways stop, his car still idling and pointing in the direction he needed to go to Carmen's house, if he needed to go quickly. Martin saw what Mark did, and he slid to a smoking stop just beyond Mark, his car still facing down the road. On the other side of the bridge the tornado churned on itself. The wind howled and cackled like a thousand ghouls laughing at their predicament. The tornado began to try and cross the bridge.

Drake saw what was happening, and reached into the back seat. His left hand found the cool wood of the staff. He grabbed it and opened the door.

"What the hell are you doing?" Mark shouted at Drake.

Drake didn't hear his brother. He rose out of the car and shifted the Staff of Orkan to his right hand. He paced towards the middle of the road, and then turned to face the bridge.

The blackness of the death storm began to sweep over the

river, the cars rocking in the wind. Churning images of ghosts filled the blackness across the bridge from him.

"Drake!" Martin shouted.

The blackness crept forward slowly onto the bridge.

Drake looked down and saw the runes on the staff had begun to glow blue.

"Du skal ikke passere," Drake shouted. The massive blackness stopped momentarily, and then lurched forward again. The winds picked up speed and threw chunks of rocks and trees against Drake making him stumble.

"Ved kraften av de Stanget av Orkan," Drake shouted as he raised the staff upward. Lightning arced off the metal end of the staff and shot into the tornado. "Være borte!"

The lightning forced the black mass to pull into itself. The spinning debris crashed into the side of the bridge, rocking it. With a thunderous moan the seething storm collapsed in on itself and was gone, leaving a huge mess of rocks and trees all over the roadway.

Drake turned and ran back to Mark's car. He came around the front, and opened the door. He held onto the staff as he climbed in, closing the door behind him.

"That was awesome!" Mark said. "Where did you get that?"

"Hurricane Ridge," Drake replied.

"What did you say?" Mark asked. "It wasn't English."

"I don't know," Drake answered. "It just came to me. I think it might've been Norwegian."

Martin started to pull away, driving down the road towards Aunt Carmen's.

"Go," Albert said as he pointed to Martin's car ahead of them.

Mark stepped down hard on the accelerator and they raced off behind Martin.

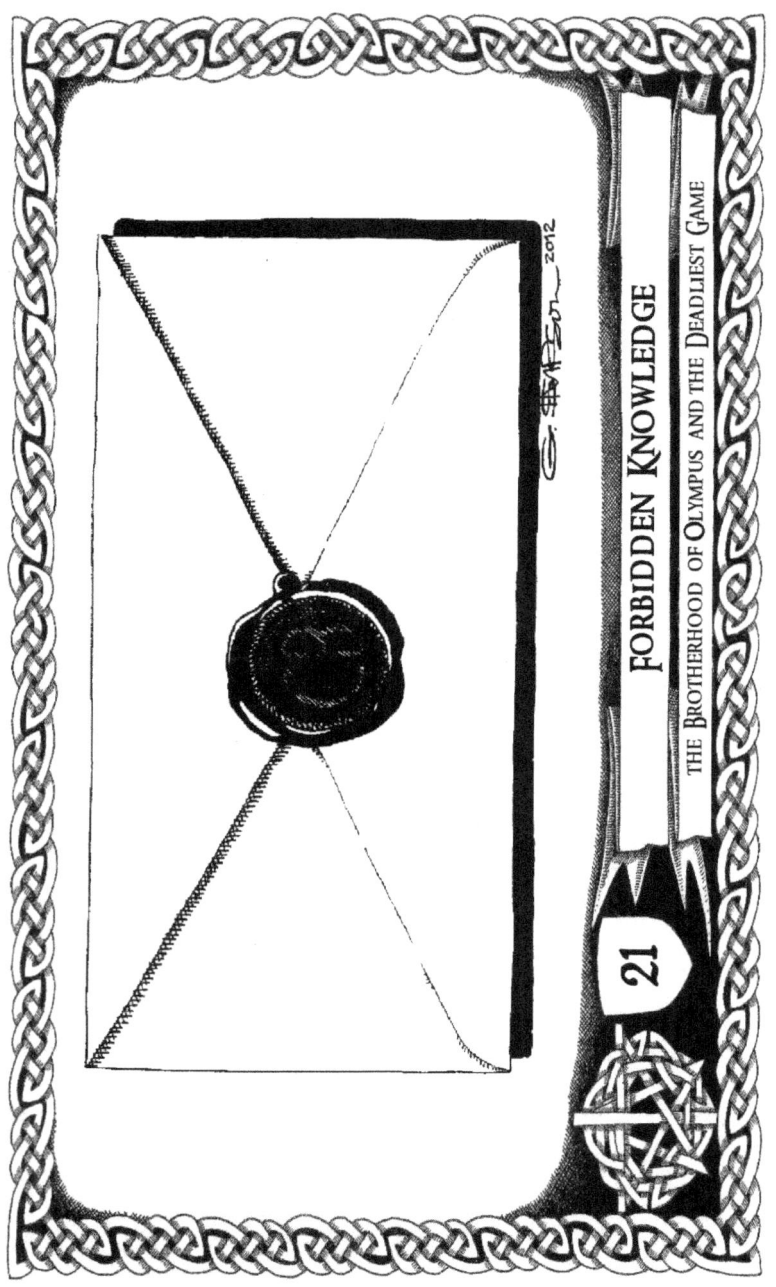

## The Council of Aunt Carmen
## Chapter Twenty-One
## June 27, 1979
## Brooklyn, Washington

They passed Sprucedale Road, and then turned soon after on the ambling private road that led them to the west. Martin pulled off the road and on to the long gravel driveway that led up to Aunt Carmen's house. There was a noticeable change in the environment when they left the main road. A sense of easiness, or peace, permeated the air. The feeling of being pursued and the lingering fear of what they had faced faded and was replaced by a nurturing calmness. Mark pulled into the driveway behind him.

The two cars, damaged, beaten, and looking worse than they ever had idled smoothly next to each other. Martin shut off his car and pulled the keys. He jumped out and came over to talk to Drake.

Mark and Drake had gotten out of Mark's car. He had left the motor running, 'just in case,' he told Drake as they exited the car. Albert climbed out after Drake. He couldn't help but notice the battered side of Mark's car.

"Oh, Mark isn't gonna like this," Albert said as he looked at the long dent in the side of the car from the tree that nearly toppled them on the logging road.

Dennis was sitting up, rubbing his head, and looking like the sunlight was too bright for his eyes.

"Drake," Martin said as he came up and hugged his brother. "Where did you learn that? Where did you get that staff?"

243

"Hurricane Ridge," Drake answered. He was still unable to explain how he did what he did, standing there facing the churning darkness. "I don't know, it just kinda happened. I'd forgotten I brought the staff, but Albert knocked it out of the blanket when he grabbed it to cover himself."

Albert perked up. That was pretty close to 'Thank Albert for saving us,' which was pretty cool to him. "It was pretty scary, huh?"

"How's Dennis?" Drake asked Martin. "Is he okay?"

"He was passed out through the whole drive here," Martin said. "I think he fainted."

"Ouch!" Dennis yelled from inside Martin's car. He had begun to notice the cuts and gashes from the blackberry briars on his arms and legs. Some of the thorns had broken off in his skin. Martin had dragged him rapidly and forcefully through the brush. "Who's the dillhole that threw me in the blackberry briars?"

Dennis got out of Martin's car to join his brothers. He walked with a grossly exaggerated limp. His brothers were amazed he could walk with the limp he possessed. He was shocked by the damage to the cars.

"What happened to your cars?" Dennis asked, assembling a feasible time line of events in his head. "You two crashed into each other and I flew out into the blackberry briars, didn't you? I'm telling Mom."

Martin and Mark looked at each other and shook their heads… and in that moment of absurdity they laughed.

It was then that they noticed Aunt Carmen was walking to them along the side of her house. She was clearly very pregnant, her long dark brown hair hung loosely beside her face, strands of her hair pulled back into a loose ponytail. She smiled at them as she approached.

"What're you guys up to?" Carmen asked as she continued to walk to them. "The radio just said that there were unconfirmed reports of a tornado touching down in the North River area, can you believe that? There's never been a tornado sighting here. It's probably not safe for you guys to be out driving around. Oh, but from the looks of your cars it seems like you know that already."

"Aunt Carmen," Martin began. "We went to find Wally's glasses. The *Spirit* board told us that if we found them we could stop the lawsuit."

"Who used it?" Carmen asked.

"Dennis and I did," Martin responded.

"Where did you two use it?" Carmen continued, searching for the precise information that would help her make sense of the situation.

"On Wally's grave," Martin replied. "But at first it wasn't Wally, it was the mordgeists, but I pushed them away through the board. Then Wally told us "

"What exactly did he say?" Carmen asked. "It's very critical that I hear exactly what was said."

"Well," Martin started, "at first it told us to find his glasses, and then that his glasses would enable us to see the truth. If we knew the truth then we could stop the lawsuit."

"That may be a good interpretation of what it said," Carmen replied. "But what were its precise answers?"

"It spelled out, 'find my glasses,'" Dennis interrupted. "And then it spelled, 'glasses see truth.' Which, made me ask, 'where they were at,' and it spelled out 'at site.' Then Martin asked, 'where at the site,' and it said, 'don't know can't see there.'"

Everyone turned and looked at Dennis in amazement. He looked back at them, shocked that they were all looking at him.

"What?" Dennis said somewhat annoyed by the staring.

"What did it say about the lawsuit, Dennis?" Carmen asked.

"Well, Martin asked, 'how can we stop the lawsuit?' And the board answered by spelling out, 'must break and burn evil,' and then it said 'good-bye' and was silent," Dennis explained.

"So it said you must break and burn evil," Carmen pondered the possibilities.

"What does that mean?" Mark asked. "Drake just broke some serious evil at the bridge."

Drake smiled, and Albert patted him on the back.

"Here's what I know, boys," Carmen began, "that *Spirit* board made a connection with some of you, and it has given gifts to you of knowledge and of power. It hasn't really given you the power beyond what you already possessed. We're a special family, with many secrets, and in time you would come to know many of them. But this board, it's thrown you into a struggle to rise up faster than you should have. I see that it pitted you against each other, and it exploited your weaknesses to try to drive you apart. The board's a powerful thing, but it's what's behind it that's even more powerful. I sense a very wicked entity, and at first I thought it was just me being a bit off in my judgment, which is why I used the board with you, Martin. But that night on my way home, I was attacked by some pretty nasty creatures on the bridge. They wanted my baby. They wanted the pure untainted life force of the La Madrid line. They wanted my child. Since then, both my baby and I've been off the grid. I've masked us and made us invisible to things that look for people like us. But I've not forgotten the list of predictions we got that night Martin, the first one was that I was pregnant. The accidents, the deaths it predicted, every one of them has come to pass so far."

Carmen pulled the envelope out from behind her.

"This knowledge," Carmen continued with tears forming in her eyes, "no one should have this much knowledge of their future. It's unholy, and as I realized after that night, it wasn't given to us freely from my brother, but some twisted entity that used my brother to hurt us."

"So what do we do?" Drake asked. "How do we fight it?"

"We never use that board again," Carmen started. "That board is a portal straight to these creatures that want to corrupt you and hurt you, and I would imagine they would try everything they could to kill you."

"That's not much of a fight," Mark added. "Sounds more

like running away."

"No, it's not much of a fight," Carmen said. "The alternative is to destroy the board."

"That doesn't sound hard," Albert said. "It's just a game, right?"

"Wait," Carmen realized something as she finally registered all of what Dennis had said about the board. "It told you two, to stop the lawsuit you had to break and burn the evil. The evil is the board. To stop the lawsuit and all the other things that have been happening—the attacks on me, your death tornado, and whatever else you have faced since that board came into your lives, you have to break it. You have to not just break it, it needs to be burned. It must be destroyed."

Albert thought to himself, 'how did Aunt Carmen know that I called that icky black storm a death tornado none of us said that name to her? It's almost like she read my mind.'

"I did, Albert," Aunt Carmen stated as Albert's eyes grew incredibly wide.

"We can break it and we can burn it," Mark said. "It's just a piece of wood, right Albert?"

Albert nodded with a smile.

"Burning it would work," Carmen said. "Just make sure you burn all of it."

The boys looked at each other, and they knew they had to do this last thing. They had to destroy the *Spirit* board that plagued them this last year.

"Come with us Aunt Carmen," Dennis asked.

"I cannot go," Carmen replied. "But I will do what I can for you. I'll go out and let them see me," she motioned down to her pregnant belly, "I will let them see *us*, and I will lead their attention away from Mom and Dad's house. It should make it safer for you."

"That doesn't sound safer for you," Mark said.

"I'll be alright," Carmen replied. "I'll draw them away. I'll give you thirty minutes, and then I'll disappear and lose them. Once this is done they'll not bother us again. It's the board that's marked us for them to see us, and I won't use one again."

Martin and Dennis got back into the Datsun. Martin started the car. Mark and Albert climbed in the Impala, and Drake waited for Albert to get in the backseat.

"Drake," Carmen stated as she handed him the envelope, "burn this too, make sure we get rid of all of it."

Drake nodded, and then climbed in the car. Mark revved the engine. The two battered blue cars began to rumble down the long driveway.

"Thirty minutes," Carmen said. "And don't let it divide you. Be safe, my nephews."

**22**

THE **BROTHERHOOD**
OF **OLYMPUS**

THE BROTHERHOOD OF OLYMPUS
AND THE DEADLIEST GAME

## The Brotherhood of Olympus
## Chapter Twenty-Two
## June 27, 1979
## Brooklyn, Washington

They quickly drove the miles of country roads towards their grandparent's house. A dark feeling had settled upon them when they left Carmen's driveway, and it had gotten worse as they drove. Albert hid under the blanket in the back seat, peering out from behind it. Drake reached back and touched his brother on the arm to reassure him. Albert popped his head up and forced a smile.

The mid-afternoon sky had darkened above them as thick dreary clouds piled on top of each other in a mammoth column, not to the intensity of the death tornado in its sheer blackness, but darker than a typical storm cloud blotting out the sunlight. As they neared their grandparents' driveway, they noticed the clouds break up and begin to move rapidly to the west before turning north. Aunt Carmen had just made herself a target.

"We have thirty minutes," Drake said to Mark. "She just left, and pulled their attention away from us."

"Then we better get this done," Mark replied.

Martin drove in first and parked. Mark followed and parked next to his brother. Albert immediately noticed that the house was dark, and their grandparents' fifth-wheel trailer was gone.

"Where's Grandma and Grandpa?" Albert questioned.

"They're at the square dancing convention by Everett, with Mom and Dad," Mark answered. "Right?"

Drake nodded.

The boys looked at each other and got out of the car. Martin and Dennis were already standing beside the Datsun. The five of them stood together in a makeshift circle between the two cars in the grey gravel driveway.

They exchanged glances, and no one spoke.

"Aunt Carmen drew them away, like she said," Drake finally said, breaking the very awkward silence.

They all nodded.

"So," Mark said. "Where's the board?"

"Up in Wally's old room," Martin responded.

Buddy the large Saint Bernard ambled over to the group and stood there contently, drool pooling on his hanging lower lip.

"So go in and get it," Mark told Martin.

"I'm not going in," Martin responded. "Besides, the front door is locked."

"Then how do we get in to get the board?" Drake asked.

"The back kitchen door, on the deck, it's usually unlocked for me," Martin explained, "if Grandma or Grandpa know I'm going to be here."

"Okay," Mark said. "So go check if it's unlocked, and then go in and grab the board. We'll wait for you out here."

"I told you," Martin asserted, "I am not going in there by myself."

"Let's send Drake," Dennis added. "He's not scared of anything."

"He does have that staff, too," Mark added, pointing at the wooden staff in Drake's left hand. Drake shook his head.

"Mark," Martin stated. "Why don't you go, you have never used the board and it wouldn't even bother you."

"Yeah," Dennis added. "Let's send Mark."

Mark shook his head.

"I know," Dennis continued, "let's send Albert. He's the smallest and it wouldn't even know he was in there."

Albert turned white at the thought.

"Dennis you go," Albert remarked as he stood up tall next

to Dennis showing that he was no longer the shortest Fraser boy. "You're the shortest."

"How about just Mark and Drake," Martin said. Drake and Mark shook their heads.

Drake was getting upset by the lack of decision making ability they possessed. The thirty minutes Aunt Carmen was buying them by risking her life was slipping away. He finally snapped.

"Listen," Drake began as he stepped into the middle of the circle and turned to face each of them as he talked. "All of you. Aunt Carmen pulled their attention away from us, she gave us thirty minutes, and we are standing out here wasting it because none of us want to go into that house by ourselves. I don't care who is youngest, or biggest, or who used the board the most, or the least, or who is more scared or not. None of that matters. What matters is that here, on this day, June twenty-seventh, 1979, five brothers stood together. Five brothers stood here with different likes, dislikes, and views of the world, five brothers who sometimes seem to have nothing in common but the blood in our veins. We don't have to like each other, we don't have to be friends with each other, but no one can remove the one thing that binds us, our brotherhood. And that brotherhood is based on the love we have known for each other since we were little. Up until this last year, none of us could have imagined a future where we weren't together. That bond was strong. This past year we have been tested, sorely tested. But through it all our hearts have been pure. We've done only what we thought was best. Even if no one else could see that, I see that, I see all of that now. Like the ancient Teutonic knights who went before us, they had five in their Brotherhood who stood together and they knew one simple truth, united we stand, divided we fall. Geez, that's even a motto of our country. Why would we let fear divide us now, as we stand here united to challenge the greatest adversary we've ever faced? I found this staff on the foothills of Mount Olympus and by its power I say this to you, my brothers. I say we go in there together, as brothers should, I say today we stand together as the Brotherhood of Olympus!"

They stood there shocked. They all knew Drake was smart, and good with words, they just had never heard him string so many together at a single time before without it being a lecture about history or science, or some other academic subject. He was convincing and certainly motivational. Drake moved back into the circle and stuck his hand in, like he had so many times playing basketball. Albert immediately placed his hand on top of Drake's, with a frightened smile. Drake raised an eyebrow to him. Mark placed his hand on top of Albert's and squeezed both hands below his to show his solidarity. Martin looked at the three of them and knew he had to join with them. He stepped in and placed his hand on top of Mark's.

The four of them looked at Dennis. He was unsure of himself, but knew he didn't want to be left out there by himself so he reluctantly placed his hand on top of Martin's. The runes on the Staff of Orkan flared a faint blue.

That moment in time, a singular event, with such a wide range of consequences that rippled through realities and dimensions unknown to them, was recorded by Elders of a mystic race, as the modern founding of the Brotherhood of Olympus.

23

## INTO THE ABYSS

### THE BROTHERHOOD OF OLYMPUS
### AND THE DEADLIEST GAME

**Ascent into Madness**
**Chapter Twenty-Three**
**June 27, 1979**
**Brooklyn, Washington**

The five brothers stood, hands on top of each other forming an uneven pentacle. Drake had rallied them in their moment of need. Now they looked at each other.

"Ready," Mark said. "Break."

Mark pushed his hand down with a chuckle and began walking around the back of the house towards the wide stairs that led up to the large back deck. Drake shook his head at the nonchalant way Mark broke their circle and followed him towards the back stairs. Martin, Albert, Dennis, and Buddy followed in that order around the house.

They walked up the stairs cautiously, the dark pillar of clouds was far on the horizon, and they all hoped Carmen was still safe.

Mark and Drake reached the back kitchen door, and then stepped to the side and waited for Martin to arrive. The house was dark inside and deathly quiet. Martin opened the white metal and glass storm door. He adjusted the hydraulic door closing mechanism at the top to keep the door propped all the way open.

"Is it locked?" Dennis asked from the back of the group.

Martin reached for the doorknob and turned it, opening the door to the white tiled kitchen. Buddy immediately turned and went down the deck stairs as fast as his large body would take him.

"What's wrong with Buddy?" Albert asked. "Come here

Buddy, Buddy," and then he attempted to whistle.  It was a whistle like sound but it was far from a whistle.

"Now," Mark added with a laugh, "you've really scared him."

Martin stepped into the house.  He turned to the right and began to silently walk across the kitchen floor in front of the deep double sinks and the window out to the deck.  Albert smiled and waved to him.

Mark looked at Drake, and then stepped in to follow Martin.  Drake took a deep breath and followed Mark.  Inside, Martin had turned to the left to face the doorway out of the kitchen into the hallway.  Across the hallway were the steep stairs down to the lower floor and the front door beyond.  Martin stepped into the hallway.  Mark followed him to the edge of the kitchen.  Drake stood behind Mark, the Staff of Orkan in his left hand.  Dennis and Albert were now inside the kitchen.  Albert flipped the light switch in the kitchen.

The kitchen lights flickered on.  Taking Albert's idea, Mark reached the central light switches at the top of the stairs and turned lights on in the living room, the hallway, and the hanging light above the landing near the bottom of the stairs.

Martin continued to sneak stealthily down the hallway, and Mark followed casting his shadow onto Martin from the hallway light.  Drake stepped down the hallway until he came to see the photograph of the five boys in DeWitt Park from 1965.  He stopped there and waited.  Dennis wouldn't come farther than the end of the kitchen.  He dared not get too close to the stairs.  Albert peered down the hallway partially behind him.

Martin put his hand to the bedroom doorknob and turned it, opening the door.  His stuff was in Wally's old room.  A lot of his clothes were scattered on the bed, some on the floor, and his Air Force uniform was hung in the open closet.  There at the foot of the bed, on a few cardboard boxes, sat the open game box.  The *Spirit* board sat on top of the empty box.

"There it is," Mark said from the doorway. "Grab it."

Martin reached out and grabbed the board. As if it began to sense why they were there, the *Spirit* board awoke.

"Let's go," Martin said as he walked past Mark and out into the hallway. He decided to be quick and break the board. He placed one end in his left hand, one end in his right and he pushed them together with all his strength. To his surprise the board gave no resistance, his knuckles crashed into each other as the board bent like it was made of rubber.

"It's pressboard," Drake said. "Pressboard doesn't bend, it breaks!"

A wind began to blow down the hallway from Wally's room, the pictures in the hallways began to flutter, or the ones in frames began to swing on their hanging wires. The wind pelted the backs of Mark and Martin, stinging like hundreds of pieces of sharp broken glass. The lights in Wally's room popped and went out with a spark. The hanging light in the stairwell swung from side to side, banging the wall, like it was on a ship in rough seas. Drake moved Mark and Martin past him and into the kitchen.

The wind whipped in the dining room door at the far end and blew back on the boys in the kitchen, pushing them back towards the hallway.

"Break the board!" Mark yelled to Martin.

"I tried!" Martin yelled back.

"He bent it end to end," Drake added. "It bent like it was rubber."

"It's a sheet of paper lacquered on a piece of pressboard," Mark rationalized. "It'll break. Let Drake and I try."

Mark reached out for the board. Drake set down the staff on the island counter in the middle of the kitchen and held out his hands to take one end of the board as well.

Martin placed one end of the board behind his belt buckle and firmly gripped the other end. He pulled the board back into his abdomen, folding it on itself again, but this time it snapped jaggedly in two pieces. Martin looked up and smiled.

The house shook on its foundation like a minor earthquake had just rumbled through. The wind stung their exposed flesh. Martin lifted the broken board up, but it held together, the lacquered paper held the two pieces of wood, damaged, and dangling, but still together.

The boys looked at the determined board. Martin took hold of each piece of the board, and twisted while pulling them apart in opposite directions. The paper tore from the wood. An ear piercing shriek rang out in the house. Martin dropped the two pieces of the broken board to the floor and held up his hands. His fingers and palms boasted large white burn blisters. He screamed in pain. Both Dennis and Martin buckled over, violently ill, vomit shooting onto the floor. The lights in the kitchen blew out in a large shower of sparks.

The house shifted, like a carnival ride. The doorway to the deck was now up, and the doorway to the hall and the stairway beyond was straight down. Martin and Mark immediately grabbed onto the counters; Dennis, on his knees, was not that fortunate. He slid through his own vomit and was falling towards the stairway, the stairway he had always feared. Horror overtook Dennis, his eyes rolled back, and he fainted as he slipped past Martin and Mark towards the flashing strobe of the stairway light below him. The stairway had opened up into a bottomless abyss beyond the flashes of the light. Hot flashes of air rumbled up out of the darkness below.

As Dennis fell out of the kitchen, an arm reached for him and grabbed his shoulder, taking grip of his shirt. Drake held onto his brother and would not let go.

"Dennis!" Drake shouted at him. "Dennis! Wake up! Dennis!"

Dennis slid further down, and Drake's grip slowly slid down his arm as Dennis swung there, being held up by his left arm. Dennis fell further in the abyss of the stairway. Drake now only had him by the wrist. Mark dropped down on the wall beside Drake and reached for Dennis. He managed to grab hold of the same wrist Drake held.

"Dennis!" Mark shouted. "Quit faking! Help us or you're going to die, you dillhole!"

Dennis turned and looked up at his brothers. Tears ran down his cheeks and his eyes were filled with terror.

"Grab our hands!" Mark shouted.

"Don't look down!" Drake shouted at his brother.

Below the suspended form of Dennis a snaking purple tentacle covered with festering sores rose out of the abyss of the stairway, searching for Dennis. It rose slowly and steadily, tapping the wall and the carpeted stairs as it neared his legs. Dennis did what anyone does when told not to look down. He looked down and saw the tentacle nearing him. He screamed in horror. Albert had slid down, and was looking through the doorway over Drake's shoulder. He screamed for the safety of his brother, right in the ear of Drake, making him loosen his grip. Dennis shifted down lower, as Drake tightened his grip once more on the outstretched hand of his brother. Mark now held more of the weight of Dennis.

The tentacle found his leg and began to wrap around it, where it touched his skin above his sock it seared his flesh. Dennis cried out in pain.

"Pull!" Mark barked at Drake. "Pull him up."

The tentacle matched their tug. Dennis was suspended between the equal forces that pulled him in opposite directions.

"Give us your other hand Dennis!" Drake yelled at him.

Martin had climbed up from the counter he initially grabbed, hoping to find his way to the door and the exit above. He now hung unto the porcelain of the kitchen sink and the cabinet door below the sink. He felt his strength failing and his blistered skin racked him with pain. He knew that when he fell he would take Dennis and perhaps Drake and Mark with him. He had to stay strong.

"Dennis!" Albert shouted in a moment of clarity. "Throw something at it!"

"What's he going to throw?" Mark asked. "He's hangin'

down there by one arm."

"The staff!" Albert said as he began to look for the staff.

"No!" Drake shouted. "He cannot throw the staff, it's too important, we need it."

"More than your brother!" shouted Albert.

Dennis heard what Albert said. Throw something at it. What could he throw hanging down here? He didn't have anything to throw, his hand was empty, and his pockets were empty, wait that wasn't right. He had carried a handful of bottle caps in his pocket since last summer when he learned how to do telekinesis with the *Spirit* board. He reached down and slid his hand into his jeans pocket and pulled out a couple bottle caps. He thought painful thoughts into those bottle caps, acidic painful thoughts, and then he dropped them onto the tentacle around his leg. They hit the tentacle and burned into its flesh, one went clean through the purple flesh, the other burned down the length of the tentacle as it rolled and tumbled into the abyss. The tentacle suddenly released his leg. Just as fast, it rose up again to grab him. He already had more bottle caps in his hand. Explosive, acidic thoughts he loaded into these bottle caps and then he released them. They blew up on impact with the tentacle like cherry bombs filled with acid and they took the end of the tentacle completely off.

With Dennis being free of the abyssal tentacle Mark and Drake began to muscle him upward. The going was slow, and their arms ached from holding Dennis for so long.

Suddenly Albert stood over the doorway looking down the hole, and he threw the staff down.

"Noooo!" shouted Drake as he saw the staff go over his head and down the hole. Albert's act of sacrifice didn't go unnoticed. A blinding blue light filled the house. Drake and Mark pulled Dennis up with a thud and they all fell on the floor, the house was back to the way it had always been. Dennis held the Staff of Orkan in his right hand.

"Nice catch," Mark said to Dennis who smiled back at him.

"I always knew that was gonna happen," Dennis announced as he stood up. "That's why I've never liked those stairs."

The rest of them climbed back onto their feet as the wind picked up in intensity. Albert screamed in horror, darkness took shape in the wind, tattered gray and black robes hung in both the dining room and kitchen doorways. The hooded robes shrouded the vile forms of the mordgeists who had tormented them for so long.

"Out of the house!" Mark yelled.

Drake helped Dennis, and Mark assisted Martin as they hurried out of the house. Albert needed no prodding and was the first out.

They regrouped on the weathered wood of the deck. Albert looked in the distance and saw the towering black cloud mass. It appeared to be moving closer and getting larger on the horizon.

"We don't have much time," Albert said as he pointed off at the blackness. They all turned and looked. The approaching darkness hardened their resolve.

"We have to get the pieces of the board out of the house," Martin said, buckled over from the pain of his hands, "and then out into the burn barrel."

"Albert," Mark ordered as he pointed to the brooms and mops hanging from the wall past the kitchen. "Get me a broom!"

Albert quickly ran over to the wall-mounted rack and pulled down a yellow-handled broom. He turned to run back to Mark and saw the red eyes of the mordgeist staring at him through the kitchen window. He closed his eyes and almost ran off the edge of the deck. Luckily Mark caught him as he ran, and continued to run, even after Mark had picked him up.

"Drake, get your staff," Mark said, taking the broom from Albert. "You're going to force them back, and I'll sweep the pieces out. I don't want to touch it and burn my hands like Martin."

Dennis gladly gave the wooden staff back to his brother. Drake held the staff in both hands, left hand above the right. Behind him Mark stood with the broom.

"Ready?" Mark asked.

"No," Drake responded, but he stepped into the house anyway. The winds tore into them, ripping their shirts on their seams. Drake looked through squinted eyes for the position of the mordgeists. The *Spirit* board pieces were to the right between the island and the sink. Drake stood tall in the kitchen. Mark slipped into the kitchen near the floor and quickly found the pieces of the broken board. Mark brought the broom down and swept the first piece over by the door in one hard push. He reached and got the bristles of the broom on the second piece and flicked it over by the door too.

Mark began to back out of the house, and he tapped Drake as he moved past him. With a sudden flurry the mordgeists descended in two directions upon Drake. He spun the staff out of his left hand and fully into his right, with a hurried stroke the staff struck the skull of the first mordgeist with a shower of blue sparks sending it crashing into the coffee mugs hanging on the side wall of the kitchen. The second mordgeist blew by, raking its skeletal fingers on Drake's left arm drawing blood through his torn shirt. Drake winced at the sharp pain in his arm. The mordgeist against the wall began to rise, and it turned to look at him. Its skeletal face, filled with sharp teeth, seemed a bit different than before. As it turned completely towards him, Drake saw that the left side of its head was shattered, its left eye was black, and fragments of bone hung on tendrils of oozing ectoplasm that blew in the wind. Its right eye flared red. Drake felt the pain and hatred radiate from it as it rushed him.

"Clickety, click, now you die!" the mordgeist shouted as it surged at him. Drake braced the Staff of Orkan before him in both hands, the head of the staff facing the oncoming mordgeist.

The mordgeist hit him, knocking him backwards. Its

hands tore at his shoulders as its shattered face lowered towards Drake. It opened its mouth, and the teeth, hundreds of teeth, each a dagger sharp point, poised to tear at him.

"Not today, you bastard!" Drake snapped back as a blast of blue lightning tore through the body of the mordgeist as he lifted the mighty staff into its body. A final surge of blue energy blew the broken skull flying into the far corner of the kitchen shattering it into hundreds of fragments.

Mark worked feverishly trying to remove the board pieces from the house. Once he was behind Drake he stepped out onto the deck and reached in to sweep the pieces out, one at a time. The first piece lay under the bristles of the broom, and he pulled it across the floor to the threshold of the door. That's where it stopped. Their grandfather had never actually installed a door jam on this back door, so there was a small gap between the door and the floor, which they always covered with a towel on the inside to keep the cold out and the heat in. There was nothing there to stop this piece of broken pressboard from coming out of the house. But there it stood. Right on the edge of the threshold and it would not budge, no matter how hard he pushed on the broom. Finally, out of frustration more than logic, he reached down and grabbed the torn piece of lacquered paper sticking up on the board, thinking it would burn him, and quickly lifted it and tossed it backwards over the deck railing in one sudden motion. Below, as the broken piece of *Spirit* board hit the green grass, Buddy turned and ran away from where he had been watching the boys.

"Drake!" Mark shouted into the windy house, hoping his brother could hear him. "Come on, we got them out!"

Drake turned and began to step out of the house. The remaining mordgeist rushed towards him as he stepped outside, stopping at the threshold as if a barrier prevented it from leaving.

"Weee ssshall hunt you forever," the mordgeist said as it towered up over Drake in the doorway. Below it on the threshold sat the final piece of the board, its torn lacquered paper sticking up.

Mark looked at Drake, they both looked at the board piece and then at the ghastly mordgeist above it.

Mark suddenly reached for the board piece with his right hand, his speed amazing Drake. It didn't impress the mordgeist, however. As his fingers grabbed the paper the mordgeists icy grip settled on his hand.

"Nnnnot over," the mordgeist hissed, its toothy mouth right above Mark's head.

"Duck!" shouted Drake. Mark did just that, but the mordgeist didn't. Instead it rose up, allowing the uppercut motion of the staff to push its skull straight up into the beam over the door with a sickening crack of the bone fracturing. The blue light that flashed off the staff ignited the ooze that flew out of the broken mordgeist, showering both Drake and Mark in shimmering blue ectoplasm that simmered and popped into vapor.

Mark rose up defiantly and flipped the last piece of the board out of the kitchen and into the yard below.

24

SUCCORBENOTH
IN FLAMES

THE BROTHERHOOD OF OLYMPUS
AND THE DEADLIEST GAME

## The Fire of Redemption
## Chapter Twenty-Four
## June 27, 1979
## Brooklyn, Washington

The Fraser boys stood on the raised back deck of their grandparents' house, all shaken, sore, ill, or wounded from their encounter in the house with the *Spirit* board and its mordgeist minions. All they wanted to do was to rest from the frantic fight, but one quick glance to the rapidly approaching black tower of clouds in the distance made them realize they weren't done. The board still sat, broken in two pieces, yet whole.

"Come on," Mark insisted, "we have to go burn it before that cloud gets here."

"Cloud of death," Albert said as he stared at it in the distance bringing back the all too fresh memory of the seething black tornado they had already faced today. Mark and Drake looked at Albert and shook their heads. "I'm just saying it seems an awful lot like the other one."

Mark walked to the edge of the deck, peered over the railing and saw the two pieces of the *Spirit* board lying in the green grass below. He started to walk the length of the deck towards the wide stairs leading down. Drake, carrying the Staff of Orkan in his right hand, followed him. Albert quickly started after his brothers. Only Dennis and Martin lingered on the deck for a moment, both feeling nauseated still, and physically exhausted from hanging over the abyss of the stairway.

Mark looked at the first piece of the board in the grass

below him. He pinched the edge of the paper with his scratched and bloodied right hand and picked it up. The grass below the flat of the board was brown and shriveled like it had been sprayed with grass killer. The irregular rectangle would never grow grass again, it would remain parched and dead, no matter what their grandparents did to it to try and revive it.

Mark quickly carried the piece of the board across the yard to the rusted hulk of the burn barrel that rested on gray cinder blocks along the fence that bordered the sweeping fields of their great-grandparents' property.

The fields were home to several of their great-grandfather's horses. Long gone were the massive Clydesdales, Percherons, Shires, and Belgians that he used to use when they horse logged the forests. Now their great-grandfather kept only a few Quarter Horses and Palominos whose white coloring made them look like ghosts of the long departed draft horses in the late afternoon mist rising up from the river.

Drake and Albert made it to the burn barrel and looked in at the piece of game board lying on the pile of ashen soot that filled the bottom three quarters of the fifty-five gallon drum. Mark went back and grabbed the second piece of the board in the same manner as he had the first. The grass below it was also ruined and in stark contrast to the lush green of the grass around it.

Martin and Dennis slowly made it to the side of the burn barrel as Mark quickly moved past them and dropped the second piece of the board into the barrel with a small thump that raised a small cloud of ash.

Mark pulled out his silver lighter from his pocket, flipped the cap open, and struck the flint with his thumb. A steady flame danced above the lighter. Mark lowered his hand into the barrel and put the flame on the underside of the torn lacquered paper. He held it there for a long period of time. The lighter finally became hot and he had to close it, but the paper didn't ignite. It didn't even darken from direct exposure to the flame.

Dennis stared into the burn barrel at the broken form of the *Spirit* board. He then had a sudden realization.

"What about the pointer," Dennis asked as he pointed at the board pieces. "It has to be burned too."

"Where's the pointer?" Mark asked.

"In the box," Martin stated. "At the foot of the bed."

"Back in the house?" Albert said as he shook his head.

"Let's go," Mark said as he motioned towards the black tower of clouds that was nearly to their great-grandfathers property.

"I can't go back in there," Martin said as he pointed to Dennis. "We'd just slow you down."

"Just send Albert," Dennis said. "He's not hurt or sick. He can just run in and grab it."

"I'll go," Drake said as he looked at Mark.

"Let's go then, little brother," Mark said as he patted Drake on the shoulder with his uninjured left hand.

Both Mark and Drake began to head to the stairs of the deck. Albert ran off after them.

"I'm going too," Albert announced as he neared them.

Mark looked at Albert and then at Drake, and shook his head.

"Albert, you're going to have the most important job," Drake said as they walked up the wide wooden stairway. "You're going to keep the door open. Don't let it close. It has to stay open so Mark and I can come right out, got it?"

"Yep," Albert said. He was proud that he had the most important job, and he was equally happy that he didn't have to go in the house to do it. "I got it."

The three boys neared the propped open storm door and the still open kitchen door. Mark looked down and saw Martin and Dennis standing beside the burn barrel, and then looked up to notice how close the black clouds had gotten. They only had a few minutes to go before it was in their great-grandfather's fields. Time was running out.

Drake thought about the burning-hot board pieces. The

pointer was likely to be equally hot or dangerous to touch. If only they had something to carry it in.

"Mark," Drake began, "does Grandma still collect grocery bags in the cupboard by the door? If she does, we can take one and put the pointer in it so we don't have to touch it and risk being burned, or worse."

"Good idea," Mark said. "Let's go. Remember Albert, keep this door open."

"I got it," Albert answered. "I got it."

"Little brother," Mark stated as he turned to Drake, "I want you to know something before we go in there. You and I have always been together, I trust you with my life, and I think you feel the same. I love you. No matter what happens, I will always be there for you. You got that?"

"Ditto." Drake nodded since he was not good with statements of emotions.

"Me too!" exclaimed Albert as he prepared for his job.

Mark and Drake stepped in to the house. Mark immediately opened the cupboard by the door and grabbed a handful of the brown paper grocery bags. He began to open one, and then he slipped a second one inside it and opened them both together.

"We're gonna double bag it," Mark said with a smile, "in case it happens to start to burn through one bag."

The two brothers turned and Drake took the lead holding the staff before him in his right hand. Mark followed him closely with the open paper bag. As they neared the hallway the house rumbled. A gust of wind raced down the hall, and the outside kitchen door slammed shut.

Albert's eyes opened wide. He turned the knob and pushed in on the door but it refused to yield.

"Holy spumoni!" Albert exclaimed as he began to throw his shoulder into the door trying to force it open. "I get one job and I can't even do it."

Drake and Mark didn't hear the door slam, nor could they hear the repetitive thumping of Albert's shoulder as he threw himself again and again against the wooden door in a vain attempt to open it.    Somewhere in the house a musical instrument began to play, a banjo perhaps.   Or was it a wind-up music box?   It plunked along at an irregular pace.   Then the warbling voice echoed down the hallway.

*Thank you for your concern, but I must refuse your aid,*
*No matter how dark it get I'm really not afraid,*

The song haunted the boys in its eerie echoing and unseen place of origin.   They turned and began down the hallway.

"Where's the music coming from, Drake?"

Drake shook his head and slowly began to advance down the hall some more.   The house shook violently and they had to put their hands on the walls to steady themselves.

*I know you're a thinkin' I'm all depressed,*
*But my life's not as bad as you seem to suggest,*

They felt like they were being watched.   They looked at the walls, the walls filled with pictures of the family, and those same pictures were now different.   Inside each of the pictures, the people had turned their heads to look at them, and their smiling faces had turned angry and full of hatred.

*Seeing shadows from the sun move across my floor,*

The photographs took life and the black and white, and color images of their family turned on them.    Little arms reached out of the pictures grabbing for them.   Angry faces shouted angry words at them, and yet the scariest of them was the incessant laughter, the cackling of hundreds of mocking images.   The dark wind blew down the hallway into their faces, yet still they advanced step by step.

*Playin' chess by myself with nothin' but pawns,*
*Watchin' Mister Rogers, and drinkin' beer,*

With the bass voice of 'Rogers' they heard Albert's shrill giggle and it made them stop and turn to look for him, but the giggle echoed around them, fading in and out.   They had no way to tell where it came from, or whether it really was Albert.

*My life ain't perfect, but I got nothin' to fear,*

The house rumbled and shook with a massive groaning that chilled them to the bone.   The house seemed to be trying to bust loose of the foundation. The shaking knocked them into the wall, and they noticed that the texture of the wall had changed. It was now slimy, like thick gooey paste, and stuck to their hands as they righted themselves.

*The shadows sometimes tell me things I don't wanna hear,*
*The darkness might consume a lesser man I fear,*

The door at the end of the hall, Wally's door, blew open and spectral light beamed into their eyes and flashed in an uneven strobe. A wave of nausea crashed over them and they both fought back the vomit that forced its way up their esophagi.

The house tore at its foundation again, knocking them into the larger portraits on the wall. The steely fingers of the animated photographs grabbed at and ripped their clothes, their hair, and their skin. The large portrait of their grandparents yelled at them, and their possessed grandfather spit at them. The gauntlet of pictures attacking them ate away at their confidence, lowered their drive, and stalled their ambition.

*In spite of your charm you really are quite nosy,*
*And after you leave me, I'll really get busy,*

Drake turned back to look at Mark. Fear had overtaken them both. Together they had faced down the wicked mordgeists, and now this chilling music, the house fighting them, the horrible laughter, and the harassment from the hundreds of photographs had stopped them. They were within feet of the doorway, yet to them it seemed like hundreds of times as far.

Mark shook his head as he looked into Drake's eyes. Then he noticed the blue charm hanging around Drake's neck. It began to shine with its own light. A spot of brilliant gold light had emerged, and that growing orb of light reassured the frightened heart of Mark.

*Seeing shadows from the sun move across my floor,*
*Playin' chess by myself with nothin' but pawns,*

Mark reached up and touched the charm, unafraid of the light. The glow radiated through his flesh and grew brighter, stronger, and more vibrant.

Drake felt his body regaining strength, his blood filled with fire, chasing the cold dampness of fear from his body.

*Watchin' Mister Rogers, and drinkin' beer,*
*My life ain't perfect, but I got nothin' to fear,*

Albert's shrill laughter came again but this time they remained focused as they advanced on the door again, the light from the star-cross charm challenging the spectral light from inside the room.

They made it to the bedroom. The light of the star-cross shone brightly. At the foot of the bed sat the planchette on top of a cardboard box. Beyond that a ghostly image of a large muscular daemon radiated, like it was stuck in a form of limbo between where it belonged and where it wanted to be. It was neither tangible nor transparent. It was caught. It stood over seven feet tall, its sinewy form radiating a purplish black light that spun about it like the storm they had faced earlier in the day. Its hideous face was framed by long, unkempt wisps of fiery red hair, like a matted mane of a rabid lion. A dark magenta glow pulsed from its eyes as it stared at them. Its eyes knew them in an instant. It knew their fears, their desires, and their dreams. Its taut, charred skin pulled back to reveal a toothy smile, a smile filled with hundreds of razor sharp interlocking fangs. Its smile dominated its face. Its mouth seemed too large for its massive head.

*Even though I know I appear quite aghast,*
*I really do appreciate you forgettin' my past,*

Drake knew who this entity was in a flash.

"Succorbenoth," Drake said its name, binding it, and the brightness of the golden light of the star-cross charm blinding it.

Mark quickly stepped to the foot of the bed, seized the pointer in one quick motion and dropped it inside the brown paper bag, before rolling the top of the bag down to secure the contents inside it.

The image of the Daemon lord faded with the pointer safely in the bag. The boys turned and advanced back down the hallway as quickly as possible.

*Thank you for visitin' me, I know you gotta go,*
*The shadows are returning and they've seeds they gotta sow,*

They dodged insults and heckling, spit and ooze, down the hallway balancing by holding onto each other as the house shook violently. They made it to the doorway into the kitchen and saw the outside door was closed.

"Albert!" shouted Mark. "One simple job, one simple job."

As they passed through the kitchen the music stopped, the laughter and chatter down the hallway ended, and the house turned silent. A pleasant, disembodied voice whispered near their ears, its breath blowing across the hairs of their necks.

"Don't do this, boys," the feminine sounding voice cooed. "Let me go, and I will give you anything you want, anything you desire."

Drake looked at Mark, worried that Mark might break and give in to this offer.

"Anything I desire?" Mark questioned.

"Yes," the voice breathed over their necks again. "Your heart's desire shall be yours."

"Then," Mark began as he reached for the doorknob, "then I want you to give me my uncle back, you big dillhole!" He jerked the door open in an instant, and Albert slumped inside with a weary smile thinking he had finally busted the door down. Mark tossed the paper bag in one fluid motion out into the yard by the burn barrel. The whispering voice rose up into a shrill shriek that hurt their ears.

Drake bent down and helped Albert up, and together the three brothers walked back onto the deck and began their way down the wide stairs. The dark cloud spire was in the fields moving upon them. They picked up their pace and started to run towards the burn barrel, Mark stooping to pick up the paper bag along the way. Gusts of wind began to pummel them as the storm moved closer.

Mark brought out his lighter and flipped it open.

"Drake, Martin!" Mark shouted as he readied the lighter

below the rolled up grocery bag. "Block the wind so I can light this."

Drake and Martin did just that, moving into a shielding wall so that the lighter could ignite the grocery bag. As the flames grew, Mark moved to the burn barrel and dropped the flaming bag on top of the two pieces of game board. The bag flamed up and burned rapidly in the gusting wind. Then the flames slowly died leaving the plastic pointer still intact sitting on the two pieces of the broken *Spirit* board. They were stunned. Why would it not burn?

"Albert, come with me!" Mark shouted in the fierce wind.

Both Mark and Albert ran towards the giant unfinished workshop beyond the deck and stairs. Drake looked at Martin and Dennis. They both looked pale and seemed to be losing their fight to stand up against the wind. Once again, Drake lifted up the Staff of Orkan and challenged the winds. The golden light of his charm leapt up onto the blue runes of the staff and a blast of golden blue light shot into the ebbing darkness. The staff formed an island within the storm, a shielding bubble that the storm broke hard on but could not penetrate. He stood there resolute of the challenge of the pressing storm that grew stronger and stronger as its center neared them.

Mark and Albert fought their way back through the fierce winds and into the power bubble Drake maintained around the burn barrel and his brothers. Albert held a thick stack of newspapers, and Mark carried a few pieces of wood and a large glass jar of gasoline.

"Let's light this thing up," Mark said as he dropped the wood and took some of the newspaper from Albert, crumpled it up and stuck it in around the board and pointer. He then poured some gas on top of all of it. Finally he took another sheet of newspaper and rolled it into what resembled a large crinkled fuse. He soaked one end in the gasoline and stuck that end inside the burn barrel. He flicked open his lighter and started the dry end of the newspaper fuse on fire.

"Step back," Mark instructed. "This should burst into

flames."

And it did just that. Gasoline-fueled flames burned the newspaper to a cinder, but as the flames receded, the *Spirit* board and pointer remained, unscarred by the flames.

Shocked and dismayed by the inability to burn the board, they felt failure looming. Drake felt his hold on the storm slipping as his arms twitched, his muscles ached feverishly as he held up the staff. He couldn't go on. In that moment of near concession, he remembered one forgotten element. Aunt Carmen had given him something, the envelope of forbidden knowledge. It had to be burned too. It was part of the board, part of the evil it had brought into the world.

"Albert!" Drake shouted as his hold over the storm lessened and the spectral images in the black churning winds pressed closer and closer towards them. "In my shirt pocket, get the envelope out of my pocket. It has to be burned too!"

Albert jumped over to Drake reaching in first one, then the other pocket of his plaid shirt before finally pulling out the folded envelope.

"Yes," Martin said as he looked at the envelope. "That must be destroyed too."

"I'm putting the wood in with it too," Mark stated as he took more of the newspaper and crumpled it up. He handed some to Dennis and Martin and they busied themselves crumpling newspaper and stuffing it into the burning barrel. Mark doused the paper with the rest of the gasoline. Next he arranged the wood in a crude pile with the board fragments. He held the envelope and flicked open his lighter. His thumb struck the flint and once again flame danced above the silver lighter. The envelope smoldered, darkened, and then lit up into flame. Mark tossed the burning letter on to the pile of gasoline soaked paper. With a powerful 'wooosh' the burn barrel erupted in a fiery ball. An unearthly shrieking pierced their souls. The board had finally begun to burn along with the wood in the barrel.

Drake tired from the strain of holding the seething dark cloud at bay with the Staff of Orkan. When he saw the board finally ignite he dropped the staff down as he fell to his knees. The powerful winds broke and fled as if they feared to linger any longer, taking with them the horrible shapes of apparitions and ghouls. Small gusts blew their clothing and hair. The flames of the burn barrel leapt high into the early evening sky. A growing mist from the river settled around the fire in a large perfect circle. At the edge of the circle of mist appeared the palomino horses on one side, and Buddy, the massive Saint Bernard stood vigil on the opposite side.

The sickness that had plagued Martin and Dennis fell off them and they stood up, free of the cramping pains. Their spirits lifted and the brothers turned and smiled to each other. Drake was helped up by Albert and Mark. Both the staff and his star-cross charm looked rather ordinary again. As they stood there in the heat of the fire they knew life would never be the same. They could not go back to where they were before this all started. Together they had survived, but they somehow knew that they might never stand together again. There were deep rifts in their relationships that would take time to heal.

Martin knew that his adult life had begun, and he could never go back to his childhood. Somehow he hoped that his brothers, as they entered adulthood, would still be his friends. He also knew that the *Spirit* board had awoken deep and foreboding powers in him that he intended to further investigate. He knew his path would always stay close to the paranormal, and he knew he possessed the La Madrid gift.

Dennis wondered, as he watched the flames, if he was ready to move on. He knew that Drake and Mark had saved him from the abyss, but he wasn't sure they were friends anymore. He, too, had learned from the *Spirit* board but he wasn't sure if he wanted to know more. He did realize that he needed to get more bottle caps. He somehow felt safer with them in his pocket, and now that he knew he could use them, well... the future could turn out pretty cool.

Albert was happy to be alive. He was pleased that he got to be part of this with his brothers. He knew that he had finally earned a place of respect with each and every one of them, though his dreams would be haunted by images he saw that day for the rest of his life. He was truly happy, except that now that the excitement had ended, he noticed that his pants were rather damp. That was totally not cool and he hoped no one else noticed.

Mark did what he had to do. He rose up and made sure they all got through this, just like he knew Wally would've done. He was proud of his brothers, especially the plucky Albert and the brainiac Drake who both stepped out of their comfort zones to help him. Unfortunately, as he stood there, a nagging feeling ate at him. He was just not ready to deal with the horrors they witnessed. He didn't want to think about them ever again, he wanted to forget this chapter in his life and move on. He just wasn't sure if he could do that with his brothers around always reminding him of this day.

Drake ached from the strain of the staff, though his spirit had returned and the sensation that nearly overpowered him in the hallway, that fear, lingered somewhere in his memory. He would never again truly be without fear, for he would always remember it. He looked forward to the coming year—life was good. He was oddly excited to be a leader at school. And he even found himself thinking of Rachel Finnegan. She was his friend and he was happy for that.

"Hey buttheads," Mark started. "Let's get going, I've got a car to fix."

"Buttheads?" Dennis replied. "I thought we were dillholes?"

"Nah," Mark answered as he walked away from barrel. "There's only one dillhole and he's in there burning."

"Buttheads, huh?" Dennis said as he followed Mark. "Interesting word, buttheads, buttheads, buttheads!"

"Stop wearing it out," Mark said as he patted Dennis on the shoulder, "or it will lose its power."

Albert ran after them, thinking he would master the power of this 'butthead' word and use it against Dennis.

Drake and Martin walked together towards the cars.

Dennis and Albert were already inside the battered blue Impala. Mark had started its rumbling engine.

"Looks like you are riding with me, little brother," Martin said as he opened the driver's side door and climbed into the car.

Drake opened the other door, reached in a placed the Staff of Orkan behind the seat, then sat down and closed the door.

Martin backed up his Datsun and waited a moment for Mark to peel out in the gravel driveway, showering rock on the hood of the B-210.

"Well, at least he didn't break anything that wasn't already broken," Drake stated with a dry chuckle.

"What about your date?" Drake queried Martin.

"I'll drop you off at home first, and clean up," Martin answered. "I think Beth will understand, that I'm a bit late, at least once she sees my car."

"You sure were awesome today, Drake," Martin said as he pulled forward in the driveway. "I want you to know, that Brotherhood of Olympus stuff you talked about? I've thought about it, and I want you to know... I'm in."

Drake smiled at his oldest brother.

"But I need to get some hardware like you've got," Martin said with a laugh. Drake laughed at the absurdity of it all.

"I think that's the last we will be seeing of that Succorbenoth or his minions," Martin said as he slowly revved his car before turning out onto the road. Mark was already a good distance ahead of them.

"I hope so," Drake replied. "I'm sure I saw him in Wally's room. He wasn't very pleasant looking and I'd be way happy if I never had to see him again. You know, I've been thinking."

"When're you not thinking?"

"Don't you think it's odd how the singular events of a moment in time, like Friday the thirteenth, 1978, can impact someone else or a family so profoundly?" Drake pondered with a sigh. "I mean, I don't think we'll ever be like we were before Wally died."

"Yeah," Martin responded as he pulled his car out onto the road and began to race after Mark who was now at the far end of the valley. "Makes me wonder what really happened that day, but I doubt anyone will ever know."

Drake nodded in agreement.

As they continued down the road they both had a sudden urge to look back at the fire in the burn barrel. The nagging temptation was nearly overpowering. But neither boy turned as they drove off to the west.

Within the flames, the fire began to take on a shape, and that shape was that of a vaguely humanoid head. The charred and tortured face of Succorbenoth turned and watched the cars disappear in the distance and with a bellowing scream it let everyone know it would not underestimate a Fraser boy again.

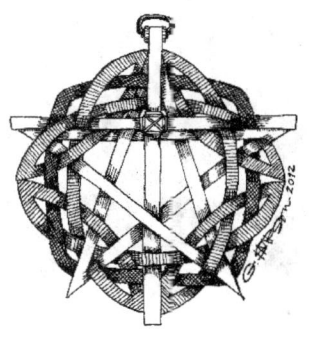

Epilogue

Nu Kua and Ganesha

The Brotherhood of Olympus and the Deadliest Game

**Council of the Wise**
**Epilogue**
**January 13, 1978**
**Tower of Infinity, on the border of the Ethereal Plane**

There was no sensation, no feeling, or any semblance of time or space. Memory too escaped him. Gone was his history, his tragedy, and his name. Yet in this absence of material relevance, there was one undeniable truth—he was no longer what he once was. Then it occurred to him that he was moving rapidly. The molecules of atmosphere coursed through him in a curious way, and within his perception he could see the tiny spirals of electrons dancing past him. He knew them as they passed through what he had become, nitrogen, oxygen, hydrogen, carbon, and that gave him pause for he had never truly known chemistry, and now he was at one with all of them.

Feelings as he had known them were gone and they had been replaced by this sense of being at one with the elements. As he focused on himself, his globular shape of pulsating energy began to morph into a more human form. Before him lay a gaseous horizon of greenish black vapor, his own form solidifying more and more as he quickly moved toward the vapor. On the frontier of the vapor he perceived a towering red spire. The scale of the structure was difficult to measure in this world of cosmic awareness. It was massive and well beyond the capability of human engineering or construction.

The red tower grew more massive as he streaked towards it. He became aware that this was his destination. As he rapidly neared the structure he was suddenly struck by a new sensation, a presence of something else far greater than him. There was a divine awe that radiated through him, similar to what he had felt standing in Paradise upon the base of Mt. Rainier, or entering the green Hall of Mosses in the Hoh Rainforest, or standing on the beach and gazing at the size and majesty of the Pacific Ocean.

And then he was inside the red spire, cocooned in white glowing light.

"Greetings," echoed a voice from tall, grey-skinned creature with long, gangly arms and legs, and an overly large ovoid head that had emerged from the radiant light. "I am Ranthalion, Keeper of the Tower of Infinity. You are Walter Reuss, son of Henry, and you are most welcome here."

"Walter," he thought, and was startled to hear his thoughts as sound though he did not speak. "I know that name. Where am I? Why am I here?"

"The mysteries of life, such as how long is forever, how big the universe is, what happens after you die, or are you alone in the vastness of this enormous universe have long been debated amongst human scholars, and dreaded by your children in the blackness of night. Many agree that most of those answers come from the faith of the individual, since human science has had difficulty quantifying these grand questions," Ranthalion answered with large sweeping motions of his spindly arms. "Few humans have had the privilege to see reality from the vantage point of this Tower, Master Reuss. From here all realms and realities are visible."

Walter noticed others had joined him and the alien-looking Ranthalion. There were many other slim gray beings, though smaller than the Keeper, busily working in the white vastness of the room in which they stood, and the auras of the divine were now among them.

"Why have you summoned us here and now, Woden?" a powerful feminine voice uttered. "We have little concern or regard for this place, this construct of Elder gods."

He noticed many beings, or entities, gathering in what appeared to be a bright, crystalline white courtyard with a large circular gazing pool filled with a mirrored black liquid, embedded into the center of the patterned glowing tiles of the floor. The entity shapes were confusing. They shifted in size and shape before him and they radiated light like stars, so much so that he knew it would have hurt his eyes to gaze upon them, if he had any.

"I have called you," began a deep voice from a large man holding a long golden spear, "because the time is now upon us. The events long foretold have begun, and war will soon be upon us."

There was a long silence following the statement.

"I summoned many of our kind, as we had agreed upon in our last Council of the Wise," the large man with the spear stated. He was now wearing gold plate armor as he became more fixed in his shape. His armor glowed like molten metal, and his undulating bright energy leapt off the end of his massive spear like flumes of smoldering plasma. "But, as you see, few have come. I fear many of our kin have wandered off in the vastness of the universe, or have barricaded themselves into their own realms. I had hoped for a larger audience. But, I am pleased with those that have arrived."

The large golden-armored man gave a quick but deliberate bow to those in attendance.

"Xièxiè nǐ, suǒyǒu de fùqīn," an exotically beautiful woman moved forward towards the gazing pool. Her features were decidedly Asian, her eyes piercing and captivating, her complexion as delicate as porcelain, her elegance was beyond measure, and as she gracefully moved Walter noticed her large serpentine form that coiled and slid across the glowing tiles from her waist down.

"Please," the golden-armored man replied, a flush overcoming his face, revealing for the first time an intricate patch over one eye, "my lady, Nu Kua, I am humbled by your presence, but not all that have gathered are fluent in Chinese."

"My pardons," Nu Kua stated as she stopped at the edge of the pool and looked into it. "I know much of creation, but

I do not know this land we see below us, how is this so?"

"This land," a tall bluish white man began as he stepped forward to join Nu Kua and the golden armored man at the edge of the pool, "is far removed from all of our realms and where we once held sway in the mortal lands of Earth. Humans have called it the Pacific Northwest, a fitting name given its geography. More precisely, it is known as Washington, in honor of one of their great leaders. It is a part of the land now known as the United States, a human democratic republic that has thrived for two-hundred Earth years. This, my kin, is a hinterland, cut off from settlement by Europeans until the latter half of the nineteenth century, more than three-hundred years after they began colonizing the Atlantic coast."

He was shaded in an aura of mystery, his features fluid and changing, but upon his head sat a majestic, overly elaborate turban of Middle Eastern design that had a blazing sun above his brow and two incredibly long plumes of symmetrical feathers.

"Bah, a hinterland it's not," a shorter man interjected as he stepped forward. He had a wide, sun darkened face, the feathers of a great eagle were in his long black hair, and he wore clothing that looked like tree bark, lined with brilliant white fur. "Thousands of generations of my people have lived upon this land, Lord Amun. My people were a proud people, and their myths and legends were borne of this land."

"K'wati is correct, but so too is Amun," a lady coursing with raw electrical energy stepped forward. Arcs of violet lightning surged around her form that seemed to shift in a rhythmic pattern from that of a young girl full of life and wonder, to a statuesque woman of unbridled beauty, to a wizened, wrinkled, and grayed matriarch, and then back again through the same unending cycle. "This land possesses a spirit through the countless interactions of people, animals, and phenomena throughout the ages. It is ripe in magic. This is a wondrous land of magic, and would likely not be the case had it not been a hinterland, for civilization would have brought science and reason, and we all know that human science and reason crushes magic wherever it spreads."

"How do you know all of this history of a land never under your dominion, Amun?" the exotic beauty of Nu Kua shifted upon the coils of her serpentine form.

"It is my nature to know," Amun responded with a curt bow. "And what the humans have called the magic of this land Lady Hecate, is animism, the concept that all things possess a spirit, that everything living and non-living are bound by this spirit. I do not have to tell any of you here, how correct that is, or how lost it is in many parts of the mortal world. As the hidden one, I gather all knowledge."

The assembled deities nodded their heads in silent agreement.

"I too seek knowledge," a short pot-bellied man stated as he moved to the edge of the pool. His radiance was yellow as his skin and he had four arms naturally attached to his squat torso. In each of his hands he held a different object. In one it was a heavy war mace, in another it was a delicate white water lily, in the third it was a golden chakra, and in the fourth it was a bit of ivory. What was most remarkable about him was his large elephantine head. His wide knowledgeable eyes were kind and full of empathy, and his right tusk was broken off near his thick yellow skin. "Wisdom and prudence are both my domains, and as the Lord of Beginnings, it was both wise and prudent that I should come to this event, long have we waited for this day to arrive."

"Aeon, Shou Lao, please join us," The golden armored man stated as he looked back and motioned for others to step forward. Two elderly forms moved to the front, adjacent to the gazing pool. One was tall, with a long gray beard, black light oozing from his darkened robes, and he carried a massive scythe propped up with both of his gnarled hands. The other was shorter, with an overly large bald head, wild white eyebrows and random white whiskers upon his jaw line, and he carried a large wooden staff in one hand and a single gold peach in the other. "As keepers of time, you both know the importance of this event."

"Aye," the taller Aeon spoke.

"That we do," finished Shou Lao. "And we are pleased to see that he has joined us. The path of his future was changed by his untimely death, but as some have seen, his part in this tale is not concluded."

"In fact," Aeon added with a gentle dip of his heavy scythe pointing in the direction of the new arrival, "we do believe that he may now become more powerful than any of us had previously imagined."

The assembled throng of entities, both the more solid around the pool and those lingering behind seemed to turn and look at him.

"Please step forward, my boy," Woden motioned.

Without any effort of his own he moved up to the edge of the gazing pool across from the gathering. He noticed for the first time a fragrance, the distinct aroma of roses, before it was lost in the heady scents of the assembled mass of powerful beings that churned through him like charged ozone.

"Tell us the prologue of this grim tale, Walter, son of Henry," Amun stated as he made a welcoming hand motion towards Walter.

"I don't know where to begin," Walter spoke from his being, shocked again that he didn't really speak, but rather thought it out loud.

"Perhaps," K'wati enthusiastically began, "I could tell this part of the tale, and same young Master Reuss the trouble, so soon after the trauma of this day has befallen him."

"If it pleases you, let me do that honor," a sultry voice emerged from the glowing entities as a tall feminine form walked forward. The powerful scent of roses flooded across the pool and into the essence of Walter. She was an angelic beauty with raven hair, a long, flaming, barbed tail enhancing her walk, and large folded, leathery wings upon her back. "As librarian of Gehenna, I have chronicled the coming of this event for many centuries."

"Daemon's are welcome here?" the shifting three-persona woman questioned as her violet lightning spiked higher and more intensely around her.

The elongated Ranthalion bowed low to the daemon.

"All are welcome," K'wati quickly answered, "provided they have an interest in these events and peacefully enter into this Tower."

"Thank you, Ranthalion, and K'wati," the daemon responded. "Rest assured Lady Hecate, I do possess a powerful interest in the success of this venture, as time will ultimately tell."

Aeon and Shou Lao both nodded in agreement.

"Tis true that the Grand Library of Gehenna possesses few rivals in any realm," Amun added, "I myself have frequented it often in my quest for knowledge."

"May I continue?" questioned the daemon.

"Yes, Countess Furfur," Nu Kua replied, as she gave a nod to the daemon. "Please do."

"As you wish," the daemon smiled. It was a radiant smile that would enrapture the hearts of men the world over.

"This was to be a story of five human boys, an uncle, a cousin, and three brothers, all descendants of Heinrich Reuss Von Plauen, the last High Lord of the Brotherhood of Olympus who ceased to exist in 1469," she began. "But, there is an equivalent council to this fair one that's dark and sinister, as most of us know. It's populated with many of my kind and many of your kind as well who harbor desires of great evil upon mankind and vengeance against many of you so gathered today. They have long known of this re-birth of the Brotherhood of Olympus, and they plotted to destroy it before it came to pass. For if they could, they might forever alter any hope of human enlightenment, enslave humanity for their own nefarious purposes, and give them the power to wage victorious war against most, if not all of you here. They struck the first blow of the war today by killing this human, Walter Reuss. With the uncle, the chosen leader of the group plucked from existence, and here with us now, things must shift. Some have always foreseen these events, and actually saw Walter as the key to the master plan. Through his death the plot has changed and now focuses solely on the brothers."

Woden, Aeon, and Shou Lao exchanged knowledgeable glances with each other.

"The five Fraser boys," the daemon explained, "residents of the greater Aberdeen area are not so different from other boys in this area of the world during this time. You see, Aberdeen is the largest town located in Grays Harbor County. The port of Aberdeen was the best on the west coast of America in the late 1800s to early 1900s, built for one cargo… timber."

"I knew that," Walter added.

"The lumber industry provided the raw materials to build the coming metropolises of the Pacific Coast as far south as California," continued the daemon with a look towards Walter that made him feel heat inside himself. "It has been recorded that Aberdeen was and had always been a logging town, through and through. From its earliest incarnation as a timber camp to the bustling small city we see today."

They looked down into the gazing pool, and the rugged landscape surrounding Aberdeen came into view. Walter was amazed by the clarity of the sight before him. People were walking on the streets below him and he could see their features.

"The wise and learned city council of Aberdeen," Countess Furfur mockingly added as she pointed into the pool, "had repeatedly denied any diversification of its industry by sticking by its timber and lumber traditions, and their families, while voting down opening its port to such things as the exportation of coal from nearby Centralia, or the importation of automobiles from the Far East."

"Look at the people," announced the amazed Walter.

"Many of the human families in the area hover around the poverty line, and there was a real potent fear of the day when timber harvesting could no longer continue at its current rate," she kept explaining even as she rolled her eyes at Walter's innocence. "Some had already seen the writing on the wall, as the environmental movement, led locally by hippies, were already advocating for more sustainable harvesting practices, if not an outright ban on tree cutting."

Some of the assembled deities were beginning to tire of the narrative of the radiant daemon, and they began to impatiently move or mill about the gazing pool.

"My sister Carmen is a hippie," Walter added as most of the gathering seemed to ignore him.

"The hippies were the bane of the loggers and the timber industry," the daemon continued. "And interestingly enough, much like Walter's sister, their ranks were filled by disenfranchised timber family members, many of whom had gone off to the new liberal state college up in Olympia."

"Enough of the regional history," the yellow, elephant headed man interjected. A few of his peers nodded in agreement. "Let us hear of the Fraser family."

"Yes, of course," the daemon obliged. "The Frasers are one of many working-class poor families who did what they could to make ends meet. They own a modest two-story house in the residential area of Hoquiam. The father, Drake, of the Clan Fraser, is a man proud of his Scottish heritage, and he spent many years of his youth in the timber industry himself."

"Drake," stated a new figure that moved to the front edge of the pool, his radiance shifted from black to white as his face changed in an equally divergent manner. There was the dark and sinister, evil visage of a man with demented eyes, followed by the serene, welcoming and wise face of a handsome man in a rapid flash of succession. "Son of Martin the Nameless, Erlking, and Master of Gates. The Erlking has not responded to any messages or envoys for many years. Some think he has died upon his throne and none may now enter his realm. I firmly believe the Erlking is the key to these trying times before us."

"Janus," greeted Amun with a slight bow. "Good of you

to join us. I see your interest has been piqued as the god of passage and gates."

"Amun," the bipolar image of a man conceded. "I am pleased you remember me, it has been a long time."

"How could I forget? When last we met, I believe our peoples were at war, and yours drove mine into hiding or slavery and destroyed thousands of years of civilization devoted to me and my kin," Amun replied.

"To the victor go the spoils, dear brother," Janus quipped. "But let us not dwell on the past when the present and future are ripe before us."

"Enough of the personal issues gentlemen, continue Countess," Ganesha urged, with a flamboyant hand gesture with his water lily. "Please."

"Very well," the daemon restarted. "Sophia, the mother, and elder sister of your Walter here, is of the La Madrid family, and she carries the Reuss line, of the fallen Hochmeister of the Brotherhood forward. Her motives are entirely her own, she acts without any influence of any otherworldly power. Her children are like a perfect storm. Their genetics mixed to just the right temperature, Reuss, La Madrid, and of course the Clan Fraser."

The group peered more intently into the gazing pool. A young man sitting in a sparsely decorated bedroom came into view. He was tall, and had straight black hair with a little wave around the ears to the back of his head. His eyes were blue and his skin was a pale, pasty white.

"Hey!" Walter exclaimed. "That's Marty!"

"This," the Countess instructed, "is Martin, the eldest of the Fraser boys. He's seventeen, and named for his paternal grandfather who died seven years before he was born. He's fascinated with science fiction. He had what he liked to call a near religious experience watching *Star Wars* last summer, a remarkable fifty-nine times."

"What is *Star Wars*?" Nu Kua queried.

"It's a cool movie," Walter responded. "About these dudes, Jedi knights, fighting a really evil dude in black armor.

His name was Darth, Darth Vader. It was pretty popular."

"Hmmmm, okay," the daemon interrupted. "It's a moving picture story of an epic battle of good versus evil set in the vastness of space."

"Intriguing," Amun stated. "I must see this *Star Wars*."

"Martin," the Countess restarted her narrative, "had grown up with an aversion to the sun, since going outside would have taken him away from his beloved television reruns of shows like *Lost in Space*, *Land of the Giants*, and *Star Trek*."

"Epic stories with such epic names, no doubt," Woden interjected.

"Are these all moving picture stories, young Walter?" Amun asked in a quieter voice.

"No, they are on the TV," Walter responded as he began to be perplexed by the enormity of the explanation. "I mean television, yeah, kind of like moving pictures but not on a screen like movies, on a smaller screen inside the TV."

"I must see this TV," Amun stated pragmatically.

"Marty," Walter said in a voice so sad it pained those around him. "I can't be dead. I have to help him and his brothers."

"You may still be of help to him, young Walter," replied Amun with the slightest hint of compassion.

The image in the pool shifted and another person came into view. This boy was standing in a meticulously cleaned bedroom. He was shorter than Martin and had the same straight black hair like his brother. Unlike his older brother, this boy had brown eyes and a dark olive complexion that reflected his partial Spanish heritage.

"And who are we gazing upon now, Countess?" asked Nu Kua.

"This is Mark, the second eldest, my Lady," the daemon responded with a slight head bow. "He is nearly sixteen. Named for a Japanese immigrant who was long ago a friend of his mother's family. He is remarkably different than his older brother. He is quite industrious, and he demonstrated a talent for mechanics at an early age when he began taking things apart to see how they worked. Typically he took apart something that belonged to one of his brothers."

"They would get so pissed off at him when he did that, too," Walter further clarified the statement.

"He is also the rebel in the family," revealed the Countess. "He has a history of defiance towards authority. He began to smoke cigarettes before he was eleven, when he was introduced to them by his uncle, over there."

The daemon pointed in Walter's direction. Walter sheepishly shrugged his shoulders in a mock expression of being sorry.

"He would be the natural leader to assume the mantle left by the death of their uncle," the Countess elaborated. "But, he has no desire to pursue it. Most notably because of his unwillingness to accept that all of this is even real. That conviction to what he sees as the truth will lead him astray."

"Truth is a fickle thing," the darkened face of Janus stated before the wizened face finished the thought. "Without equal measures of intelligence and compassion applied, of course."

"Of course," Amun concurred with an air of distrust.

"This Mark, through all his outward strength, there is an underlying weakness," the porcelain face of Nu Kua looked saddened as she stated her observation. "The dichotomy that exists in him pains me."

The image in the gazing pool shifted again, this time focusing onto another boy who was dressed in athletic gear and was putting on a sweatshirt.

"This, my Lords and Ladies, is Drake," the daemon spoke with a new tone, almost like a sense of pride.

"Another Drake?" Janus queried anxiously. "Could this be the one long foretold, or is it the father I have come here for?"

"I cannot say, Lord Janus," the Countess slyly responded. "Though he is the middle child, and was named after his father, he is not officially a junior or a second. He has been called Drake, Jr. by many of his relatives and it does get on his nerves. He's very aware that his legal name does not include the junior moniker, and he would prefer to be known as the second."

"It's still years to come before people in this region will raise the name of Ken Griffey, Jr. to icon status," Shou Lao stated. "And that act will change the name junior in young Drake's mind."

"Intriguing," Ganesha said as his large head tipped to one side.

"Drake is extremely introverted," continued the Countess. "But he has found comfort in his near insatiable quest for knowledge. His memory is vast, and populated with as much knowledge as he can acquire. As a librarian, I am partial to this boy."

"I am warming up to this one as well," Amun announced boldly. "The quest of knowledge is virtuous."

"Being a wall flower has its benefits, as well," the Countess added with a warm smile. "He developed an ability to observe from a detached perspective, and this in turn enhanced his artistic skills he inherited from his mother. Nearly all of his peers know he's excellent at drawing. The quirkiness of his character can best be described by noting one of his proudest accomplishments, which is not even of his doing. He shares a birthday, September twenty-second, with both Bilbo and Frodo Baggins of *The Lord of the Rings* fame."

"Is that a television moving picture story as well, Walter?" question the coiling Nu Kua.

"Ummm, no, it's a bunch of books," Walter explained. "Although they did just make a cartoon movie of *the Hobbit*, I doubt they'll ever be able to make a real movie of *The Lord of the Rings*."

"I know of this story," Woden added with a raised eyebrow. "It is a heroic epic on the grandest of scales, my grandson Magni has read it to his son StanLee. Magni is quite a connoisseur of Midgard literature. He even named his child after a very prolific Midgardian scribe, who he favors."

"Drake," interrupted the daemon, "is what many would describe as a hopeless optimist, and the intellectual resource of his siblings. He is the one I would strongly recommend we focus on, to convince to lead this new group. He doesn't believe he is much of anything right now, but in time I believe he will be a shinning star in the coming war—if he ever believes in himself. He is also seemingly bound by eldritch magic of an unknown source to the words of his uncle. For example, he is unable to cry, a simple human emotion, because of what Walter once told him."

"I had no idea I did that to him," Walter shamefully apologized. "We were just kids, how could I know?"

The image in the gazing pool shifted once again. This time a younger boy came into view. He did not have similar features like his older brothers. He was short and had a mane of unruly dirty blonde hair.

"This is Dennis," the Countess started with an audible sigh. "The fourth Fraser boy is three years younger than Drake, which is the biggest age gap between any of the brothers. Dennis looks more like his maternal grandfather's side of the family, Walter's father, Henry Reuss."

"Yes, Germanic, and the descendent of our long lost High Lord, undoubtedly," Amun added.

"Teutonic, more precisely," Woden clarified.

"Dennis had been born sick and spent many of the first months of his life in the hospital in Seattle," the daemon continued. "His ill health completely shifted the Fraser parents' focus away from their three older children, and that was particularly hard on Drake, who had been the baby of the family until then. Dennis still has a tendency to get ill easily, and his older brothers have been forced to baby him."

"He doesn't like the stairs at my house, he's very afraid of them for some reason, and somebody has to walk him past them to use the bathroom," Walter added.

"As Dennis grew," she stated, "he demonstrated that he was calculating, and quite bright. Dennis is the brother most likely to side with the one he thought would win, in any dispute. His future is open, it hasn't been foretold if he will fully join the reborn Brotherhood, and perhaps this is due to the cloudiness that Drake causes in the timelines going forward. But I wouldn't discount him or any of the Fraser boys."

The gazing pool image moved in the direction Dennis was pointing, but did not dissolve as it had before. Sitting in a loose pile of dirty clothes on the floor was the youngest boy in the family. He was making odd facial gestures for the amusement of his brother.

"This is the youngest Fraser," the daemon started with a curt smile. "Albert turned eight years old on New Years Eve 1977, and he is already nearly as tall as his older brother Dennis. He is the prototypical baby of the family. He gets attention from his parents for nearly everything he does, and gets away with things his older brothers never could have at his age and in some cases still cannot. He is spoiled. But in many ways he is just a child seeking acknowledgement from those who already give it to him freely. His future is more of a conundrum than even that of Dennis. Where he goes is not known, perhaps this is due to him being a casualty of the war."

"A conundrum," Hecate interjected with a spark of purple lightning. "I do love a puzzle."

"A war casualty?" Aeon questioned. "My dear Countess, this has not been discussed before, the sacrifices of the Frasers has already been a grievous topic among those of us who see the streams of time. The fates of the three oldest during the war are well observed, but we have always believed the younger boys would emerge unscathed."

"What do you mean sacrifices? Why my nephews?" Walter questioned. "What does all of this mean?"

"My dear boy," Woden answered, "as it has been told, you were born to be the leader, and the Dark Council knew that. So the forces of evil and hatred struck against you and all of us, by ending your mortal life. And now the task falls to your nephews."

"So I'm just dead?" Walter exclaimed. "This is the end of the story for me? I have to be able to help them. If I was so damned special I should've some ability, some power to do something to help them avoid these casualties and sacrifices?"

"No, you are not allowed. In time perhaps, if you can achieve what few have ever tried." Amun stated flatly. "But you must now travel the ethereal plane until you find what you have lost. And be wary of trying to contact your nephews, the consequences could be deadly."

"But, I'm already dead," Walter replied. "Oh, you mean for them. I should warn them, is that possible?"

"Yes, it is possible," Janus added. "You must be cautious. The minions of the enemy will be quick to exploit you to wreak havoc amongst your kin. Your family may seek a way to communicate with you. Your loss is most grievous to them."

"Your journey is just beginning, Walter Reuss," Hecate interjected. "Should you master the challenges that lay ahead of you, you may become more powerful than the Dark Council imagined."

"What do you mean?" Walter questioned. "This is all very confusing, and very hard to believe."

"And why has it begun today, Woden?" Ganesha added. "The symbolism of the date will not be lost upon humanity."

"Ganesha, long have we known each other, and in all that time, have I ever misrepresented myself?" Woden responded.

"No," the elephant-headed man replied.

"I did not choose the date," Woden explained. "The Dark Council plotting against us all chose it precisely for that reason. It will forever more carry the onus of a dark mark, and will enable them to use it for their own sinister means in the future. Just as it happened on this date in 1469 when the Brotherhood of Olympus last walked this Earth."

"It is Friday the thirteenth, a very regular occurrence actually, because there is always at least one of them every year," Aeon explained in ancient voice. "But it is also a day steeped in modern phobia, like black cats crossing your path, walking under a ladder, opening an umbrella indoors, or even breaking a mirror. Each of these carries connotations of bad luck or evil portents."

"Luck only exists for those individuals who make things happen for themselves," Shou Lao stated philosophically.

"Unless one is a leprechaun," added Aeon. "Take heed of that Countess Furfur, for your doom is written upon such luck."

"None of the Frasers have possessed this fear," the Countess added with disdain for the black robed god, "although that may change after today, and the very dynamics of the Fraser family will change on this day as well."

"'Tis true," Woden stated. "Their paths in life will be forever altered, and life as they have known it will never be the same."

"What is our course of action, since war is now upon us?" K'wati questioned.

"Open war will not begin for a number of years yet," Shou Lao stated with raised eyebrows and a toothy smile.

"Our lot is to attempt to recruit those of our kin who might share our sentiment," Amun pronounced regally, "while we watch and attempt to aid the formation of this new Brotherhood, in a manner that does not violate the Covenant of Reason, thus preventing the Dark Council dominion over the Earth."

"When the time comes," Woden added, "the forces of my realms, Asgard included, shall answer the call of the horns of war."

"Let us hope that our forces, as grand as they may be, shall be enough to defeat those of our dark kindred," Janus said as he looked painfully into the mirrored black of the gazing pool. "I fear the cost of this war shall be high, for all those involved, and some of us may cease to exist entirely."

"Wait," Walter interrupted as he stepped forward into the assembled gods. "Can't some of you see the future? You knew about me hundreds of years ago, right? Can't you use that knowledge to avoid all this war stuff?"

"Young Walter," Woden responded earnestly. "'Tis true that some amongst us may see the future, but it is the heart of humanity, born with freewill that ultimately will shape the outcome of this war. We here hope that our champions choose well, and that the best possible outcome emerges. None of us wants to blink from existence, nor do we want to even contemplate losing this looming war."

"Ranthalion," Amun asked their host, "where do the loyalties of your race lie?"

"Lord Amun," the Keeper responded with an exaggerated bow, "my people and my kin in the other great Towers will abide by our neutrality as deemed by the Elder gods who created us and our Towers. I am sorry I cannot offer more than that."

"Perhaps," Ganesha added, "your view may differ once your Towers are laid siege to by the Dark Council."

"Mayhaps," Ranthalion replied gracefully. "Although that probability is highly unlikely, even the Dark Council as you have aptly named them, respects our neutrality."

"Are we thus adjourned Woden?" Hecate asked as she moved next to Walter. "I will escort Walter Reuss into the ether and guide him as I may before his challenge commences."

"Aye," Woden agreed as he raised his spear upward, the golden plasma leaping upward into the heavens. "We are adjourned, may the fortunes of war bring blessings upon each of you, and should any of us fall may the choirs of Valhalla forever sing our names."

# Glossary of names, locations, phrases, and items

**Aeon.** (æ·än) He was the god who was the personification of time, from the Greek pantheon of mythology. He was also known as Chronos, not to be confused with the Titan Cronus. In art he was depicted as an old wise man with a long, gray beard bearing a long handled scythe. Images of him form the root of the "Father Time" myth.

**Amun.** (ăh·mən) He was the god of creation, the wind, and knowledge, from the Egyptian pantheon of mythology. He created himself, represented the essential and hidden knowledge, and was the champion of the poor. Later he became known as Amun-Ra and assumed the titles of sun god, and the Lord of the Sky. In art he was depicted as a tall, slightly blue-skinned man who wore an intricate turban adorned with two massive Nile Goose feathers.

**Caul.** (kawl) A child born with a veil of flesh over their face is said to have been born in the caul. In medieval times the appearance of a caul on a newborn baby was seen as a sign of good luck. It has also been considered an omen that the child was destined for greatness. In modern times those born with the caul have been documented by some researchers as possessing supernatural abilities.

**Chalat'.** (chă·lăwt) They were the indigenous people of

the western Olympic Peninsula who lived in the shadow of Mt. Olympus. They resided in the river valleys carved from the glacial runoff from the mountain. This is the ancient name of the people of the Hoh Rainforest, also known as the Hoh Indians.

**Chehalis**. (shə·hā·lĭs) They were the indigenous people to the south of the Olympic peninsula who lived in the Chehalis river valley. The river empties into Grays Harbor and the Pacific Ocean. The Chehalis were the trading partners with the Olympic Peninsula people and the Cowlitz and Chinook to the south.

**Chimakum**. (chə·mă·kŭm) They were the indigenous people of the eastern Olympic Peninsula who lived on the northern shore of Hood Canal. According to Quileute tradition, whose language was very similar, the Chimakum were a remnant of a Quileute band that had been carried away in their canoes through a passageway in the Olympic Mountains by a great flood and deposited on the other side of the peninsula. They were a warlike tribe who often fought with their neighbors.

**Covenant of Reason**. (kŭv·ə·nənt ŏv rē·zən) This agreement was signed by the greater powers that once influenced the day-to-day lives of mankind that banned them from contact or intrusion into the lives of men. It was agreed to by the benevolent powers as being necessary to keep the benign powers from running havoc over the mortal world, even though it cost all of them their ability to be directly involved in the development of humanity. Many banished individuals have plotted for centuries how to circumvent the agreement and once again enter the mortal world. Some of the benevolent have prophesized that a war over the Covenant looms somewhere near on the horizon of time.

**Daemon**. (dæ·mən) These were evil beings of greater power and influence over the lesser demons and devils of various netherworlds. Often seen as being akin to demigods within netherworld pantheons, many were the offspring of gods or goddesses and lesser demons or devils. They often ruled over dominions or keeps within these netherworlds.

**Doquebatl**. (dōk·ă·băt'l) He was the greater spirit of change to the Klallam people. This was another name of K'wati. *See K'wati.*

**Du skal ikke passere**. [Norwegian] English translation— You shall not pass.

**Duwamish**. (dū·wă·mǐsh) They were the indigenous people of the far eastern Olympic Peninsula who lived on both sides of Puget Sound, consisting of most of modern day King County. One leader of the tribe, Chief Seattle, was credited with leading the Duwamish, Suquamish, and Klallam in conflict that resulted in the end of the warlike Chimakum people in 1847.

**Elder god**. (ĕl·dər gǎwd) Deities of primal forces, who had dominion over Earth and many other realms before the pantheons of gods that rose to prominence during the early days of human civilization, but have since been nearly wiped from all history and memory. They constructed many wondrous things, including the Tower of Infinity, before they disappeared.

**Eldritch magic**. (ĕl·drĭch mǎj·ǐk) Magic from an archaic source, often synonymous with wizardry, that could also be described as being eerie, or weird in nature. One plausible origin of the root word being from the Middle English word, elfriche, which meant elf kingdom or fairyland; usually a magic or magical item of greater power.

**Ethereal Plane**. (ē·thər·ē·əl plān) A realm or plane of existence that connects many other realms together, it borders many of the known planes and some of the undocumented planes. It is a dark, windswept land of blackish green vapor. Some mystics have claimed that humans could travel trough the ether to visit these other realms. It is the home of the Mordgeists, and a place where many spirits gather with unfinished business before moving on to another plane of existence.

**Ganesha**. (gə·nā·shə)  He was the god of wisdom, prophecy, and prudence, remover of obstacles, from the Hindu pantheon of mythology.  He was also known as the Lord of Beginnings and would be invoked before a task began.  In art he was depicted as a short, pot-bellied, yellow-skinned man with an elephant head that had a broken right tusk.  He had four arms, one holding a shell, another holding a chakra, another holding a mace, and the final one holding a water lily.

**Gehenna**. (gĭ·hen·uh)  A fiery and ice-filled series of realms beyond what is known as Earth.  In some mythology, this is a place of torment for lost souls after death.  It lies beyond the ethereal plane of existence and is home to many dark citadels of daemonic powers.  One such place is the Great Library of Gehenna, located on the side of an ever-erupting volcano, said to hold infinite knowledge.

**Guizor**. (gī·zôr)  The ruling caste of the huisum race, few of them still exist, and all of them are revered for their wisdom. *See Ranthalion.*

**Hecate**. (hĕk·ā'tē)  She was the goddess of fertility, later associated with Persephone as queen of Hades, from the Greek pantheon of mythology.  She was also known as a goddess of the underworld, magic, witchcraft, necromancy, crossroads, gates, and doorways.  In art she was depicted as three women—a young maid, a statuesque matron, and an old crone.

**Hoh Rainforest**. (hō rein·fôr·ĭst)  It is one of the largest temperate rainforests in the United States, located on the western side of the Olympic Peninsula.  The trees of the forest are nearly all covered in long blankets of mosses and lichens.  Some of the old growth trees, Sitka Spruce and Western Hemlock, grow as high as 312 feet, and 23 feet in diameter.  It is also home of the Duncan Tree, the largest western red cedar in the world.

**Huisum**. (Hu·ēs·əm)  The gray skinned race of neutral observers created by the Elder gods who still serve their long lost creators through the technology of the Towers of Ominous Power.

**Hurricane Ridge**. (hûr·ĭ·kān rĭj) It is a mountainous area in the northern part of the Olympic National Park, accessible from Port Angeles. At an elevation of 5,200 feet, it was named for its intense gales and winds. From this location many of the mountains of the Olympic range are viewable, including Mount Olympus to the south.

**Janus**. (jā·nəs) He was the god of doorways, passages, gates, bridges, and all beginnings from the Roman pantheon of mythology. He was also known as a god of the past, present, and future. In art he was depicted with two faces, facing the opposite directions.

**Kalaloch**. (kălā·lŏk) This is the name of the Pacific Ocean coastal area of Olympic National Park, just to the north of the Quinault Indian Reservation. It features prominent rock outcroppings and wind swept beaches. Destruction Island, the largest island off the coast of Washington, can be seen from the beaches and cliffs of Kalaloch. When spoken of by locals, the name sounds like 'Clay-lock.'

**Klallam**. (klăl·lŭm) They were the indigenous people of the northern Olympic Peninsula who lived in the windswept valleys of the mountains and along the coast of the Strait of Juan de Fuca. They were a peaceful people who shared camps and villages with other tribes, like the Makah, S'Klallam, and some tribes of what is now British Columbia.

**K'wati**. (k·wăt·ē) He was the god-like spirit of change and enlightenment for many of the indigenous people of the Pacific Northwest mythologies. Known as the 'Changer,' he was the greater spirit who created mountains, rivers, and gifted the peoples of the region with the abilities they needed to survive. In art he was depicted as a wise man wearing cedar bark clothing lined with white fur, often seen with either a broad woven cedar hat, or eagle/thunderbird feathers woven into his hair. He was also known as Doquebatl by the Klallam.

**Leprechaun**. (lĕp·rĭ·kŏn)   One of a race of elf-like creatures often referred to in Irish folklore and mythology. According to most sources, they were often slightly mischievous, protecting a hidden treasure, and somehow connected to rainbows.

**Lilac**. (lī·lŏk) [Syringa vulgaris] It is a flowering plant common to much of the United States and in herbology it has been used for its powers of exorcism and protection. Lilac has been used to drive away evil where it has been planted or strewn.   In New England, lilacs were originally planted to keep evil from the property.

**Makah**. (mä·kä) They were the indigenous people of the far northwestern tip of the Olympic Peninsula who hunted gray whales in the Pacific Ocean.   They were a peaceful people who shared camps and villages with other tribes, like the Klallam, and some tribes of what is now British Columbia.

**Mordgeist**. (môrd·gīst) They were inhabitants of many netherworlds; their origin was lost in antiquity, whose name literally means 'death spirit.' They have often been seen in locations where humans have recently died, or will soon die. They are harbingers of death. They have often worked for daemons, gods, or spirits with greater power or force, making them quite mercenary in their activities. In art they have been depicted as skeletal creatures, shrouded in gray robes and mists, with unnaturally long teeth and glowing red eyes.

**Nu Kua**. (nü kwä) She was the goddess of creation, from the ancient Chinese pantheon of mythology.   She created mankind from the mud of the Earth.  In art she was depicted as remarkably beautiful woman with jet black hair, with a large, coiling body of a serpent below her waistline.

**Pacea fie cu tine regele meu**. [Romanian] English translation—Peace be with you, my King.

**Plane**. (plān) A level of existence or reality with finite, or near infinite borders, where laws of physics, energy, and time are mostly consistent, our contemporary Earth exists within one such plane. It has been speculated by many that alternate realities or divergent timelines may exist within the plethora of planes. Travelling between planes requires powerful magic, talismans, or established gates or portals. Some of these planes of note include, but are not limited to, the Ethereal, the Astral, Gehenna, Asgard, the Abyss, Gladsheim, and the Prime Material—where Earth as we know it exists.

**Queets**. (kwēts) They were the indigenous people of the western Olympic Peninsula who lived to the south of the Chalat', and the north of the Quinault. They were absorbed by the larger Quinault tribe after the 1855 Treaty of Olympia, and have since disappeared as a recognized tribe.

**Quileute**. (kwĭl·ē·yūt) They were the indigenous people of the western Olympic Peninsula who lived to the north of the Chalat', and the south of the Makah. Their language was not of the Salish family; instead it was of the same origin as the Chimakum. According to their tradition, K'wati transformed wolves to make the first of the Quileute.

**Quinault**. (kwĭn·ălt) They were the indigenous people of the western Olympic Peninsula who lived to the south of the Queets, and the north of the Chehalis. They were given one of the larger reservations in Washington as a result of 1856 Quinault Treaty, though they have not thrived economically.

**Ranthalion**. (răn·thăl·yən) Keeper of the Tower of Infinity, and Lord of the Garrison of Infinity, he was of the guizor caste of the huisum race that was created by the Elder gods to serve as guardians of the mythic Towers of Ominous Power. The huisum were made to be neutral observers, scientists, chroniclers, and collectors of life in all its forms. Many gods, daemons, and other greater powers have sought to control them over the eons, but the huisum have managed to remain neutral.

**Raven**. (rā·vən) He was the god-like spirit of creation and trickery for many of the indigenous people of the Pacific Northwest mythologies. Known as the 'Trickster,' he was the greater spirit who dropped the stone as he flew that formed the land humans later inhabited. He was always seen as playing an angle or attempting to outsmart mankind for his own benefit. In art he was depicted as a black bird, or as a spry man with black hair and mismatched clothing, often containing baubles or colorful feathers.

**Red Pepper.** (rĕd pĕp·ər) [Schinus molle] It is quick growing tree that is invasive in the northern South America, Central America, and southern North America, and in herbology it has been used for purification, healing, and protection. Red pepper has been used to cure illness and to bind evil from entering protected spaces.

**Rose.** (rōz) [Rosa 'Mister Lincoln'] It is a flowering plant common to much of the United States and in herbology it has been used for its powers of luck, protection, healing, love, love divination, and psychic powers. Roses and the wood of the plant itself have been used to as protection when they are carried.

**Salish.** (sā·lĭsh) Family of indigenous languages that were interwoven along the coastal regions of what is now British Columbia and Washington, primary amongst these was the Skagit-Nisqually or Lushootseed. Many Salish terms were incorporated into the Chinook Jargon, which consists of terms and words from the languages of all the trading partners, used amongst indigenous people, the French, the British, and the Americans. A number of these words are still in use in the region as place names, rivers, mountains, and other things.

**Sésquac.** (sés·kwŏch) This is the Salish name of a 'wild man' who lived in the forest. The Sésquac, or Sasquatch, lived in the mountainous regions of the forests and was equally feared and revered by the indigenous people of the region. They were described as large ape-like proto-humans, covered in long hair, and standing between seven and twelve feet tall in some legends.

**Shou Lao.** (shō lă·ō) He was the god of longevity and knowledge, from the ancient Chinese pantheon of mythology. He also ruled over the date of death for every living thing. In art he was depicted as a small man with a very prominent bald head, bushy white eyebrows and random white whiskers, he often was shown carrying a staff and a golden peach.

**S'Klallam**. (sklăl·lŭm) They were the indigenous people of the northern Olympic Peninsula who lived in the valley of the Elwha River and the shadow of Hurricane Ridge, along the coast of the Strait of Juan de Fuca. They were a peaceful people who shared camps and villages with the Klallam.

**Skokomish**. (skō·kō·mĭsh) They were the largest group of nine tribes that comprised the Twana, an indigenous people of the eastern Olympic Peninsula who lived along Hood Canal, a fjord-like inlet. Skokomish means "river people" or "people of the river" in the Twana language. They like most of the tribes on the Olympic Peninsula relied heavily on fishing for their survival.

**Squaxin**. (skwăks·ĭn) They were a group of seven Salish clans of indigenous people who lived along the south eastern edge of the Olympic Peninsula. Consisting of the Noo-She-Chatl, Steh-Chass, Squi-Aitl, T'Peeksin, Se-Heh-Wa-Mish, Squawksin, and S'Hotle-Ma-Mish people, the Sqauxin lived along several inlets on the southern end of Puget Sound.

**Staff of Orkan**. (stăf ŏv ôr·kăn) This was an ancient wooden staff, said to have been crafted from a branch of Yggdrasil, the World Tree. It was imbued with powerful magic, the primary one being control over weather, hence its name 'Orkan' which is Norwegian for hurricane. It has long been in the possession of Woden in his armory. It was an item crafted of Eldritch magic.

**Star-Cross**. (stăr-krôs) This is the combination of two powerful symbols, the pentacle and the cross. The pentacle has long been used to represent the divine, or spirit over the four elements. It is a symbol of great power over the spiritual world, but has often been mistaken for the corruption of the symbol when it was inverted with a single point facing down, and two points facing up in a goat horn analogy. The cross, from Christian theology symbolizes divine forgiveness, divine power, and sacrifice. The combined symbol was first used by the Brotherhood of Olympus sect within the Livonian

Brothers of the Blade, that later became an autonomous subdivision of the larger Order of Teutonic knights.

**Strait of Juan de Fuca**. (strāt ŏv wăn də fyū·kǎ) The eighty mile long, fifteen mile wide waterway that separates the northern coast of the Olympic Peninsula and the southern edge of Vancouver Island, named after the Spanish sailor who reputedly discovered it in 1592.

**Succorbenoth**. (sū·khôr·bən·ŏth) He was a daemon who served many of the rulers in the netherworld known as the Abyss. He had dominion over gates, and has often linked to any daemonic incursions unto Earth because of his ability to make gates from the netherworlds to Earth through the manipulation of human hosts on the Earth side of the gate. He has also been linked to the death of Walter Reuss. In art he has been depicted as being a massively tall humanoid surrounded by a purplish-black aura, with a lion's mane of fiery red hair, and an overlarge smile filled with many interlocking fangs.

**Suquamish**. (sū·kwǎ·mǐsh) They were the indigenous people who lived north of the Squaxin, up and down the Puget Sound, but centered primarily on the smaller Kitsap Peninsula which was separated from the Olympic Peninsula by Hood Canal. They all wintered together in a village centered around Old Man House, the largest longhouse on Puget Sound.

**Tower of Infinity**. (tow·ər ŏv in·fǐn·ə·tē) One of a series of mythical towers built by the Elder gods that predate the rise of the Old gods, such as Woden, Amun, and Nu Kua. Each tower was given dominion over an aspect of reality. The Tower of Infinity granted visitors the ability to see into the infinite streams of time and space. Some Towers of Ominous Power, like the Tower of Infinity were in fixed locations, while others have been known to move by some unknown force or magic.

**Twana**. (twăn·ǎ) They were a larger group made up of nine tribes of indigenous people who lived along the eastern coast of the Olympic Peninsula. The Twana consisted of the Dabop, Quilcene, Dosewallips, Duckabush, Hoodsport, Skokomish, Vance Creek, Tahuya, and Duhlelap communities, within those communities there were at least thirty-three settlements.

**Være borte**. [Norwegian] English translation—Be gone.

**Ved kraften av de Stanget av Orkan**. [Norwegian] English translation—By the power of the Staff of Hurricanes.

**Veni, Vidi, Vici**. [Latin] English translation—I came, I saw, I conquered.

**Woden**. (wō·děn) He was the All-Father, greatest of the Aesir, and leader of Asgard, from the Norse pantheon of mythology. He was also known as Wodanaz or Odin. He has been known as a god of war, battle, victory, death, wisdom, magic, poetry, prophecy, and the hunt. Wednesday was named after him, 'Woden's day.' In art he was depicted as a large man with a long white beard, bearing an eye patch, often seen with a large golden spear (Gungnir), two ravens (Huginn and Muninn), and an eight legged horse (Sleipnir).

**Xièxiè nǐ, suǒyǒu de fùqīn**. [Chinese] English translation—Thank you, All-Father.

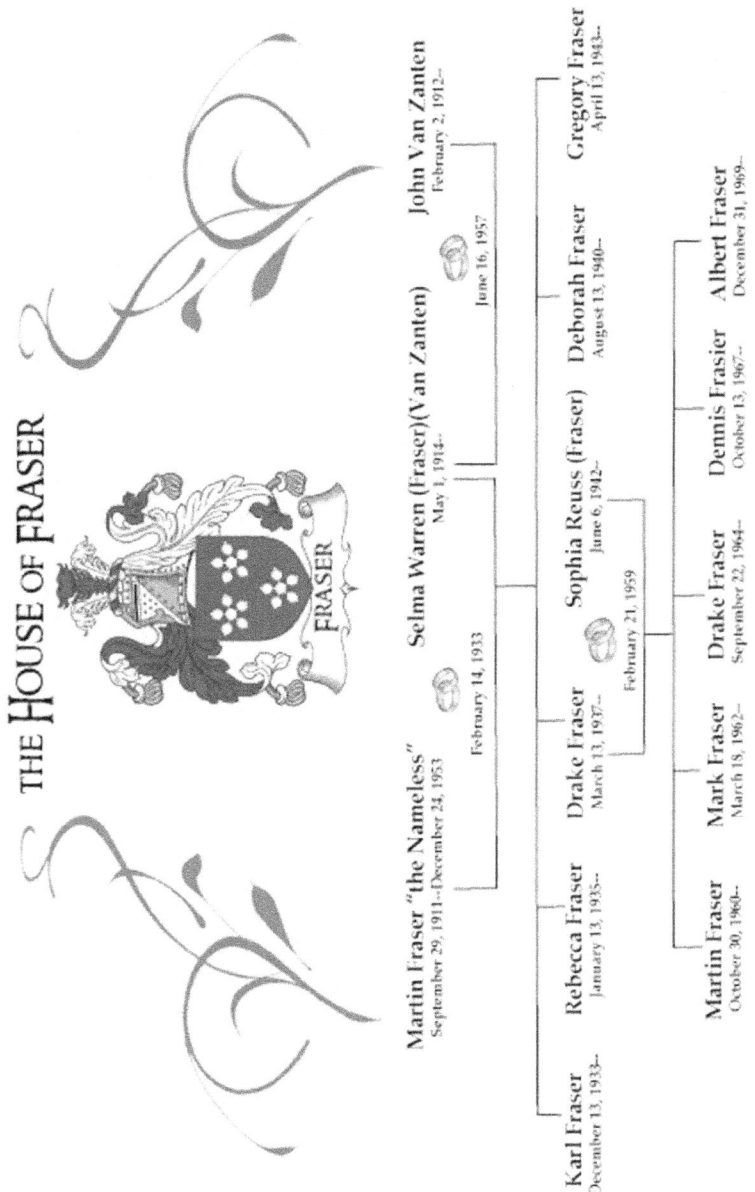

THE HOUSE OF FRASER

FRASER

Martin Fraser "the Nameless"
September 29, 1911–December 24, 1953

Selma Warren (Fraser)(Van Zanten)
May 1, 1914–

John Van Zanten
February 2, 1912–

February 14, 1933

June 16, 1957

Karl Fraser
December 13, 1933–

Rebecca Fraser
January 13, 1935–

Drake Fraser
March 13, 1937–

Sophia Reuss (Fraser)
June 6, 1942–

Deborah Fraser
August 13, 1940–

Gregory Fraser
April 13, 1943–

February 21, 1959

Martin Fraser
October 30, 1960–

Mark Fraser
March 18, 1962–

Drake Fraser
September 22, 1964–

Dennis Frasier
October 13, 1967–

Albert Fraser
December 31, 1969–

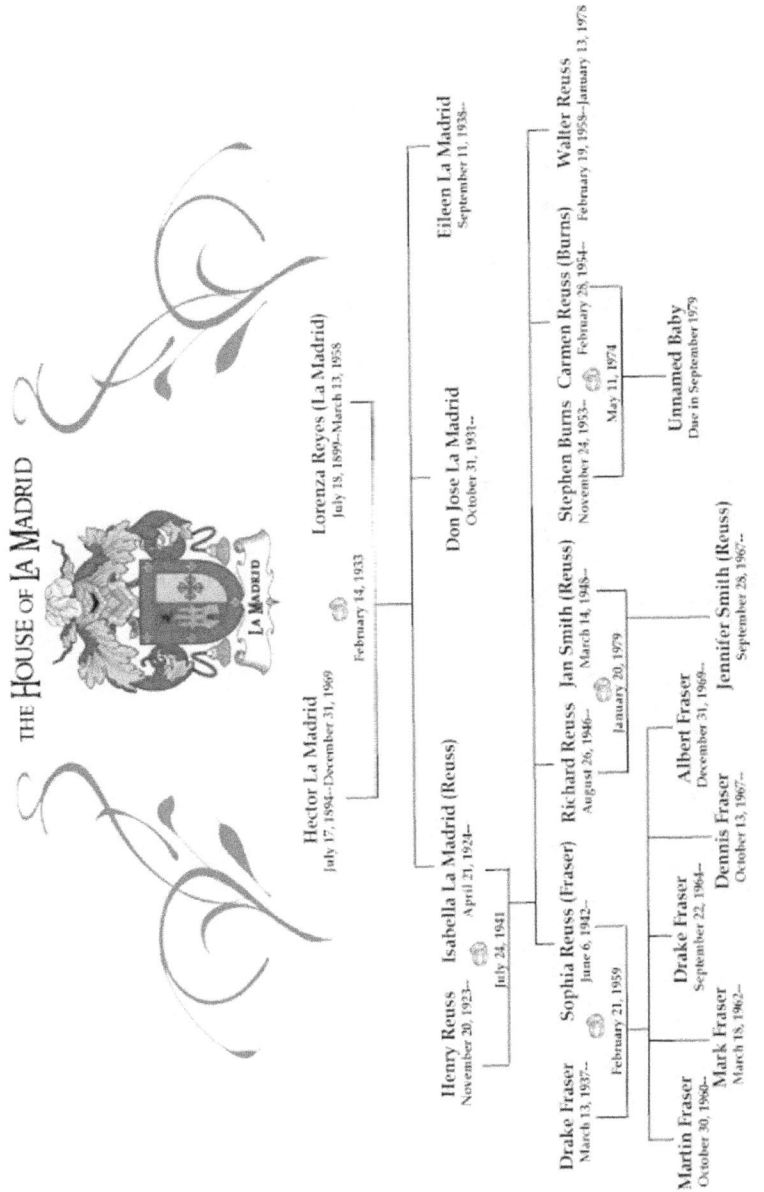

THE HOUSE OF LA MADRID

LA MADRID

Hector La Madrid
July 17, 1894–December 31, 1969

Lorenza Reyes (La Madrid)
July 18, 1899–March 13, 1958

February 14, 1933

Fileen La Madrid
September 11, 1938–

Don Jose La Madrid
October 31, 1931–

Walter Reuss
February 19, 1958–January 13, 1978

Isabella La Madrid (Reuss)
April 21, 1924–

Henry Reuss
November 20, 1923–

July 24, 1941

Richard Reuss
August 26, 1946–

Jan Smith (Reuss)
March 14, 1948–

January 20, 1979

Stephen Burns
November 24, 1953–

Carmen Reuss (Burns)
February 28, 1954–

May 11, 1974

Unnamed Baby
Due in September 1979

Jennifer Smith (Reuss)
September 28, 1967–

Sophia Reuss (Fraser)
June 6, 1942–

February 21, 1959

Albert Fraser
December 31, 1969–

Drake Fraser
March 13, 1937–

Drake Fraser
September 22, 1964–

Dennis Fraser
October 13, 1967–

Martin Fraser
October 30, 1960–

Mark Fraser
March 18, 1962–

315

THE HOUSE OF REUSS

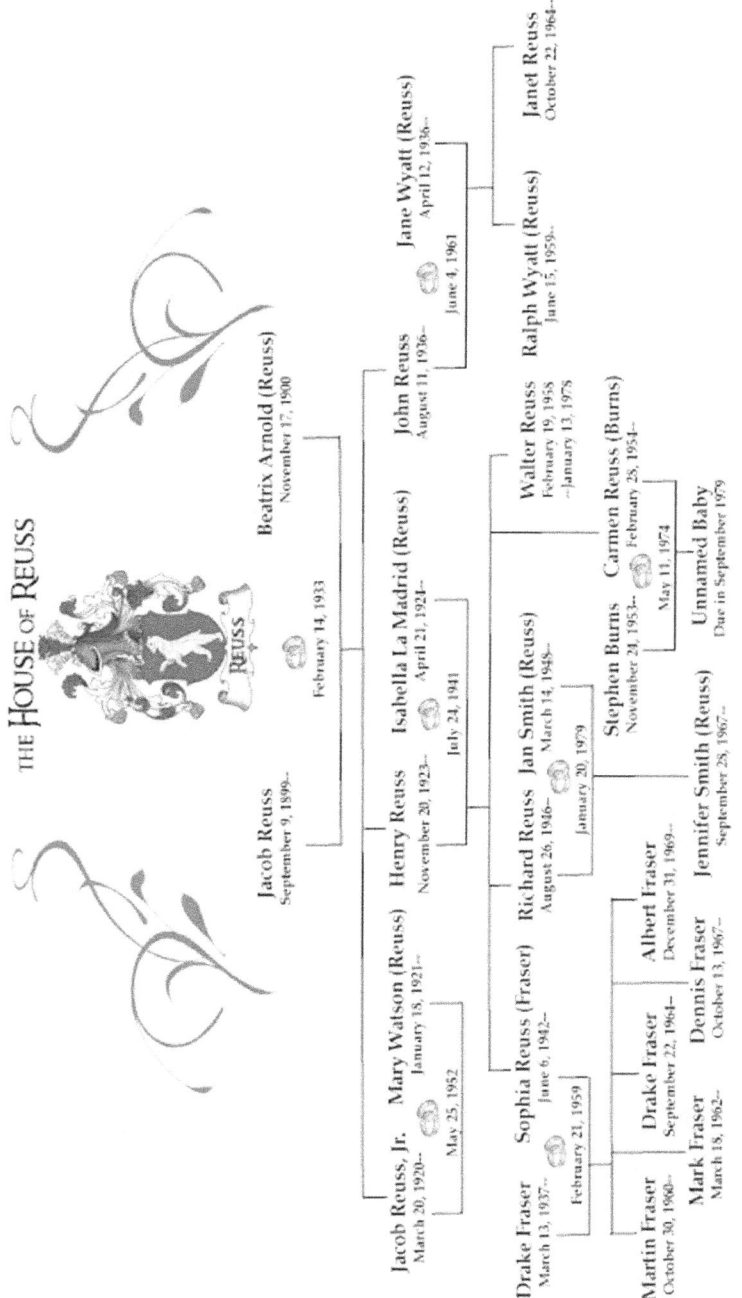

Jacob Reuss
September 9, 1899–

February 14, 1933

Beatrix Arnold (Reuss)
November 17, 1900

Jacob Reuss, Jr.
March 20, 1920–

Mary Watson (Reuss)
January 18, 1921–

May 25, 1952

Henry Reuss
November 20, 1923–

July 24, 1941

Isabella La Madrid (Reuss)
April 21, 1924–

John Reuss
August 11, 1936–

June 4, 1961

Jane Wyatt (Reuss)
April 12, 1936–

Ralph Wyatt (Reuss)
June 15, 1959–

Janet Reuss
October 22, 1964–

Drake Fraser
March 13, 1937–

Sophia Reuss (Fraser)
June 6, 1942–

February 21, 1959

Richard Reuss
August 26, 1946–

Jan Smith (Reuss)
March 14, 1948–

January 20, 1979

Stephen Burns
November 24, 1953–

Carmen Reuss (Burns)
February 28, 1954–

May 11, 1974

Walter Reuss
February 19, 1958
–January 13, 1975

Unnamed Baby
Due in September 1979

Jennifer Smith (Reuss)
September 25, 1967–

Martin Fraser
October 30, 1960–

Mark Fraser
March 18, 1962–

Drake Fraser
September 22, 1964–

Dennis Fraser
October 13, 1967–

Albert Fraser
December 31, 1969–

# DISCUSSION GUIDE

Between the publication of the first edition of this book and the second edition, which is part of the larger Brotherhood of Olympus Saga, the author attended a number of book clubs and classrooms that had read the Deadliest Game. It became apparent through his discussions with book club members and middle and high school English teachers that providing a resource of guided questions could be extremely valuable for anyone looking to add a book to their club, or classroom literary circles. The author enlisted the aid of two English teachers with nearly 30 years of experience between them to craft a set of literary questions for his books, aligned to CCSS. Questions, comments, feedback, and of course photos of examples of student work can be directed to the author's website:

**https://guysimpson.net**

## Chapter 1: The Unexpected News – the accident

Page 13 – Wally told Drake as a youngster, "Crying only makes it hurt worse."
-What message is being reinforced by this statement?
(CCSS.ELA-Literacy.RL.8.3, CCSS.ELA-Literacy.RL.8.4)

-What implications does this have on Drake and his future?
(CCSS.ELA-Literacy.RL.8.3)

*Extension*:
How does this account demonstrate the power of words?
Identify a statement from a family member or loved one that has stuck with you. (CCSS.ELA-Literacy.W.8.3)

## Chapter 2: La Madrid Gift – Psychic abilities

Page 25 – As Drake ventures down the hallway, consider, what is pulling him toward the door? (*Read and predict*)
(CCSS.ELA-Literacy.W.8.3)

*Extension:*
Many people have what can be considered psychic abilities, like the La Madrid Gift. Why do they sometimes feel compelled to conceal those abilities?

*Activities:*
-Research a culture which fully embraces the idea of people possessing psychic abilities. Report your findings via a visual display. You may compare and contrast dissimilar cultures. (CCSS.ELA-Literacy.W.8.2, CCSS.ELA-Literacy.RL.8.9, CCSS.ELA-Literacy.RH.6-8.6, CCSS.ELA-Literacy.RH.6-8.7)

-Generate a list of terms associated with people having psychic abilities. Then, label them as having negative or positive connotations. (CCSS.ELA-Literacy.L.8.4, CCSS.ELA-Literacy.L.8.5, CCSS.ELA-Literacy.RH.6-8.8)

## Chapter 3: Only the Good Die Young

Page 39 – The first use of the Fraser brother's term, dillhole. "It's only 8:30 dillhole."
Siblings often create slang terms for each other.
-How can these be considered terms of endearment? (CCSS.ELA-Literacy.L.8.4, CCSS.ELA-Literacy.L.8.5)

-How do nicknames/terms strengthen family bonds? How can they also be destructive? (CCSS.ELA-Literacy.L.8.4, CCSS.ELA-Literacy.L.8.5, CCSS.ELA-Literacy.RL.8.4)

*-Author note:*
This is the first mention of the ratchet noise that is pervasive in the earlier chapters and then reappears near the end of the book as a repetitive "clicking." The use of the onomatopoeia was intentional to build a connection between the mordgeists and the readers. The first actual clicking occurs with Wally's turn signal for the turn he never got to take.

## Chapter 4:  I'll Always Be Young

Page 44 – Notice the initial sounds of the mordgeists, as they begin talking.
-What is the author's purpose of using a sound similar to what we hear described in chapter 3 when Mark is working on his car?  (CCSS.ELA-Literacy.RL.8.4)

-What events occur in chapter 4 that link back to previous chapters? Find examples of looping, reference to prior events. (CCSS.ELA-Literacy.RL.8.1, CCSS.ELA-Literacy.RL.8.3)


## Chapter 5: Lilacs and Roses – Introduction of Miss Furfur and Rachel Finnegan

-What are you starting to notice about Drake's personality? (CCSS.ELA-Literacy.RL.8.3)

-Or, which of Drake's personality traits are becoming more pronounced/solidified?

Page 54 – "Girls have cooties," is another instance of Wally's words influencing Drake.

-How is Miss Furfur different from other girls Drake knows? Describe how she is different enough that he has to ponder Wally's message when interacting with her.  (CCSS.ELA-Literacy.RL.8.1, CCSS.ELA-Literacy.RL.8.3, CCSS.ELA-Literacy.RL.8.6)

Miss Furfur grants Drake and Rachel access to the secret archive room.
-What is the appeal of the secret room? (CCSS.ELA-Literacy.RL.8.1)

Pages 60-61 – Identify key elements of foreshadowing located in this chapter.  What subtle hints does the author give the reader? (CCSS.ELA-Literacy.RL.8.1)

## Chapter 6: Ten Thousand Lakes – Transition/change

The author fills in some of the background story for the reader.
-How do family dynamics and decisions made by Drake's parents affect his character? (CCSS.ELA-Literacy.RL.8.3)

-Many changes occur in chapter 6 – Identify the most significant ones and describe the impact those might have on Drake. (CCSS.ELA-Literacy.RL.8.1, CCSS.ELA-Literacy.RL.8.2, CCSS.ELA-Literacy.RL.8.3)

Page 70 – "Young Drake...his encyclopedic mind at work, recorded all of this and one day it would help lead him to a discovery of his true heritage."

-What is an encyclopedic mind? (CCSS.ELA-Literacy.L.8.5)

-This is an example of which figurative language? (CCSS.ELA-Literacy.RL.8.1, CCSS.ELA-Literacy.RL.8.4, CCSS.ELA-Literacy.L.8.5)

-The second part of the quote is an example of which literary device? (CCSS.ELA-Literacy.RL.8.1, CCSS.ELA-Literacy.RL.8.4)

## Chapter 7: The Spirit Board – Introduction to the Game

Page 77 – Drake has a brief encounter with an old man he describes as, "...a pirate Santa Claus." Why would the author include this interaction? (CCSS.ELA-Literacy.RL.8.1, CCSS.ELA-Literacy.RL.8.3, CCSS.ELA-Literacy.RL.8.4, CCSS.ELA-Literacy.L.8.5)

Page 78 – The boys discover the Spirit Board when looking for games in the campground Rec Room.

-What prior knowledge or background do you have of Spirit Boards? Other names? (CCSS.ELA-Literacy.RL.8.6, CCSS.ELA-Literacy.RL.8.9)

-How are they portrayed in the media, movies especially? (CCSS.ELA-Literacy.RL.8.6, CCSS.ELA-Literacy.RL.8.9)

-How does the author use text structure to convey the mode of communication used by the board? Or, how does the board talk to the boys? (CCSS.ELA-Literacy.RL.8.5)

-Who takes the most interest in the board? (CCSS.ELA-Literacy.RL.8.1)

-What implications do you think this will have for him? (Prediction) (CCSS.ELA-Literacy.RL.8.1, CCSS.ELA-Literacy.RL.8.3)

## Chapter 8: If a Picture Paints a Thousand Words – Back to the Library

Pages 90-91 – After Mark questions the validity of the secret room at the library, Miss Furfur once again opens the door for Drake and Rachel. What explanation could be used to support the existence of the door and the archive room?

-During an afternoon of research, Rachel asks Drake, "If you could know anything about your future, what would you want to know?" Describe and explain what you would want to know. (CCSS.ELA-Literacy.RL.8.6)

-If you could ask about the future would you ask a question? Why or why not? (CCSS.ELA-Literacy.RL.8.6)

If so, what would it be? (CCSS.ELA-Literacy.RL.8.6)

Would you ask about anyone else? (CCSS.ELA-Literacy.RL.8.6)

Do you consider any questions off limits? (CCSS.ELA-Literacy.RL.8.6)

## Chapter 9: Must be Your Lucky Day – Spirit board at Payless

Page 98 – This is the first mention of lights flickering around Drake when he walks under the Payless sign. What do you make of it? (CCSS.ELA-Literacy.RL.8.1)

-What is it that allows Drake to talk to Miss Furfur, considering he usually tries to avoid most girls? (CCSS.ELA-Literacy.RL.8.1)

Page 101 – "The ride home was in silence…it was somehow longer than it should have been." Describe situations where time seems to expand or slow. What causes that feeling? (CCSS.ELA-Literacy.RL.8.1, CCSS.ELA-Literacy.RL.8.6)

At this point, the Spirit Board establishes itself as a primary character.

-How is the use of an inanimate object as a character in this book different from other stories you have read? Consider the interactions between it and the boys. (CCSS.ELA-Literacy.RL.8.3, CCSS.ELA-Literacy.RL.8.5, CCSS.ELA-Literacy.RL.8.9)

## Chapter 10:  Torn Asunder—the Spirit board spells EVIL

Page 110 - Drake dreams of a black stone tower and begins to put some of the pieces together.  He is starting to see the correlation between Miss Furfur's arrival and the archive room in the library.  How do you feel they are connected? Support your position using facts from the text.

Page 113 - Drake runs into Rachel, on her birthday, and she has a gift for him that she makes him promise to wear for her.  How is the author using symbols to advance the story, or change the flow of the story?

Identify the type of influence, positive or negative, each female character has on Drake.

Why did the board spell – E.V.I.L.?

Author note:
The Star-Cross introduced.

## Chapter 11:  Madame Chavali – Psychic bookstore visit

Page 124 - Drake and Rachel visit a psychic book store and the store keeper states, "What will be may be, and what may be will be, unless you choose to do neither, then nothing will remain."

-It seems to be circular talking, but what do you think the store keeper is trying to tell Drake and his friend?

Pages 125-128 - The mystic tells Drake, "You will be a king, a king by your own hand." She foretells of many castles, a tower, great daemons and the Fraser brothers being in grave danger. She tells him to keep the brothers together and to trust in himself.

-What might this mean?

Why might it be important to keep his brothers together?

## Chapter 12: Brothers Divided

Page 133 - Martin explains to Dennis that if they focus they can move the bottle cap.
Martin later tells Drake, "We are learning things beyond your ability and knowledge."

Drake prides himself on his intelligence; describe how the "beyond your knowledge" statement might have made him feel?

## Chapter 13: The Loop

Notice how the author describes the geography and the locations where Drake visits with his family.
-What is the author's purpose for describing the Olympic Peninsula, the Hoh Rainforest and Hurricane Ridge?

What is the significance of this setting?

How do these relate to the map at the beginning of the book of the Olympic Peninsula?

Pages 157-163 - Drake dreams about visiting Mount Olympus.
Why does the author include the dream scene?

What does it reveal in terms of the purpose for the existence of the Brotherhood of Olympus?

At first, Drake thinks the visit to Mount Olympus must be a dream.
How does Drake finding the Staff of Orkan under his sleeping bag affect the dream perception?

## Chapter 14: The Deal – Martin makes a major mistake

Page 169 - Martin's friend, Tom, tells him that he can take money from his register at work a little at a time, and they can pay it back the next week when they get paid.
Martin listens to his friend and takes the money to buy things for his party. What insight does this give about Martin's personality?

Why wasn't Tom punished?

Was Martin trying to protect his friend and friendship by taking all the blame?

Page 172 - What is the significance of their dad kissing Mark and Drake on the forehead?

Martin is given the choice by the Hoquiam Police to join the military or go to jail as a consequence for his actions. Has something like this ever happened before, historically or in other literature or media, explain your position?

How can parents be affected by the actions or behavior of their child?

## Chapter 15: Changes Bearing Gifts

Page 163 - Rachel tells Drake about the herbology book she used to make charms for Drake.
What is herbology?

Page 164 - Drake hangs the charms over the doors and sprinkles the ground pepper around his house just as Rachel directed, and later that night Dennis comes out of his coma.

Many people believe in lucky charms and superstitions. What are some superstitions that you are familiar with or have heard about?

Using citations, explain who does Rachel believe is behind the troubles facing Drake and his family?

How has Rachel's role in the story changed from earlier chapters?

## Chapter 16: Carmen of the La Madrid Family

Page 189 - "Martin snuggled on the couch, he was home and yet he would never be at home there again."
How can his home not be his home anymore?

How does Martin's interaction with Tom when he visits his old school help illustrate that point?

Page 191 - Aunt Carmen is described as a hippie and a flower child.

What images are associated with those two terms; do they have negative or positive connotations?

Why is this information about Aunt Carmen important?

Pages 191-196 - Aunt Carmen and Martin are using the Spirit board and it tells them of what the future might hold for their family.
Why do you think the author spelled out the Spirit board responses letter by letter rather than simply stating what was said?

The author choose to use the Spirit board as a character with dialogue, how has this 'character' developed during the story? What are its end goals?

Page 197-200 How did Wally's apparition in the backseat of her car frighten his sister? What benefit resulted in his sudden appearance?

Author note:
Chapter Illustrations: provide an Easter Egg reveal, what do they spell?
Chapter 7, Page 74
Chapter 9, Page 96
Chapter 12, Page 130
Chapter 16, Page 186

## Chapter 17: The Coming Storm – Photograph of the Boys 1965

Page 181 - As Drake is looking at old photos and his family he thinks to himself 'that the family has turned the corner in a philosophical way.'

What does the author mean by philosophical way?

Give examples from the text.

How does the wrongful death lawsuit change the temporary tranquility of what could have just been a somewhat 'happy ending' to the book during the middle of chapter 17?

Page 207 – Photo of Drake, Mark, Martin, Uncle Wally, his dog Tippy, and their cousin Ralph—what is the importance of this picture? Use examples from the text to support your position.

Pages 208-209 - Drake returns to the old photograph and realizes, 'This is his destiny, and now he must rise up to face it.'
What do you think is Drake's destiny?

## Chapter 18: Of Presidents and Librarians

Page 212 - Rachel nominates Drake for class president.
Why does Rachel nominate Drake?

Why does Drake vote for the boy who was nominated against him?

Identify what is Drake's moral dilemma in this chapter?

Page 219 - Drake writes a note and leaves it in the empty archive room.
-What do you think Drake wrote on the note?

 Why did he remove the books from the library?

Page 220 - Miss Furfur tells Rachel, "We both know who we

both are, and neither one of us is fooling the other."
-What did the author mean by this?

How have the roles of Miss Furfur and Rachel Finnegan changed?

How might this foreshadow their roles in future stories?

## Chapter 19: The Eyeglasses

Page 226 – the Spirit board tells Martin and Dennis to, "Find my glasses," and, "Glasses see truth," to help them fight the lawsuit. How might seeing the truth be linked to Wally's missing glasses?

Page 229 - The sight of the piece of yellow metal gives Drake a sudden chill.
Have you ever had a similar feeling, what caused it?

What is the significance of the eyeglasses resting in a small field of clover?

What other uses of clover has the author used in the book?

Pages 230-232 - A disembodied voice yelled at them to 'get out.'
Who or what might have been this voice?

## Chapter 20: Flight to the Bridge

Pages 236-237 - The brothers are trying to outrun the death tornado as they 'zipped by' and 'skidded' and 'tires squealed'. What other words could the author have used to describe the flight to the bridge?

Page 213 - Drake shouts, "Du skal ikke passere," and the blackness stopped.
Why does the author use a foreign language?

Would the statement have the same impact if it had been in English? Why or why not?

This is the first time, since the death of their Uncle Wally, that the Fraser brothers act together in a unified way. What brings them together?

Yes, their lives are threatened in a dire situation, but is there a greater purpose?

## Chapter 21: The Council of Aunt Carmen

Page 246 - Aunt Carmen tells the brothers, "That board is a portal to these creatures."
What is the best definition of portal in this context?

Pages 247-248 - Aunt Carmen tells Drake, "Make sure we get rid of all of it," after first saying, "Just make sure you burn all of it."
What is the effect of the repetition?

Page 248 - Carmen tells the brothers, "Don't let it divide you."
What is it?

Explain why she issues this warning?

## Chapter 22: The Brotherhood of Olympus

Page 253 - Drake tells his brothers they are a brotherhood. "United we stand, divided we fall."

How does this brotherhood compare to other examples of brotherhoods you know?

How does this chapter add to your understanding of the title?

Drake's choice to step into the middle of his circled brothers was a dramatic shift in his character as he stepped into a leadership role, something that he had always avoided. What was Drake's motivation and what effect does this have on his brothers?

## Chapter 23: Ascent into Madness

How does their grandparent's house change once the Spirit board is attacked?

Page 260 - The stairway turns into a bottomless abyss with a snaking purple tentacle.
When does the author first mention Dennis' fear of the stairs?

Page 261 - Dennis does what anyone does when told not to look down.
Why do people do the opposite of what they are told?

When did the author first introduce bottle caps as a psychic tool?

## Chapter 24: The Fire of Redemption

Page 271 – Drake tells Albert, "You're going to have the most important job," implying something more as well. How does Albert respond when he can't keep the door open?

Page 272 - Mark states to Drake, "Little brother, I want you to know something before we go in there. You and I have always been together, I trust you with my life, and I think you feel the same. I love you. No matter what happens, I will always be there for you. You got that?" How is the author using foreshadowing in this section of the book?

How has the house further changed as Drake and Mark enter it?

How does the author describe the change in the surroundings once the Spirit board starts to burn?

Page 282 - As the brothers drive away, they have a sudden urge to look back at the fire, but neither boy does.
Why does the author end the story in this way?

How does the author use foreshadowing of future stories in the last pages of this tale?

## Epilogue: Council of the Wise

What was the author's purpose for including this retelling of the events surrounding the death of Walter Reuss?

The author included mythological characters from around the world in this story, and details a world behind our world where a struggle for the future of humanity is taking place. How does this knowledge affect your understanding of the story?

Does it change your views on the characters?

You see that Rachel's belief that Miss Furfur was more than just a librarian was correct, why might an underworld Countess act alongside gods long seen as being just and supportive of humanity?

## Overall Questions and Activities

- How does the author create opportunities for the reader to interact with the text?

-What are the advantages of the story being told in third person? (CCSS.ELA-Literacy.RL.8.5, CCSS.ELA-Literacy.RL.8.6)

-What effect does the looping of events in early chapters have on your interpretation of the plot? (CCSS.ELA-Literacy.RL.8.5)

Use of Mythology – What background knowledge does the reader employ to fully appreciate the mythological references? (CCSS.ELA-Literacy.RL.8.9)

Text features/graphics – How do the illustrations enhance the story, or add to the reader's understanding of the text? (CCSS.ELA-Literacy.RL.8.5)
Do they enhance or detract from the book?

CCSS
Reading Literature: Key Ideas and Details 9.1, 9.2
Reading Literature: Understanding Craft and Structure

History/Social Studies: Integration of Knowledge and Ideas

Writing: Research to Build and Present Knowledge

FATE

THE BROTHERHOOD OF OLYMPUS
AND THE TOWER OF DREAMS

*This tale is based upon actual events...*

**To Everything There is a Season**
**Chapter One**
**Autumn 1979**
**Hoquiam, Washington**

Being sophomore class president was not really as bad as he thought it would be when he was elected into the position at the end of his freshman year. Nearly all August he dreaded coming back to school. By Labor Day those feeling had turned to anxiety. He knew he had to stand in front of the entire student body, almost six hundred kids, and say something into a microphone about his fellow tenth-graders. As a painfully shy, introverted bookworm, that was not his proverbial cup of tea. The odd thing about time was that it continued to pass at the same incremental rate whether you wanted it to go faster, slower, jump ahead, or just stop. It was like waiting for what seemed like forever for a desired holiday with presents, or how quickly the last days of summer dwindled away if you didn't want to go back to school. Time was a fickle concept at best.

Tuesday, September fourth, brought the inevitable welcome back-to-school assembly to Drake Fraser. He had prepared a speech that merged the message of Abraham Lincoln at Gettysburg, with the logical ramblings of Mr. Spock. It was a page and a half long. He practiced reading it, twice. He dressed in his hooded basketball sweatshirt from the year before, crisp new blue jeans, and his new Converse All-Star tennis shoes. Both the jeans and the shoes were his new school clothes for the year.

Drake had grown over the summer he stood an

imposing six foot, four and one-half inches tall, but still lacked much girth. His straight black hair was now past his ears in length, in a rough bowl style. His Spanish, dark olive complexion had darkened over the summer as it always did from his time spent outside. He stood nervously next to the other class presidents, silently fidgeting, along the wall of the gym. He took the moment to review his speech one last time.

"My fellow sophomores, in the course of human events," Drake mumbled to himself as he began to read his handwritten monologue. The time slipped away, and the Associated Student Body advisor, Mr. Dawson, took over the microphone from the varsity cheerleaders.

"Thank you varsity cheerleaders," Mr. Dawson stated with his mouth a bit too close to the microphone. "And now, here are your three returning presidents to welcome each class back, sophomore Drake Fraser, junior Daphne Young, and senior Steve Hanson. Please give them a round of applause."

"Psst... Fraser," interrupted Steve. Drake had been reading his speech so intently that he didn't hear the introduction. "Let's go."

Drake and Steve followed Daphne to the center of the gym floor and they stood awaiting Mr. Dawson. Steve and Daphne waved to some of their friends and classmates to an increased amount of noise. Drake stood holding his speech. A noticeable tremor had started in his hands, and panic was welling up in him.

"First let's hear from your sophomore class president, Drake Fraser," Mr. Dawson's voice echoed through the gym. He turned and handed the microphone to Drake, who looked at it like it was an alien device. Time seemed to freeze. He noticed the gym full of students and staff, their eyes upon him. Even the kids who normally didn't pay attention, like his brother Mark, were looking at him, waiting.

"Drake," Daphne quietly encouraged him. "You have your speech, read it, they're waiting."

"Come on, man," Steve added with a slight nudge. "You can do it."

Drake had to react. He looked at his paper, and it was blank. His heart beat so violently he was sure it would rip through his chest. He decided in that moment to improvise. He thought of something calming from the past year, raised the microphone, and opened his mouth.

"I'm very good at integral and differential calculus," he began in a low voice, barely audible through the sound system. The gym quieted and his voice grew stronger and louder. "I know the scientific names of beings animalculous."

The students in the gym were hanging on his words, trying to figure out the cryptic yet lyrical message he was delivering. The message was not lost on the choir, band, drama, and most of the art kids, and a particular blonde girl who caught Drake's eyes, who all started to sing with Drake as he finished his speech.

"In short, in matters vegetable, animal, and mineral," Drake stated as he held the microphone very close to his mouth, his voice now echoing through the large space. "I am the very model of a modern Major-General."

The students singing along with his spoken words stood and clapped loudly, bringing his brother Mark to his feet, along with a quickly rising contingent of other students. Drake handed the microphone to Daphne, and he felt the heat of his body temperature radiate from him. He remembered very little of the rest of the assembly, or the first day of school, for that matter.

By the first Friday of school, many of the routines of the prior year had returned. Drake sat in the lunchroom at a table occupied by fringe kids, outsiders, invisibles, or socially awkward brains. He received more recognition from students passing by, but no invitation to join another table, though he never sought one out either.

He waited and hoped Rachel Finnegan would rejoin him

for lunches, like she did for most of last year. But through the first week he didn't see her at lunchtime. He'd thought a lot about her, how she infuriated him by nominating him for class president, how she always pestered him about his artwork, how she hung out with him at the Hoquiam Public Library for most of last year, and how she gave him the medallion which he still wore on her birthday two summers ago. She was in his mind, and despite the words of his deceased uncle Wally, 'girls have cooties,' still haunting him, he'd come to realize that he liked her. He liked her long blonde hair, her cheery attitude, her infectious smile, and her endearing support she'd demonstrated for him and his family.

He sat quietly and ate his somewhat warm 'hot' lunch.

"Hullo Drake," rang the familiar tone of Rachel as she appeared before him on the opposite side of the table. She stood there, her hair pulled back in a loose ponytail, wearing a green V-necked sweater and a knee-length black skirt. She looked down at him and he smiled, forcing his dimples to pop out. Rachel felt the temperature rise in the room. "Are you just gonna look at me, or are you gonna invite me to sit down?"

"Please," Drake said as he began to rise. He couldn't recall ever seeing her in a dress before, or wearing green, despite his insistence that she was Irish. "Join me."

"Thanks," she cooed as she tucked her skirt behind her, and sat down. "By the way, using the Major-General's song from the Pirates of Penzance was simply brilliant as your welcome back speech. The high school did that show last year. Very topical, Mister President, most of the kids still know that song. Didya like how we all sang the last part with you?"

"I didn't sing," Drake responded as he set down his fork. "I'm not a singer, you're the singer, remember?"

"Oh, that's right," she toyed with him as she opened her brown paper lunch bag. "You're an artist and all around genius, not a singer."

"I never said that," Drake interjected as he watched her.

"I know," Rachel said with a sly smile, "but that doesn't mean you aren't. Besides, that's my opinion."

Drake sat and forced himself to eat since he didn't like to eat while others watched him. Fortunately, Rachel was also occupied eating so it wasn't like she was staring at him like she did the first few times she sat with him last year. He thought of tangents and angles to try and broach the subject of liking her. Every one of them sounded completely lame in his head.

"Whatcha thinking?" Rachel queried as she studied his face doing what appeared to be mental gymnastics.

"Nothing," he quickly retorted.

"Oh, okay," she replied as she twirled a loose part of her hair with the index finger of her left hand. "How was your summer?"

"Well," Drake began as he pondered how to tell her all of the events of the summer, "you know Miss Furfur never came back to the library, right?"

"Yeah, good riddance," she responded with a wrinkled face. "I didn't like her Drake, she's a daemon and she threatened me. Didya know that?"

"Uh uh," he answered. "She isn't a daemon."

"Whatever," Rachel immediately rebutted. "What about your grandparents and the lawsuit? And that nasty Spirit Board game your brother had?"

"I don't remember you being that interested in all of that, Rachel," he replied as he ate, taking careful precaution to avoid talking with food in his mouth.

"Duh," she said with a giggle. "Don't you remember me hanging out in the library doing all that research with you? Of course I'm interested."

"Well," he began to explain, using his hands more to describe what he was saying "the Spirit Board turned evil. It attacked us, or at least whatever was using it attacked us. It wrecked both of my brother's cars with a black tornado of death."

"Wow," she interrupted. "Really?"

"Yes," Drake continued intently, "and then we had to go into my grandparent's house to get the Spirit Board and burn it, but it was like haunted, and I had to fight mordgeists with my staff. My brother Dennis almost got pulled straight to Hell by a nasty purple tentacle and we all nearly died. But the board wouldn't burn because we'd forgotten some of it in the house."

"Wow," she responded again as she ate her orange, slice by slice. She struggled not to smile, that was like the most words Drake had ever said to her at one time. She was very happy, yet tried her best to remain serious. "That sounds incredible and really scary too."

"Well, we eventually got it to burn," Drake added as he moved his hands with an enthusiasm Rachel had never seen. "And when it did, I think it broke the cycle of evil. A few weeks later, in fact, the lawyers told my grandparents that the truck driver's family had dropped their lawsuit against them."

"Cool," she added as she watched him talk, carefully observing his body language. "Well, I'm glad you're okay, you and your whole family, right?"

"Yeah my family's okay now," Drake pondered about his family, his four brothers, his parents, his aunts and uncles, and his grandparents, as he replied to her question. "And you know what else is cool?"

"What's that Drake?" Rachel asked a question to his question.

"Well," he began with a spark in his eyes, "before we went into the haunted house I made us into a team, like heroes or something."

"Like the Superfriends?" she asked.

"No," he quickly answered. "Not like superheroes. Although that'd be really cool, too. We're like Knights of the Round Table, you know, we became the Brotherhood of Olympus."

"Oh, that is awesome Drake. I get the brotherhood thing, cause you're all brothers and all," she stated a bit confused by his gushing information to her. "But why

Olympus? Why not the Brotherhood of Fraser? Or the Brotherhood of Aberdeen? Or the Brotherhood of Grays Harbor? Or…"

"Hmmm…" Drake interrupted her before she took that tangent any further and then he responded thoughtfully. "I'm not sure, except that I recall being told that is what we should be called in a weird dream I had a couple years ago. Some god, I think he might've been Odin, you know, the chief god of the Norse pantheon. He told me all of that, and gave me a magical staff."

"Okay," she responded as she peered at him with doubtful eyes. She knew there were some very sinister forces at play last year around Drake and his family, Miss Furfur the daemon librarian was one, but getting magical weapons from ancient Norse gods was a bit of a stretch. "Drake Fraser, you're still a very weird boy."

Drake blushed. People around them began to clean up and get ready to go to fifth period.

"What do you think of my necklace?" she questioned, tactfully changing the subject as she raised it out from her pale skin above her cleavage. "It's a four leaf clover, and I put it under polished glass and made a charm out of it. I also made this bracelet the same way. Do you like 'em?"

Drake looked at both of the pieces of jewelry with admiration of her workmanship.

"Those are cool. You're very good at charm making," he said as he thought of his own medallion he wore that she had made. "But, Rachel, I do have another question for you. I noticed you're wearing a green shirt."

"Sweater," she interrupted.

"A green sweater," he continued, "and you have new jewelry made of four leaf clovers. Did your dad finally admit to being a leprechaun?"

"Drake Fraser, you take that back!" she snapped. He wasn't sure if she was being playful, or angry.

"I'm sorry," he said. "I didn't mean to offend you."

"It's time to go back to class," Rachel said as she rolled

up her lunch sack with a simple smile. "And Drake, you really need to get a clue about how girls work. Maybe you can look that up in the encyclopedia."

Drake wished there were such entries in the encyclopedia to help him better understand people, especially girls. Unfortunately, he never got to tell her that he liked her that day.

By late September, Drake had been having lunch with Rachel every day. He still couldn't muster the courage to talk to her about his feelings. He was getting comfortable talking with her during lunch though, and even began to forget about his inability to eat while someone watched him.

He also spent more time with some of the kids in his art class. He was by far the most accomplished at drawing in the entire school. Two of the guys in his class, who sat at his table of four, actually recruited him to come over after school and try playing bass guitar for their band. Bill Thompson and Pete Mason had both long admired Drake's artwork. They played guitar and drums and needed a bass player for their garage band, so they thought they would see if Drake could play.

Two or three times a week the guys would gather in Bill's garage. They had a trap set in one corner, and some amplifiers in another with a few twenty-five foot cables running out to guitar stands and microphones. Drake didn't like the look of the microphone, since it conjured up images of being made to talk in front of the whole school. But over time he learned a few bass progressions, could read a bass line on sheet music, and, most importantly, could keep a steady rhythm to blend the drums into the guitar.

They christened the name of their band FATE. Drake drew up a stylized logo, with each letter having an arrow-like end. They used their band name to work on a project in art. Each student had to make an album cover, paint it on tag board, and have it graded. The three boys made the self-titled first album, *FATE*, the second album, *The Rising Dead*, that featured a skull on the cover, and the third album, *Twisted Fate*, which had a giant screw going into a thick cluster of arrows all pointing away from each other. Drake drew the titles for each of the albums, along with some of the other more artistic details. He completed and turned in The Rising Dead album and earned an "A" grade on it.

By early October, Drake was writing some lyrical poetry that Bill and Pete were putting to music. Drake still didn't like to sing, but could be heard on a couple of their cassette tape recordings singing backing vocals. The three of them decided if they were going to be more than just a garage band in Aberdeen they would need a singer. There were many garage bands in the greater Grays Harbor area, and sometimes they would jam with other bands or musicians in the area. Two musicians they spent time with were Kirk Arrington, a classmate of Mark's and Duke Erickson, a fellow sophomore, but unfortunately they also played drums and bass and neither of them wanted to be a lead vocalist. Drake enjoyed learning more complex bass riffs from Duke, who had been playing bass for a few years already, and whose nose he accidently broke in PE during eighth grade. Duke had always blamed the other kid next to Drake, and Drake had never felt up to taking the blame for it. He kind of just kept the status quo by remaining quiet about it.

Basketball would be starting up soon and Drake, as the tallest kid in school, would once again be the center. He knew he'd have to balance his time amongst all the things he was doing. He'd met a couple times with his oldest brother Martin when he was home from his duty assignment at Fairchild Air Force Base (AFB) to discuss the emotional high they felt with the whole founding of the Brotherhood of Olympus. They'd often sit and discuss possibilities until early in the morning and dream of a day when they could do something again to make a difference in the world.

Drake didn't realize it at the time, but he was beginning to blossom as an individual. The future, indeed, looked very bright for young Mr. Fraser.

# ABOUT THE AUTHOR

Guy T. Simpson, Jr. is the author of the Brotherhood of Olympus Saga. He is an award winning artist and illustrator, possessing a graduate degree in education from The Evergreen State College. He has worked as a middle school science and leadership teacher in rural Washington State, as well as a plethora of other jobs throughout his career. He still resides in the Pacific Northwest with his wife, three college student children, and a number of dogs and cats. He is currently at work on the third installment of the Brotherhood of Olympus Saga.

For more information see the author's website:
**www.guysimpson.net**

Now Available:
## THE BROTHERHOOD OF OLYMPUS
### AND THE
## TOWER OF DREAMS

Coming Soon:
## THE BROTHERHOOD OF OLYMPUS
### AND THE
## DREAM STONES

www.ingramcontent.com/pod-product-compliance
Lightning Source LLC
Chambersburg PA
CBHW070159260626
47160CB00002B/389